I0645573

Openings

Book I in *The Hayek Chronicles* Series

James S. Peet

Openings

James S. Peet

2022

First Printing: 2022
Enumclaw WA 98022

ISBN 13: 978-0-9996093-6-1

Cover art by Keith Draws: https://keithdraws.wordpress.com/

To buy this (and future) books by James S. Peet in an e-book format, please go to **www.jamespeet.com**.

James S. Peet

To fellow geographer and world traveler
Dave Jeschke, aka Dave Jaskey
1959-2020

To all Vietnam Veterans
Welcome Home!

CONTENTS

ACKNOWLEDGEMENTS

Special thanks to all that made this novel possible: Becky Rush-Peet - the original alpha reader/editor; Shannon Page, my editor, and; Keith Draws who did the cover art.

WASHINGTON

1

Tim Bowman didn't intend to open a portal to a parallel Earth, it just happened.

The half-Irish, half-Japanese Buckaroo Banzai wannabe was actually working on an attempt at a matter transporter. As a kid in his early twenties, he had watched all the *Star Trek* television shows and decided that he should be able to figure out some way to make the show's transporter a reality. Several decades later, with a Ph.D. in physics in hand, here he was in a small metal shed on his ranchette just outside the small town of Selah, Washington, finessing his latest attempt. His buddy, Dave Jaskey, was sitting on a swivel chair watching him. Dave, dressed for the cowboy action shoot the two were planning on attending shortly, was holding onto a lever-action rifle he had brought with him to show Tim. It sat, forgotten, in his lap as he watched Tim begin the start-up process for his machine. Where Dave was sitting, he could see the imposing profile of Mt. Rainier, Washington's largest mountain, through a window at the far end of the shed.

The machine was a simple-looking affair, consisting of two metal-framed gateways separated by about fifteen feet, and a control panel fed by a standard electric cord from an outlet on the shed's wall. The control panel was linked to both gates. According to Tim, once it was activated, one should be able to walk through the opening of one gate and appear from the other. Naturally, Dave was skeptical.

A sacrificial chicken was in a cage next to the first gate. The plan was to push the chicken through the gate and have it emerge from the other. Tim had considered using a goat but figured his wife would be more upset to find one of her milk goats missing than a chicken that had stopped laying eggs. Besides, he figured, it's a chicken. If it died, it wouldn't be missed.

Tim finished fiddling with the control panel, and then said to Dave, "Well, here goes nothing." He flipped a switch and a humming sound emanated from the two gates. Dave's eyebrows raised in surprise.

"Well, at least something's working," he said.

Tim left the control panel and practically ran to where the chicken sat. Opening the cage, he pulled the squawking bird out. Standing to the side of the gate, where he could keep an eye on the other gate, he reached around and threw the chicken through. It disappeared from sight. He stepped back for a better look at the exit gate, frowning.

"Where's the damned chicken?" he asked.

Dave shrugged. "Beats me."

Tim hurried to the opening of the second gate and looked through it. All he saw was the shed's floor and space between the two gates. His frown deepened, creating deep furrows on his forehead. He ran back to the first gate, and this time actually looked through the opening.

"What the hell?" he muttered.

Dave got up from his perch and walked over to stand by Tim.

"What the hell is right," he said.

The two men saw the chicken, but instead of standing on the floor of the shed, either outside the second gate or between the two, it stood on the ground of a high desert, just like the land surrounding Tim's ranchette. Off in the distance, they could see a mountain that looked just like Mt. Rainier. But they couldn't see any signs of civilization, just an untouched natural environment. Dave did a double-take, looking at the mountain through the gate and then at the mountain through the window.

Tim was just about to reach down and grab it when the bird squawked and tried to run away. Its little bird brain had recognized danger, but too late. A tawny bundle of fur leaped in; the two men stood in shock as a large cat with two long fangs bit down on the bird, ending its squawking with a flurry of flying feathers.

Both men stepped back, shocked. Dave grabbed a cartridge from the leather pistol belt around his waist and loaded it into the rifle. He brought it up and aimed it at the lion. The motion caught the attention of the large beast. It turned to face them, dead bird dangling from its mouth between two scimitar-like fangs. It laid its ears back and crouched as if to attack.

At that point, Dave had had enough and shot the animal between the eyes. It dropped like a stone, still clutching the dead chicken between its jaws.

"What the hell is it?" Tim asked.

"From the looks of it, a freakin' saber-tooth tiger," Dave said, working the lever on the rifle to eject the spent casing, and loading another cartridge from his belt.

Tim stepped back toward the gate, and then, gingerly, poked his head through it. He looked around for a minute, then pulled his head back and turned to Dave.

"You look and tell me what you see, so I don't think I'm crazy."

Dave did. When he looked back at Tim, his eyes were wide, the whites showing vividly around the blue irises.

"A herd of woolly mammoths? Did you just invent a time machine, or what?"

The two men dragged the lifeless saber-toothed tiger through the gate and into the shed, dead chicken in mouth and all.

"I don't think so," Tim said. "You're the astrologist, can't you figure it out this evening?"

"Astronomer," Dave absently replied. It was a standing joke between them.

"I'm not sure I want to try taking any pictures at night from there," Dave said, nudging the dead lion with his cowboy boot. "Not if there's more like this. Why don't you shut this thing down until we figure out what we're doing?"

"Probably a good idea," Tim said. Giving the lion a wide berth, he went over to the control panel and turned off the machine.

"So, we've got a couple of options here," Dave said, "Either you developed a time machine and found a way to the past, or you've opened up a portal to an alternate universe, giving us access to another Earth where the megafauna still roam."

Several hours later, the two men stood by the metal frame, which Tim was beginning to think of as "the gate." Tim had powered up the gate briefly almost a half-hour ago so Dave could take a look at the night sky. After a quick glance, the astronomer had Tim shut down the gate.

"Interesting. Looks like the same night sky."

That caused Tim's eyebrows to rise.

"And?"

"We'll find out shortly."

As Dave began to ready the equipment, he said, "Y'know, time travel ain't real. Think about it, you go back in time, guess what? You're in a different place. Not only is the Earth spinning around the sun, our solar system is also moving away from the center of the universe. Has been since the Big Bang. Anything go back ten-thousand years, it'll be in space light years away." Dave then became silent, focusing on his preparations.

After watching Dave mess with the various pieces of equipment, Tim was beginning to get antsy.

"So, how long will this take?"

Dave finished attaching the large-format camera to an equally large telescope mounted on a small floor dolly, basically a frame with little roller wheels. "Not long. We'll need to push this through, find the right stars, trigger the shutter release, give it a couple of minutes, maybe five, for three eight-second night shots, then reel it back in."

"You think you'll be able to figure it out?"

Dave shrugged. "Shouldn't be too difficult. Stars move. All the time. All we have to do is locate Barnard's Star and measure its proper motion."

Tim recalled the term from early astronomy classes, but that was more than twenty years ago, before his neighbors selected him to go kill little brown people in Southeast Asia.

"Proper motion?"

"Yeah, you know. The movement across the sky. It's the angular motion across the sky with respect to other stars, usually more distant."

"So, what makes this Barnard's Star so important?"

"That bad boy practically zips across the sky." Dave stopped working on the camera to look up at Tim. "It's sorta like the race car of stars. To give you an idea, it's moving so fast that it covers ten point two-five arc seconds per year, the same distance in the sky as the moon is wide about every 170 or so years."

"And, that's fast?"

"Dude! It's practically hyper-velocity for stars. Plus, it's close. Only about six light years away."

"If it's so close, why do we need the telescope? Can't we just use the camera?"

Dave sighed. As if addressing a particularly slow student, he explained in further detail. "First, it's not very luminous, due to its size. Small star, doesn't kick out much light. It's only about fourteen percent the mass of our sun, and probably about twenty percent the size. Because of that, it's cooler and dimmer. I'm talking about 2,500 times less powerful than good old Sol. Basically, it's a red dwarf. That means, without a telescope to bring it into focus, we might not be able to find it, let alone take a picture."

"Oh."

"Yeah, oh. Now, let me finish this up. Good thing it's summer. Wouldn't have this opportunity in winter."

Tim waited patiently as Dave finished getting the camera/telescope combination set up. Finally, Dave stood painfully from the squatting position he had been in for the past hour and announced, "Okay. Good to go."

"Want to me open the gate now?"

"Are you crazy? Do I look like I'm prepared? If there's more of Mr. Smilodon's clan out there, I want to be ready for them."

Dave went over to the wall where he had leaned his rifle earlier in the day, after dispatching their predatory visitor.

Picking it up, he checked to ensure it was loaded, despite having loaded it after the afternoon's excitement.

"Okay. Now I'm ready."

Both men wore revolvers in cowboy-style holsters. Tim had elected to use the same type of lever-action rifle Dave possessed. Tim pulled the lever down slightly, ensuring that a round was in the chamber.

"I'm ready."

While Tim had served in the Marine Corps, Dave had served in the Air Force. Tim always felt that giving Dave anything more than a .22 was a waste, but he wasn't about to argue with the addition of Dave's 45-70 lever-action rifle. It was identical to what some of the cowboys used to carry during their heydays in the 19th century, and threw a pretty hefty slug, proven to take down Smilodons.

The plan was to open the gate, and while Dave took the star shots, Tim would serve as security, keeping any and all hungry critters off Dave. That is if they could duplicate opening the gate.

Tim turned on the machine, and when he heard it humming, looked over at Dave. Dave nodded. "Yep, it's still dark. Cover me."

With that, Dave pushed the dolly through the gate with one hand, holding his rifle with the other. Tim rushed over to stand by the gate and keep watch while Dave stepped through the gate and aligned the telescope, facing it toward the south.

Several minutes passed before Dave said anything.

"Got it."

Tim could hear the camera shutter click. Even though it was only eight seconds, it seemed like an eternity as he cast his gaze about, looking for threats. Finally, the time was up, and the shutter closed.

Dave extracted the film and loaded another film holder, all by touch, taking less than a minute to do so. While Tim kept watch, he checked the camera/telescope alignment again, then took another photograph. Immediately, he looked up and around, checking his surroundings, bringing his rifle.

The wind could be heard whistling through the sagebrush. The quarter moon was barely up but provided enough light for the men to inspect their surroundings. They scanned the landscape but didn't see anything moving. Tim could smell the dry, dusty scent of the sagebrush and a slight hint of lodgepole pine.

The shutter closed again.

For the third time, Dave changed the film holders and made sure the camera/telescope combination was properly aligned. He then pushed the button on the cable attached to the camera shutter release. The shutter clicked open.

Finally, after eight agonizing seconds, the shutter closed for the final time.

"That's it. Let's reel her in."

Tim stepped further back into the shed, rifle at the ready, while Dave pulled the dolly back. Once both men and the camera/telescope combination were back on solid concrete, Tim rushed over and shut the gate down.

Both men breathed a sigh of relief.

"Well, that was fun," Dave said, as he began disconnecting the telescope from the camera.

"How long do you think it'll take to find out?"

"Couple of hours. It'll take about an hour to process the film. Luckily, I've got some recent star shots at home, so I don't need to go to campus."

"How accurate will it be?"

"Close enough for government work," Tim said with a grin.

He set his rifle against the shed's wall and tucked the film holders under his arm.

"I'll call you after I've developed these."

Tim nodded, lost in thought.

2

It was almost two hours later, well after midnight, before the phone rang. Tim's energy for the past couple of hours had managed to transfer itself to his wife, who, despite the hour, was still awake because of the heightened tension. She had gotten used to this feeling years before. It happened whenever Tim was working on something new. Luckily, she didn't have to work, and they didn't have any kids, so it wasn't too much of a strain on her to be awake.

Veronica, who had just stepped into the kitchen to get a final glass of white wine, didn't even have a chance. Despite being in the kitchen where the phone was attached to the wall, she was almost knocked over by her husband as he raced for it.

"Yeah?" Tim answered, not even noticing her look of shock. She folded her arms across her chest and glared at him, to no avail. He was totally preoccupied with whatever was being said on the other end.

Tim's look went from one of expectation to one of dismay.

"You're shitting me. It's today? Are you sure?"

A slight pause as Tim listened to the caller. Veronica could hear talking from the other end, but couldn't make out what was being said.

"Okay. See you in fifteen."

Tim hung up the phone, a dazed look on his face.

"It's a bit late for company. Want to fill me in?"

Tim turned toward his wife. Her questioning blue eyes were framed by a pale, oval face, surrounded by a mass of dark hair. To him, she was the epitome of black Irish.

"You know that experiment I've been working on?"

"Yeah, the transporter. Did it work?"

"Well, yes, and no."

Arms still crossed, Veronica canted her head and raised one eyebrow. "Care to elucidate?"

Along with being drop-dead gorgeous, at least according to Tim, she was also bright and well-educated, so he wasn't taken aback by either the look or the question.

"It's not a transporter."

"Then, what is it? A time machine?"

Tim could hear the humor in her voice.

"Noooo. I think it's a portal to another universe?" he answered, more as a question than a statement.

Veronica dropped her arms to her sides. Her eyes widened. Tim could even see her irises constrict and her nostrils flare.

"You mean like, to another planet-type universe?"

"No, more like the multiverse."

"Multiverse?"

"Yeah, you know. Same planet, different timeline. Multiple universes, hence, multiverse."

Veronica crossed her arms against her chest again and leaned back against one of the kitchen counters. "Explain."

"Okay. You know how time is pretty much linear, right? Things flow along, pretty much in chronological order?"

Veronica nodded. "Yeah, that's why we call it *chrono*logical."

"Well, what if, instead of doing one thing, somebody did something a little different. For example, what if Hitler hadn't declared war on the US? We would have only fought the Japanese, and the Nazis would probably still occupy all of Europe, maybe even Great Britain. What if we never developed the bomb? Fighting might have raged on for years, and my parents might never have met in occupied Japan when they did, so I was never born. Or, what if the South had seceded through the courts, rather than going to war? We'd now have a Confederate States of America."

Veronica nodded.

"That creates a branch in time. Imagine this happening gazillions of times. It's like having a big old oak tree with branches going out, but all going up."

Veronica raised her eyebrow again.

"Now, imagine being on one branch, but then having the ability to step over to a neighboring branch, much like what a squirrel does on a regular tree. That's what I think I've done."

At this point, both of Veronica's eyebrows rose, almost to her hairline.

"Let me get this straight. You think you've opened up some sort of portal to a parallel Earth?"

Tim nodded.

"And what makes you think that?"

"Follow me."

Tim headed for the back door out of the kitchen.

The two stood inside the walk-in freezer in the shed, looking at the dead Smilodon, which had been gutted and hung from a hook.

"Ever see one of these in real life?"

Veronica stared at the dead cat. Reaching out, she touched the fur. The two long teeth, with her chicken still clenched between them, were visible.

"It's real," she said, in wonder.

"Damned right, it's real. Almost ate me, too."

Veronica turned toward Tim. "What do you mean, almost ate you?"

Tim described that afternoon's adventures, while she had been shopping in town, then went on to describe what he and Dave had been up to during the evening after supper.

"So, that call was from Dave?"

Tim nodded.

"What'd he say?"

"Barnard's star is in the same place it is here."

Veronica's brows furrowed.

"What's that mean?"

"Whatever I found on the other side of the gate exists at the same time we do. Basically, different Earth, same time."

"With saber-tooth tigers?"

"And woolly mammoths."

Veronica looked back at the gate.

"Holy shit!"

"Exactly, holy shit."

Dave showed up as the two Bowmans were walking back into the house. His dusty, beat-up Ford Bronco Roadster cast its light across the house, allowing them to see the final steps into the kitchen.

Tim walked through the house and opened the front door just as Dave was about to knock on it.

"C'mon in."

Dave stepped in and nodded at Veronica standing in the opening between the kitchen and living room.

"Evening, Veronica."

"Good evening, Dave. I hear you've got some interesting photographs."

Dave turned toward Tim, who shrugged.

"I told her."

Dave nodded. "Okay. Well, where do you want to see 'em?"

"Kitchen'll do."

In the kitchen, Dave pulled a series of eight-by-ten-inch photographs from a portfolio and set them on the counter. They showed white dots on a black field. He separated the photos into two groups of three.

"Ones on the left are from the observatory last week. Ones on the right are from tonight."

Tim couldn't see a difference between them. "Which one's Barnard's star?"

Dave pointed to a small dot. He then pulled a small transparent ruler from his shirt pocket.

"Here's the constellation Ophiuchus. Note this star," Dave said, pointing to one of the stars near Barnard's star.

Dave handed Tim the ruler. Tim noticed it was metric. "Now measure it here and on our photos."

Tim did so, and was surprised to see the measurements were equal distance. "How accurate is this?"

"Accurate enough. I'm sure we could take more, better star shots, but I don't think it'll make any difference. Either way, if the other side were in the past or the future, or even a different planet, the stars wouldn't align as well as they do here."

Tim considered the photo some more. Staring at the two series, he was abruptly brought back to the present when Veronica spoke up.

"So, what are you going to do now? Call KIMA?" She was referring to the local CBS affiliate television station in Yakima, and the oldest station in central Washington.

Tim shook his head. "Naw, I don't think so. Let me think on this a bit." He turned toward Dave. "You haven't told anyone, have you?"

"Not yet. Petra's out of town visiting her mom, and the kids are with her."

"Good. Don't."

Veronica gave him one of those looks that said *What are you really thinking?*

Tim noted the look. "I've got an idea, but let me sleep on it." He turned back to Dave. "What time can you be here tomorrow?"

"Hell, I can stay tonight, if needed."

"Not necessary. How about eightish?"

"That works. You want to keep the photos?"

Tim nodded. "Yeah, you might as well leave 'em here."

3

During what was left of that night, Tim and Veronica barely slept. Tim's mind was going a mile a minute, so when the sun finally began to peek over the horizon shortly before five, he got out of bed and went into the kitchen to fix coffee.

The coffee had barely finished brewing when Veronica, not showing quite the bedhead that Tim had, but eyes totally bloodshot from lack of sleep, came in and helped herself to a cup.

She took a sip and sighed with contentment. "Best part of waking up. So, what's the mighty hunter thinking?"

Just at that moment, the kitchen phone rang. It was the type with a spiral cord long enough to walk around the entire kitchen and even into part of the living room. Sometimes, Tim would inadvertently wrap himself up in it while talking, not paying attention to the fact that he was walking, talking, and turning simultaneously.

"Hello?"

"It's me," said Dave. "I'm awake. Okay to come over?"

"Yeah. Now's fine, but why so early? I thought we'd agreed on around eight"

"Figured if you were like me, you probably didn't spend much time sleeping last night."

Tim chuckled.

"You got that right."

"Great. On my way. Coffee made?"

Tim looked over at Veronica who was taking another sip from her cup.

"Yeah, but the way Veronica's going, might not be much when you get here."

"Tell her not to drink it all."

Without even saying goodbye, Dave hung up, leaving Tim with a dial tone buzzing in his ear.

Tim hung up and said, "That was Dave. He's on his way over."

"I somehow figured that out," she said dryly.

Barely fifteen minutes later, Tim heard Dave's Bronco pulling up on the gravel driveway. Dave had bought the blocky vehicle, saying he needed something with four-wheel drive to get to his mining claim on the Naches River, in the Cascade Mountains east of Yakima.

Tim had recommended a jeep, but Dave shot that idea down, saying, "AMC sucks. New jeeps aren't worth crap. Ford's are more reliable." Tim had countered with "Ford: stands for Found On Road Dead."

Tim was a bit of a jeep fanatic, owning the same 1962 Willys CJ-3B he had bought second-hand while in high school. But he had to agree with Dave. Jeeps made by AMC were total crap. If he thought hard enough about it, Tim would have to admit that all jeeps were probably pieces of crap. It reminded him of the saying about Land Rovers turning drivers into mechanics since 1948. jeeps had been doing that since 1941. Of course, the great thing about jeeps was they were easy to fix and didn't cost an arm and a leg to do so. His '62 Willys was real easy to fix and could cross just about any terrain thrown at it.

It wasn't just the standard jeep that Tim loved; he also had two other Willys: a pickup truck and a station wagon. All three Willys were stored in a pole barn next to his inventor's shed.

Dave hopped out of his sport-ute and made his way to the front door. Before he could knock or ring the doorbell, Tim opened it.

"Hey."

"Hey," Dave replied. As he followed Tim into the kitchen, he asked, "So, what's the plan?"

Veronica handed Dave a cup of coffee, then leaned against the kitchen counter, also waiting for Tim's announcement.

Tim said, "Dave, other than that claim you've got on the Naches, where else is there gold around here?"

"Depends on whether you're talking placer or lode. There's some placer mining all along the Naches, and on Blewitt Pass, but if you're serious about gold in these parts, you'd have to consider Swauk Creek, up near Liberty."

"Where's that?"

"Up Highway 97, between Ellensburg and Leavenworth."

Veronica nodded. "I remember passing it when we went to Oktoberfest last fall. South of Blewitt Pass."

"Yep. That's the one. Of course, all of those areas have mining claims on them already, so what are you thinking, Tim?"

Tim rubbed his stubble-covered chin.

"What if all that gold's in the same place on the other side of the gate?"

Dave took a sip of coffee.

"Interesting concept. So, you're thinking we go through that gate, pick up a bunch of gold, and then what?"

Veronica echoed, "Good question. Then what, Tim? Did you forget about that rather large-toothed predator you met yesterday? And, how would you get there and back? Who's gonna open the gate for you?"

She set her cup down on the counter, causing it to bang loudly.

"And if you think I'm gonna sit there with the gate open and a shotgun in my lap while you go gallivanting off on another planet, possibly getting eaten along the way, you've got a different think coming, buster."

Tim could tell his wife was royally pissed. He wasn't about to piss her off any further, so he took care with his next words. "No, I don't expect that. What I'm hoping is that you'll help. I can show you how to work the gate. It's really not all that difficult. You operate it a bunch until you're comfortable. That way, you don't

have to sit there with a shotgun. And believe me, if we go, we'll be
going in armed for bear."

"I still think it's stupid."

"Is it, really?" Dave interjected. "Think about it, Veronica. Here's
a chance to explore a new planet, one possibly without humans.
And along the way, possibly get rich. You and I both know what
Tim makes teaching at YVC. The same as me. It's okay, but we'll
never be rich. And, how'm I'm gonna pay for college for my kids? If
we go over and get a bunch of gold, we'll be set for life."

Dave became even more animated. "Hell, why think small? We
could even start our own country. I don't know about you two, but
I'm beginning to really hate what this country's become. I know I
didn't go to Vietnam like you did, Tim, but I did serve in Thailand
during the war, and I got the exact same treatment you did when I
got home—spat on by a bunch of ungrateful draft-dodging hippies.
And it doesn't look like anyone's learned a damned thing since.
Reagan invaded Grenada, sent troops to Lebanon. For what? Maybe
it's time to take a big leap forward and get out of Dodge, if that's
possible."

Both Tim and Veronica were taken aback by Dave's outburst.
Tim seldom talked about his experiences in the war or when he got
home, but this struck a chord in him. He looked meditative.
"Y'know, Dave's got a point. Why think small?"

"Are you serious?" Veronica looked from one man to the other.
"You have no idea what's out there. For all you know, you found a
zoo, and maybe Nazis are running the country."

"Only one way to find out," Dave replied.

Veronica looked over at Tim, who was rubbing his chin again, a
thoughtful look on his face.

"Are you seriously considering doing this?"

Tim looked at her. After a slight pause, he said, "Actually, yeah.
Either with or without you. I'd prefer it to be with you, 'cause
that'll make our lives a lot easier."

Realizing that she was placed in a no-win situation, she relented.
"All right. Show me how to work the damned gate."

It didn't take long for Tim to show Veronica how to operate it. As everything was already calibrated, all it took was for her to flick a switch and power it up. Dave suggested not only writing down everything, such as how to operate and calibrate the machine, but also how to repair it if anything went wrong.

"I'll take some photos of the current calibrations. That way, if anything gets jostled, she'll have good, solid reference material to refer to."

Tim thought those were good ideas, so while Dave went to get his camera, he began writing up everything he could think of about the construction and operation of the gate. Dave came back, took pictures, then disappeared again. It wasn't until late in the morning, approaching noon, before Tim was finished writing everything up. As he put it in a three-ring binder for his wife, Dave returned with the photographs. They were placed in plastic sleeves, which were then placed in the binder.

He handed the binder to his wife. "Here you go. Everything you need to know on how to operate and fix the gate."

Taking the binder, she asked, "What now?"

Tim grinned. "Now, we prepare."

They went back into the house. While the men sat down with sheets of paper and pens at the dining room table, Veronica made lunch.

Tim started writing. "First things first: safety. I'm thinking rifles and pistols. I'm bringing my .45-70 and 1911. You?" The .45-70 Tim referred to was a lever-action rifle identical to the one Dave had killed the Smilodon with. The 1911 was an automatic pistol used by the US Military.

".45-70, same as you, and a Smith & Wesson 29. It's a forty-four magnum, a bit more powerful than your 1911. Want me to loan you my spare?"

"How's the recoil?"

"Trust me, if you have to use it, you won't notice. Just hold on tight."

Tim nodded. "Why not both, the 1911 and the 29?"

"How much weight you want to pack?"

"Good point. Okay, so we're not gonna go that far the first time. How far you figure to get to where the gold is on the Naches?" Tim was referring to the Naches River, which separated the cities of Yakima and Selah, feeding into the Yakima River, a tributary of the Columbia River.

"Depends on where we go. Just to the mouth of the river's about two miles, so figure on an hour. My claim is up near the American, which is about an hour's drive away. To go there'd probably take us days." The American River was a tributary of the Bumping River, which fed into the Naches on the east slopes of the Cascade Mountains.

"Think we can find gold near the mouth?"

"Don't see why not. Let's try there first, then move upriver if the pickings are slim. Of course, if you really want to get a lot of gold, we're gonna have to go a bit further."

Tim looked at him expectantly, pen held over his sheet of paper.

"Baker City."

"Baker City? You mean, like, in Oregon, Baker City?"

"That's the one. Everything I've read and seen makes it seem almost as good as the California goldfields."

Tim dropped his pen and raised his hands, palms up. "Hell, why not just go to California, then?"

"Too far. We can get down to Baker City and back a lot faster on horseback or shanks mare than we could California."

"Shanks mare?" Veronica set down plates with sandwiches in front of them, looking at Dave.

As the men moved their sheets of paper to make room for the food, Dave said, "Yeah, shanks mare. You know, walking."

Veronica raised her eyebrows. "I've never heard that phrase." With that, she returned to the kitchen for beverages.

"Hmm. How long you think it'd take to get to Baker City?"

Tim took a bite of his sandwich.

Dave took his time, mentally calculating the distances and expected travel times. "It'll probably take about ten days to get there by horseback, maybe three weeks on foot. Figure a couple of weeks to get the gold. All told, expect to take a bit over a month or so. That is, if we take horses. If we walk, double that."

"What about if we float down most of the way?"

"Huh. I hadn't thought of that. With or without horses?"

"Either way. If we build a big enough raft for the horses, equipment, and us, do you think we'll be able to float down the Yakima to the Columbia, then across to Oregon? That'll save us some time."

"Except the time spent building a raft."

"There is that."

Veronica returned with the beverages and a sandwich for herself. "Are you thinking of taking Bucky?" She was referring to their buckskin-colored quarter-horse.

"If we go by horse, he's the only one I've got and know. Unless you've got another horse I could take." The last was said with a mischievous grin.

"Well, you certainly aren't taking Cinnamon." Tim had already guessed there'd be no way Veronica would let him take her quarter-horse. The damned equine was more pet to her than working horse.

"Take off five days."

"What?" This came from both Tim and Veronica in synchronicity.

"Take off five days," Dave repeated, setting his sandwich back on his plate. "If we raft down the Yakima and cross the Columbia, we should be able to shave off five days of travel." Dave looked expectantly between the couple.

"I suppose we could do that. Just means bring a chainsaw, axes, and rope."

"No, it doesn't. Let's take some empty 55-gallon drums, lash 'em together, and put some planks on top. Fast, easy, and stable. And besides, we don't even know if there's sufficient wood in the area that would be good enough to use as a raft."

The two men agreed on that as a plan of action and set about developing a list of equipment to take. Dave focused on the mining equipment while Tim developed a camping list.

"So, you think the two of you are going to be able to do this by yourselves?"

Tim nodded, taking a bite of his sandwich. Some of the mayonnaise oozed out and smeared his fingers. After chewing for a bit, he swallowed, licked the blob of mayonnaise off his finger, and responded to his wife.

"Yeah, why?"

"I'm just curious as to how two guys are going to get any real work done if one's got to be on constant guard."

The two guys in question looked at each other.

"Um, yeah. You might have a point," Tim conceded, less than graciously.

"So?"

"So what?"

"So, are you going to try and find some others to go with you, or are you gonna try this with just the two of you?" Veronica asked, exasperated.

Dave shrugged. "Up to you, man. Your gate. I'm just along for the ride" Dave took a bite of his own sandwich and decided to keep quiet and just watch the interplay between husband and wife.

Tim put his sandwich down. "I don't know. I guess I hadn't thought that far."

"Maybe you should. I have no desire to be a widow." Pointedly looking at Dave, she continued, "And I'm sure Petra would feel the same if she knew what you two were up to."

"Hey, don't bring me into this. This is Shogun's plan."

"All right. I'll bring some others in. Who do you suggest?"

"What about some of your war buddies, like that Lewis character?"

"Don?"

"Yeah, him. Isn't he into the whole outdoor thing?"

Tim thought about. He remembered Don Lewis, who was in the same squad with him in Vietnam, lived near Seattle but spent as much time as possible in the mountains, hiking and hunting. Don was a history teacher for a high school, but was a pretty steady character.

"Yeah, Don might work. Unless he's teaching summer school, he might be up for it. Let me give him a call." Tim held up his sandwich. "After lunch."

Tim called Don shortly after lunch, and managed to convince him to come over to the dry side without giving anything away. All he had to say was, "Don, I need you here. It's important. Can you come?"

There was no way Don was going to refuse such a simple request. Maybe it was because he was an adventurous soul, or maybe it was because he was curious. But Tim suspected it was because Don wouldn't be alive if Tim hadn't shot the Viet Cong sapper that was trying to kill Don one night. Tim could still see the knife blade as it rose up behind Don's back, just before he shot the sapper in the face. At night, the sapper sometimes came back to life, and Tim was forced to shoot him over and over. He never told Veronica about it, but somehow, she knew. Maybe it was because he would bolt upright in bed, bathed in sweat, and panting as if he'd just run a 200-yard sprint. Or, maybe it was his shouting at Don to duck and screaming "Die, motherfucker, die!" while still asleep, thrashing about in the small double-sized bed they shared. Somehow, she knew.

"He said he'd be here later today."

"That's fast." Veronica was surprised.

"Yeah, well. That's Don. He's bringing his oldest kid with him. Wants him to get some highway driving experience."

"How old's the kid?" Dave asked.

"Probably at least fifteen by now. Find out when they get here."

A bit more than three hours later, while the afternoon sun still beat down on the dry landscape, a beat-up yellow jeep CJ-5 pulled into the driveway. From the passenger side emerged a small, almost elvish man with graying hair and a bona fide cookie-duster mustache. He looked older than his forty-two years. From the driver's side emerged a lanky youth with bright red hair. The two made their way to the house as Tim stepped out and greeted them.

Immediately, the older man gave Tim a hug, then said, "Tim, you remember Jack?"

Tim held out his hand. The young man facing him was a much older version of the toddler he'd first met a couple of years after returning from Vietnam. The last time he'd seen the boy was a couple of years ago when he had been in Seattle at a conference and spent an evening at Don's house, drinking wine and scotch, and feasting on alder-smoked salmon.

"Welcome, Jack. It's been a few years. You've put on quite a few inches."

"It's great to see you again, Dr. Bowman," the youth said, grasping Tim's hand and beaming from the compliment.

"How was the drive?"

"Pretty scary, until once we got over the pass."

"Not used to highway driving, are you?" Tim chuckled.

"No, sir. Not used to driving. I just got my learner's permit last week. Dad's had me driving everywhere."

"You'll get used to it. Tell you what, why don't you go inside and grab a pop or something while I talk to your dad."

Jack agreed.

Don watched him go, then turned to Tim. "So, what's up?"

"Follow me. You're not gonna believe until you see."

Keeping his mouth shut and eyes open, Don followed Tim around the back of the house to the shed. Dave was waiting inside, holding his rifle. Dave nodded a greeting toward Don, who returned it, as Tim took Don to the freezer and opened the door. He didn't say a word, just watched Don's expression. He wasn't surprised to see the look of complete and utter shock come over his friend's face.

"What the hell, over? Is that really a saber-tooth tiger?"

"Yep, and the proper name is Smilodon."

"Where'd you get it?

Tim pointed to the gate.

Don walked over to the inert gate and looked through it.

"How?"

Tim went to the gate's control panel and flicked the switch to power it up.

"Like this."

Immediately, the landscape behind the gate changed from the interior of the shed to the exterior of the parallel planet, with Mt. Rainier clearly visible. They could feel the afternoon heat coming through the gate, like a warm blanket comforting them in the air-conditioned shed.

Taking a glance through the gate, Don turned back to Tim. "Is it okay to step through?"

"Let Dave go first. He's armed."

Dave stepped through the gate, quickly moving his head around, scanning for threats.

"All clear. Come on through."

Don stepped through the gate, then stopped and stared.

"Hooooly shit! This is amazing!"

"Ain't it, though?" Tim had stepped up to the gate, but not through it. He didn't want to have all three of them on the other side if it shut down.

"Are those mammoths?" Don pointed off in the distance.

Dave shaded his eyes and looked toward where Don was pointing.

"Yep. Either woolly or Columbian mammoths, considering where we are."

"C'mon back and let me shut this down," Tim said.

Once the two men were safely back in the shed, Tim shut the gate down.

Don looked at Tim and Dave in wonder.

"Let's get a beer and talk." Tim gestured toward the door.

"So, the basic idea is to get a team together and get some gold? What about after that?" Don took a sip from his bottle of beer and looked from one man to the other. They were sitting on the back porch, watching the sun start its descent past Mt. Rainier. The only clouds visible were on the tops of the distant mountains.

"Well, that's where it gets interesting. How do you like how our country's become?"

Don's eyes squinted. "I don't. You know that. It's becoming less and less free and more and more of a cesspool."

Tim grinned. "So, what do you think of starting our own country?"

Tim didn't think it was possible for Don to squint any harder, but Don proved him wrong. His eyes practically became slits, the wrinkles at the corners of them even more pronounced.

"Whatchu talking about?"

"I'm talking about starting our own country. One founded on freedom, like our founders envisioned, but even more so. Look, we go over, we get some gold. We get better outfitted and go back. Once we've got enough gold, we move over and build our own society. Just like old-time pioneers, only better equipped and better financed."

Don looked out over the landscape, took another sip of beer, then set the bottle down on the armrest of his wooden Adirondack chair. "One condition."

Tim squinted his own eyes.

"What's that?"

"The boy goes."

"Huh?

"The boy. He goes with us."

"You mean Jack?"

"Yeah. The kid's way more prepared than any of us. Eagle Scout, already knows how to ride and shoot straight. Bagged his first elk at thirteen. Plus, he's young. And we're gonna need young."

Don looked at Tim, then Dave.

"Ain't any of us spring chickens. The boy goes, I'm in. He doesn't, you can count me out."

"What'll his mom say?"

Don grinned. "She'll say the same thing I bet you guys say all the time, 'Yes, dear'."

Tim chuckled at that. Dave guffawed and spewed beer out his nose. As he wiped it off with his arm, he continued to laugh.

Turning more serious, Don asked, "So, we going in on foot, horseback, or what? We could take the jeep if needed."

"Horseback at first. When we get, back I'll make another gate, one big enough for jeeps and trucks and maybe an airplane. If we do well enough, Dave was saying we should try for more gold-heavy areas, such as the California goldfields."

"How you gonna get across the Columbia with horses?"

Dave chimed in. "Rafts. We're gonna take some 55-gallon drums down to the Yakima and make some rafts that we'll float all the way down and then across the Columbia to Oregon."

"Yeah, that makes sense. What about California?"

Tim leaned forward, holding his beer with both hands between his legs. "That one's a toughie. Considering the distance, and what's out there, I don't think that's in the cards for some time. Not unless we can get some sort of plane over there. That means we'll need something that can either fly about a thousand miles round-trip or carry enough fuel with all of our other supplies to refuel and fly back. And, it'd have to be one that can land on water. As far as I know, there aren't any airfields over there."

"Speaking of which, what do you actually know about the other side?"

Both men shrugged. Tim said, "Same as you. It looks like the same Earth, but with megafauna from the Pleistocene. No signs of human habitation, but we've only had a couple of quick peeks through the gate. Enough to be certain it's Earth in the same time, just different."

"Well, if you need a pilot, Jack's already got his license. Single engine at fourteen, just got twin-engine rated. I reckon, if we have enough money, I can get him seaplane rated."

"Hell, if we find enough gold, I'll get him a seaplane," Tim said with a grin.

"Now, I know you two've got horses, but what about spares? Keeping a horse in Kirkland is a bit difficult, if you know what I mean. Ain't like I live in Enumclaw." Kirkland, across Lake Washington from Seattle, was an easy commute for Don. Enumclaw was a small cow-town southeast of Seattle, known for its dairy farms and horses.

"I'm sure we can wrangle some up for you," Dave said. "Along with a couple of mules to carry stuff. Don't know about you guys, but I don't think carrying a bunch of mining equipment on the same horse I'm riding is a smart thing."

"Can you handle that, Dave? You're the one with all the contacts."

Dave nodded. "Sure. I know of several for sale. If they wind up missing, I doubt if anyone'll cry over them."

"You're not gonna steal them, are you?"

"Damn, Tim. You think I'm that stupid? No, I'll just buy them. I'm just saying that if they die or get eaten on the other side, nobody'll miss 'em."

"Ah. Gotcha."

The meeting ended with Tim agreeing to let Jack join them and Don agreeing to go on the trip.

"I'll tell him on the drive home. Matter of fact, I'll drive so he can take some time to really think about it. Last thing I need is for him to be thinking so hard about it he runs us into the back of a tanker truck."

Just then, Jack joined them. "Tell me what on the way home?"

Don looked at the youth, then decided to tell him now. The look on the boy's face made Tim glad that Don hadn't waited until they were on the road. The boy might have yanked the steering wheel to head back to Selah immediately.

Tim explained that he and Dave would get most of the required things, but wanted Don and Jack to bring their own weapons and camping gear.

Dave said, "Let's keep weaponry simple. One rifle, and one or two pistols. Rifles should be .308 or better, and pistols should be .357 magnum or better. We'll be bringing .45-70 lever-action rifles and a .44 magnum. What do you guys have to bring to the party?

"We've both got .30-06 hunting rifles. I've got a .38 I can bring."

"Ditch the .38. It barely works on humans, and I sure as hell wouldn't trust it to work on something as nasty as a saber-tooth tiger. Get a couple of .44 magnum revolvers. Spend a couple hours getting familiar with them, using .44 Special loads. They're lighter, so training will be easier. How many rounds can the rifles hold?"

"I don't know. Three, maybe four. They're just regular hunting rifles."

"Got anything that'll hold more?"

"Just my Ruger Mini-14."

"That ain't gonna do. Cartridge is too small. While you're getting the revolvers, pick up a couple of rifles. Either something like this," Dave held up his lever-action rifle, "or something that's magazine fed. Minimum .308 or 7.62 NATO.

"If you can afford it, get an M1A, or maybe a Garand; the original M1 or the Tanker model. Either works well. The original uses 30-06, but the Tanker model is smaller, lighter, and uses 7.62 NATO. It's not really for Tankers, that's just a marketing ploy. They're made by Fulton Armory My preference would be the M1A. Either way, you'll be able to have more rounds available if needed."

As Dave listed off the weaponry, Don ran his thumb and forefinger down the sides of his mustache, looking a bit pensive, with his eyes reverting back to the squint the others recognized as him being thoughtful. "I think I can come up with something. So, why are you going with that old-fashioned cowboy gun?"

"'Cause I'm good with it, and it works, as evidenced by what's in the freezer."

Tim smiled. "Can't argue with experience."

For the next couple of hours, the three men and Jack sat and discussed the options, planning for what they hoped were all the eventualities. Actually, the three men discussed. Jack just sat there, taking it all in, occasionally asking a question or two.

They decided to meet back at the Bowmans' ranchette in a week to cross over and begin their quest for fortune.

Supper that evening was served on the back deck, overlooking Mt. Rainier. The horses in the fenced pasture below him were engaged in their usual behavior, ignoring the "monkeys" on the deck while grazing and keeping a wary eye out for any tigers that might be disguising themselves as small paper lunch bags. Tim sipped a glass of wine, a rather sharp merlot, one in which it seemed the liquid was absorbed in his mouth rather than making the passage down his throat when Veronica set down their plates. Along with a bottle of red wine from one of the new, local wineries, she served a meatloaf smothered in ketchup, garlic mashed potatoes, and grilled veggies. She knew Tim didn't particularly care for meatloaf, but as Dave had so rightly pointed out, the salary of a community college instructor wasn't quite up to being able to have steak every day, even if they lived in a farming community. Besides, they had a ton of ground meat in the freezer, and if Dave kept shooting wild animals in their shed, they'd have even more.

"So, have you guys figured out what all you're doing?"

Tim set the wine glass down and picked up his fork, nodding. "Well, we're gonna load up for bear, then go find some gold."

With a grin, he plopped a bite of the meatloaf in his mouth and began chewing.

"Seriously, that's all? What if something goes bad, like one of those saber-tooth tiger things, or worse? Have you guys even tried to find out if there are humans on the other side?"

Tim finished chewing, swallowed, then took another sip of wine.

"We're bringing radios, first aid kits, and guns. That's about all we can plan for in the event of dangerous critters. As to humans, I haven't a clue how to know if any are there, other than to see them, which we haven't so far."

"What about radio? Have you tried to see if you can pick up any radio or television broadcasts?"

Tim looked at his wife in wonder. *Why the hell didn't we think of that?*

"Can't say we even thought of that. Looks like we've got a bit more research to do tomorrow."

This time a forkful of garlic mashed potatoes made its way into Tim's mouth, while a pensive look crossed his face.

Veronica recognized the faraway look in her husband's eyes and didn't even bother to try and engage him in conversation until he returned to Earth.

Fortunately, the trip to Tim's never-land wasn't too long, and he was back among the conversant in just a couple of minutes.

"How long you think you'll be gone?"

"We're planning on a month. You okay with that?"

"I guess. Why so long?"

"That should give us enough time to get to the Baker City area, hunt around, and if we find some gold, have enough time to dig out enough to make it worthwhile."

"Okay. If anyone asks, what do I tell them?"

Tim shrugged. "Just tell 'em I'm at a conference."

Eyebrow rose. "For a month?"

"Okay, not a conference. I don't know. Maybe some retreat or something." A pause. "I know, I'm helping out at a summer camp for geeks. Physics camp. Somewhere on the East Coast."

4

Early the next morning, Tim and Dave decided to go hunt for some hominids.

Dave, the ever-present lab assistant extraordinaire, held up the small, battery-operated shortwave radio with optional power cord. "How you gonna tell the difference between a broadcast here and one there?"

Tim held up a pad of lined paper. "First things first. Let's find out what we can hear, and write down the frequencies. Once we've got them down, then we open the gate, put the radio there, and start scanning. Anything we don't already have might mean it's originating from over there."

For the next half hour, the two men listened to the radio, tuning it from one end of the spectrum to the other, including not only shortwave broadcasts but ones on the traditional AM and FM frequencies as well. At one point, they caught the British Broadcasting Corporation, or BBC, and listened as the newsreader talked about world reaction to the hundreds of people killed in the Golden Uprising in India, when the Indian Army removed militant religious leaders from the Harmandir Sahib, or Golden Temple, complex in India's Punjab province. The broadcast then segued into President Reagan talking about his much-touted Star Wars program, with the successful shootdown of a missile in space for the first time. Tim wasn't sure how he felt about that story. He didn't like seeing the military-industrial complex getting fed more, but he also didn't like the lack of the best equipment to face his country's enemies with.

As expected, they also picked up the local Spanish-language station, KDNA, and the local pop-40 station, KFFM. Tim had Dave pause on KFFM while the station played Tina Turner's "What's Love Got To Do With It."

The two men looked at each other and nodded, with slight smiles on their faces. "Ain't CCR, but ain't shabby," Dave finally said, referencing Creedence Clearwater Revival, a rock band from the late sixties and early seventies.

While Dave tuned, he would read off the frequency, which Tim would write down. Soon, they were finished, and Tim had several pages in his chicken-scratch writing.

"Okay. Let's do this."

As Tim walked toward the gate controls, Dave set the radio down in front of the gate, turned, and walked over to where his rifle was leaning against the shed wall. After checking to make sure a round was chambered, he returned to the radio, which was now blaring out "On the Dark Side" by John Cafferty and the Beaver Brown Band. Tim recognized it from the movie *Eddie and the Cruisers* from the year before.

"Ready," Dave announced.

"Starting up."

Tim, still holding the pad of paper, flipped the on switch, and within seconds Dave could see through the gate. He could feel the fresh morning air enter the shed. Holding his rifle at the ready, he approached the gate, then stepped through it. Tim watched anxiously, picking his own rifle up, and approached the gate.

Within seconds, Dave was back in the shed. "All clear."

"Keep watch while I run this thing." Tim picked up the radio and stepped through the gate. Over his shoulder, Dave watched, rifle at the ready, half in and half out of the gate. A foot in both worlds, as it were.

Tim set his rifle down next to him and spent the next several minutes scrolling through the stations and radio bands, listening.

With each chirp of the radio, he would consult his list, then move on to the next frequency.

In less than ten minutes, he was done. He looked up and around, finally taking in the surrounding landscape.

"Nothing?" he heard from behind him.

Picking up his rifle, he stood. "Nope. Not a thing. If there're any humans out here, they either haven't advanced to the level of wireless communications yet, or they're so far ahead of us, our technology would be stone-age."

"Well, grab that stuff, and let's shut this down. Lots of work to do, still."

A week later, the Lewises' faded yellow jeep drove up the Bowmans' driveway in a cloud of gravel dust. This time, Don was driving.

As soon as the jeep's motor shut down, the father and son team exited the vehicle. Tim hadn't quite reached them when he saw Don gesture to Jack, telling him to leave the equipment in the jeep for now. Both men wore newer cowboy hats, broad-brimmed to keep the sun off them, short-sleeved shirts, jeans, and laced-up boots.

The two men shook hands while Tim welcomed them back. He could see that Jack's eyes were shining with excitement about the upcoming adventure. Letting go of Don's hand, Tim turned to Jack and took his.

"Ready for a little adventure?"

"Yes, sir. I sure am."

"Know what adventure is, son?"

Jack looked at him quizzically. "Uh, I'm not sure what you're thinking, sir."

"Adventure usually means somebody else in deep shit in a faraway land. Your dad and I have already been on our adventures. You ready to go on an adventure?"

Don laughed heartily at that. Jack just nodded awkwardly, turning a bright red. Tim suspected that the boy blushed easily, especially with all that red hair.

Tim suggested they gather their gear and carry it to the shed. He watched Jack as the young man gathered his equipment. Nothing about the youth's actions indicated he was anything but proficient. The first thing he did was strap on an LBE, or Load Bearing Equipment, harness. It consisted of a web belt, web suspenders, two canteens, and two ammo pouches. An empty holster hung down from the right side. He slung a pack over his back with ease, and then pulled a rifle off the bottom rack of a gun rack attached to the jeep's roll bar. It appeared to be an M1A, the civilian version of the M14. Keeping the rifle pointed in a safe direction, he drew the bolt back, inspected the chamber, then let the bolt slide back. He obviously wasn't taking it for granted that it was empty. Slinging his rifle over his shoulder, he turned back to Tim, waiting for further instructions. In the meantime, his father had completed the same action from the opposite side of the jeep.

It was only after Don had slung his pack on his back that Tim noticed a canvas-covered tube attached along the side. Jack appeared to have the same item on his pack.

"Planning on going fishing?" Tim knew a fishing rod case when he saw one.

"Where we're going? Hell, yeah. Likely to be crawling with hogs." Don was referring to the summer-run Chinook, or king salmon, by its irreverent nickname, due to their size.

"Good point. Anyhow, Dave's waiting for us in the shed." Tim then noticed that neither Lewis appeared to have any handguns, despite both having holsters attached to their LBEs. "Say, did you bring any pistols?"

Don nodded.

"Yep. In the packs. Didn't want anyone to see Jack hauling around a hogleg on the way over."

"Makes sense."

"You might not need the packs. We've got saddlebags and a couple of pack mules."

As the threesome headed toward the shed, Tim could see his and Veronica's horses in the pasture. They had been joined the day before by Dave's horse, two mounts for the Lewises and a couple of pack-mules. Tim wasn't sure about the mules, as they seemed ornery beyond belief, but Dave swore by them. "Can carry more than a horse," was his excuse. Saddles were set along the top rail of the fence closest to the shed. Two of them didn't look like the normal Western saddle.

Don saw the equines, also. "Think I'll keep the pack."

"Get any riding in?"

Don rubbed his butt as they walked. "Yep. Maybe too much. Spent the week doing nothing but riding and shooting. Guess we're as ready as we'll ever be. What's with the weird saddles?"

"Pack saddles for the mules. Dave thought of everything."

"Hope he thought of bringing some butt balm. My ass is still hurting, and I doubt it's gonna get any better."

Tim heard Jack laugh quietly at the comment.

In the air-conditioned shed, they found Dave standing next to a pile of gear. "Ah, good, you're here. I won't have to do all the packing of this stuff by myself," he said.

The Lewises set down their packs and approached the pile.

"What all is it?" asked the elder Lewis.

"Radios and placer mining equipment. Shovels, breaker bars, gold pans, small gold sacks, and a couple of sluice boxes. I've also got a metal detector. That should save us a bunch of time. Any of you ever pan or prospect before?"

Tim and the Lewises shook their heads.

"It's pretty simple. First step, find some gold-bearing areas. That's where the detector and pans come in handy. Once we find some gold, we set up the sluices and just shovel gravel into it. I'll show you how to do it when we get to where we're going."

"What about food?" Don asked.

Tim pointed to a small pile of boxes across the room. "I've got a bunch of freeze-dried stuff over there. We'll have plenty of water available, so no sense carrying heavy cans or such." Dave pointed to another pile, this one consisting of leather bags. "Front and back saddlebags. One set goes over the saddle horn, the other behind the seat. Grab one of each, then load up a week's worth and pack 'em up. I'd like to be out of here within the next half-hour or so."

Dave then left the shed while the others picked through the freeze-dried packets, selecting their favorite foods for a week's worth of eating.

"You gonna take any?" Don asked, looking at Dave as he entered the shed, holding onto several canteens.

"Got mine already. Here."

He passed out two canteens to each person. When Tim took his, he realized they were already filled. "Thanks."

"You'll strap these over the saddle horn, one on each side, over the saddlebags."

Looking around the small group, Dave asked, "Everyone ready?"

In his best John Wayne imitation, Tim said, "We were born ready."

"Well, if that's the case, let's go saddle up the horses, pack the mules, and get on out of here."

It took longer than Tim expected, but finally, the horses were saddled, all the supplies had been packed or strapped on, and the three men and the boy were ready. Each of the travelers wore wide-brimmed hats, holstered pistols, and in the Lewises' case, LBE and packs. Tim and Dave had decided to carry small packs with basic survival equipment, spare ammunition, and a water-filled Army surplus canteen in them. Dave had made sure each person also carried in their individual packs laminated topographic maps of the areas they'd be traveling in. Everything else—tents, sleeping bags, spare food, more ammunition, and the mining equipment—were either on their horses or on the pack mules.

Dave had volunteered to lead the pack mules, not trusting the others. That left Tim and the Lewises to maintain guard as they traveled.

Dave had joked, "Hey, I'll be the first mule-skinner on this planet, whatever the hell we're calling it."

Don had quipped back, "You'll also be the first teamster." He then had to explain to Jack how the terms came about. "A teamster is somebody who drives draft animals, either mules or oxen. A mule-skinner is a teamster who leads a mule train."

"Mule train?"

"A bunch of mules with leads tied between them. They're strung out, one behind the other, just like a bunch of train cars."

Tim, standing by and listening to this interchange while holding onto the reins of his horse, called out to Veronica.

She came out the back door, drying her hands with a kitchen towel.

"We're ready."

Veronica nodded, ducked back into the house, and in less than a minute came back out empty-handed.

Tim led his horse toward it the shed as Veronica walked in ahead of him. As Tim entered the shed, his horse reluctantly following him, he called to Veronica and gestured toward a pump-action shotgun leaning against the wall next to the door.

Her eyebrows rose before she walked over and picked up the weapon.

"Just in case. Make sure you're holding on to it and ready to use it when you open the gate."

She checked the action and saw it was loaded.

He pointed to a transceiver set up near the gate. "We've got a transceiver with us, one that can be powered with a hand-crank. We'll try to call every other day around 5 PM, so open the gate then. All you need to do is turn on the radio and listen. If you hear us, just reply with a simple 10-4 or Roger. That way we'll know you got our call, and we can give you an update.

"We should be back in a month, but depending on what happens, it might take a bit longer. Dave told Petra, and she's agreed to help out while we're gone, and to be here when you open the gate."

Tim could see Veronica's relief when he told her that.

He gave her a kiss. "We'll be back soon."

By this time, the others had made their way into the shed, which was becoming decidedly crowded, with five humans, four horses, and two mules. Luckily, Tim had moved almost everything else out days before.

He handed his reins to Don, then reached up and extracted his rifle from the rifle case attached to the right rear side of the saddle. A brief check to see that it was loaded, then he took up position in front of the gate.

He glanced over to Veronica. "Okay, open it up." Then, he turned his attention back to the gate, rifle ready for anything.

The gate hummed briefly, then the wall behind it disappeared, replaced with the high desert, folded landscape of the western edge of the Columbia Plateau with Mt. Rainier visible in the distance. Near the gate, Tim could see the pile of plastic blue barrels, wood planks, canvas tarps, a tool chest, and rope that he and Dave had transferred over the day before. They were undisturbed, as was the orange flag flying upon the makeshift flagpole. Dave said that was so they could easily find the gate on the way back.

It didn't take the group long to transfer from Earth to the parallel Earth. As each man crossed over, leading his horse, rifle in hand, he would mount up and move out of the way for the next man, keeping an eye out for any threats. Fortunately, none were visible.

In the distance, they could see a herd of mammoths, it must have numbered fifty or so. Tim looked back at Jack and saw the sheer look of amazement on the youth's face.

"Pretty amazing, isn't it?"

"Yes sir!"

"Well, keep your eyes open. This ain't Mt. Rainier National Park. There're hungry, nasty critters out there."

With that, Tim turned back to continue his scan, starting off close, then moving out, a habit that returned from his days in Nam.

A quick look back at the gate, and he could see Veronica standing on the other side, shotgun held in her left hand, clearly not prepared for action. She blew Tim a kiss with her right hand. Tim caught the kiss in the air and returned the gesture, getting a sad smile in return. Veronica then disappeared from the gate, which shut down a couple of seconds later.

That was it. The three men and a boy were now all on their own on an unexplored planet. No people in sight, and no chance of rescue if things went bad.

It was exhilarating!

OREGON

5

"Okay, let's get this show on the road," Tim announced. "First stop, Yakima River. Let's unload the gear then come back for the barrels. We should be able to drag most of them to Wenas Creek, then float them down to the Yakima. They're pretty light, empty."

Tim led the group, with Dave behind him leading the mule team, followed by Jack, then Don. Don kept turning in the saddle, constantly checking behind him while the others looked mainly to the front and sides.

They headed south until they ran into a small creek, which they took to be Wenas Creek. Dave made a professional judgment that it looked deep and fast enough to be able to float the barrels down. As they followed the river downstream, Tim realized that it wasn't the same on this Earth as on theirs, which was a good thing. Instead of heading further south, cutting through the small town of Selah, this Wenas Creek went straight east, toward the Yakima River. At least, Tim hoped the Yakima River was there. All around them was familiar terrain, but lonely looking, without the heavy hand of man modifying it.

Not long after that they arrived at the mouth of the creek where it emptied into the Yakima. Fortunately, a gravel bar was on the downriver side of the creek, so grabbing the floating barrels and dragging them ashore would be an easier task than fighting the river. Especially if a barrel or two floated out of the creek and into the river. They unloaded most of their equipment, keeping their personal gear with them and the spare food on one of the pack mules. The mule let its displeasure be known when it discovered it was the only animal still packing, by trying to kick Dave. Dave, though, was too smart for it, ducking the kick and swatting the mule on the rump with a loud "Quit it!" The mule simply responded by laying its ears back on its head.

On the trip back to the barrels, everyone was on a heightened sense of alertness. Despite this, Dave had to comment, "Everyone be alert. The world needs more lerts." This elicited a groan amongst the others, even Jack, who Tim could hear mutter, "Can't even escape dad jokes on an uninhabited planet."

Even before they arrived at the site, Tim could see the orange flag flying in the light breeze. *Hmm. Looks like Dave was right. Those orange flags really do stand out.* The barrels soon came into sight, the blue starkly contrasting with the dusty-green color of sagebrush surrounding it.

Before they dismounted, Tim asked Don and Jack to keep watch. Don recommended letting Jack keep watch while he helped move the barrels. "I'd like to get these things down to the river and get the raft set up sooner rather than later."

Tim agreed, so the three men dismounted, stacked their rifles, and then began the process of using the mules and three horses as draft animals. The barrels had two loops of rope around them, connected by a third piece of rope. Dave had explained to Tim the day before that he had rigged them up this way to make them easier to transport and easier to rig a raft with. Toward that end, Dave showed him what he had in mind when he took one of the canvas tarps and laid it out. One end of the tarp had some rope interwoven between grommets. Dave attached two lengths of rope at either side of the end of the tarp closest to the mule, then attached the other ends of the rope to the mule's pack saddle.

"See? Instant sled. Now, let's load some planks on this, and barrels on top."

They set the planks on the canvas first. It was only when they were putting the two-by-twelve-inch planks on the canvas that Tim noticed there were two one-inch holes drilled on either end of each plank. It took him a second to realize that Dave must have done it as a means of securing the planks to the barrels with rope. The holes also served to secure the planks to the tarp.

After the planks were set in place, the men rolled the plastic barrels onto them. A rope was strung from the top end of the tarp, through the ropes on the barrels, toward the back end of the tarp. At the back, they tied the rope through one of the holes in the center plank. They managed to get a half-dozen barrels set on a canvas sled that way.

The next four sleds took less time to rig up, now that the men knew what they were doing. All this time, Jack had been keeping watch, not saying anything, just looking. It was only when the last knot was tied and the men were taking a much-needed water break that he spoke.

"Bear coming this way. Big one, too."

Each man grabbed his rifle from the tripod where they had been stacked and held them at the ready.

"Does it look like it's deliberately coming this way, or just meandering?" his father asked.

"Mostly meandering. If you guys can get the horses moving, he might not even know we're here."

Tim turned toward the others. "Sounds like a good plan. Dave, let's get this show on the road."

Dave nodded, shouldered his rifle, then went to his horse, gathering its reins. He led his horse, now surprised to discover that it had been drafted into being a draft animal, and gathered up the lead of one of the mules. "I'm ready. Let's go." He began walking, leading the horse in one hand and the mule in the other, toward Wenas Creek.

Tim followed Dave's lead, put his rifle in his rifle scabbard, took his horse's reins and the lead of the second mule, and began walking them toward the river. Don, with only his horse to lead, held onto his rifle, just in case.

Jack, meanwhile, brought up the rear, rifle resting on the front of his saddle, while he looked around in all directions, paying particular attention to the bear. He commented that the bear looked bigger than any other he'd seen before.

"Might be grizzly," his father said.

"Naw, hump's not as prominent. And it looks like it chased a car and caught it."

That caused some confusion among the adults. "What do you mean, 'chased a car and caught it'?"

"Face is all squished in, like the car stopped and his face ran into it."

"Short-faced bear," Dave grunted.

Tim looked toward the astronomer, now leading two equine companions in front of him. "What's a short-faced bear?"

"Like a grizzly, only bigger. Lots bigger."

"How do you know this shit?"

Dave stopped and turned, looking at the others. "Look. We've obviously stumbled on a place where Pleistocene fauna still exists. Don't you think it's a pretty good idea to know what the hell's out here? I know this shit 'cause I read up on it earlier this week." Unstated was the follow-up question of "why the hell didn't you?"

"Well, clue us in once we get set up for the night."

Dave nodded, turned around, and continued the journey to the creek.

The creek's location was easily identifiable, even from a distance, due to the plethora of cottonwood trees lining its banks. Tim couldn't remember a time he had seen so many near the creek, let alone ones as big as these, many of which were more than six feet in diameter. He even spied one that looked almost ten feet in diameter. Once at the creek, the men led their horses between two of the massive cottonwoods into it, until all the sleds were floating in the water.

Dave stood in the cool water, looking downstream briefly, then turned to the others. "We can either cut these loose and float them down like this, and gather them up at the river, or keep them tied on and walk 'em down. I vote we just walk 'em down. You?"

Tim shrugged. "Any reason why?"

"Yeah. Less chance of losing any, and less work for us," Dave said with a grin. "Besides, our boots are already wet, and they ain't gonna get any wetter, so we might as well."

Don piped up, then. "I agree. Let's just keep moving. I'd like to get as much distance between us and that big-ass bear."

"Okay. Let's do it," Tim said, glancing back in the last known direction of the bear.

They finally arrived at the mouth of the river and had the draft animals pull the barrels and planks up on the gravel bar. Tim was relieved to see the supplies they had left on the bar earlier untouched. As with the creek, the river was surrounded by massive cottonwoods. Tim checked the branches of those closest to them, seeking out any possible predators. To his relief, none were visible. He began the process of removing the tow rope from his horse.

"Dave, why don't you untie your sleds and get on watch with Jack?"

Dave nodded at Tim's couched-order request, rapidly undoing the knots on his saddle. After his horse and mule had been relieved of their burdens, he mounted his horse, drawing his rifle from his scabbard, and took a small ride around the gravel bar.

Tim and Don finished untying the ropes, then hobbled the horses and mules to prevent them from wandering off too far.

Dave, astride his horse, gave brief instructions to the two men on the ground about how to assemble the raft. "Put the barrels side by side, with the rope between the two rope ends facing up. You're gonna want four rows of five barrels."

Fortunately, the barrels weren't too heavy, so they were able to get them arranged fairly quickly. It was a simple matter of picking up a barrel by the ropes wrapped around the end, then laying it next to another one. Once all the barrels were in place, Tim called to Dave, whose attention was facing outward, looking for any threats.

"Now what?"

"Slide some of the two-by-twelves through the middle ropes, between the barrel and the rope."

Tim began to see what Dave had in mind. Soon, there were planks stuck over the barrels and under the ropes, with a row of barrels all connected by a single plank. Once that was done, Dave had them lay the remaining planks in the spaces between the secured planks.

"Now, you see those holes at the ends? Weave rope through them, tying them together. Make sure you do an over and under weave."

Tim and Don followed Dave's instructions, and soon a raft was assembled. It looked big enough for the four humans and six equines, but Tim wasn't too sure about how to keep the horses and mules on it. That's when Dave pointed to several two-by-fours that had been brought along.

"Use those for railings. It'll stop those stupid animals from trying to step off the raft and into the water."

When all was said and done, they had a small raft with a railing around most of it, along with a couple of oars that Tim hadn't even seen before, and a couple of poles. When he asked Dave about them, he just shrugged. "Punt poles. Good for pushing the raft."

Tim looked at his watch and realized it was barely two o'clock. "Let's heat up some water and eat lunch, then shove off. I'd like to get some miles behind us today."

Dave suggested that they cut down from a riding guard to a standing guard while they cooked and ate. "Smoke from the fire should keep any wild animals away," he reasoned. When he saw the confused looks on the others' faces, he clarified. "Look, wild animal smells wood smoke, it usually means a fire. A wildfire. Ever get stuck in a wildfire?" The others shook their heads. "Sucks. Big time. So, if you're a smart critter, and you smell smoke, you get the hell outta Dodge. Capisce?" At this, they nodded, immediately grasping the concept.

"Okay, let's get a fire going, then," Tim said.

Jack immediately went to gathering up driftwood that was lying on the edges of the gravel bar near the river bank.

Lunch over, the next step was loading the raft. Dave suggested holding off on loading the horses and mules until everything else had already been loaded and strapped down. "Look, we can afford to lose the horses, and even most of the food, but we can't afford to lose the mining gear."

Tim and the others had to agree with him, so their first task was loading and securing the mining equipment and the radio. Only after they had everything secured did they begin the process of loading the horses.

The horses were the easiest to load, but still not easy. Trying to get them aboard the craft took some doing, including actually mounting them and whacking them on the rumps with the reins. The mules, on the other hand, made dealing with horses look easy. More time was probably spent trying to load the stubborn animals than it took to build the raft, but eventually, they were all aboard, and none of the mules connected their many kicks with any of the humans.

"Keep them in the center, away from the edges," Dave cautioned. "No sense having them all get on one side and capsize us."

Tim was beginning to wonder if building the raft wasn't one of Dave's dumber ideas. Even though they were barely off the gravel bar and into the Yakima River, the vessel dipped and bobbed, enough to concern him.

"You sure this'll hold?"

"Only one way to find out. Let's take her out. If anything's gonna happen, it's gonna happen out there," he replied, expansively waving his hand downriver, his other hand holding onto an oar.

"All right, let's spread out. Tim, you and Jack push off. Don and I'll use the oars to steer."

Tim, rifle slung over his shoulder, set the pole into the water until he felt it strike the river bottom. Looking at Jack, who had done the same, he nodded. "Let's do this."

The two began pushing on the poles, eventually forcing the small craft away from the gravel bar. As he pulled the pole up to repeat the process, moving his hands down the pole to readjust it for pushing off again, river water flowed off it, soaking his hands.

The horses and mules were distinctly uncomfortable with the motion of the small raft, and it took the combined efforts of Dave and Don to keep them under control, while Dave still held onto his oar. Fortunately, the river was swift enough to move them on, but without the whitewater that would have made the journey dangerous.

"Keep an eye out for rapids, logjams, and sweepers," Don warned.

Even with his limited time spent on the river, Tim knew what a logjam was, but he had never heard of a sweeper, other than something used to clean carpets in a house.

Before he could ask for clarification, Jack saw the confusion on his and Dave's faces and explained that a sweeper was a tree that had fallen down into the river, with its branches both above and below water.

"Really nasty stuff, if you get caught in them," the youth explained. "Some call 'em strainers, but mostly we just call 'em sweepers, because they tend to sweep canoes and rafts under them, drowning whoever's in the boat. I helped out on a rescue last summer when I did a Boy Scout trip down the upper Yak."

"Anyone have any idea what we can expect, rapids-wise, that is?" Tim asked the group. All he got were shrugs in reply. "What, hasn't anyone ever floated or canoed between Selah and the Columbia?"

"Not me," Dave replied. The Lewises shook their heads.

"We've done the Yakima Canyon and from Cle Elum, but that's about it," Don said. "Are you saying you've lived in Selah practically your whole life and you've never floated down from there?"

Tim shook his head, and the conversation died.

They soon passed the Naches River, and the increased flow from the small river helped in both depth and speed.

While keeping an eye out for hazards, Tim reflected back on his life, wondering how it was possible he wound up where he was when he was.

Born in Japan in late 1947, the outcome of a mixed marriage between a Boston Irish soldier from Selah, Washington, and a Japanese college student, he was luckier than most. Even though fraternization between soldiers and Japanese civilians was originally banned, that loosened up in late 1946. His father, Richard Bowman, called Dick by his friends (and enemies), found a way to court Hiroki Ito, who was working at the base PX as a part-time cashier, and eventually convinced her to marry him, over the objections of her remaining living relative, an elderly aunt who had managed to survive the US Air Force's firebombing of Tokyo.

It wasn't until 1951 that Hiroki and five-year-old Tim were given permission by the US government to immigrate, joining Dick in Selah, where he managed a small apple orchard for his family, who had migrated from Boston when he was a teen. Hiroki was better off than most Japanese war brides. Despite the racism of the US at the time, and particularly the hatred of Japanese due to the war, Dick's aging parents accepted her with grace, particularly since she had presented them with their only grandchild, a precocious, adventurous boy. It also helped that the Bowmans employed Japanese migrant labor before and after the war, so there were plenty of Japanese-Americans, both Issei and Nisei, around to smooth any friction between Hiroki and the white residents of Yakima County.

Had it not been for Dick's drinking problem, which led to him beating both Hiroki and Tim, life would have been perfect. Eventually, Dick drove off the road one day in a drunken stupor, crashing his car into a telephone pole. Unfortunately, he wasn't wearing a seatbelt and was catapulted through the windshield into the pole, crushing his skull and snapping his neck. Not the type of injury one recovers from.

For the next several years, Tim worked in the orchard, picking up the slack for his missing father, attending school, and eventually graduating as valedictorian of the Selah High School class of 1964. From there, it was off to Central Washington University, where he finished a four-year degree in physics in two and a half years, taking classes during the summer to finish early and, hopefully, enter a graduate program. That's when his plans fell apart. Rather than getting into grad school, he was placed on a wait-list, along with several other promising students. It seemed that just about everyone was trying to avoid the draft and the military's increasing involvement in Vietnam by going to school. Graduate schools were inundated with male applicants, and with limited space, had to turn down many aspiring scholars. Unfortunately, Tim's draft number was low; the only reason he had managed to avoid the draft so far was with a college deferment. That ended upon graduation.

So, while waiting to get into grad school, Tim was notified by his neighbors that he had been selected for induction into the armed forces of the United States and was to report to his local draft board. They took one look at the healthy young man, and it was off to basic training for him as one of the few Marine Corps draftees. Six months later he was in South Vietnam, M14 in hand, out on patrols. That's where he met Don.

A year later he left South Vietnam, physically whole but definitely having issues that went unresolved. It might have had something to do with killing people. Or maybe it had something to do with seeing friends shot, blown up, stabbed, get bamboo punji sticks through their legs, and generally messed up, with his occasional killing of other humans thrown in. Nobody really recognized post traumatic stress disorder, or PTSD as it became known, when Tim first came home. Pretty much everyone said, "Get over it." They certainly didn't want to talk about it, nor hear what he might have to say. Furthermore, Tim didn't feel like talking about his experiences with those who hadn't gone, so he buckled down and worked on his doctorate in physics, after finally getting off the waiting list.

While most newly minted Ph.D.s wanted to teach and conduct research at prestigious universities or work on exciting things, like nuclear weapons, all Tim wanted to do was return to the Yakima Valley, the last place he had really ever known peace. There, we wanted to teach physics, and try to develop a transporter beam based on the *Star Trek* series he watched before and after his time in

Southeast Asia. Luckily for him, Yakima Valley College was hiring, and being a local boy, they picked him over other, similarly qualified physicists, despite his half-Japanese heritage.

It was at YVC where he met Dave Jaskey, the local astronomy instructor. The two hit it off, and Dave was the one who laid the moniker Shogun on him. Tim figured that was better than Jap or Nip, both of which he had constantly heard growing up.

Mind occupied on the past, he was rudely brought back to the present by exclamations from the Lewises. Thinking there was some sort of threat, he set the pole down and unlimbered his rifle. It was then he saw that everyone was looking into the relatively clear waters of the river. Looking down, he beheld a sight he never thought he would see: the river was filled with fish—salmon and steelhead. It looked like a living carpet of them in the water. Tim had never seen so many before.

"Probably what it looked like before the damned dams went in," Don said, referring to five dams that had been constructed across the river beginning in the 1880s.

"Hey, Dad. Can I fish?"

"Not now. Wait until we pull in for the night. I don't reckon we'll be lacking for fish wherever we are on this river."

Shortly before six o'clock, Tim suggested they pull in and set up camp. They had only been on the river for a couple of hours, but it was enough for the animals to get used to it. Besides, the men were getting hungry. Tim bet that the animals were, too.

Don suggested they land on a gravel bar on the west side of the river. "That way, the morning sun'll wake us up, and we can get an early start."

"How would it differ from staying on the east bank?" Dave asked, steering toward the nearest west bank gravel bar.

"Trees aren't so close, they'll block the sun. See the size of them monsters?" Don gestured toward the humongous cottonwoods looming over the river. "If we're on the opposite side, the sun's rays'll hit us earlier."

It didn't take very long before they had drifted far enough downriver and spotted a gravel bar that suited their needs. Within minutes, the raft was grounded and the horses and mules disembarked. The browse nearby was good enough that, once hobbled, the animals were happy to graze.

As Tim was getting a fire ready, Don broached the subject of having Jack do some fishing.

"Makes sense to catch and eat something rather than using up our limited supplies."

Tim found it hard to argue with that reasoning.

"Okay, but one of you needs to keep watch. We've still got tents to set up."

Don agreed to set up the tents if Dave would keep watch. Dave had no problem with that. Bad enough he'd have to share a tent with Tim, he didn't really want to spend time setting up the tent.

Tim had barely gotten the fire started when he heard a commotion from the river. Looking over, he could see Jack backpedaling up the bar, then walking downriver, his rod bent nearly double.

"Don't get too far," he yelled to the youth. Jack nodded, but stayed focused on the fish he was fighting.

Slowly he made his way back upriver. He was about twenty-five feet upriver from the campsite when Tim saw a Chinook salmon break the surface, flying high into the air. Jack took that moment to reel the big fish in just a little more. Tim was amazed: he had never seen a salmon that big. *Geez. That thing must weigh well over fifty pounds.*

It was clear that Jack was struggling, but it was also clear he didn't really want any help right at the moment.

Don finished setting up the tents and made his way over to Jack. Tim could see him ask the young man something. Jack vigorously shook his head.

Ten minutes later, Jack finally managed to bring the hog up to shore, dragging it away from the water as fast as he could walk backward. It still bucked and flapped its tail up and down, slapping the stones as it was dragged across them. As Jack held the line tight, his father picked up a stone and smashed the flopping fish on the head, killing it instantly. Jack gave the line slack and Don unhooked the hook. After Jack reeled in the slack line, he set his pole down on the pile of packs on the gravel bar, then just sat down, arms limp as noodles.

Tim grinned at him. "How's it feel?"

"Exhausting. I've never caught one that big before." The boy's grin was infectious.

"Not many can claim they have, nowadays."

"Look at the size of this thing," Don said.

Looking over at the older man, Tim saw he was holding the salmon up by the gills with both hands. Its head was almost level with his shoulders and the tail was touching the ground. The fish was easily five feet long.

"Must weigh about seventy-five or eighty pounds," Don said, setting the fish back down. "Good job, Jack."

Jack just grinned.

Supper that evening consisted of grilled salmon and freeze-dried vegetables. Tim found it hard to believe that such a huge, powerful fish could produce such tender fillets. Of course, Don's method of cooking helped. The fish had been placed on a grill over a bed of coals; fresh shavings of alder were added to the coals, producing a slight smoke. This transcended into the creation of a tender, alder-smoked grilled salmon, to rival some of the finest restaurants in Seattle.

While they were eating, the salmon in the river began a process Tim had seen only once before, jumping out of the water and slamming down into it on their sides. Each large salmon that came down sounded like a small gunshot, the report was that sharp. Dozens of them were doing it at the same time, creating a sound that reminded Tim of one of the many firefights he had been in. Fortunately, it wasn't quite the same, so it didn't cause any ugly issues to raise their heads.

"I wonder why they do that?"

"'Cause they ain't got middle fingers," said Don, which caused the men to chuckle, and left Jack looking a bit bewildered. Don didn't bother to explain his comment to the confused lad.

After supper, Tim took over the cleaning, scraping the grill off with river sand as he washed it, and drying it before packing it away. Each person washed their own equipment, which consisted mainly of a fork and aluminum plate for each. The empty bags from the freeze-dried portions were rinsed to remove any food remaining, and stored in a plastic garbage can. It didn't matter to the four that they might be the only people on this new Earth, the old "pack-it-in/pack-it-out" ethos was strong in them; Jack mainly from backpacking trips and scouting, and Tim and Don from their days humping in the boonies of Vietnam, trying not to leave anything useful for Charlie to use.

The fire was stoked, and a ready supply of wood was gathered. They decided to keep two-person watches. The last thing they needed was something spooking or killing their horses and mules. The plan was to do a rotating watch, where one person would relieve one of the two-man watch after two hours. That way, nobody would be on watch more than four hours, and each of them would be able to get a few hours of sleep. It would also, hopefully, ensure that somebody was awake at all times.

Tim and Dave took the first watch, while Don and Jack crawled into their tent. Tim cautioned Dave about looking into the fire. "You don't want to lose your night vision, so when you feed the fire, keep one eye closed."

They used their saddles as backrests, sitting on blankets set over the gravel. It was enough to keep them less than comfortable, which was good for staying awake. Rather than face the fire or each other, the two men had set their saddles such that they were back-to-back. Close enough to talk quietly without disturbing the sleeping Lewises, and they could keep watch over the small camp.

As the smoke drifted across the camp, the moon slowly rose in the east. Tim hadn't paid too much attention to the phase of the moon as he was getting ready for the trip, so he was surprised to see it was almost full.

"Is the moon waning or waxing?"

Tim could feel Dave shift, probably looking at the moonrise.

"Waxing. Should be full in a couple of days."

They were quiet for some time, listening to the night sounds. Some, Tim recognized, such as the ho-ho-hoo hoo hoo call of a great horned owl, or the chirp of crickets, or the yipping of coyotes. Others, he had heard only in movies, such as the howl of a wolf. Or the roar of a lion. That one got him concerned. Dave commented on it. "Lucky for us, that one's pretty far away. Got the horses attention, though."

Tim looked over at the hobbled animals and saw them staring in the direction of the howls, ears pricked forward.

"This is gonna be interesting," Dave said.

"How so?"

"Think about it. On Earth, most animals have come to fear man. We've been hunting and killing them for millennia. Here, I doubt there's another person out there, other than us. Nothing to fear. Why should they? Now, here we come, with our guns. What do they know about that? I bet all they see is some pale, slow, tasty-looking snack. Hell, the only thing that gives our predator status away is our eyes."

"Our eyes?"

"Yeah. Binocular vision for tracking prey. Something most herbivores don't have. You ever notice that cute, warm, fuzzy critters, like bunny rabbits, bambis, and such, have eyes on the sides of their heads?"

Feeling Tim nod, Dave continued, "That's so they've got a wide field of view. Able to see a threat coming from just about any direction. Predators have eyes in the front. Matter of fact, there're only three types of vertebrates with forward-facing eyes: primates, predatory mammals, and birds of prey. If you've ever looked at an owl or hawk's face, you'll know what I mean.

"That means, whatever's out there, ain't afraid of us. So we better be damned careful and keep an eye out. Else we'll be somebody's meal."

The thought of that sent a chill up and down Tim's spine.

The first night passed slowly. Because of the rotating watch schedule, everyone was able to get about six hours of sleep. It might not have been a straight six hours, but it was better than four, even if some of it was still during the evening's extended twilight.

Daylight came early, and within an hour of the sun rising, the expedition was back on the raft, floating down the Yakima toward the Columbia River.

The next couple of days passed like the first, with the day spent floating downriver, stopping for meals and toilet breaks, and to let the animals graze briefly. Nights were spent camped on gravel bars, eating fresh-caught salmon or steelhead for supper, and taking turns on watch over a smoky fire. Without a cooler or means to preserve their catch, the leftover fish was disposed of in the river after each meal. It wasn't all easy, though. There were several stretches of rapid water with sweepers and mini-log jams that required all hands on deck for evasive action. They even had to unload and portage around a couple of the rapids. Those took several hours each time.

The landscape changed as they entered the water-scarred wasteland of basalt known as the Channeled Scablands, larger rocks in the water making it more turbulent.

Finally, they reached the mouth of the Yakima, where it fed into the mighty Columbia. All three men had been on the Columbia or driven through its gorge at one time or another, and knew of its infamous winds. They were pleasantly surprised to see that the winds weren't blowing at gale strength that day.

"How far we gotta go down the Columbia?" Tim asked.

Dave consulted his map. "About twenty miles. It's about ten miles to the mouth of the Snake, then about another ten to the Walla Walla. We'll wanna pull out at the Walla Walla. No other good rivers nearby, and the overland distance would be about the same regardless of where we land.

"Besides, it wouldn't be good to be stuck on this thing if the winds kicked up. Ain't nobody got a life vest, and these horses probably wouldn't stand for it."

Tim looked at the other, who just looked back at him, waiting for him to make the decision. "Okay. Let's do it."

And, they did.

6

They hit a series of rapids about six miles downriver of the Snake, which had them worried a bit, but they managed to get through them without incident. Fortunately, the weather stayed with them across the Columbia, with the wind only kicking up slightly in the late afternoon as they pulled into the mouth of the Walla Walla River. A sandbar extended across part of the river mouth so they grounded the raft and disembarked the horses and mules. They then unloaded the equipment and stacked it nearby.

At Dave's suggestion, the four of them used the mules to move the raft away from the river. The thought of it catching the wind and being blown into the river, to eventually make its way to the Pacific Ocean, stranding them on the Oregon side, wasn't something they wanted to consider. It took some struggling, but soon the unwieldy craft was secured on the far side of some large cottonwoods adjacent to the river. It was Tim's first time using mules as draft animals; all the other times Dave had handled them. He found the situation less than amusing. The animals were stubborn, cantankerous, and just plain mean.

"Naw, they just don't like you," Dave said, laughing, when Tim announced this.

A short time later, the animals were hobbled and staked out, contentedly grazing on the sparse vegetation.

Over the next half hour, the group established camp, got a fire started, and Jack took up his usual late afternoon occupation of getting some food for supper. Tim watched as the youth expertly cast upriver, letting his line drift down. At the end of the drift, Jack would lift up on the pole, raising the tip, then drop it to reel in the line. Tim knew that the lift up was in the hope of having a hook set into a fish's open mouth. It didn't happen this time, but it was a common enough occurrence that the act was natural to the teenager.

Looking about, Tim saw Dave tending the fire and Don keeping an eye out for hungry critters. It was amazing the numbers and types of animals they saw just floating down the rivers. Along with the now-ubiquitous mammoths, they saw vast herds of elk, the typical mule deer, numerous bears, both grizzly and short-faced, and predators not seen on the North American continent for generations. Those that scared Tim were the ones he had the least experience with: Smilodons; North American lions, which differed from their smaller cousins the mountain lions; dire wolves, and the American cheetah. Normal predators he thought he could deal with, but Dave disabused him of this notion earlier, as they drifted down the Yakima and Dave lectured the others again on the variety of fauna that might exist in this here-and-now other Earth.

"Look, ain't none of them grown up fearing man. As far as they know, we're just a couple of hairless bipedal meals."

Tim watched Jack roll his eyes as Dave spoke, recognizing that the teen was likely bored from hearing the same thing again and again. Tim couldn't blame him, but it was still good information to keep in mind.

Everyone, including the animals, were glad to finally be ashore for good. Well, for good until they had to cross the Columbia back into Washington.

Tim looked across the river. "Hey, guys. I've been thinking."

"Ooh, bad move."

"Nooooo!"

"Seriously though," he continued, undeterred, "I think we oughta come up with a name for this place. Something that reflects what we want it to be. For example," he waved across the river at the far shore, "rather than calling that side of the river Washington and this side Oregon, why don't we come up with our own names? Maybe names that honor those who lived here before the white man."

"Uh, Dr. Bowman," Jack quietly said, raising his hand as if asking for permission from a teacher to speak.

"Yeah, Jack?"

"Aren't we, like, the only humans here? I mean, we haven't seen any other humans since we got here, and we're mostly white."

Tim looked at the youngster. He was about to argue with him, then recognized the veracity of his statement. "You're right, Jack. I guess I meant, let's honor those who lived in the area on Earth first by naming places after them."

For the most part, they all agreed, but Don had a non-Native American suggestion for naming the entire planet. "How about Hayek?"

The two college instructors looked at each other, then back at Don.

"I think it's brilliant," Tim said, with Dave agreeing with him.

Jack had a puzzled look on his face.

"What's a Hayek?"

"Not a what, but a whom," his father replied. "Friedrich Hayek. He's an economist who wrote the book *The Road to Serfdom*. Pretty much the libertarian's bible. He's also a Nobel Prize winner, for economics, and one of the greatest advocates of classical liberalism, along with Milton Friedman. I don't know if you remember the documentary we saw by Friedman, *Free to Choose*." Jack shook his head. The documentary had come out when he was only nine, so it wasn't something he was likely to watch back then. "Regardless, Friedman was one of Hayek's disciples, if you will. Went on to preach about classical liberalism, mostly to people who probably didn't listen or didn't want to hear what he had to say, which would be most politicians."

Don went on to explain the concept of classical liberalism to his son, describing it simply as a political ideology that puts the rule of law, civil liberties, and economic freedom above all else. "It's basically the concept that the Libertarian Party is founded on, but probably not as loose about things as libertarians are."

"Well, heck, if you're gonna name the planet Hayek, you might as well name the first city Milton," Dave chimed in.

"Why not Friedman?" Tim asked.

"Naw. Too formal."

"Okay, Milton it is, just as soon as we found it."

"What about states or provinces?" Don asked. "Most states were either founded with ethnographic or natural boundaries, except in the US and Africa where a lot had geometric boundaries."

Don then had to explain to the others the differences between the boundary types. "Real simple, ethnographic just means boundaries based on people, like where languages change, or religions. Natural, well, that's things like rivers and mountains and oceans. Geometric just means lines drawn on a map. Most of the Western US is like that, and a lot of Africa, since the Europeans decided to split it up at the 1884 Berlin Conference."

"Wouldn't it make sense to make it based on bioregions?" Jack asked.

"Actually, that's not a bad idea," Don said. "Think about it, in Washington, we've got five distinct bioregions; well, actually nine, but who's counting?"

"Nine?" Tim asked. "I can only think of five—the coast, the Puget Sound, the Cascades, the Columbia Basin, and the Rockies. And, politically, really only two, East of the Cascades and West."

"Yeah, well, most biologists and geographers split the Cascades into three regions, the North, West, and East, and you forgot the Blue Mountains in the southeast corner, and the Okanogan Highlands," Don replied. "But, if we were to break it down, I think the Coast would be one, the Puget Sound lowlands another, the Cascades combined, and everything between the Cascades and the Rockies would be one."

"Okay, who wants to be the cartographer for this?" Dave asked in jest.

Jack raised his hand.

"Yeah, Jack?" his father asked.

"Oh, I'm just replying to Mr. Jaskey. I'd like to do that. Be the cartographer, I mean."

"Fine, but do it when we get back. I'd rather you focus on the task at hand while we're here. Your mother would kill me if you got killed."

After a night spent at the fork of the Walla Walla and Columbia Rivers, the small group began the overland trek to where Baker City was on Earth. It turns out the topographic maps they obtained on Earth were a fairly close match to what they found on Hayek, as they were now thinking of the planet. The major differences, of course, were that the river courses were slightly different and there were no cultural features, such as cities, towns, roads, bridges, or fast-food restaurants.

Looking at the maps, Dave told the group, "Looks like our best bet is to follow the Walla Walla until it forks, then take the South Fork just past where the South Fork Walla Walla Trailhead is. There's a creek that flows into the river just where the river turns west from a north leg. That'll put us up on the plateau just north of Tollgate, and from there, we can pretty much follow the route of 204 down to Elgin, and from there, it's straight south to Baker City."

"How far we talking?" Tim asked.

"Give or take, about a hundred twenty-five miles, maybe more. At least four days, maybe five. Another day or so if we go up to where Sumpter is. That's a pretty good placer mining area."

The hardest parts were going to be getting over the mountain range between where they were and where they were going, along with staying near water in the otherwise arid basin.

"Well, let's get this show on the road. Same order as before?" Tim asked.

Dave nodded, grinning. "Yeah, you get up front so the big hungry critters can eat you first and give us time to get away."

The routine for the next four days was pretty much identical. Ride for eight or nine butt-breaking hours, set up camp, eat, collapse, rise, and ride another eight or nine hours. Eventually, everyone except Dave would ride point, even Jack. But Jack was never allowed to ride "tail-end Charley". That always went to one of the two combat veterans. Dave continued his role as mule-skinner.

Tim was in the lead as they approached the area that was Baker City on Earth. As he rode, he scanned the sagebrush-covered hills, then paid particular attention to the wooded area lining the Powder River. As they rode close to the river, he could see it was full of spawning salmon with the occasional beaver dam and lodge. They were almost at their destination, with evening fast approaching. It wasn't twilight yet, but give it another couple of hours, then things would start getting harder to see. The good thing about summer in the high latitudes of the Pacific Northwest was that they could reasonably expect to see until well after nine o'clock at night.

They all got used to scanning the landscape around them, starting near then looking further afield. They also got used to paying attention to the horses and mules, as the animals were usually the first to warn of predators close by. First, they would flatten their ears behind their heads, then they would shake their heads, and then, if the predator was too close, they would whinny and rear up. The first time this happened to Tim, it caught him by surprise. He was used to riding, but not when a horse was scared to death. First came the ear flattening, then the head shaking and foot stomping, then rearing up. Tim almost fell off, but barely managed to hang on.

Dave, riding behind Tim, yelled up, "Something must've spooked him. Look around."

Doing so while the horse frantically backed up to Dave and the mule train, Tim finally saw what had the animal upset, and couldn't believe his eyes. "It's a freakin' lion!"

Less than a hundred feet away stood a lone male lion, bigger than any lion Tim had ever seen in a zoo or on television.

"Shoot it!" shouted Dave.

Tim slid off his horse, rifle in hand, and brought the rifle up just as the lion started its charge toward the horse.

Tim fired, worked the rifle's lever-action, ejecting the spent cartridge and loading another, and fired again. The second shot seemed to stop the lion, but it wasn't enough, so Tim fired twice more, not even hearing the loud gunshots in his adrenalin-fueled state of mind. The lion lay sprawled out in front of him, blood leaking out of numerous wounds into the dry earth.

"Look around, they travel in packs," Dave yelled to the others.

Seeing that the lion he shot no longer presented a threat, Tim cast about looking for any more. Fortunately, it appeared to have been a lone lion.

"What the hell happened?" Don asked, riding up.

"American lion," Dave said. "Cousin to the African lion, only bigger. Went extinct in North America about 12,000 years ago. Guess it thought Tim and/or the horse would make an easy meal."

"All I heard was some shouting and shooting. Next time, let's get a telephone going. First person yells what they see, second one yells what the first one said, and so on until the last person knows exactly what the hell's going on." Looking down at the dead lion, he continued, "Well, looks like we're having super-tabby for supper tonight. I've heard mountain lion tastes good. I wonder how these guys taste."

It turned out American lion was as tasty as mountain lion. At first, Tim, Dave, and Jack were a little leery about eating cat, but the smell of the cooking feline was enough to win them over, and the lion steaks were not only rare but very tasty.

As had become the norm, they dkept the fire going, having verified that the local fauna didn't really like smoke, as evidenced by no nightly disturbances the previous nights.

As they ate, they discussed their plan of action for the next several days.

"Way I see it," Dave said after swallowing a bit of fire-roasted lion, "we could start placer mining here, or, we could head up to Sumpter and placer mine there, and likely get more gold. It's about twenty-five or so miles away. If you've ever been to Sumpter, then you've likely seen the tailings left over. Lots of gold pulled out of there. River's a little shallower, which would make our job easier."

Jack, being far less knowledgeable than the older men, asked, "What's a tailing?"

"Best way to describe them," Dave said, "is it's the stuff left over after you extract whatever you want. In this case, all sorts of gravel, mud, and whatever was pulled out from under the river, run through a big rotary drum, and whatever wasn't gold was tossed out the back. All the gold wound up in the drum in a floating dredge. Of course, they didn't get all the gold, so some of it's still in the tailings."

Tim said, "I'm thinking we should at least do some placer mining here, see what we can find. If it's good enough, I don't see the sense in going any further."

"Tim's got a valid point," Dan agreed. "I don't know about you guys, but my butt sure could use a break for a couple of days."

That evening, when Tim tried to check in with Veronica, all he got was static. When he told the others, Dave said, "I thought that might happen. Not enough signal strength. Next time, let's find a bigger transmitter."

"Yeah, but then how do we power it? It's all a trade-off one what to bring. Jeez, I hope Veronica's not too worried."

Early the next morning, the group assembled all the tools necessary for placer mining. Dave showed the others how to set up the portable sluices, and how to set them in the river. The sluice boxes were nothing more than a couple of pieces of aluminum welded together with a flat bottom and shallow sides. On the bottom were several crosspieces, with pieces of outdoor carpeting between them.

"The way this works is you set it into the river so that water flows through the sluice. Then you shovel gravel into the top. The water will wash the lighter stuff away leaving the gold. Big nuggets get trapped by the riffles," here Dave pointed to the crosspieces, "and the smaller stuff'll get stuck in the carpeting.

"I recommend one of us use the metal detector to find the bigger deposits, one keep guard, and the other two shovel gravel. We should switch off every thirty minutes or so, as shoveling is hard work."

The men could see that Jack was more excited about finding gold than standing guard, so he was "allowed" to be one of the first to shovel. While Dan stood watch, Dave got the metal detector unpacked and assembled. It was one of the newer underwater models, and it took a bit of fiddling with before he had the balance right. Stepping into the relatively cold waters of the Powder River, he began sweeping the machine in front of him. It only took a couple of sweeps before he stopped, pointed to where the detector's coil was, and yelled, "Here. Dig here!"

Stepping back, he watched as Jack lifted the first shovel of gravel and dumped it in the sluice. The gravel muddied the water in the sluice, and Jack dropped another shovelful in. Reaching down, Dave pulled some of the bigger rocks out, looking at them before tossing them back in the river, downstream of the sluice. "Gotta give the water room to move things," he said to Jack. "Reach in and shove things around."

Jack did so, repeating Dave's actions of pulling rocks out, checking them for gold, then tossing them back in the river. Finally, the muddy water cleared, and stuck behind the riffles and in the carpeting were gold nuggets and a thin layer of gold flakes. Placer gold! The edges of the nuggets were sharp, not rounded like the young man had expected.

Picking up one of the nuggets, his eyes widened. He could only say, "Wow," in a hushed voice.

"Wow, exactly," Dave said, taking the nugget from the boy. "See how the edges are sharp, not worn down?"

Jack nodded.

"That means it didn't travel far. Had it been pushed downriver a fair ways, the edges would have been beat smooth. That means we're near the mother lode.

"Put the nuggets in that bag over there. We'll empty the carpeting in a while."

After a half-hour, the four traded places. Dan took up guard position while Tim shoveled. Jack was shown how to operate the metal detector and Dave took his place on the shovel.

"Remember," Dave told Jack, "we're looking for as much gold as possible, as fast as possible, so don't waste time chasing weak signals. You hear a strong signal, let us know. Weak signal, keep moving. We can always come back later for the rest of this stuff."

The four kept up the rotating shift until lunchtime. Unfortunately, while all were in good shape, none were actually prepared for the rigors of placer mining, as evidenced by the blisters that developed under gloves.

As they ate leftover lion and reconstituted dehydrated vegetables, Tim commented, "I bet we're all gonna be hurtin' pups tomorrow."

"What's this tomorrow stuff, Shogun? I'm a hurtin' pup now," Dave said from his location under one of the many massive black cottonwood trees.

"How you doing, Jack?" Don asked his son.

"I'm fine, Dad. You want I should shovel more?"

"And let us old folk take it easy?" Tim joked.

"Well, I am a bit younger," the boy said, grinning over his fork.

Several days of placer mining and numerous blisters later, the four had a rather large supply of gold nuggets, pickers, and dust bagged up. Most had never heard the word "pickers" applied to gold before, only nuggets, flakes, and dust. Dave explained that it referred to small nuggets, almost too small to pick up, but which made a distinct clinking sound when dropped in one of the metal gold pans. Another term for them was clinkers.

All told, they had several bags full of raw gold, an amazing amount for the short time they had been mining.

"This is nothing," Dave said, as the four looked in awe on the small leather bags full of gold. "Just wait until we get a dredge in here. We'll be able to pull out a lot more."

"How much is it worth?" Jack asked. He had never seen much gold before, and this was a large amount. More than any of them had ever seen.

"Well, figure we got about a hundred pounds. Off course, that's Avoirdupois pounds, not Troy pounds."

"Huh?" Tim said for all of them.

Just as if he were back in the classroom, rather than in a high desert valley, Dave took on his lecture mode. "Avoirdupois pound, the system we normally use, where one-sixteenth of a pound is an ounce. The Troy system was set up by the British a long time ago, about seven hundred years, with a Troy pound having twelve Troy ounces. Most stuff is measured using the Avoirdupois system, except precious metals and gunpowder, which use the Troy system.

"Both are based on the use of grains as weight, so a Troy ounce weighs 480 grains and a regular ounce weighs 437.5 grains. That means a Troy pound is five thousand seven hundred sixty grains as opposed to seven thousand grains for a regular pound. The grain was based on the ideal weight of a single grain of wheat back in the Roman times.

"So, knowing that we've got about a hundred pounds, or about seven hundred thousand grains, that's about," Dave looked up to the sky, mentally calculating, "fifteen hundred Troy ounces. At about three-hundred seventy bucks an ounce," again, his attention turned inward, calculating, while his eyes looked at the sky. When the answer came to him, he smiled and looked at the other three. "At about three-hundred seventy dollars a Troy ounce, that comes out to about five hundred fifty thousand dollars."

"A half a million?" Tim gasped.

"Holy smokeroonie, Batman," was Don's response.

"Yeah, if we can get it all back and then sell it. Of course, we'll still need to pay taxes on the sale, so figure on about half of that going to Uncle Sugar, so we wind up with a bit under two hundred eighty kay."

"Ouch," was all Tim and Don had to say.

"Did I hear you right, Mr. Jaskey? We've got to give up half of what we earn to the government?"

"Yeah, Jack, you heard right. That much money and we've got to pay half to the government."

"That just doesn't seem right," the teen said.

"Gotta pay for them wars, roads, bridges, and other such stuff," Dave said.

"What if it's a business, and we don't pay ourselves much?" Tim asked.

"Good question. You'll want a good accountant for that," Dave replied.

"So, we could set up a business when we get back, sell the gold, buy everything we need to come back, and write it off. I'm betting that'll drop our tax rate. Anyone know what corporate tax rates are?" Tim asked.

Everyone shrugged. With the exception of Jack, who was still a minor in high school, the other three were all public employees, teachers with no knowledge of business.

"Well, let's connect with a CPA when we get back and set up a business. Since I'm the one who invented the gate, anyone have a problem with me getting fifty percent of it? If so, I'll just destroy the gate and we walk away with what we've got."

Everyone agreed that destroying the gate would be stupid. "Besides, even if I only have one percent, I'm willing to bet I'll be a multi-millionaire before long," Don said.

"Multi-millionaire? I'm betting billionaire," Dave said. "Think about all the people that would love to leave Earth, and then think how much we can charge them. Hell, we've got a monopoly here. And if you've got a monopoly on something people want, they'll pay whatever they can afford to get it."

That caused the others to become a bit introspective. It's one thing to talk about becoming a millionaire, but a billionaire?

"Here's a thought," Don said. "Let's assume that Tim gets fifty percent of the company, that leaves fifty percent for the rest of us. Shouldn't we think about leaving some wiggle room for potential investors?"

"Why?" Jack asked, clearly confused. If they had all this gold, why would they need more money?

"Simple, son," Don said, "because we may not have enough money on hand, and we can use the shares of a company to either get other people to invest their money with our company or get banks to loan us money using the shares as collateral."

"What's collateral?"

"It's something you put up, so in case you can't pay on a loan, they can take it. Sort of like the house. If I can't make the payments, the mortgage company can take it from me."

"Oh." Thinking about it for a moment, the teen asked, "So, like if I was to buy something, like a car, on credit, the company that loaned me the money has a physical thing they can take from me if I can't pay?"

"Exactly."

"How much do you think we should set aside?" Dave asked.

"I'm not greedy," Don said, "but whatever we bring back from this trip should be our contribution, and if we keep forty percent or so set aside for investors, that means we each get two and a half percent. So, figure on five hundred and fifty thou for ten percent, that means we could probably raise another two mil or so, if needed." Don's face split into a wholly unfamiliar expression—a grin. "Heck, I don't know about you guys, but I've never had a hundred thousand before, especially for only a couple of weeks' work. Just imagine how much we'll make with more mining, and whatever other fees we get people to pay to come over."

All agreed that the breakdown in company shares would be more than equitable.

"Meanwhile," Tim asked the group, "let's consider our next step. Do we come back here or head for California?"

"We try heading for California on horseback, we wouldn't get there for some time," Don said. "If we got there, that is. Look at all that's around us. We've been lucky so far, but how long'll that last?"

"What if we fly?" Jack asked.

"How?" his dad replied. "No runways at either end and the terrain in California gold country is hills and mountains, mostly mountains."

"Can't we do like they did in Laos and Vietnam during the war?" the young man asked. "You know, airdrop a crew to build a rough airfield, then bring the plane in with fuel bladders or drums?"

"How do you know this stuff?" Tim asked in wonder. Few of his students seemed to have the types of smarts young Lewis had.

The boy blushed, the red rising up his face to the red roots of his hair. "I read a lot, and I watched a lot of documentaries about the war. Plus, I love planes. I'm hoping to become a pilot."

"I thought you already were one," Dave said, more in the way of a question than a statement.

"Oh, I've got my pilot's license, sir, but I'm talking a real pilot. You know, a commercial pilot's license and a job flying for an airline."

"All that's well and good," Tim said. "But you got to remember, the gate's barely big enough for a horse. I don't see how we could get a plane through it."

"Build a bigger gate?" Dave asked.

Tim thought about that for a bit. "Y'know, I think it's just possible. Let's try when we get back."

The trip back to Selah was almost as uneventful as the trip to the goldfields, with the major difference being they wound up riding most of the way, other than the brief trip across the Columbia River. As with their brief time on the Columbia between the Yakima and Walla Walla Rivers, they had to deal with a minor set of rapids as they passed through the Wallula Gap on the Columbia. Or, what passed for minor on such a big river as the Columbia. As with the first time, they managed to get through these rapids without incident, landing on the north shore of the mighty river for the nearly one-hundred-mile overland trek back to their starting point.

As they crossed over the dry basalt of the first set of ridges, Don looked about at the landscape, taking in the hot, dusty scent of the land, and declared, "Y'know, this looks like it'd be prime wine country for quality reds."

"What, this area?" Tim asked. "Hell, nobody even lives here on our Earth. Horse Heaven Hills they call it. Ought to call it Horse Hell Hills."

After getting over the anticline that formed the hills, they dropped into the lower Yakima Valley. Another day's journey had them almost at Union Gap, which separated the upper and lower Yakima Valleys. Rather than head through the gap and push on the remaining ten or so miles to their destination, they waited as a herd of Columbia mammoth passed through it on their way into the lower Yakima Valley, trailed by some dire wolves. The wolves took some interest in the outlanders, but decided to avoid them when Dave shot their leader when it got too inquisitive; read it was about to attack him.

That evening, at the five o'clock check-in, they managed to reach Veronica and let her know that they would be home the next day. Needless to say, Tim could hear the relief in her voice during the brief conversation, knowing that they were all still alive.

Finally, after a bit more than three weeks on the trail, the small party saw the orange flag indicating the gate's location. Tim glanced at his watch. They still had an hour before noon; he suggested they unpack the mules and hobble all the animals. "No sense having them stand around with all that weight on them," he rationalized.

While Don and Jack stood guard, Tim and Dave unloaded the pack mules, then hobbled them. They decided to keep the horses saddled and ready to go at a moment's notice, but did do a bit of a compromise by putting each horse on a picket line, tying the ropes off to trees rather than actually pounding a picket pin to tie the rope to.

The first time they had used picket lines, Dave had explained to the group that horses had to be trained to work around picket lines. "Otherwise, they think it's a snake and they'll try to run. Not good for the rope or the horse. Seen too many horses with broken legs because of that."

Tim looked at his watch every hour, or so he thought, and saw the minute hand slowly creep from 11:15 to noon. Exactly at noon, the gate opened, just where they thought it would. Cheering broke out among the four, as the gate rapidly expanded enough to show the interior of Tim's workshop. Petra stood at the entrance holding the shotgun, a huge smile on her face. She was a small, thin woman with a ready smile and a quick wit. Tim could see what Dave saw in her, more for the mental than the physical.

Dave called out to Don and Jack, "You guys keep watch, we'll get everything over to the other side."

Several minutes later, all animals and equipment were in Tim's shed, and while Tim and Dave stood guard from just outside the gate, the other two joined them. One last look and the four stepped into Tim's shed and Veronica shut down the gate.

Tim didn't even have time to turn around and greet his wife before she tackle-hugged him. Kissing him fiercely, she then let go, wrinkling her nose, and said, "You stink. You need a shower."

It was then that Tim noticed there were others in the shed. Don and Jack were surrounded by a woman and two other red-headed children. The woman was Don's wife, Eileen, and their two children, Jack's siblings, were Maureen and Kathleen, both just about to enter teenhood.

7

That evening Veronica and the other ladies laid out a feast for the men beyond anything they had experienced over the past several weeks. None of them, including Jack, could seem to get enough fresh vegetables.

As Tim took a break from eating his spinach salad, he said, "We need to find a way to have fresh veggies on future trips. Man, I didn't know how much I missed these." The other men just nodded as they ate, occasionally taking breaks for swigs of beer, another thing that had been sorely missed on Hayek.

The time spent after crossing over and before the "welcome home" feast involved taking care of the horses and mules, ensuring they were safely in the pastures, cleaning and putting away equipment, taking long, hot showers, and discussing future plans, said discussion being done over a few drinks while waiting for supper. To say that the women were suitably impressed by the large amount of gold was an understatement.

When Tim had told the women about forming a corporation and buying more equipment, Petra suggested a CPA who could help out. "He works with a lot of businesses, so he'll know what to do. You'll also want a lawyer to set up the corporation."

Dave took a sip of his whiskey and asked, "Does he know how to keep his mouth shut? I don't know about the rest of you, but I think keeping this on the low down is the best move."

Don answered, "I don't think he needs to know much. Just tell him we're forming a mining company and need to buy equipment with the gold we've found. Let him figure out what we need to legally and financially do. We do the rest."

"So, you guys think you'll find a plane we can afford?" Tim asked. "It's gotta be able to drop a small bulldozer out the back so we can build airfields, like those Air America guys Jack was telling us about." What Tim didn't say was that he had seen Air America in action in Vietnam, and knew some of their capabilities.

It turned out that Jack knew a fair amount about airplanes and field expedient airfields, and told the older men about the Central Intelligence Agency's airline operation, Air America, that operated in Laos during the Vietnam War. The company had numerous cargo airplanes and had to develop airstrips in remote areas, mainly because the craft they used were STOL—Short Take-Off and Landing. One way of doing so was to drop a small crew with some portable equipment and construct a dirt runway. Another way was to lay down perforated steel planking, also known as Marston Matting. Ten-foot sections, each weighing less than seventy pounds, could be connected together to provide an airstrip, just by laying the planks down on the ground, over the standing vegetation.

There were a number of cargo planes that Jack knew about, but only a couple that would be able to airdrop small bulldozers or Marston Matting.

"What we need is something with a rear door and ramp. That pretty much limits us to de Havilland Caribous, Lockheed C-123 Providers, or C-130 Hercules. And good luck getting either of the last two."

That left the choice of planes as either a de Havilland Caribou or a seaplane, for operating off lakes and rivers. If they could afford the Caribou, they'd buy that, drop in by parachute, and build an airfield. If not, they would fly to either Lake Tahoe or the Sacramento River, then walk to the South Fork of the American River, where gold was known to exist. Landing on the Powder River, which they had just left, was out of the question. There was insufficient water; not only was the river too shallow, but it was also too narrow. Any plane they attempted to land on it would probably have its wings sheared off by the trees lining the riverbank.

Tim was barely awake and hadn't even made his way into the kitchen where he could smell fresh coffee brewing, when the phone rang. He heard Veronica answer it, then shout for him, "Tiiiimm! It's Dave."

When Tim came into the kitchen, Veronica handed him the phone. As he took it, he pantomimed drinking. Veronica immediately understood and got a coffee mug out of the cupboard while Tim began talking with Dave.

"Yeah?"

"I spoke with that CPA this morning," Dave said.

"Already? What time is it?"

"After nine. What, you just get up?"

Tim looked at his watch, then scratched his head, doing no damage whatsoever to the bedhead he had awoken to, then accepted a fresh cup of coffee from Veronica. He answered, "Yeah, damned phone was ringing. Woke me up."

Dave laughed. Tim took a sip of coffee, waiting to hear what Dave had to say.

"Anyhow, he recommended we get a lawyer and draw up a charter for our company, and that we form it as a corporation. He said we should start out as an S corporation."

"What's that?"

"Apparently, there are two types: C and S. C corporations are the big guys, lots of investors, publicly traded. That kind of thing. They get taxed at a corporate level, and whatever goes to the shareholders gets taxed as long or short-term capital gains or income tax. So, sorta like getting double-taxed.

"S corporations are smaller, less than a hundred people. They're still corporations, just have a slightly different structure and get taxed differently. There is no corporate tax. Instead, the shareholders get taxed on their portion of the profits as regular income. So, if we used the gold to buy a plane for the company, then split the rest of the money between us, we only get taxed on our share. We can also expense the plane and other equipment, deducting the full cost, instead of taking the tax deduction as a depreciation over a bunch of years."

"Hmm. So, we set up the company, sell some gold, buy the plane, and we can write all that off?" Tim asked.

"Yep, along with any costs to actually mine."

"Any downside to going with the S corporation?"

"Yeah, we can't have foreigners or companies as shareholders."

"That's fine with me. What about a lawyer?"

"Yeah, the CPA recommended a guy named Bob Poe. He's in Yakima. Supposed to be a good business lawyer."

Tim took another sip of coffee as Dave asked, "You want I should call him?"

Nodding, then realizing Dave couldn't see the nod, Tim replied in the affirmative.

"Will do," Dave said. "Talk with you soon. Oh, yeah, we meet with the CPA at one o'clock, after lunch." Dave hung up, then Tim turned and hung up the phone as Don walked into the kitchen, bedhead and pajamas on full display. He didn't even have to say anything, Veronica just handed him a cup of coffee. The Lewises had spent the night with the Bowmans, the adults in the spare room and the kids in the living room. Jack had claimed the sofa while the girls were forced to sleep on air mattresses on the floor. The only kid still sleeping was Jack. It had been a long, hard three weeks.

Smelling the brew before taking a sip, Don asked, "What'd Dave find out?"

Tim explained.

"Sounds good. We should probably have everything set up before selling even one ounce of gold."

"Yeah, I think so, too. I think the next major step is finding the right aircraft and other stuff."

"We'll be checking on that starting when we get back home," Don said, looking back through the door at Jack. "Leastways, he'll be doing most of that." Turning back to Tim he asked, "What do you think about using some of that gold to pay for flying lessons for all of us? I was thinking about this last night, and I really don't see any of us returning to teaching. Do you?"

It was a subject they had all danced around, both while on Hayek and once they returned home. Tim loved teaching, as did Dave and Don, but the pay just wasn't there. Tim was fortunate that he had inherited enough from his grandparents that he could afford his small ranchette, but Dave and Don weren't in the same class. Dave did a little better teaching at the community college level, but he supplemented his income by teaching an evening class each quarter at Central Washington University in Ellensburg. Winter driving between the two cities, while only forty to forty-five minutes, could sometimes prove quite treacherous, and Petra wasn't all too thrilled about Dave's schedule or commute.

As a father supporting a family of five on a teacher's salary, Don had it the hardest. Eileen was a stay-at-home mom, not having transitioned into the career mom move that so many other women were doing, focusing on raising her kids and being there for Don when he got home, even when getting home meant another four or five hours of work in the evening.

Tim had also been giving serious thought about not returning to teaching. The prospect of exploring this new world was much more enticing to him than lecturing students about quantum particles and quarks.

Veronica broke the silence. "Why go back? Not only will you make a lot more doing this, but it's also more fun. I haven't seen you guys this charged up in, like, forever. I don't know what you were like before Vietnam, but I know what you've been like since returning, and I'm seeing a totally rejuvenated man. When was the last time you had any nightmares?"

Tim had to think about it. Certainly not while they were on Hayek. "Not since before I opened the gate."

"Exactly. Do you want to return to how it was?"

Both men shook their heads. It was at this moment that Jack joined them. "Return to what?" he asked.

"Our old lives," his father answered.

"Why would you want to do that?" Jack asked in wonder. "I mean, exploring whole new worlds, that whole Star Trek thing. Heck, I don't even want to go back to school."

"Yeah, well, you need an education," his father said, taking another sip of coffee.

Jack, not having been offered coffee by Veronica as the two men had been, found a mug and poured his own. It was a habit he had picked up on Hayek. Adding a spoonful of sugar, he turned back to the adults. "C'mon Dad. You think I'm not gonna learn on Hayek? I'm sorry, but what can they teach me at Lake Washington High School that I won't learn with you, Dr. Bowman, and Dr. Jaskey?"

"I can think of many subjects," Tim said, preempting Don. "Literature, geography, sociology, psychology, economics, just to name a few."

Jack leaned back on the counter, cup held in both hands. "How many of those are important when opening a new world? Geography and economics I can see. But most of what we learn in high school is pretty much useless for this new world. From what I see, knowing business, geography, and how to fly and shoot straight means a lot more."

Tim was impressed with the perception of the young teen. "Are you sure you're only fifteen?" he asked, jokingly.

Jack smiled. "Sometimes Mom thinks I'm ten." Then he turned more serious. "Let me ask you, Dr. Bowman, how much of what you learned in high school do you use? How much did you use when you and Dad were in Vietnam? How much do you think you used when we crossed over? I know I learned a lot more about geography just studying all the maps and listening to you guys discuss biomes and watersheds and economics than I learned in school so far.

"What I do know is that knowing how to shoot, and more importantly, when to shoot, or when not to shoot, is more useful than knowing what some dead author wrote a couple of hundred years ago. Knowing how to navigate is more important, in my mind, than learning how to conjugate a Latin verb. I could go on, but the reality is, I learn more with you and Dr. Jaskey and Dad when I'm over on Hayek. Do you think I would have learned about classical liberalism in high school? I can tell you now, most teachers probably don't even know what it is."

At this Don chimed in, "Gotta admit, you're right about that. Most don't. They're pushing for socialism, not even recognizing just how bad it is."

"See! That's exactly what I'm talking about. You want me to learn? Keep me out of high school!"

After the Lewises had left, Tim pondered what Jack had said. Modern education was only getting worse, pandering to the lowest common denominator. And, from what he could see, they were pushing the whole "college for all" when the world still needed tradesmen. Why did an HVAC specialist need a college degree? Sure, it was nice to be educated, but to what degree? And, couldn't those interested in a liberal arts degree learn on their own? Perhaps, with guidance, they might even learn better.

The question remained, though. What education would be necessary for this brave, new world they found? He was still pondering this, considering taking on the task of developing a high school and college curriculum when the phone rang.

It was Dave and he had been in touch with the attorney, Bob Poe. "Says he can fit us in this morning at ten-thirty, if you're free," Dave concluded.

Tim glanced at his watch. It was almost ten. "Where is this guy?"

Dave gave him an address on Pendleton Way, about a block from the courthouse. It was about fifteen minutes away.

"Give me that address again," Tim said, grabbing paper and pencil. "I'll see you there."

Tim had barely enough time for a quick shower. Before hopping into the stall, he told Veronica where he was going and asked if she wanted to join him at the attorney's office. "After all, you're part of this too."

She agreed, and as soon as Tim was dressed, the two of them got in the Willys station wagon and headed out. Before they were out of the driveway, both had rolled the windows down to get some air flowing. The Willys wasn't air-conditioned. "Promise me you'll buy me something with air-conditioning before summer's out," Veronica said as she moved her hand, sticking out the passenger window, in an up and down fashion, much like an airplane's wing, her black hair floating about her face in the automobile generated wind.

Parking in downtown Yakima was a struggle, but the two still made it to Poe's office in plenty of time. Dave and Petra were waiting in the lobby. They didn't have to wait long before Poe came out of his office. He was a young man, barely into his thirties, but already going bald. His horn-rimmed glasses accentuated his youth, rather than lending an air of age and wisdom. That was fine with Tim. Age and experience were good, but sometimes youth and flexibility were more important.

Poe introduced himself then invited them into his office, where there were barely enough seats for all of them.

"So, Dave says you guys are onto something pretty important and want to start a company. Is that about it?"

Tim answered for all of them. "That pretty much sums it up. Just how confidential is what we say gonna be?"

Poe started into the typical lawyer spiel about attorney-client privilege and Tim stopped him. "Yeah, we know all that. My question is, do you know how to keep your mouth shut? I'm not talking client-attorney privilege, I'm going beyond that."

The young attorney stared at Tim. During his short career in the law, he wasn't used to having anyone interrupt him. "Well, uh, attorney-client privilege means I can't really talk about what my clients do with anyone, unless, of course, it's illegal. This isn't illegal, is it?"

"Does that include your wife?" Tim asked.

"I'm not married."

"Okay, then. What we're doing isn't illegal. Highly unusual, but not illegal. We need to know you're not gonna say anything to anyone. Period, dot, period. You understand?" Tim was quite emphatic, leaning forward from the edge of his seat.

Again, Poe nodded.

"If this goes the way we think it's gonna go, we'll probably need in-house counsel. Is that something you might consider?"

"Well, I've got my business here, and…"

Tim interrupted him again. "Not to be snarky, but a small office near the courthouse probably doesn't bring in the big bucks. I'm talking big bucks. We need to know if you can be quiet, discreet, and do what we need."

Poe looked back and forth between the four seated across from him. Leaning forward and placing his elbows on the desk, which had obviously seen better days, shoulders hunched forward indicating intense interest, he asked, "How much are we talking?"

"That depends. If you're counsel, likely millions."

"Is there a buy-in option?"

The four hadn't expected that. They were just looking for an attorney who would set up their business. Tim and Dave looked at each other. Years of being together paid off, as they silently agreed.

"Depends," Dave said. "How much can you contribute?"

"Tell me what the venture is, and I'll decide." Poe was clearly playing hardball, for which Tim respected him.

"Before you say anything, I recommend you actually retain him as your attorney," Veronica said. "That way we might be able to stop him from blabbing. Even if we have to sue him."

Tim was impressed with his wife's forethought.

"Yeah, that'd probably be a good idea. Can you draw up a quick contract stipulating that you're our attorney of record?"

Opening a desk drawer, Poe pulled out a small, single-page document and set it on the desk. "Will this do?"

One at a time, the four perused it.

"Yeah, that'll do," Tim said.

"Great, let me get my secretary to fill in the names. I'll be right back." Poe was up and out of the office with the document in a flash.

"Ooh, these legal dogs are bloody greedy," Dave said, paraphrasing a line from one of his favorite movies, *Paint Your Wagon*, in a fake Scottish accent.

A few minutes later, Poe was back with the agreement. Tim and Dave's names were on it, but not the wives. "Sorry, I didn't have everyone's names on it, but this should suffice," Poe explained.

Tim looked at the agreement and passed it back to Poe. "We're a team. Put their names on it, then we'll talk." Sitting back in his chair, he waited with crossed arms until Poe picked up the document and left the office.

Several minutes later, Poe returned with a new document. This time, both Veronica's and Petra's names were on it.

First Tim, then Dave, reviewed the document, then signed and dated it. Dave passed the document on to Veronica who signed it. Once Petra signed it, she handed it to the young lawyer. It wasn't until Poe signed and dated that the four were willing to talk.

Tim started the conversation. "We're not businessmen, but don't take us to be stupid. We've both got Ph.D.s, so we're pretty bright. We just don't know business. A CPA recommended we seek out a business attorney and your name came up."

Poe nodded. He seemed to do that a lot. Elbows on his desk, hands in front of him with fingers interlaced, hunched forward in interest.

"We've found a way to mine gold. A lot of gold."

"And, you've got permits and mining rights?"

At this, Tim and Dave grinned. The women, though, looked nervous.

"We don't need no stinking permits," Dave said.

Tim also answered. "No, no permits and no rights. Don't matter. Where we go, you don't need 'em."

"You mine anywhere in the West, you need one or the other," Poe replied.

"What if it's not in this country?" Tim asked.

"Well, then, you'll likely need import licenses."

"What if we're not importing it across international borders?" Tim said. "All we want to do is sell the gold as a company. Can you set it up for us, or should we go elsewhere?"

"I believe so. If it's not coming from the here, and not being imported, then where *is* it coming from?"

"Elsewhen," was Tim's simple answer.

"Elsewhen?" Poe parroted, a confused look on his face. "Not elsewhere?"

"Elsewhen," Dave repeated.

What followed was an educational discussion in which Poe learned of the gate and the profits that would likely be gained.

Again, he asked, "How can I get into this?"

Both couples recognized his greed and interest. The question was, could he be trusted? Tim decided to test him. "You ever kill a man?" he asked.

Poe was taken aback. "No. Why would I?"

Tim leaned forward. "I have. Several times. And I'm willing to do so again."

Poe picked up on the implied threat. "If you think I'm going to blab about this, with the potential here, you can forget about it. If what you say is true, then I want in. No need for any threats."

Leaning back in his leather upholstered chair, Tim said, "No threats, just statements of fact."

Poe nodded. "I get you. So, I can draw up the papers, shouldn't take more'n a day or so. What kind of legal structure are you looking for?" He picked up a legal yellow pad and pen and took notes as the men spoke.

Dave mentioned the CPA's recommendation for an S corporation and Poe agreed. "Easy to set up, just need to know names and shares or percentages to assign each one, based on their contribution, or basis. How many people are we talking about, how many shares, and what amount to contribute."

Tim looked up briefly, calculating. "Three people to start with…"

"Make that four," Dave said.

"Four?" Tim looked at Dave.

"The kid gets his own share."

Tim looked at Veronica, who simply nodded.

"Make that four, and…" again, he looked up, mentally calculating how much each person contributed. "Figure on $137,500 per person. Equal shares, except me. I get fifty percent of the company *plus* a further equal share. If it weren't for me, we wouldn't even be here now. If we go with assigning everyone's contributions to a total of ten percent of the shares, that leaves us with forty percent free for investors. So, each person would get two and a half percent of the company. How many shares can a company have?"

"As many as a million, if you want," Poe answered. "But the maximum number of shareholders it can have is a hundred, and they can't be other corporations, partnerships, or foreign investors. This can make it pretty hard to raise a substantial amount of money."

"We're not worried about that. Can we set it up where there's shares still available? I mean, shares we don't own, but people can buy into?"

Poe nodded. Again. "I can set up the number of shares on the articles of incorporation, and get a CPA to assign a value for each share. The company doesn't have to issue all the shares. You raise money by selling shares."

"How do we know how much to charge for each share?" Veronica jumped in.

"Well, a CPA will usually determine the company's worth, then assign a value, which they call par. You can then sell the shares at par when seeking investors. Things they take into account to determine this are assets, risk, stage of start-up, management team. Now, as far as I can tell, one of your greatest assets is this gate. Do you have a patent application in yet?"

Tim shook his head. "Nope. Not gonna patent it. I figure if anyone else can figure out what I did, they're welcome to it. Odds are, though, is that they won't."

"Sort of like Coca-Cola, huh?" the young attorney said, to which Tim just nodded.

"Okay, so, let's see if I've got this straight." Poe looked down at his notes. "You'll be wanting to set up an S corporation with a million shares, with Tim getting half, or half a million shares, plus equal shares from $137,500, based on what the CPA determines is par. Does that sound about right?"

The four nodded.

"Mind you, the par might only be a fraction of a cent, what we call penny stocks. Are you good with that?"

This time they either nodded or shrugged.

"Once we go public with this, the price will rise."

"Oh, you can't go public. To do that, you need to be a C corp," Poe said, hands coming up in a stopping motion and eyes widening.

Tim laughed. "I don't mean publicly traded, I'm talking about when we go to the press and let the public know what we're doing. Gold mining is just the beginning."

"Just the beginning?" Poe asked, one eyebrow rising almost to his hairline.

"Yep. We're planning on opening the planet up to settlement for like-minded individuals. So, we also need something that stipulates that all land and sea are the property of the company. We figure people will pay big bucks to leave this Earth for one with less regulations and more opportunities. On top of that, we'll own all the land, so people will have to buy or lease land from us. We'll need you to write up some ironclad agreements on that—we'll always want right of first refusal on any sale. Also, anything that comes through the gate will be charged both transit fees and tariffs to run whatever government we set up, which is going to be as minimal as possible. Sort of like what America was before Woodrow Wilson."

Poe leaned back in his high-backed leather chair, clearly overwhelmed with the scope of what he was dealing with. Leaning forward after a second, pen and legal pad in hand, he said, "So, on top of forming a corporation, you're going to want me to develop a real-estate transaction form, like a deed or patent, and some sort of constitution?"

"Yes on the first two, but no on the third," Tim said. "No constitution, but we do want you developing an agreement that anyone crossing over to Hayek accepts responsibilities for their actions and agrees to abide by the rules and laws."

"Why no constitution?"

Tim and Dave looked at each other, then at their wives, and finally back at Poe. "Because we figure that's something the founding fathers, that being us, ought to develop. We just need to be sure we've got something in place that people will legally recognize."

"Gotcha. So, one corporate charter with articles of incorporation as an S corp, a deed or patent for land with the right of first refusal, and some sort of responsibility statement or agreement?"

Looking over at the other three before responding, Tim finally said, "Yeah. That about sums it up. Also, any chance you'd be willing to give us a generic non-disclosure agreement for our meeting with the CPA later today? We'll also want the articles of incorporation as soon as possible so we can get the ball rolling."

The meeting that afternoon with the CPA involved only Tim, Dave, and the CPA, whose name was Jeff Shimazu. Shimazu was, like Tim, a product of an American soldier and a war bride, only this time the father was a Nisei, one of the famed 442nd Regimental Combat Team made up of Americans of Japanese descent. His mother was French, who had decided marrying a Japanese-American and moving to America was a lot better than living in 1945 war-torn southern France.

Jeff was a few years younger than Tim, who was surprised that he recalled the man from high school. There weren't many mixed Japanese-Anglos in their small high school, but for some reason, the two had never really mingled. Likely because Tim was a senior when Jeff was a freshman.

Jeff remembered Tim and welcomed him warmly, along with Dave.

"So, how can I help you? Dave mentioned you wanted to form a corporation and needed some help."

Tim pulled the non-disclosure agreement from his battered briefcase. "Before we talk, would you be willing to sign this?"

Shimazu looked over the agreement, shrugged, picked up a pen from his desk, and signed and dated the document. Passing it back to Tim, he leaned back in his chair, brought his hands up in front of him and laced his fingers together, waiting.

Tim briefly looked at the agreement to be sure it had Shimazu's real name on it before putting it away. Looking at Shimazu, he developed a big grin.

"What do you know about the multiverse?"

8

Three days later, Tim and Dave were in possession of copies of their Articles of Incorporation, copies of an Internal Revenue Service form indicating they were electing to be an S corporation for tax purposes, and documents that explained the value per share for each of the million shares issued by the new company: Parallel, Incorporated.

Poe and Shimazu had managed to come up with twenty-thousand dollars each as a way of buying into the firm. There was no way either of them wanted to miss out on the financial benefits of a company that would ultimately make them rich, along with providing them with a bolt-hole in case the Cold War turned hot. While Yakima didn't have much to worry about as a target for a nuclear strike, other than the Yakima Proving Grounds, it was on the downwind side of multiple possible targets on the other side of the Cascade Mountains.

Included in the papers were contracts for Poe as the legal counsel for Parallel, Inc. and for Shimazu as the Chief Financial Officer. Tim was listed as the Chief Executive Officer and Dave was taking the role of Chief Operations Officer. The only ones without defined C-suite roles were Don and Jack. Tim had felt Don would make a good Field Operations Manager with Jack as his assistant.

Shimazu had calculated par at a bit over eighteen cents a share, based almost exclusively on the gold mining operation. He didn't want to even write up anything on the gate, mainly because of the believability factor. "Who would believe this if they didn't actually see it?" he had asked Tim and Dave at their initial meeting. "I'm not even sure I believe it." The next morning, he did, as he and Poe had made their way to Tim's ranchette for a demonstration.

All told, each original member was assigned 25,000 shares at five and a half dollars a share, except Tim, who had 525,000 shares.

Dave had joined Tim at Tim's ranchette when Poe and Shimazu had brought the papers over. The four were sitting on his deck overlooking the mountains and reviewing the documents and having morning coffee when the phone rang. It was Don. "We found a plane," he said without preamble.

"What kind?" Tim asked

"A seaplane. A Grumman Goose. We'll be by later today with the particulars. Got room for the kid and me?"

Tim grinned. He hadn't told Don and Jack about their interest in the company yet. "Yeah. When should we expect you?"

"Be there by lunch."

"Great. See you then."

Stepping back out onto the deck, Tim told the others of the conversation. Both Poe and Shimazu looked at their watches. Poe said, "I can be back then. Still got lots of work to do at the office until this thing takes off." Shimazu nodded. "Me, too."

"Good, see you guys then," Tim said, as the two professionals put down their empty coffee cups and stood.

Don pulled into Tim's driveway just before lunch. Travel time between Kirkland and Selah was only a bit over two hours. Jack was driving, this time with more confidence.

Veronica had prepared lunch for the entire crew, as Petra had joined them, so Tim waved Don and Jack onto the back deck.

"We've got a CPA and lawyer in on this," Tim told them. "Once they saw what we were up to, they jumped in with both feet, along with twenty kay each. They should be here shortly."

"Forty thousand more?" Don asked. "Good, cause I think we're gonna need it. Should we tell you what we found or wait until the other show up?"

"Let's wait," Tim said. "Shouldn't be too long, anyhow."

Within ten minutes, both Poe and Shimazu arrived. After introductions, and while eating, Don told them what they had found.

"Turns out we don't have enough for what we wanted, which was a DeHavilland DHC-4 Caribou." Looking at Tim, he said, "You might remember them from 'Nam as the C7 Caribous. Those planes are great for short fields and could get us down there with room to spare. If we build an airfield in California, we could even bring enough fuel to fill up and get us and the gold home again. Trip down with fuel, trip home with gold. Sounds pretty sweet. As a frame of reference, it's got a slightly better payload than a C-47 with a shorter take-off and landing distance.

"Anyhow, we don't have enough for one; they're about eight hundred thousand each. But, we do have enough for a seaplane, specifically a Grumman Goose."

"Weren't those made during World War II?" asked Dave.

"Yeah, but they're still going strong," Don said. "And the great thing about 'em is that they can land on water." Turning toward his son, he said, "Jack, show them what you've got planned."

Nervous, but with a confidence born of knowledge, Jack laid a road map of the western US out on the table. "Since we can't afford a Caribou, and don't have the ability to build an airfield without one, Dad and I decided on a seaplane to get us there. It had to meet a number of criteria, among them being a decent range, the ability to land on water, twin engines, and a decent payload. That pretty much left us with either the Canadair CL-215, a PBY, or the Grumman Goose, Albatross, or Mallard. The CL-215 is about the same price as a Caribou, which means it's out of our price range. I couldn't find any PBYs for sale, which leaves us with looking at Grummans. There aren't any Albatrosses for sale, and the Mallards are a lot more expensive than the Goose, so we recommend getting the Goose, specifically the G-21G model." Looking about, he said, "We managed to find one of those for sale.

"With a crew of two and carrying six or seven passengers, it can go almost seven hundred knots, or about eight hundred statute miles. It's got five hundred eighty-six gallons fuel capacity if we want to maximize the distance. Take-off distance on water is about a thousand feet, and it needs about fifteen hundred feet to land. That's our big limitation. Not too many bodies of water in California with that kind of length, and landing on one of the rivers doesn't look too appealing. At least, not to me." He grinned, shyly.

"To get down and back, we'll need to ferry fuel down and stash it at various spots. Avgas, or aviation gas, weighs about six pounds a gallon. As a frame of reference," he said, unknowingly mimicking his father, "water weighs over eight pounds a gallon. So, if we wanted to carry a couple of bladders of fuel with two hundred gallons, our payload would be fifty-nine hundred pounds, just for fuel. Max take-off weight is twelve thousand five hundred pounds, and empty weight is about fifty-five hundred pounds, so we've actually got room for almost sixty-six hundred pounds of payload, which includes anyone riding inside."

Jack looked around at the assembled adults, making sure they understood. Said adults were quite impressed with what the fifteen-year-old was relaying to them.

He continued, "Anyhow, we figure we need to establish at least two refueling points. One half-way between here and the California goldfields, one at or near the fields, and maybe a third one, just in case. Our best bet is to establish the first fuel depot at either of the lakes in the Newberry Caldera, near Bend, Lake Abert near Valley Falls, or Goose Lake on the Oregon-California border. Our final destination would be Donner Lake, north of Lake Tahoe."

"Why there instead of Lake Tahoe?" Tim asked.

"It's a little closer to the goldfields," the youth answered. "I figure, since I'm going to be the pilot, I won't be spending much time walking. You older guys," at which Jack smiled, "are the ones that are gonna have to walk in with equipment and walk out with the gold, until we finally get an airfield put in. So, the closer I get you to the goldfields, the less complaining I hear."

The older men laughed, recognizing the truth in Jack's statement. None of them looked forward to walking several days lugging equipment and then gold.

"How much fuel are we talking about, and how are we gonna access it?

"Good point," Don said. "The kid already thought of that."

"Yes sir," Jack continued. "I recommend we establish fuel depots at all three lakes on the way down, putting in at least a thousand gallons at each site. We can use a couple of two-hundred-gallon fuel bladders and fill up empty thousand-gallon bladders on site with either a manual pump or an electric pump. That way, when we're on our way back, we can maximize our payload capacity and keep our fuel weight down. In other words," he wrapped up with a grin, "we can carry more gold back."

The five men and one youth looked at the map intently, each figuring out what it would take.

"One other thing," Jack said. "We could probably air-drop a bunch of stuff once you're at the goldfields. Things like rockers, shovels, picks, breaker bars, maybe even a dredge and fuel."

"Can you do that?" Dave asked.

"I haven't yet. But I'm sure with some practices, I could."

"Probably need to bring some smoke with us," Tim said. The last time he had used smoke was in Vietnam when they were bringing in a helicopter for a medevac.

"Smoke?" Poe asked.

"Smoke grenade," Tim said. "You pull a pin and colored smoke pours out. Lets something in the air see where you are."

"I vote we go with Goofy Grape," Don said with a smile. It was a joke only the Vietnam veterans understood.

"How much does this plane cost?" Tim finally asked.

"Two hundred thousand," Don answered.

"That'll leave us with about three hundred fifty, I mean, three ninety with Poe and Shimazu's contributions," Tim said. "Which begs the next question: where can we sell the gold, now that we're a business?"

Shimazu spoke up then. "I've been doing a little digging. Turns out one of my clients does some recreational panning, but he's been bitten by the gold bug hard and knows a fair amount. He might even be interested in going with you if you want an extra hand.

"Anyhow, the first step is to find a gold assayer. They'll buy panned gold, but it won't be at gold spot prices. Those are paid by traders for refined gold, which turns out to be ninety-nine point nine-nine percent pure. Usually in gold bars, or bullion as it's called. Figure on probably getting sixty to seventy percent of the spot price when you sell."

"So, you mean instead of five hundred fifty thousand dollars, we should expect only about three hundred eighty-five thousand or so?" Tim asked.

"If you're lucky," Shimazu responded. "It might even be as low as three hundred thirty thousand."

"Damn," Don said, shaking his head. "How do we make it so we get more?"

"Refine it yourself and make it as pure as possible, from what I understand," Shimazu replied.

"Does this client of yours know how to do that?" Tim asked.

Shimazu shrugged. "Don't know, but I can ask him."

"Okay, so let's say we've only got about three hundred seventy thousand to work with. Two hundred kay for a plane. What else?"

"Fuel bladders and maintenance," Jack immediately piped up.

Don said, "Engineering equipment to build a runway and other major camp infrastructure."

"Mining equipment," Dave said.

"A bigger gate," Poe added.

"Yeah, that last one's a bit nebulous, but shouldn't cost too much," Tim said, cupping his chin in his hand. After thinking for a minute, he said, "All right. Here's what we're gonna do. Jeff, you talk with your mining buddy and see about selling the gold. I'll work on the gate. *If*, and this is a big if, I can scale the gate up to get a plane through it, then we buy the plane." Turning to Don and Jack, he asked, "Can you do a layaway with an escape clause?"

Don nodded. "I think so. Plane's been on the market a while."

"Do it then. Let's put down ten percent. Give the seller whatever sob story you can, but be sure to get some sort of escape clause with minimal fee. If I can't get the gate scaled up, no sense in losing more money than we have to."

Turning to Jeff, Tim said, "You said your client might be interested in going gold hunting? Two questions: can he keep his mouth shut, and can we do this with just giving him a share of the gold? I don't want to give out company shares if I don't have to."

"He was an investigator with the Attorney General's Office. He knows how to keep his mouth shut."

As the meeting broke up and each man went his own way, Dave pulled Tim aside. "Think you can scale this thing up big enough to fit a plane?"

"Not sure. Only one way to find out, though."

"If you can, then maybe we should rent a hangar at Yakima Air Terminal."

Tim considered it. "What are you thinking?"

"Once you confirm you can scale, we set up the gate in a rented hangar. Bring in enough equipment to build our own airfield, and move it through the gate to Hayek surreptitiously. Build the airfield on Hayek, then move the plane over. Once we get enough gold, we get a Caribou, like the kid said, and move that over. It'll help with operations. I suspect that within a year we'll have enough money and infrastructure to notify the world and start the whole migration process."

"A lot of this hinges on whether or not I can scale the gate."

Dave grinned at Tim. "Then what the hell are you doing talking with me? Get your ass in that shed."

It took almost a week, but Tim, with Dave and Veronica's help, finally managed to make a larger version of his gate. It was almost as tall as his shed. Not quite big enough for an airplane, but certainly big enough for a truck. He wasn't sure if it would work, but he made sure all the electronics and settings were identical to his original gate. He also made sure it was separated from the original gate, which would serve as their control. He wanted the original gate open when he opened the larger version to make sure they were on the same planet.

With Dave and Veronica standing beside him, Dave with his lever-action rifle and Veronica with the pump-action shotgun, and with no little amount of trepidation, Tim plugged in the gate controls. Ensuring the settings were the same as the original gate, he turned the on/off switch to activate it. Immediately, the view from in front of the gate changed from a shed wall to the dusty hills of eastern Washington. Because the new gate was facing a different direction than the old one, the view wasn't of Mt. Rainier, rather it was of the Cascade Mountains toward the south, with Mt. Adams's snowy peak showing through.

Dave went to the first gate, rifle at the ready, and looked through. "Looks clear. Let me walk around and see if it's working." With that, he stepped through the smaller gate and a couple of seconds later reappeared on the other side of the larger gate. Stepping back into the shed, grinning, he said, "Looks like it works."

"Hot damn!" Tim yelled. Veronica practically leaped in the air in excitement.

"Now that we know it works, you want to shut it down?" Dave asked, looking backward to ensure no hungry Pleistocene critters were making their way toward him.

"Sure," Tim agreed, doing as Dave suggested.

"What now?" Veronica asked.

"Now we let the others know, get the plane, and start moving equipment."

A couple of quick but somewhat cryptic phone calls, and all the partners knew. Don had already put a deposit down on the plane and Jack had become seaplane rated. Don was also learning how to fly. Dave spent some time looking at mining and used engineering equipment. Poe had lined up hangar rental at Yakima Air Terminal, a hangar big enough for a Caribou, but nothing else. It would have no problem fitting the smaller Grumman Goose.

When asked why Tim kept the gate in Selah, rather than moving it closer to their future operations in California, he simply said, "The more people see or hear about it, the less likely we'll be able to maintain control until we're ready to make an announcement.

Besides, I like operating from home. It makes me feel comfortable."
Making the inventor uncomfortable was not on the agenda of any
of the partners, even if it meant more time flying on Hayek. Even if
it meant spending more money upfront.

Shimazu told Tim that his client, the former Office of the
Attorney General investigator, was interested in helping out. "I
made him sign an NDA before I said anything. Says he's happy to
do it for a quarter-portion of his share of the gold if he's allowed to
move over to Hayek permanently once things are up and running."

"Did you tell him that the portion would only be from the forty
percent of the company not owned and that he wouldn't get any
shares of the company?"

"Yep. He's fine with that. Just wants some gold and a place to
go."

Thinking about what the former OAG investigator wanted got
Tim to thinking about how they would divvy up land. As it stood,
all land on Hayek, including the lakes, rivers, and oceans, was the
property of Parallel, Inc.

"Guess it's time to start finding a surveyor, if we're going to be
selling, leasing, or handing out land." The more he thought about it,
the more he realized they should also start planning for the City of
Milton, to include all necessary infrastructure. He told Veronica
about this, and she said she'd look into it.

Tim figured it would take at least another week to build a gate
big enough for the planes, but he saw no reason not to start getting
ready on Hayek.

The team planned on moving equipment over immediately from
the shed, along with building a small airstrip. Don found a deal on
some surplus Marston Mats, the ten-foot-long by fifteen-inch-wide
steel strips with holes punched through them to reduce the weight
down to sixty-six pounds, used to make field-expedient airstrips.
Hooks on one side of the mats aligned with slots on the other side,
to allow them to be hooked and locked together. Enough mats laid
out on the ground made for a decent runway. Tossing gravel on top
made it even better. The goal was to create at least three runways:
one outside the shed's gate, one outside the hangar at the airport,

and a final one in California. The second strip was only going to be a transfer point, with planes transiting from the Yakima Air Terminal, mostly taking off, with few landing, other than for necessary mechanical maintenance. All future flights would be between the strip by the shed and the one in California. As such, more time would be spent prepping those fields. The strip behind the hangar would just have planking laid down for only fifteen hundred feet, which was still above the minimum take-off distance of barely twelve hundred feet the Caribou needed. The strip behind the shed and the one in California would initially be two thousand feet long, with likely expansion once things were up and running.

While Tim, with Veronica's help, worked on the hangar gate, Dave and Don worked on getting the Milton strip, as they were now calling it, up and running. The Yakima Air Terminal strip would be second, and once enough gold was flowing, and a Caribou bought, the California strip would be built.

Tim was sure his neighbors were wondering what he was up to, with forklifts, bulldozers, and then long, heavy crates being delivered to his ranchette, but he didn't let them in on the secret. Some were the type he'd rather leave in the dark.

Recognizing that trying to build an airstrip while not getting eaten by the local fauna was a bit tricky, Don convinced Tim to allow him to recruit some help. He found a somewhat suspect firm holding itself out as providing "executive protection and home fortress development." Upon talking with its CEO, Lenny Gross, a Vietnam veteran who had worked with MACV-SOG, Don got the firm signed up with one of Poe's ironclad non-disclosure agreements. He figured anybody that had worked with the ultra-secret agency Military Assistance Command Vietnam - Studies and Observation Group, running operations into North Vietnam, Cambodia, and Laos, would know how to keep their mouth shut. Don had told the CEO that the job would be in an area with lots of dangerous animals and that everyone should have, at a minimum, an M1A with several magazines. "If your guys can bring M14s, I'd recommend that," headed.

"We gonna be crossing international boundaries?" Gross asked. This wasn't too much of a problem. Doing so with firearms, particularly fully-automatic firearms, was.

"Not really," Don said, smiling. Then he proceeded to let Gross in on the secret, reminding him of the NDA he had just signed, which included a one-million-dollar penalty for discussing it with anyone. The CEO was disbelieving at first, but agreed to take the gig on condition of ten thousand dollars up front. "I'll have my guys show up armed and ready."

Most of those Gross employed were Vietnam veterans, like himself. Some were former Navy Seabees, engineers who had served in construction battalions in Vietnam. Others were just regular infantry, but combat tested. Nobody who hadn't been shot at was brought to Selah. Don and Gross didn't initially tell them where they would be working, just saying, "It'll be dangerous and interesting and in rough conditions," and had all of them sign Poe's non-disclosure agreement.

Upon entering the shed, many of them had looked confused. All they saw was the gate, which meant nothing to them, some construction equipment, and piles of surplus army tents, cots, and cases of C-rations, the combat rations that many had eaten in the field while serving in the Army. Some of them laughed at the piles of tents and food. That is, until they were told to dig out their rifles. Most of them had brought M1As; a couple had M14s. It was then that Tim approached the gate controls.

"Lock and load, gents. Lock and load," Don said, slapping a magazine into his rifle's magazine well, jacking the action open and letting it slam forward, chambering a round. The rest followed suit.

"You expecting bear on this here job?" one of the older vets asked jokingly. Don just smiled, and then Tim turned on the gate, commenting, "Maybe a cave bear."

Dave and Don stepped through, rifles ready, looked around, then turned back to the assembled group of armed men. "Well, what are you waiting for?" Don asked. "An engraved invitation? Get the lead out."

With that, the men stepped through the gate and onto Hayek with exclamations of surprise and wonder. Having only recently crossed over for the first time, Tim understood their feelings.

The head Seabee looked around, and announced, "We should have this strip done in two days. Bring the dozer through, then the fuel wagon, and then the roller." The equipment he referred to had been rented for a month from a local construction equipment rental firm. Jeff had said it would be cheaper than buying equipment, and fewer headaches if it broke.

Tim went back to working on the gate in the hangar, and each afternoon when he and Veronica returned home, they saw the pile of Martson Mats sitting outside the shed shrink in size. Popping into the shed for a quick look the second afternoon, Tim was amazed to see the airstrip complete, and what appeared to be a road heading south. When Tim asked the lead Seabee, Doug Murphy, why there was a road, the man said, "Dave said you were gonna build another airstrip where the Yakima Air Terminal is. We figured, why move stuff in and out of the hangar if we can continue using this gate. Fewer people to see and play guessing games. Give us about a week and we'll have the road punched through. Well, good enough to take the Martson Mats, anyhow."

At about seven miles, that meant they were putting in a mile a day of road. It reminded Tim of the construction of the cross-continental railway in the 1800s when a good day was laying a mile of track.

"You laying down gravel?"

"Naw, just scraping and running a roller over it," Murphy said. "We figure to haul the mats over using a tractor, so we don't need much. Biggest thing is building a couple of bridges over the Naches River and a couple of creeks. Of course, we got plenty of trees we can use for that.

"Speaking of gravel, sure would be good to put some on those Marston Mats. You okay with us ordering a bunch? Probably need about six hundred cubic yards."

"How many truckloads would that be?"

"Ballpark? About forty. We could move that much stuff in a couple of days. Make for a nicer runway."

"What would it cost?"

"About thirteen bucks a cubic yard, so figure on about a bit under eight grand."

Tim didn't have to think too long. Even though they hadn't sold the gold yet, they still had the forty thousand put up by Poe and Shimazu, less the ten thousand paid to the security firm, a thousand used for the hangar rental, a thousand for equipment rental, and two thousand for salaries. The plane wouldn't be purchased until the gold sold, and from what Jeff was saying, that should be in a couple of days.

They were into this for less than fifteen thousand so far, and still had some wiggle room. He wanted a decent runway, and they had the funds. "Go ahead and do it."

While Tim worked on the gate, Don left the airstrip to Dave and worked on getting the Goose. Jeff worked on selling the gold, and the Seabees built the connecting road and distant airstrip. Dave had spent some time getting more weaponry. He also brought in an old Africa hand, Lee Orange, who used to run safaris in Rhodesia to teach everyone how to handle weapons in dangerous animal situations. Anyone who had faced down lions, hyenas, and cape buffaloes in their natural environment, and lived to tell about it, was somebody worth listening to.

At one of the evening gatherings on Tim's patio, after everyone had knocked off for the day, Dave introduced Lee to the group, which included a bunch of the Seabees and other veterans. "Now, I know just about every one of you've carried a gun into combat, either the M14 or the M16. Some love 'em, some hate 'em. But we're not going into combat. We don't have the logistics train to support those kinds of weaponry, along with the legal means. Hell, it costs two hundred dollars just for the damned tax stamp to own a fully-automatic rifle. And, I know most of you brought M1As and M14s while you've been building the airstrips. Those work great for what you're doing, now. But they won't work for what we've got planned. They're too damned heavy. Lee here is gonna tell you what we should, and will, be carrying."

"Thanks, Dave," Lee said in his clipped Rhodesian accent, standing up to be better seen by all, a glass of whiskey in one hand. "How many of you have ever been on a safari in Africa?"

He was greeted with a sea of shrugs and head-shaking.

"Thought so. Well, let me tell you, I've been on hundreds. And on not one of them did I ever carry anything other than a break-action or bolt-action rifle. And the reason for that is, they don't break. Well, at least, not as often as a semi-automatic rifle does. They're also lighter, usually by several pounds. How many of you carried an M14 when you were a teen or in your early twenties?"

This time a bunch of hands rose.

"Do you think you can carry it, and as much ammo as you carried back then, now? I've seen some of you on the other side holding your M1As. You look tired. There's a reason for that. You're older, and the guns are heavy. Loaded with a twenty-round mag, those things weigh over ten pounds."

Reaching behind him, Orange pulled up a rifle. This one was a small, scoped bolt-action rifle, one clearly modified, as seen by the large detachable magazine.

"This is the type of rifle you need to be using. A simple bolt-action rifle chambered in 7.62 NATO, with a detachable ten-round box magazine. If you need more than ten rounds, you're dead," he finished with a chuckle. The others joined in, the macabre sense of humor fitting them.

"Why 7.62, you might ask? Simple. It's got the ballistics that work and surplus ammo is cheap for practice. Most people recommend good hunting bullets that expand. That's not what we're taking. Instead, we'll continue to use full metal jacket. Again, why? Because you're not going hunting. If you've got to use your rifle, it's because something big and nasty is attacking you. You want to stop that big nasty, and the best way to do that is to break bones. For that, you don't need or want expanding bullets, you want something that's going to penetrate and hit hard, not lose its energy. In Africa, for the really big game, we used solid hard bullets—in other words, full metal jacket. It'd be best if we were using .300 Nitros, but we've got what we've got. Mind you, this won't do for a cape buffalo, but it'll work on most of what you're likely to deal with." This time he grinned. "But don't go using it on a mammoth—you do *not* want to piss one of those furry jumbos off.

"How many of you have ever used a bolt-action rifle?" he asked the assembled men, many of whom raised their hands.

"Is this how you used it?"

Cycling the bolt to ensure an empty chamber, Orange pointed the rifle at the wall, making sure not to fan anyone with the gun barrel, pulled the trigger, eliciting a loud 'click' from the firing pin, then operated the bolt, all while keeping the rifle shouldered.

Just about everyone nodded on seeing this demonstration. Orange lowered the rifle and looked around. "On safari, that would get you killed. Can anyone guess why?" Mostly blank stares greeted him.

"Because sometimes, the animal you're shooting has a mate you didn't see. And if all your attention is focused on looking at the target, you lose track of other things. Let me show you how you should really do it."

Once again, Orange raised the rifle to his shoulder and pulled the trigger. This time, instead of keeping the rifle up, he lowered it to the ready position, cycled the bolt rather forcefully, glancing down into the chamber as he did so, then scanned around as he brought the rifle back up for a second shot.

Lowering the rifle a second time, he said, "Notice what I did there. Let me walk you through it." As he did, he mimicked his previous actions. "First, I fired. Then, I lowered the rifle to the ready position. That gave me a second to see what else might be in front of me. As I reloaded, I looked down to ensure my old cartridge left the chamber and the new cartridge fed properly. You'll see I also slammed the bolt home. That ensures the cartridge seats properly. I could probably just push it forward like many of you have been taught, but if that cartridge doesn't seat properly, the rifle won't work. If the rifle won't work, I'm dead. So, don't be gentle. It's hardened steel, you're not. Slam it home.

"Finally, before bringing the rifle up to fire again, I did a quick scan around me. That's just in case Simba's buddies have decided that I make a better prey than predator. If I don't look around, I might get an ugly surprise.

"This is how we did it in the bush, and this is how you'll do it over there. Trust me, it'll keep you alive."

Dave stood, and all eyes went to him. "We've got our local gunsmith working on modifying a bunch of Savage Model 110 rifles right now. They'll still be chambered for .308, but he's reaming out the chamber a bit to better fit the 7.62 NATO round. The .308 is a hotter round with more pressure, but it can take a 7.62, which is just a hair longer.

"He's making the stocks lighter and replacing the barrels with eighteen-inch fluted barrels. He'll also be making magazines that can hold ten rounds, replacing the sights with ghost ring sights, and mounting one-by-four variable scopes. They should be ready in a few more days. We'll be issuing them on Hayek, but just to make this clear, this is company property, not yours. You lose or damage it, you pay for it."

One man asked, "What if we want to keep our own rifle?"

"You can do that if you want," Dave answered. "But you're still going to have to train on our system. If that doesn't work for you, the door's over there," he finished, pointing to the shed door. "Just remember the NDA you signed."

The man shook his head. "Naw, I ain't leaving. This is too much fun, and I kind of like the pay." The rest of the men laughed. The pay was more than usual, and the excitement of being on a new planet fit the craving for adventure most of them had.

Dave nodded. "Keep in mind, if your rifle fails and somebody dies because of that, it's on you."

"I'm gonna recommend we each bring a pistol," Dave said. "We may have to stow them away in the luggage, based on the law, but they might come in handy."

9

Before Tim could wrap up constructing the terminal gate, Don and Jack flew into the field with the Grumman Goose, parking it inside the big hangar. Built in the mid-1940s, the plane was showing its age. Tim got a chuckle out of the new nose art, a Gadsen flag snake with "Don't Tread On Me" underneath.

"Trying to tell people something?" Tim asked, as Don exited the plane.

"Damned right I am," Don said, shaking Tim's hand. Looking at the partial gate, he asked, "So, how long before it's ready?"

Jack joined them, and Tim nodded toward him while answering his father. "Should wrap up tomorrow. Give it a test, and if all goes well, we move the plane through as soon as the boys extend the road and runway here."

"How close are they?"

"From what I hear, they're just on the other side of the wall. Both airstrips are built, just needs a bit of fine-tuning."

Don nodded.

Turning to the teen, Tim asked, "So, you ready Jack?"

"Yessir. Also got Dad trained enough to at least take-off, land, and fly fairly straight," the boy said with a grin.

Changing the topic, Tim asked, "Have you two picked up your new rifles?"

"What new rifles?"

Tim explained about them and the training regimen, and suggested Don call Dave. "They've set up a shooting range on the other side, right near here. Far enough away that the noise isn't coming through the gate and bothering the neighbors."

"Might be a good idea if we do that before taking the Goose over," Don said. "I got a bit tired lugging that M1A around. Don't get me wrong, it's a great gun, but I'll take a lighter rifle with the same punch over it any day of the week. Eileen's picking us up soon, but we can be back tomorrow or the next day. Will that work?"

"Let me check," Tim said. "Why don't you guys go home and spend a day with the family, at least? I've still got at least another day on this thing, like I said. No sense going over late in the day."

Rather than getting back to working on the gate, Tim spent the rest of the afternoon listening to Jack as he pointed out all the things the Goose had, including the collapsible fuel bladders they bought.

"We got three one-thousand-gallon fuel bladders and a two-hundred-gallon bladder. We'll leave a thousand-gallon bladder at each of the lakes, fill them up, and then be able to do some serious gear hauling," the young man explained. It was clear he was proud of his work, and excited. For a fifteen-year-old to have this kind of responsibility was a big thing, particularly nowadays.

After Eileen picked up the Lewises, Tim drove home, using the short commute time to think of the immediate future. The gate would be finished by late morning or early afternoon at the latest. He could have stayed late and finished the job, but he knew that people who worked late sometimes made mistakes. In this case, the mistakes could well prove fatal.

Most of the security personnel were staying on Hayek now, so for the first time in a week, he actually had the house to himself and his wife. That could prove interesting, if nobody else showed up. They had decided to shut the gate down while people were on the other side, mainly because they didn't want any Pleistocene critters, particularly of the carnivorous type, crossing over to Earth and making a nuisance of themselves.

The list of things he needed to do or plan for seemed to grow exponentially since becoming the CEO of a corporation. Along with trying to keep a major secret, which he doubted would remain secret for long, he needed to plan expeditions, develop a survey for land grants, plan a city, work on a constitution, and the list went on.

Is this really worth it? he thought as he approached his ranchette. Looking at the destruction to his driveway caused by trucks bringing in equipment and gravel, he wondered. Then he stopped in his driveway, halfway between the road and his small rambler, taking in the view of his house and shed. Not even a carport or garage to protect the cars, just the pole barn. This was all he had to show for over forty years on this planet. It was all he had provided for his wife. True, it was more than some, but a hell of a lot less than others. And considering his retirement account, even less.

He gripped the steering wheel of the Willys wagon, and just stared, his mind going through multiple iterations. Finally, a smile stole across his face. *I've done it! I've actually opened a portal in the multiverse. And with that comes enough gold and opportunities to likely make me rich beyond my wildest dreams. No more Hamburger Helper for the Bowmans anymore.* Putting the wagon back in gear, Tim completed his drive down the now-damaged driveway.

Entering his home, he was greeted by the smell of something wonderful cooking. It smelled like stew, but with a scent not of beef, chicken, or pork—more like venison. Veronica had also opened a nice red wine, a local vintage from one of the start-up vineyards in the area. she handed him a glass as he came into the kitchen.

"Smells good. What is it?" he asked, taking a sip of his wine.

"You like? Apparently, some poor animal got a bit too close to the camp and the guys took him out. They gave us some." Then she shook her head. "Well, not just 'some'. They gave us a pretty big piece. It's hanging in the shed, waiting to be cut and frozen. I kind of lopped off enough to make a nice stew."

Tim took another sip of his wine, swallowing the acidic liquid then breathing out through his nose to enhance the flavor. It held a hint of blackberry. "So, what kind of critter are we having for supper?" he asked, taking another sip.

"Would you believe mammoth?"

Tim snorted wine through his nose in surprise. After wiping his face and getting over his coughing fit, he asked, "Are you serious? Mammoth?"

With a small smile, Veronica turned back toward the stew, picking up a wooden spoon and stirring. "Well, they weren't sure if it was a woolly mammoth, Columbian mammoth, or a mastodon, other than the fact that it was big, hairy, had tusks, and was wounded. It apparently had a broken leg and a bunch of bite marks on it. Probably did the poor creature some good putting it out of its misery."

Tim contemplated that while he continued to sip his wine. *Hunting rules and regulations; must develop,* he thought. There was a lot he needed to develop, and soon, as fast as things were moving. "I'm thinking we should have a meeting with the other shareholders, before the next trip."

"What on?" Veronica asked, setting the spoon down and covering the stew pot with a lid. She picked up her wine and took a sip, looking over the glass at Tim.

"We need to make some sort of rules. Y'know, like anyone crossing over has to abide by. Like, no hunting just for the sake of hunting. Hell, I don't even want people hunting unless they have a real reason, like hunger. Look at what happened in the past. Most of the North American megafauna was supposedly killed off by over-hunting. If it weren't for modern conservation, most of the larger mammals in America would likely be gone by now. Did you know that the bison, which once numbered in the millions, was down to less than a thousand at one point? I don't want to make that mistake on Hayek."

"Well, if you're going to put those kinds of restrictions, then you better think long and hard about others, like what if there's another human species there?" Veronica asked.

Tim's eyes widened. "Wow! I hadn't really thought about that since the first week."

"You should," Veronica said. "Look what happened when the Europeans landed in the New World. Millions dead, just from diseases. How do you think you'd feel being a harbinger of death?"

"Not good," he said. "Okay, we know there're are no humans here; at least we haven't seen anything to indicate there are, so I think we're good to go. But we'll need to set up a protocol on future gate openings."

"Future gate openings?"

"Sure," Tim said rather excitedly, waving his glass around for emphasis. "Future gate openings. You know, like for other timelines. If we can open one, we can probably open more than one."

Veronica took a gulp of wine. "Do you mean to tell me you actually think you can open up more timelines?"

Tim nodded. "Why not? Remember, think of time like a tree, the branches branching out as it grows. On one timeline, the South bombards Ft. Sumter and starts the Civil War, but what if they decided to go to court, or maybe have an amendment passed to secede? One simple decision, taken or not, can alter the future of a timeline and create a split, a branching if you will.

"Now, like a squirrel hopping from branch to branch, we can hop from timeline branch to timeline branch. We just need to figure out exactly how we're doing it, and then fine-tune things. Heck, we could even go to a timeline in which the atom bomb was never invented, and the United States had to actually invade Japan to win World War II, which means a world similar to ours, but without nukes."

"Or without you," Veronica said.

"There is that," Tim acknowledged.

"Does that mean you're a multiverse squirrel?"

Tim just shook his head. "Well, let's talk about this more over supper, which smells like it's finally ready."

There was a knocking at the door.

"That'll be Dave and Petra," Veronica said, turning to get some bowls down from a cupboard. "Go let them in."

"Well, that's unexpected," Tim said. He grabbed the bottle of wine, which he set down on the dining room table as he passed it. Opening the door, he was greeted by the sight of Dave and Petra, Dave holding two bottles of wine.

Stepping into the small house, Dave handed the bottles to Tim, one of which was cold, with condensation dripping into Tim's hands and onto his shirt. "Veronica invited us over, and I figured since we didn't have to put up with those security types, we might be able to enjoy a couple of good wines," Dave said as Petra headed toward the kitchen to help Veronica.

"Close the door. Food's ready, so we might as well eat, drink, and be merry," Tim said, turning back to the table. "I'll get a corkscrew and open these."

"Smells good, Veronica," Dave called to the kitchen. He was rewarded with, "Thanks, Dave."

As Dave took a seat, Veronica and Petra emerged from the kitchen with bowls of stew and spoons, setting them on the table. While Petra joined Dave, Veronica returned to the kitchen. Tim opened the new bottles, which he set down next to the already partially consumed one. Veronica returned with two empty glasses for Dave and Petra, along with her mostly empty glass.

Tim held up the bottles. Dave pointed to the red and Petra said, "I'll have the white, please."

After pouring the drinks, Tim held up his glass. "A toast."

The others raised their glasses.

"To prosperity in the new world."

Everyone nodded, and after they clinked glasses, sipped their wines.

"Well, dig in," Veronica said, waiting for the others to taste the stew so she could judge their reactions.

Those eating couldn't help but be surprised by how good it was. All of them, without actually saying so, had been expecting something tough and with a gamy taste, but the meat they bit into was tender and had more of a nutty flavor, a bit like bison, but not quite.

All talking stopped for the next several minutes as the two couples made their way through their bowls of stew. Eventually, the feeding frenzy slowed down, as first Veronica, then Petra, took a break to sip some wine. Realizing that they were probably making pigs of themselves, the two men decided to also slow down for a wine break, but Tim found it hard, considering just how good the stew was.

After taking a final sip from his glass, and while he was recharging it from the bottle of red Dave had brought, Tim brought up the subject of multiple universes and planets.

For the next several hours and all three bottles of wine, they discussed the limitless possibilities and how they should best be approached. The topics went from exploration to opening for settlement, and how best to do that. Eventually, they concluded that planets should be classified, and those with humans best to be avoided, "but not totally," Dave said. "Think about the technological advancements some civilizations might have made, such as flying cars and things like that. If we limit ourselves to only exploring unoccupied planets, then we miss out on such things."

The others agreed. "How about this," Tim put forth, "if the planet's unoccupied, it's a Class III planet. Class II for planets occupied by neolithic people, like cavemen."

"And Neanderthals," Veronica jumped in, "or any other hominids. Let's not leave it to *homo sapiens* only. I say we do it for all hominid species."

"Sure, why not?" Dave said. The agreement was unanimous.

"Class I for timelines that have some sort of civilization, ranging from agricultural revolution up to our level?" Tim asked the group.

"Why not limit Class I to pre-industrial," Dave asked, "and assign another class to industrial?"

Tim shrugged. "I dunno. I sort of consider if you've reached one level of civilization, that should count for most of them."

The four batted this one around, eventually deciding to use Class I but with additional lettering to separate pre-industrial from industrial. Anything between agricultural revolution to pre-industrial would be Class IC and industrial, including their own timeline, would be Class IB. Anything beyond the industrial capability of their timeline would be considered Class IA.

Figuring out if a planet was occupied was pretty simple when it came to industrial societies, but as Tim and Dave discovered, it was a different matter for pre-industrial ones.

"They've got no radio, no television, no telegraphs or telephones, so we've really got no way to remotely identify them," Dave complained. "So, what do we do?"

"Aerial surveys," Tim answered, burping slightly from all the wine and food. Looking at the bottles, he realized they were drained. *Time for something completely different*, he thought.

"Oh, sure. Let's fly a Spooky around taking pictures. I'm sure whoever's out there won't be suspicious. No, not at all." The Spooky was a military cargo plane outfitted with weaponry designed to provide close air support and was devastating to anyone on the ground that became its target.

"No, seriously Dave, consider this," Tim replied. "We find some high-flying plane, like a U2 or something similar, and fly patterns, taking pictures. Anything resembling agriculture should be easy to find. And if we don't see anything, then we send in ground teams. Hell, we could set up a whole organization just for exploration!"

"How would you pay for that?" Petra chimed in.

Tim puzzled over that for a moment, then cracked a huge smile. Leaning forward in his recliner (they had all moved from the dining room to the living room by now), he asked, "How much would you pay to get away from this planet and start over again? Think of all the people who hate what it's like here. If we can offer them a way out, along with technological support, such as being able to bring in the things they like and need, like tools and medicine, I'm betting millions would be willing to migrate to another planet."

"Not sure I would want them on Hayek," Dave muttered, letting his latent antisocial side show through.

"I'm not talking about moving to Hayek, I'm talking about opening other planets and letting them migrate to them! Think of the possibilities. We move them over, and charge them money," Tim said.

The others could see the potential in Tim's idea, and the discussion moved on to how it could be done and how much to charge.

"For Hayek, since it's our home, I don't want just anyone coming over," Tim said. "What we want are like-minded individuals and families, people willing to work, but also willing to pay to move over and be with us. But they also have to be willing to abide by the constitution and laws we have in place."

"Then we better get those completed, and like right now," Dave said.

"What kind of constitution are you guys thinking of?" Veronica asked.

"Sort of a mixture between the US constitution, the Swiss Constitution, and the philosophy in Heinlein's novel *Starship Troopers*." Veronica made a 'come-along' gesture, asking for a further explanation.

"First, it'll be a federal system, which means each canton will have its own constitution and laws, but the federal law will supersede all other laws," Tim said. "I think a parliament with two chambers or houses would be best, with an executive branch and a judicial branch. And term limits. Definitely term limits. No career politicians. Serving in government should be a duty, not a way to gain power and riches. Also, limit the role of government to protection of the public and the public good. That means no unilateral military action by the executive branch. We already saw how LBJ abused that. Any military action requires a declaration of war. Nothing less! No 'use of force' or 'war powers act' bullshit. And no preemptive wars. The only wars allowed will be those in which Hayek is physically attacked. As a matter of fact, I recommend we have the non-aggression principle as part of the constitution."

"I can get behind that," Dave said.

"What's the non-aggression principle?" Petra asked.

"It means you can't initiate aggression by attacking or threatening an individual, or in a country's case, an individual or another country, especially if it's to try and get what you want," Tim said. "That doesn't mean you don't fight to protect yourself, or in a country's case, fight to protect your citizens, it just means you can't initiate the force. A little different from pacifism, where no force is allowed."

"So, if we get attacked, say by the Soviets, how can we react?" Veronica asked.

"Well, we can basically respond by killing or capturing those soldiers that attack us, but I think another acceptable response would be to go after those that authorized the attack."

"You mean attack the Soviet Premier?"

Tim answered Veronica. "Yeah, I think that's acceptable. Take out the head, the body dies. If we only attack those that initiated the aggression, we'll probably have more public support on our side. Not just from our citizens, but likely from others. Especially if we develop a good PR team that can get the news out. 'Hey, bad guy leaders attacked us, we only killed the bad guy leaders, and didn't kill those not involved.'"

"Good selling point," Veronica said, "but how would you do that?"

Tim grinned. "We've got a gate. Just open a small portal in their office and send in a strike team. Kidnap or kill them. Personally, I'm all for killing any politician who thinks it's acceptable to send others to die for their ideas."

"Sounds good to me, but who gets to vote?" Petra asked.

Tim became a bit uncomfortable.

"You ever read *Starship Troopers*?" he asked, looking at all three of them.

Only Dave nodded. The two women just shook their heads.

"In that novel, the only ones who could vote were those that volunteered and served in the military, or Federal Service as it was called. I'm thinking something similar. If you're not willing to put your life on the line for others, then you shouldn't be allowed to be a part of the decision-making process."

"You're saying I wouldn't have the right to vote?" Veronica asked, her tone a bit chillier than a few moments ago.

"Basically, yeah. Not unless you were willing to do some sort of service that would put your life on the line," Tim responded. "Look, voting is all well and good, and democracy, as Winston Churchill said, is the worst form of government out there, except for all the others. But, unfettered democracy has a way of destroying what it's trying to preserve. Look what's happening in the US right now. Congress keeps voting to give people money through grants, programs, infrastructure, subsidies, or loans. Why? Because then those people vote for them. It's a vicious cycle that feeds into our ballooning deficit. I believe it was Alex de Tocqueville who said, 'The American Republic will endure until the day Congress discovers that it can bribe the public with the public's money.' Most people don't ever put themselves in harm's way, giving themselves up so that others might live. So, no, unless you're willing to put your life on the line for others, then I don't believe you should be allowed to vote, or even be a member of the government."

"Hmmph. I'm not too sure I like that," Veronica said, but not in quite as chilly a tone as her previous question.

Tim smiled at her. "When was the last time you voted?"

Veronica was taken aback. Tim knew she didn't vote, always claiming the politicians were all dirty and didn't want to 'feed the beast' as she called politics. "What's that got to do with it?"

"A lot. You're not interested enough to vote here, and since you're a woman, you don't have to worry about getting sent off to war. If you don't have any real skin in the game, should you be allowed to make choices for those who do?"

That comment made both women uncomfortable. Petra finally responded, "Yeah, well it's our husbands and sons who get sent off to war, so, yeah, we do have 'skin in the game,' as you so rudely put it."

Dave interjected. "I think that's something we should put to a vote with all the shareholders. How about this, if you served a year or two in a position that directly puts your life on the line for others, you can vote and hold office. This would apply to not only the military but also police and firefighters."

Picking up on the theme, Tim added, "How about if we require militia service from every adult, and after a certain number of years, a lot more than one or two, then they become eligible to vote? That way we aren't excluding people, just making them sacrifice a bit for the opportunity to have a say in things."

"What about conscientious objectors?" Veronica asked. "That would pretty much exclude them."

"Not really. If a requirement to migrate or live on Hayek is service in the militia, then they can either elect to serve in a non-combat role or leave. Pretty damned simple, in my mind," Tim said. As the only combat veteran in the group, he was firm about this.

"Are you proposing both a military and a militia?" Dave asked.

"Yeah. Why not?"

"That'd be an awfully big, and expensive, military," Dave responded.

"Not really. We have a small defensive force controlled by the federal government, and a militia controlled by the canton governments. The whole purpose is defense, so we don't need a lot of the big, expensive equipment that most governments have. We won't need a navy, other than to protect people from pirates that might arise, so no expensive nuclear carriers or subs. We won't need a nuclear deterrent. Heck, we could probably get away without having any armor. If you think about it, tanks are basically an offensive weapons platform. The whole concept of blitzkrieg is based on armored units. So, instead of armored units, we have anti-armor units, small teams armed with anti-tank missiles."

"How are you thinking of paying for it?" Dave asked.

"I think that one's pretty simple. First, we have a fee to migrate to Hayek, make that more than enough to outfit each migrant with their basic militia gear, and then enough to help with the cost of the military. Add on tariffs for any goods moving through the gates, along with the actual transport fees, and that should be sufficient. Look, the US was funded almost exclusively with tariffs until Wilson got Congress to pass the Sixteenth Amendment, allowing for a personal income tax. Without that, there's no way the US military-industrial complex could have grown so big. So, at the federal level, no income taxes and no property taxes, just tariffs on goods moving through the gates."

As the group had run out of wine, Veronica pulled a bottle of scotch from the liquor cabinet and poured herself a finger. "As you guys are discussing all this, have you figured out how you're going to staff everything?"

By the end of the evening, the quartet had developed a nascent constitution, consisting of a bicameral legislature, with one side being elected by citizens and the other side being appointed by the canton's executive branches, with one appointed legislator per canton. Citizens were those who had served in a position that directly put their life on the line for others for at least two years, or until such time as injuries sustained in the line of duty made them incapable of further service. This included military, peace officers, firefighters, and any other occupation that the legislature deemed as such, as long as there was a direct nexus between the job and putting one's life on the line. Those who served in the military reserves, peace officer reserves, or as volunteer firefighters for ten years were eligible for citizenship, as was any resident involved in defending Hayek from invasion. All others living on Hayek were considered residents.

All members who served in the legislative, executive, and judicial branches had to be citizens.

The elected legislators were limited to two three-year terms and the appointed legislators were limited to one six-year term. Only elected legislators could introduce bills, and those had to pass with a super-majority of a two-thirds vote. All bills were limited to a single topic, with a further caveat that any bill with more than one topic was automatically null and void. Any budget-related bill had to pass by a super-majority of three-fourths in both legislatures.

The executive branch was limited to two three-year terms, just like the elected legislators. The executive would be elected by the legislative branch and would serve as both head of state and head of government, including serving as the commander of the military. Tim argued quite vociferously against allowing the executive branch to have the power of executive orders except in direct support of laws passed by the legislature. He cited Roosevelt's infamous Executive Order 9066, which interned Americans of Japanese descent in concentration camps, as a reason for his rationale. It was hard for the others to argue against him on that one.

The judicial branch would consist of magistrate courts, courts of appeal, and a superior court. The courts of appeals and the superior courts were restricted to five and nine judges respectively, but always an odd number. As with the US constitution, judges were appointed by the president and approved by the appointed legislature.

The federal government was restricted to protecting the citizens and public good from harm by others and to protecting the rights of the citizens. Treaties, in the sense of trade or defense agreements between nations, weren't allowed. All actions between citizens and other nations would be by individuals, with the exception of requiring the government to aid those whose rights were being violated by aggression. Citizens' rights were simple: the right to self-ownership, self-defense, privacy, and private property ownership. The right of self-ownership meant that everyone had complete control over their body, able to do with it whatever he or she wanted, as long as it didn't interfere with the rights of others.

As Parallel, Inc. claimed sole ownership of the planet, the issue on how to address that was dealt with by acknowledging it in the constitution and acceptance of the private property ownership in existence prior to the constitution. The federal and canton governments would manage lands entrusted to it as parks, conservancies, or nature preserves as such, and any land sold to the government had an automatic right of first refusal by Parallel, Inc. in the event the government wished to dispose of it.

They also agreed to the simple statement of responsibility drawn up by Poe, to be signed by all migrants and residents who wished to be considered adults in terms of signing contracts and entering legal agreements. "Much better than some arbitrary age thing," Dave said after they re-read it.

10

Due to the late night and the amount of alcohol consumed by all, the Jaskeys spent the night in the spare room, so in the light of a late morning, they all got a chance to review what they had written.

"I think with a little tweaking, it'll do," Tim said after reading the draft constitution. "We should run it by the Lewises, Poe, and Shimazu."

"Let's just make sure Poe doesn't try to lawyer it all up. It should remain clear, easy to understand, and not subject to any misunderstandings, like the whole 'general welfare' clause has been."

"Veronica, would you mind typing this up after we're gone?" Tim asked. He was a good typist, but he had a lot of other issues that needed dealing with, such as completing the terminal gate.

Veronica not only agreed to type up the documents but also made breakfast for everyone, strong coffee and flapjacks covered with sweet cream butter and hot maple syrup. It was much appreciated.

After breakfast, Tim and Dave went out to the shed to open the small gate. Both men brought their new bolt-action rifles, both secretly hoping they'd be able to operate them the way that Orange had taught them. As Tim opened the gate, Dave stood ready, prepared for anything. They were greeted by one of the security personnel who informed them that things were pretty quiet, at least, ever since the incursion by the wounded mammoth. The

Seabees were down at the air terminal airstrip, doing who knows what, but likely building something. "Those guys are like little beavers," the guard said, "always building."

Tim wanted to coordinate with the Seabees on opening the terminal gate later in the day, which meant getting word to them. While the security team had radios, the range wasn't quite sufficient to reach all the way to where they were working without a radio repeater, which hadn't been erected yet. That left either walking or finding another way to get to the construction site and talk with the crusty ex-sailor.

"Why don't we take one of your jeeps?" Dave asked. Given that Tim considered them the best vehicles ever made, it made sense, and Tim was surprised that he didn't think of it. Sometimes he really did fit the stereotype of an absent-minded professor.

Tim and Dave returned to the shed and shut down the gate. They didn't want it open when they drove the Willys jeep in. Within minutes, they had the jeep in the shed, the larger gate open, and transited through it into Hayek. Making sure the guard kept a close watch on it (they didn't want their spouses surprised by any unwanted predators), they took the dirt road south.

As they drove along the rough road, both men kept an eye out for anything dangerous. Despite the appearance of normalcy, both knew that was only an illusion. Tim had placed his rifle on the floor behind him while Dave kept his at the ready. Fortunately, they didn't encounter anything more dangerous than a small herd of glyptodons blocking the road, all of whom scattered after Tim came to a sliding stop, throwing up a cloud of dust.

"Good brakes," Dave commented, watching the armored mammals, some almost as big as the jeep, scuttle away through the sagebrush.

"Yeah, not your standard jeep brakes," Tim said, putting the jeep back into gear and continuing along the road. Despite having seen glyptodons before, he was still awed by their presence. "Still can't believe they migrated this far north," he said, thinking about how on his Earth they had only gotten as far as Central America on their northward migration from South America.

"This place is certainly a study in biology and migration patterns," Dave agreed.

In a bit over twenty minutes, they finally arrived at the airstrip under construction. This airstrip, unlike the one near the shed, wasn't getting a layer of gravel, yet. Instead, all the ex-Seabees were doing was scraping the ground flat and installing the Marston Mats, of which almost all were already down and locked in place.

Tim was greeted by the head engineer, Murphy, whom he had learned everyone just called Luther, despite that not being his real name. This was taken from the musical *South Pacific,* and he could see why. Like the Luther Billis in the musical, this Luther was also comedic, irreverent, and willing to do what needed doing to get the job done.

"How they hangin', prof?" Luther asked after pulling a stogie out of his mouth.

Showing he wasn't just some academic egghead, but had actually been there and done that, Tim replied, "To the left, chief, like always. How goes the strip?"

"We'll be wrapped up this afternoon, in time for you to bring that bird over. Of course, might take a bit of refining, as we're not a hundred percent sure where the back of that hangar is, but we're damned close."

Tim nodded. "Okay. I'll be, hopefully, opening the gate after noon, before five. You guys keep your eyes open and have some mats ready in case we need to extend the strip any. Last thing I want is to have the gate open and some stranger walks in."

"Completely understand," Luther said, taking a drag on the stogie and letting the foul-smelling smoke drift about his head. "Of course, what might be worse is opening the gate to a different timeline and being greeted by something decidedly unfriendly."

All could agree to that.

Dave accompanied Tim to the Yakima Air Terminal to assist in completing construction of the terminal gate. After they pulled the jeep into the hangar, Tim turned on the lights while Dave pushed the hangar doors closed, sliding them across their tracks until they connected in the middle. While not quite one hundred percent closed, it was more than enough to ensure no passersby would casually glance in and see what they were doing.

After several hours of work, they were interrupted by Veronica and Petra, who entered the hangar through a side door, bearing lunch. Tim could smell the Kentucky fried chicken almost immediately as the women entered the vast space, it was so overwhelming.

An impromptu picnic took place in the hangar, with the four of them sitting on the concrete under one of the Goose's wings.

"I got the documents to Bob and he's making copies and reviewing them," Veronica said after wiping her chin of some of the Colonel's finger-licking wonderfulness.

"What'd he say?" Tim asked.

"Not much, just that he'd look at it and wants to meet this evening. I invited him over for supper, along with Jeff and the Lewises." Looking about the hangar, her gaze lingered on the almost completed gate. "How long?" she asked, and picked up an original-recipe chicken leg.

"Maybe two more hours. Almost done," Tim said.

There was a knocking at the small side door, which then opened and all five Lewises entered. They, too, had brought the Colonel's finest and were soon seated on the floor with the others.

Don wanted to know when they'd be ready to move the Goose over to Hayek, so Tim had to go through the entire explanation all over again.

True to Tim's prediction, it took a bit over two hours to complete construction of the gate, the electronics and tuning the longer part of it. Finally, though, they were ready to test. Dave did a quick walk around the inside of the hangar, looking out at every possible viewpoint, ensuring no bystanders were standing by to witness the gate operation. Once Dave was finished, he returned to the gate, rifle at the ready. Don and Jack were also standing by, rather than sitting in the cockpit of the plane as Tim had expected. Don had explained, "No sense sitting in a cockpit if you open a gate and all hell explodes. At least, this way, Dave'll have some extra firepower." Tim also had his rifle, but rather than being at the ready, he had it leaning against the gate's control panel.

"Ready?" he asked Dave.

Dave nodded.

Looking at the father-son team, Tim held up his fist, thumb extended upward. Don looked over at Jack who nodded, then answered Tim with his own thumbs up gesture.

"It's a go," Tim said, starting the gate controls. Within a minute, the gate was open, showing the dusty terrain of an unoccupied Yakima Valley. Well, mostly unoccupied, except for the armed men standing by, an orange windsock on a pole barely moving in the slight breeze. Recognizing Luther, Tim yelled over to Dave, "See if they need anything to move the Goose. I want it out, now."

Dave ran through the gate in his shambling gait and spoke briefly with the head Seabee. Returning, he said, "They just need to run about twenty feet of mat. Said it'll take less than ten minutes." Tim nodded.

Luther lied. It didn't even take ten minutes; they were done in five. Instead of starting the Goose's engines, Tim hooked a cable between his jeep and the Goose and pulled the small plane through while Don and Jack sat in the cockpit. Fortunately, it was level ground, else the jeep wouldn't have been able to do so, with its limited towing capacity and small four-cylinder engine.

The small plane was soon on the runway, and after Tim unhooked the cable and moved the jeep out of the way, Jack began the start-up procedure. Within minutes, the engines were running and the propellers spinning. Jack slid open the small window on the side of the cockpit and yelled, "Clear?"

Tim looked about, saw nobody was in front of the plane or near it, and held up his thumb, shouting "Clear!"

Jack returned his attention to the cockpit, then looked up. The two propellers spun even faster and the sound of engine noise grew. Slowly at first, then with greater speed, the small airplane started down the makeshift airstrip. Before it reached the end of the metal, it rose slightly above the ground, then continued up, banking slightly to the right. It was clear that Jack was making a beeline for the airstrip at the main gate.

Tim watched the plane briefly, then waving to the others, jumped back in his jeep and drove it back to the terminal gate, where Dave joined him. Tim parked just short of the gate, shut it down, then got out and went through the gate. He figured the jeep would be safer on Hayek than unattended in the hangar. Once inside the hangar, he shut the gate down.

The plan was to have Veronica come pick them up after Jack successfully landed at the main gate strip. That way, they would know that Jack and Don made it, and they wouldn't have to open the hangar's large door, exposing an empty hangar where a plane should be.

The two men decided to have an impromptu celebration, pulling out a couple of beers from a small dormitory-style refrigerator that they had in the hangar office. They figured they had time for one before Veronica would arrive, and they were correct. They had just tossed the empty cans into the garbage can when they heard a car horn tooting outside.

Outside, they found Veronica waiting in the Willys wagon. She promptly slid over the front seat to allow Tim to drive.

As he got in, he asked, "Well?"

"They made it. Jack circled about a couple of times before landing, just to see what he could see," she answered, smiling.

That brought a smile to Tim's face, too. Dave said, "Awesome," from the back seat.

As soon as all three were buckled, Tim put the Willys in gear and drove back to the ranchette.

Upon returning to the ranchette, the Bowmans and Dave found Don and Jack sitting on the back deck. Don had helped himself to a beer and Jack had a can of pop.

"How'd it go?" Tim asked as he approached the intrepid airmen.

"Kid done well," Don said. "Easy up, easy down."

Tim looked at Jack. "It went well, sir. As Dad says, easy up, easy down. Landing on the airstrip here was actually easier than I expected. They did a great job with it."

Tim sat down in one of the deck chairs, joined by Dave, while Veronica went inside.

"How soon do you think you'll be ready to start?" Tim asked, looking between the two.

"I'm ready now," Jack said.

"We can go tomorrow if we've got everything ready," Don said. "Once we load up an empty thousand-gallon bladder and a full two-hundred-gallon bladder, we'll be able to go. Just say the word."

Veronica returned holding three cans of beer, the condensation leaving wet trails down the sides. Tim accepted the proffered beer and, after thanking her, said, "Tomorrow. Let's do it tomorrow. Sooner we get this show on the road, sooner we'll have more money to invest."

"Done," Don said, taking a swig from his can. "You want we should take anyone with us to act as security?"

"You think you need it?"

"Might be handy if the plane goes down," Don replied.

Tim thought a second, then nodded. "Okay. Ask for volunteers from the security team. Dave and I are gonna focus our energies on getting back to Oregon to get more gold." Tim took another sip. "Also, work out the logistics on building an airstrip in Oregon and another California. We probably won't be able to do it until we get a 'Boo, though."

"Boo?" Veronica asked. "What's a boo?"

"Caribou," Tim said absently, then turned to his wife. "It's what we called the C7 Caribou in 'Nam. Civilian version is the de Havilland DHC-4."

Veronica nodded.

Tim turned back to Don and Jack. "Also, plan on doing a supply run for Oregon. We're heading back for more gold soon and it'd be easier if we didn't have to carry everything."

"What are you thinking?" Don asked.

"Like Jack said before, drop off the mining gear near where we need it. Also, food. If some of those security guys are willing to go with us, we'll need a fair amount, along with feed for the horses and mules."

"Why take horses and mules? You should just take some jeeps," Don said. "Get a couple of pontoon boats, a couple of fifty-five-gallon drums, and that should do you."

Tim and Dave looked at each other.

"Y'know, he's right," Dave said. "While it's a bit steep getting up out of the Walla Walla Valley, it's not impossible. What's the tow capacity of your jeep?"

"According to the manual, a thousand pounds, cross country."

"Figure a trailer might weigh between three and five hundred, that gives us about a five-hundred-pound payload. We float down on a pontoon boat like we did last time, you won't use much gas. Figure on about five hundred miles round trip, max. More likely closer to three hundred. We're looking at, what, fifty gallons of gas? And, if we've got a pontoon boat or motor barge operating, not even that. We can easily fuel a barge from here. Well, close to here."

Tim cupped his chin in his hand and thought about it, everyone else quiet, just waiting to hear what he would say.

Finally, he uncupped his chin, leaned back, and took a deep draught from his beer. Setting the can down on the chair's arm, he said, "You're right. No reason why we couldn't put a powered barge or pontoon boat in the Yakima and take it across the Columbia. Even if it could only carry one jeep and trailer, we could make a couple of trips. Make sure we've got at least two, maybe three jeeps. That would also allow us to bring in some gas-powered dredges and find a lot more gold a helluva lot faster. Let's do it!"

11

Early the next morning, Tim operated the gate while Don, Jack, and several of the security personnel took the fuel bladders through, along with a towed fuel tank that reminded Tim of the ubiquitous "water buffaloes" from Vietnam. Not the actual animal, rather the towed water tank used to bring potable water to the various forward operating bases, or FOBs. Instead of water, though, this tank contained aviation gas.

Dave was sent out to find a boat that could carry a jeep and trailer. After a morning of looking at various types of pontoon boats at local dealers, Dave came back to the ranchette at lunchtime to describe the problem. "Doesn't seem to be anything that'll work just right," he said. "All they've got are fishing or party boats. Nothing that's good for hauling gear and horses."

When Luther, who was eating a sandwich in the shed with Tim, heard this, the crusty Seabee just said, with a mouth full of food, "Get a Higgins boat."

"What?" Dave asked, not understanding the man through a half-masticated sandwich.

Luther swallowed. "Get a Higgins boat."

"What's a Higgins boat?" Tim asked.

"LCVP. Landing craft, vehicle and personnel. You remember, boats used to storm Normandy."

"Huh," Tim grunted. "Where could we get one or two, and how much would they cost?"

Luther shrugged. "Beats me. You'd be lucky to find one in operating condition." Then he had a thought. "Actually, I bet you'd probably find some companies in Seattle or BC making landing crafts for the Inner Passage trade. You could look up there. Should be some making aluminum ones, which would be lighter to haul over here. Come to think of it, you might want to get yourself a little fleet. Maybe two landing crafts to cross the Columbia and a couple of aluminum boats or arhibs for passengers."

"Arhibs?" Dave asked.

"R H I B," Luther answered, pronouncing each letter individually. "Stands for rigid hull inflatable boat. It's what the SEALS used in 'Nam." Both men nodded.

"Got it," Dave said. Turning back to Tim, he said, "He's right. We should probably get a landing craft or two and a couple of powerboats. I saw some RHIBs for sale in town, about a thousand bucks each. Want I should pick them up?"

"Yeah, but make sure they can carry four to six people. Figure we'll need an operator and at least two passengers and gear, especially for the trip back. It'll have to be able to navigate the Yakima. I figure we can probably drive some jeeps down to the Columbia and use a landing craft to get them over, but once they're on the other side of the river, I might have to leave them there."

Luther smiled. "So, you want I should build a dock or landing area on the Yakima?" The man was having way too much fun on Hayek.

"Yeah," Tim said, nodding. "And a road to haul the boats there."

"Will do. I'll get my boys on it right away. Shouldn't take more'n a couple hours."

After lunch, Dave went back to Yakima to purchase the boats. Tim decided to hit the Selah city library and peruse the phone books for Seattle, Bellingham, and Vancouver, British Columbia, for boat brokers. He figured they'd be the best place to start.

His Willys CJ-3B jeep was still on Hayek at the Yakima Air Terminal gate area, so he elected to take the Willys pickup truck, leaving the wagon for Veronica, in case she needed to go anywhere.

I may not have much, but at least I've got enough Willys for everything, he thought as he pulled out of the driveway, not even realizing that he now had a lot more than not much.

Arriving in the small town, officially called a city, Tim found parking near the library, and was soon inside the air-conditioned building, talking with a reference librarian.

"We've got yellow pages for Seattle and Bellingham, but not for British Columbia," she explained, showing Tim where the phone books were kept. Thanking her, he pulled the books off the shelves and took them to a nearby table, where he began going through them, jotting down the name and phone number of every boat broker listed. He also decided to note boat builders.

In less than fifteen minutes, he was done. Putting away the two phone books, he thanked the librarian again and made his way back out into the summer heat. Fortunately, Selah was a small town with that small-town vibe, so when he got into his pickup truck, it wasn't a stifling hot vehicle; the windows he had rolled down when leaving his home were still down.

When he got home, he started making phone calls. On his third call, he found a broker in Bellingham who had a small landing craft for sale. Almost ten years old, it was an aluminum model. It weighed only three thousand pounds but had a payload capacity of six-thousand pounds, which meant it could be towed by a pick-up truck and could easily handle a jeep and three or four passengers. That would mean each jeep/trailer combination would require two trips by boat. Tim didn't think that to be much of a problem. The seller was asking twenty-five thousand dollars for it, but the broker thought he might be willing to come down a bit, as he was recently divorced and needed the money sooner rather than later. Having a boat for sale wasn't quite the same as having money in hand from a boat sale. Tim agreed to meet the broker the next day.

After hanging up, he sought out Luther and got him to agree to go with Tim the next day. Tim figured Luther's expertise would come in handy.

Shortly after dawn, Tim and Luther began the three-hour journey to Bellingham, a small port city on Puget Sound, about an hour-and-a-half drive north of Seattle. Soon after getting on I-82, they crossed over Selah Creek on the Fred G. Redmon Bridge, the longest concrete arch bridge in America. Tim briefly looked out over the almost fourteen-hundred-foot span into the deep canyon formed by Selah Creek, but immediately returned his attention to the road. For some strange reason, the Willys wagon had a tendency to swerve in whatever direction he was looking, and the last thing he wanted was to drive over the edge and plummet more than three hundred feet to the canyon floor.

Up and over the long anticline known as Manatash Ridge they went, descending into the windy, lodgepole pine-covered flatlands near Ellensburg. They had a couple of routes they could use to get to Bellingham from Ellensburg; they could either take I-90 across the Central Cascade Mountains toward Bellevue, just east of Seattle, or take Highway 97 north to Highway 2 and then across the North Cascades. They elected to take the northern route, despite the added time. They had planned on having breakfast in the quaint alpine town of Leavenworth, which had elected to switch from a declining logging town to a faux Bavarian village economically fueled by tourism several decades earlier.

They passed through Ellensburg, which was still pretty much of a ghost town at that time of the morning. Unusual strong morning winds blowing through the passes rocked the wagon as they made their way to Highway 97 on the other side of town.

Slightly more than a half-hour later, they drove over Blewitt Pass. Looking at the creek beside the road, Tim thought of Dave's discussion on gold being here.

Pulling into Leavenworth, Tim parked in front of Kristall's, a restaurant located on Highway 2 in downtown. It was barely six-thirty when they took their seats in the faux Bavarian restaurant, where they ate a hearty German breakfast of an omelet, boiled potatoes garnished with parsley, and a slice of Black Forest ham, not Tim's usual fare. He wasn't sure if he was glad or disappointed not to be served sauerkraut.

An hour later and the two men were back on the road, eventually crossing over Steven's Pass and dropping into the Puget Sound lowlands. They arrived in Bellingham well in time for an early lunch, but rather than take a break, they headed straight for the boat broker. Neither man was exactly hungry after their large Bavarian breakfast.

When they arrived, they found the broker, a man about their age, just closing the door to his small sales building. Tim could see the 'closed' sign in the door through the window. Seeing two potential customers, the man stopped, turned to them, and asked, "Can I help you?"

"Yeah," Tim said. "I'm the one that called about the landing craft yesterday."

"Oh, right, the small aluminum one," the man said, and held out his hand. "Jeff Davenport."

"Tim Bowman," Tim said, grasping the man's hand. Nodding toward Luther, he introduced the Seabee simply as "This is Luther." Luther and Davenport shook.

"So, let's take a look at this here landing craft," Luther said. "That is, if you don't mind?"

Davenport smiled. "Take a coffee and donut break at the local diner or show a boat to potential customers? What do you think? Follow me, it's back here."

Davenport took them to a boatyard with a multitude of working boats and sailboats parked on "the hard" as the broker called it. Most of the boats, especially the sailboats, were held upright by the use of boat stands. Eventually, the three made their way to a section where several landing craft were resting. Clearly, they were an animal of a different color. Rather than the rakish lines of the various sailboats and other powerboats, these had flat prows, clearly meant to drop and serve as ramps for whatever cargo they were carrying.

Among the landing craft was one that was different, painted bright yellow rather than the typical gray of the others. It looked used, but not abused. The bottom paint had been scraped to bare aluminum. Tim didn't know what he was looking at, but he walked around it, nevertheless. Luther, who did know what he was looking at, did the same. The difference between them was that while Tim looked, Luther bent down, prodded, poked, and even got on his hands and knees to look at the bottom of the hull as best as possible. He took several opportunities to bang his fist on it, using the edge of his hand as a sounding board.

Eventually, he stopped, looked at Davenport, and asked, "How seaworthy is she?"

Davenport shrugged. "She came in under her own power. Engines were recently serviced, so, pretty much good to go."

Luther pulled a stogie out of his shirt pocket, inserted it into his mouth, and began patting himself down for a light. It was clearly a show, as he found his Zippo lighter in his front pants pocket, where he always kept it. Flicking the lighter open with his thumb, then striking the wheel, he lit his cigar. He took a drag, then slowly released the smoke while snapping the Zippo lid shut, releasing the tension that had also been building up in all three men. "How much?"

Davenport looked back at the boat, then turned back to Tim and Luther. "Owner wants twenty-five kay."

Luther went into a coughing spell, holding out his hand as he did so. After he recovered, he asked, "Twenty-five kay? What kind of wacky tobacky is he smoking? That thing's not worth fifteen, let alone twenty-five."

Twenty-two thousand dollars later, Parallel, Inc. was the proud owner of a landing craft, the first vessel in a fleet that would grow over the years.

Luther managed to get the broker to throw in a trailer and transport to Selah, as the vessel was too big for Tim's wagon, or any other vehicles they had on hand.

As part of the celebration, Tim took Luther and Davenport out to lunch at one of the local roadside diners, where they dined on steelhead, lettuce, and tomato sandwiches, something not readily available in Selah, or usually on Tim's budget.

12

Tim and Luther returned to Selah via I-90, crossing over Snoqualmie Pass in the mid-afternoon. Most of the snow was gone from the pass, with only lingering patches at the higher altitudes. An hour later they were back in Selah.

Pulling into his driveway, Tim was surprised to see two RHIBs on small boat trailers on the ground outside the shed. Each had an outboard motor attached to the stern. As Tim and Luther exited the Willys, they were greeted by Dave. "How'd it go?"

"Well, we found a landing craft. Being delivered tomorrow."

"Guess we'll start having to call you Admiral, now," Luther joked.

Turning to the former Seabee, Tim raised an eyebrow in question.

Luther waved his hand at the two RHIBs, saying, "A captain controls one boat. An admiral controls a fleet. You've got more than one boat, so that means you command a fleet, Admiral."

"Wouldn't that be a commodore, since the fleet is pretty small?" Dave asked with a grin.

Luther replied more seriously, "I think you're right. I recall reading something recently about the navy reinstating the rank." Clapping his hands together, he declared, "Looks like you're Commodore Bowman."

Tim shook his head. "Whatever. I think I'll just go by Tim." Looking at the boats, he asked Dave, "You got a plan for these?"

Dave nodded. "Yep. We're gonna use the jeep and take them down to the Yakima, where the guys are building a small dock."

"What do we have that can haul something bigger?" Tim asked. "We need to haul the landing craft down, and that weighs about three tons."

Shrugging, Dave said, "Not sure. I'll ask around. I'm sure if somebody's got a big pickup, like a Dodge D-100, that'd work."

Just as he said that, a beat-up-looking Dodge D-100 turned into the driveway, raising a small rooster-tail. The red paint was fading, but they could all see it was an early 1960s model. "That would do," Dave said, "as long as it's got a slant six or better."

The old truck pulled up behind Tim's Willys, and an older gentleman popped out of the driver's side. White hair going bald on top, sturdy brush clothes, and round glasses made him look like the caricature of an aging explorer. Looking about, he waved at the small group by the shed. "One of you guys Tim Bowman?"

Tim raised his hand. "That'd be me." He was curious as to who the man was and why he was here. He wasn't a neighbor, or at least not one Tim recognized. Glancing over at the other two, he got raised eyebrows and shrugs.

As he reached Tim, he held out his hand. "Ken. Ken Wilson. Jeff Shimazu said you might be able to use me." He was greeted with a blank stare. "Said you needed a prospector?"

At that, recognition hit Tim. "Ah, right," he said, shaking the older man's hand. "Well, we could certainly use some expertise on the matter." Tim waved him over to the shed. "Jeff said you already signed an NDA?" This was said more as a question than a statement.

"Yep. Sure did. What he told me got me even more interested."

"This won't conflict with what you used to do?" Dave asked him, perhaps a bit more cautious than Tim.

Ken shook his head. "Nope. Not only am I retired, but I don't see how anything that you're doing is illegal. Well, maybe not getting your passport stamped." He grinned at that last one. "So, show me what you're using so I can figure out what we need."

"Can't," Tim said. "We left most of it on site. But it wasn't much, a couple of sluices, breaker bars, and shovels. Oh, and a metal detector."

"That last was a good choice. Bet it saved you some time."

Tim and Dave nodded.

At this point, Veronica came out onto the back deck and yelled over at the men, "You guys want some drinks? Maybe a cocktail?"

Tim looked at the others, getting nods in return. He yelled back, "Yeah. Be there in a minute." To the men, he said, "Might's well talk about this over drinks, if that's okay by you, Mr. Wilson."

"Just call me Ken," Wilson said, "and show me a good drink and I'll be more than happy to help out."

Once settled on the deck, beers in hand, Ken had Dave and Tim describe their expedition, with special emphasis on the tools they used and the water conditions.

"If it's anything like Warshington," Ken began, pronouncing the state's name with an R in the first syllable, like many native Washingtonians, "then the snowmelt was probably pretty fast, leading to some high water."

"Cold, too," Tim agreed.

"In that case, it's probably slacked off some, since then. Which means you'll be able to probably get to some areas in the Powder River you couldn't before. You planning on going back on horseback?"

"Actually, we were just working on that," Tim said. "We've got a landing craft coming tomorrow, which we plan on using to take some jeeps and trailers across the Columbia. Those inflatable boats you see over there," Tim pointed to the RHIBs, "are gonna be used to ferry men and supplies up and down the Yakima and Walla Walla Rivers. Jeeps'll be used to get from the Walla Walla to the Powder River."

Ken nodded. "Sounds like a plan. You're gonna need the jeeps, along with trailers, to bring in the dredges and fuel you'll need to run 'em."

"Dredges?" Dave asked. "You mean like those big things you see in the historic gold mines?"

Ken laughed. "No, no, no. I mean small, portable, hand-operated dredges. You get somebody in neoprene waders or a drysuit, and maybe a snorkel or scuba gear in the water, they manhandle a four-inch tube that sucks up gravel and such from the riverbed, and drops it onto a sluice box."

"Doesn't that chop up smolt and other small fish?" Dave asked.

Ken laughed. "Old wives' tale. Sure, it'll suck 'em up, but it also spits 'em out the other end, none the worse for wear. Think about it, all it is is a four-inch-wide tube sucking gravel and water up and spitting it out into a sluice box. Nothing's getting ground up, chopped up, or sent through some magical choppy-grindy thing.

"Here's how it works. You got a pump, usually gas-powered. That pump operates to push water through a hose, usually at a pretty high pressure. That hose is connected to a suction nozzle, which is connected to the dredging tube. As the pump pushes the water up the suction nozzle, it creates a vacuum, what we call the venturi effect. That means, water from the dredge tube opening gets sucked up into the tube and then expelled out the other end. No water goes through a pump." Ken looked around, seeing if there were any questions, then went on.

"Of course, the big problem comes from salmon eggs. If there are any eggs still buried in the gravel, they get sucked up, spit out, and generally don't become salmon. That's why the state doesn't let us dredge at certain times of the year."

"When is that?" Tim asked, leaning forward in his chair.

"Depends on the river," Ken said, "and the salmon runs."

Tim made a come-along gesture to get Ken to explain.

"You know that salmon don't all run up the river at the same time, right?" Ken asked. The others nodded. "Well, then, if you got a run in June, then another in August, and another in December, then you've got a lot of eggs in the gravel, or redds as we call them, just waiting to hatch. And, that could take two to three months for each run.

"Now, the Powder River, where you're heading, historically had two runs, chinook and steelhead. So, if you're hoping to dredge without impacting the salmon runs, you're gonna have to do so after they hatch and become fry. Figure you got until September before the salmon run gets into full swing, so that'll give you a couple of months of dredging."

Then Ken looked more sharply at Tim and Dave. "Unless you don't care about the salmon."

Tim held up his hands in front of him. "No, no. Definitely want to save the salmon. That's part of why you're here. We want to be able to get the gold with minimal impact to the environment. We know it's impossible to have no impact, but the last thing we want to see is wiped out salmon runs and extinct megafauna."

"Megafauna?" Ken asked. "What kinds?"

Dave took over the discussion. "So far we've seen Smilodons, or saber-tooth tigers as most people know them, an American lion, Columbia mammoths, glyptodons, a short-faced bear, and I think a couple of guys have even seen some giant sloths and giant beavers."

Ken's eyebrows rose, almost reaching to his balding, but tan, pate. "Daaamn," he exclaimed softly.

"Yep," Tim grinned. "And you should see the salmon runs."

Taking another sip from his beer, Ken set the bottle down on his thigh. "When do we begin?"

"Can you start tomorrow?"

"Hell, I could start right now," was Ken's response.

"Yeah, no," Tim said. "You don't want to go over to Hayek with a beer or two in your system. How are you with firearms?"

"So-so. Qualified every year with my issue revolver. Why?"

"Remember those megafauna we mentioned?" Dave asked. Ken nodded.

"Some are a bit unfriendly. We've got a firearms training process we're requiring everyone to go through. Let's run you through it tomorrow. Say about eight?"

"I'll be here," Ken replied.

True to his word, Ken arrived early the next day, ready to learn. In the back of his beat-up truck was a contraption Tim had never seen, a portable gold dredge. He also had everything needed for a couple of weeks in the field: a pack, canteens, a tent, and a sleeping bag. When Tim saw all the equipment, he asked, jokingly, "What's your wife going to think?"

Ken paused for a moment before answering. "Don't matter what she thinks. She's dead."

Tim didn't know what to say for a moment, then stammered out an apology, which Ken brushed off. "No need to apologize. Been a couple years." He shrugged. "That's one of the reasons I jumped on this. Wife's gone, kids are grown and moved to California. No real reason for me to hang around, other than to wait and die my own self."

Tim could only nod. *There but for the grace of God*, he thought briefly. "Sorry to hear that," he said.

"Yeah, that's life," Ken shrugged. "But, this, now this is exciting! When can I see it?"

"Considering all firearms training is on the other side, now looks like a good time. Leave your gear in your truck and follow me. You'll be taking everything over when you cross, anyhow." Tim turned and headed for the shed. Ken followed him.

When they entered the shed, Ken looked about, curiously. "Looks like a normal shed."

"It is, until I open the gate," to which Tim pointed. "I'll do so as soon as the others join us."

"Others?"

"Yeah. Dave's gonna take the boats over, and Lee Orange, the firearms instructor, should be here shortly. Want some coffee?"

The two men were enjoying a second cup of coffee in the shed when they heard the sound of a vehicle pulling up outside. Looking out the window, Tim could see it was Dave, in his Bronco. Lee Orange was riding shotgun. The two men got out, and while Dave made a beeline for the shed, Lee reached into the back of the Bronco and pulled out two rifles. Dave walked in, said hi to both men, then helped himself to a cup of coffee from the Mr. Coffee machine in the corner.

Lee entered, holding one rifle with the other slung over his shoulder. "You must be Ken Wilson."

When Ken answered that he was, Lee handed him the rifle he held. "Boss thinks you should have this, so here you go. We'll spend some time on it on the range. You ready?"

Taken aback by the abrupt manner of the foreigner, Ken could only nod and say, "Uh, yeah. Guess I am." Tim and Dave smiled.

"You'll get used to him," Dave said. He turned to Lee. "Let me finish my coffee before we open the gate. It's gonna be a long day as it is."

"Right, think I'll join you," the Rhodesian said, helping himself to the coffee. Rejoining the three men, he asked, "Any others crossing over today?"

Tim shook his head. "Nope, but we'll be moving a bunch of boats over and bringing in gear. I want to be on the way in the next couple of days."

Orange nodded, taking a sip of his coffee.

"So, is that a gold dredge?" Dave asked.

"Yeah. Figured I'd bring it by, show you how it worked, and see if it's something you think we should get," Ken replied.

"How about we try on the Naches later today? Maybe after lunch?" Tim asked.

All agreed that'd be a good test.

Coffee finished, Tim had the others prepare for the gate opening. "Ken, why don't you bring your truck through. Dave, get the doors, and I'll prep the gate."

Once the truck was in the shed, Dave closed the doors, while Ken sat in the truck, engine still running. He wasn't sure what to expect, but Dave and Lee got their rifles ready. "Never know when an unfriendly over-sized tabby might want to jump through the gate and eat you," Dave said. Unknown to Ken, he was speaking from experience.

Tim got behind the controls for the larger gate and said, "Here goes." With that, he opened the portal to Hayek. One of the security team was standing by, and when the gate opened, he waved them through, declaring it was "all clear."

Putting the truck in gear, Ken slowly drove through the gate after the two men had stepped through it. Tim called to him, "Be back by noon. I'm hoping to have the landing craft here by then, and we'll need your truck to pull it through.

Dave came back a couple of minutes later, driving Tim's jeep. He parked on the Hayek side of the portal, just far enough away from the gate to let things through. "Let's get those boats over. I'll hook them up and tow them to the river when we get them over."

Tim opened the shed doors, making sure nobody was around, and the two men manhandled the trailered boats through the shed doors, then through the gate. Once both boats were over, Tim returned to the shed, waved to Dave, then shut down the gate. It was now a waiting game, mainly waiting for the landing craft to arrive.

13

At noon, Tim opened the gate and Dave, Lee, and Ken returned, this time all three riding in the truck, which now had an empty bed. Ken apparently was still in awe. "How'd it go?" Tim asked, once the truck had been parked outside.

"Not bad," Lee said. "We've at least got him trained in the basics."

"And we got the dredge to the Naches," Dave said, referring to the Naches River, a gold-bearing stream between the gate and the airstrip located at the terminal gate site.

Looking about, Dave commented, "No landing craft, yet?"

Shaking his head, Tim replied, "Nope. Broker called shortly after you left, said it'd most likely arrive between twelve-thirty and one. Might's well eat something while we're waiting."

Tim led the three men inside his small house where they enjoyed a lunch of leftover mammoth stew. While they ate, Ken described the portable dredge in more detail, explaining its operation and where they could get more. Ken recommended getting at least three dredges, and enough drysuits to outfit three teams for each dredge.

"Why a drysuit instead of a wetsuit?" Tim asked.

"Better protection from the cold," Ken replied. "All a wetsuit does is warm up water that gets into your suit, and if the water is freezing cold to begin with, you have a shock. Do that a couple of times and it wears you out pretty damned fast. Drysuit's better for that. Costs more, but you get what you pay for. Of course, if you plan on doing this a lot, especially in the winter, you'll probably want to hook up a water heater on the dredge and pump that through some wetsuits. Allows you to work longer in cold water."

"Let's just start with the drysuits for now," Tim said.

As they were finishing up, they heard a horn. Tim dropped his spoon and empty bowl in the sink, leaving it for later (or more likely, for Veronica to clean up), and went outside, hoping it was his landing craft. Sure enough, it was. The truck driver, seeing how tight the driveway was, elected not to drive up it and was waiting on the county road. Tim hustled out to the road to talk with the driver, while the others crowded in front of the door to watch.

Within minutes, Tim was back. Gesturing to Ken, he asked, "You got a trailer hitch on that truck of yours?"

Ken nodded. "Two-inch ball, too."

"Okay, he's gonna drop the boat out on the road. I'll need you to hook it up and bring it in. As soon as he's gone, we'll take it in the shed and over to Hayek."

Ken started for his truck while Tim returned to the truck on the road, standing by while the driver disengaged the trailer from his truck. Once the trailer was disconnected, he went back to his truck and returned to Tim with a receipt for the tow. The man got back in his truck, and before pulling out, looked around at the dry Washington desert and shook his head.

Once Tim was sure he was gone, he gestured for Ken to pull the pickup truck in front of the trailer. The two men worked to hitch the trailer to the boat, and once it was connected, Tim said, "Take her to the shed."

Ken hopped in his truck, started it back up, then slowly eased the truck and trailer down the gravel drive toward the shed. As he approached the building, Dave opened the doors. While the truck fit, the trailer partially extended outside. Tim looked at that and thought, *How do I open the gate without anyone from the road seeing it?* His neighbors still didn't know what he was doing, and had yet to query him.

As he walked down the driveway, the solution came to him. Entering the shed, he said, "Lee, I want you armed and ready at the gate, just in case. Ken, keep your motor running. As soon as I open the gate, I want you through it." To Dave, still near the shed entry, he said, "Dave, keep an eye out on the road. You see anyone, holler. I want to open the gate when we can be sure nobody else can see in. As soon as that trailer clears the doorway, close the doors." Dave acknowledged with a nod.

Getting behind the control panel, Tim made sure all the settings were correct, then looked over at Dave. "Clear?"

Dave held his hand up. "Wait one, car coming."

A couple of seconds later, he looked around, then back at Tim. "Clear."

"Powering up," Dave said, giving warning to Ken and Lee. Lee took up a ready position obliquely to the gate, ensuring he had a view toward the other side but wasn't in the way of Ken driving the truck through. The gate open, Lee stepped through and looked about, then stepped back. "All clear."

"Go, go, go," Tim practically yelled. Ken gunned the engine, and then slowly pulled the truck and trailer through to Hayek. As soon as the rear of the trailer had crossed the shed's threshold, Dave shut the doors.

"Dave, Lee, you want to hook Ken up with Luther and get that thing down to the river?"

Lee was already stepping through the portal when Dave replied. "Sure." Dave, who had left his rifle inside the shed so no drive-by onlookers would see it, grabbed it, checked to ensure it was loaded, then stepped through the portal.

"Shutting down," Tim said, loud enough for the others to hear him on the other side. Dave waved in acknowledgment, and then Tim shut down the gate.

Then Tim decided to pursue, yet again, another errand. They needed at least two more four-wheel-drive vehicles and trailers; while he had two, he had no intention of using his own wagon or pick-up truck for the expedition. Instead, he wanted to get two more Willys jeeps, and he knew just the spot to find them.

Fifteen minutes later, he was in Yakima, at a store specializing in four-wheel-drive vehicle parts and supplies. Sure enough, the cork board near the entrance had a number of four-wheel-drive vehicles for sale. Several of them were older Willys jeeps, and Tim took down the number for every one of them.

Returning home, he called the first number and got lucky. The man on the other end was somebody Tim knew from four-wheeling, and he was willing to let his jeep, an old World War II Ford GPW, go for five hundred dollars. "It's kind of beat up, and ain't really something you'll want for highway use," the man said as a reason for the low price. The trailer it came with was also of World War II vintage, but still roadworthy. Tim told him he'd be over in a half-hour with the money. The man said he'd hold onto the jeep until then. "Not like anyone's called about it since I put the ad up."

Tim's fourth call was also successful. This time the jeep was a 1953 Willys CJ-3A, an upgraded civilian version of the venerable World War II jeep. Tim agreed to a price of one thousand dollars, as long as the owner threw in the trailer. Like the Ford MB, the CJ-3 had seen some rough four-wheeling duty and had a few "dings and dents." As long as the engine and other mechanical stuff was fine, Tim didn't really care what it looked like. He got the address from the owner and said he'd be by in about an hour.

Tim hurried over to pick up the first jeep. While he didn't know much about boats, he certainly knew a fair amount about cars, specifically, Willys jeeps, and the Ford GPW was nothing more than a Ford production of the vehicle. Tim climbed under the hood to check out the engine, then crawled under the jeep to check out the frame, suspension, and body. A quick trip around the block proved that the jeep could run. With the owner's approval, he took it on a nearby dirt track, trying out all three gears along with the high- and low-gear four-wheel-drive. All worked.

Tim paid the man cash, got the title, and said he'd be by later with somebody else to pick it up.

The second jeep he inspected was also in sound shape, and the owner wasn't kidding about dings and dents. It looked like he had slammed it into a pretty big boulder from the dent on the passenger side. Fortunately, the frame appeared to be straight, and after taking it for a test run, Tim became the proud owner of a 1953 Willys CJ-3A jeep.

Returning home, he found Veronica there and got her to ferry him to pick up the jeeps. Before heading home with the second one, he stopped in at the four-wheel-drive store and loaded up on spare parts and several new mud-snow tires, the waffle pattern tire world-renowned for the older jeeps.

When he arrived back at the ranchette and glanced down at his battered Timex, Tim saw it was almost five o'clock. He was betting that Dave, Ken, and Lee were probably waiting on the other side. *I really should see about putting a gate with a generator on the other side, just in case something happens on this side.*

Stopping the jeep and laden trailer in front of the shed, Tim jumped out opened the shed door, then drove it inside. Parking it in front of the big gate, he got out and went over to the small gate's control panel. He picked up his rifle, which was still next to the panel, ensured it was loaded, then opened the gate. Glancing up, he waited, and then was rewarded by seeing Dave, Lee, and Ken step in front of it on the Hayek side. They were accompanied by Don and Jack Lewis.

"We really should put a gate on this side," Dave said as he and the others walked through the portal into the shed.

"I was just thinking that. We'll need a generator, at least fifteen amps. I'm thinking just a small gate."

Dave shook his head. "Naw. I'd build two, a small one and a big one. Make it somewhat portable, so you can move it if you have to."

"I think I'll start with a small one," Tim replied, shutting down the gate, then opening the larger gate. "Why don't you drive that jeep and trailer over? No key needed, just hit the starter button." Turning to Lee and Ken, he continued, "There's a second jeep outside, why don't one of you get in it and get ready to drive through?"

Ken volunteered and was out of the shed in seconds.

As Dave drove the first jeep and trailer through the gate, Tim said to Lee, "See if the coast is clear. If so, open the doors and tell Ken to go on over."

Lee was on it, cracking the double doors and stepping through them. Paying attention to what Dave was doing, he waited until Dave had crossed over, looked around for any potential observers, then shoved the doors opening, saying, "Go, go, go," to Ken, just as Tim had done earlier. Ken put the jeep in gear and rattled his way in through the doors, into the shed, then through the portal. Tim yelled, "Just park it anywhere and come on back." Ken stopped the jeep with the rear of the trailer barely feet from the portal. Turning off the engine, he climbed out and joined Dave as he was making his way back to the portal. Seconds later, the two were back in the shed, the shed doors were closed, and Tim had shut down the gate.

As Tim led the men back to ranchette, where Veronica, wisely, had pulled out several cold beers for them, he asked, "How'd it go?"

"Not too bad," Dave said. "Ken's truck was able to pull the landing craft with no problem, and the Seabees had scraped out a road to the river, so it was just a matter of getting the truck turned around and launching the boat."

"All three boats good to go?"

Dave nodded. Turning toward Don and Jack, Tim asked, "How'd the plane stuff go?"

"Pretty good," Don said. "We managed to get in two runs yesterday and two today. We've almost got the first refueling site set up. Figured we'd come home for the evening and head back out tomorrow."

"How much longer do you think before we'll be able to head to California?"

Don looked at Jack, who said, "Figure on another week or so, sir. It takes a couple of days to set a site up, and each one is further away than the previous one, which means we've got to burn some of the fuel we're transporting just to get home."

By then, the small group had made it to the house's deck, where they were greeted by Veronica, holding the cold beers out. "Eileen called," she said to Don, as she handed him his. "Said she'd be here by six." Turning to Dave, she handed him the other beer. "Petra's on her way. Should be here any minute."

Tim made a gesture of "what, no beer for me?" to which Veronica rolled her eyes. "Your beer's on the table. Jack, Lee, can I get you guys something?

Lee requested a beer and Jack said he'd be happy with root beer, if she had one.

The men had no sooner sat down at the table on the deck when a dusty Ford Bronco pulled up. Tim said, "Petra's here."

When Petra got out, she waved and hollered, "Hey, can one of you help me with these pizzas?"

Jack practically levitated out of his seat at the word 'pizza' and ran over to help her. He returned with three boxes from a local pizzeria.

The pizzas were distributed sans plates, each person just eating a slice from the box. As usual, some sauce managed to make its way from Tim's pizza to his shirt. He didn't even notice.

"Dave was thinking I should build a couple more gates and put them over on the other side," he said, more to Veronica and Petra than to the men.

"Why not just move the small gate over?" Veronica asked. "That way, you've got one over there just in case. You can work on more gates after you get back."

Tim and Dave looked at each other with that "why didn't we think of that?" look. Rather than admit they hadn't thought of it, Tim said, "That's a good idea. Think that's just what I'll do tomorrow," and then promptly took a large bite, heading off any questions.

"So, when are you guys thinking of heading out?" Petra asked. Unlike Tim, she took a dainty bite of her pizza. *That's how she remains so thin*, Tim thought, between bites.

"I don't know about the others, but I'll be ready as soon as we get another dredge," Ken said.

"And drysuits," Dave added.

"And masks, snorkels, and more breaker bars," Ken continued.

Tim swallowed his mouthful and chimed in. "Probably in two days. We need what these guys said, I need to move the gate over, we'll need a generator, and we'll need fuel for the jeeps and boats and food. That about sum it up?"

The other men nodded.

14

Two days later, the original small gate was on the other side, the jeeps were fueled up, and a second dredge and all the other dredging equipment had been purchased and moved over to Hayek. They were unable to find a third dredge in the short time they had, but Veronica said she'd look for one while they were gone.

Before the expedition headed out, this time fortified with a six-man team from the security firm, Tim got the generator running and tested the small gate from the Hayek side. It took him a little fiddling before he found the right timeline (at least, he hoped it was the right timeline). There were a couple of times he opened the gate and had to immediately shut it down as it was clearly not the timeline he came from, such as the one that had what looked like a miniature feathered velociraptor, and the one where he startled what looked like a group of Neanderthal hunters about to make a kill on a giant sloth.

Once they had the right timeline dialed in, Tim shut the gate down and secured the control panel with an aluminum cover he had made just for that purpose that morning. "No sense somebody messing with it and screwing things up while we're gone," he said to Veronica.

Turning to Lenny Gross, who had decided to head up the security firm on Hayek, he said, "Okay. We've got a connection from here back to our original timeline. Make sure no animals trample it and nobody messes with it."

Gross nodded. "Not to sweat. I'll have Luther build a berm around it, with a small opening."

Within a few days, the team began the second gold expedition to the Powder River. Don and Jack were flying back and forth between what was Oregon, California, and Washington on Earth, so they weren't involved. Dave took the first of the teams down. Each team consisted of a jeep and trailer, a driver, and two security personnel. Dave also took one of the portable dredges, leaving the other one to be brought by Ken. Tim would bring food and fuel. As it took a full day for the landing craft to make the journey from the put-in point to the landing spot on the Walla Walla, it would take three days to move all the equipment. It turned out the landing craft could handle a jeep, trailer, and a couple of passengers. To ensure that adequate security was at the landing site, several of the security personnel rode down the river in the RHIBs, taking up position before Dave arrived. All six of the men had agreed to dredge for gold for a portion of it.

Finally, on the third day, it was Tim's turn to load up. The yellow landing craft was pulled up on the downriver side of the gravel bar where they had launched the original blue-barrel raft, ramp down, waiting for him. As he wanted to ensure he could drive straight off the landing craft and onto land, Tim worked with some of the security team to unhook the trailer and back it onto the craft. After it was in place, Tim backed the jeep onto the craft. Once loaded, Tim reconnected the trailer to the jeep. The security team left the landing craft, leaving it occupied only by Tim and Luther. Luther was already wearing a personal flotation device and tossed one to Tim, saying, "You ride in my boat, you wear a vest."

After strapping it on, Tim found it was awkward slinging his rifle onto his shoulder, so he held it in one hand. *At least I'll be able to set it down once we're underway,* he thought.

Yelling that he was casting off, Luther raised the bow ramp of the craft. When it finally clunked into place, he started the engines and backed it off the gravel bar. Swinging the lightweight craft about in the current, he then began the long trip down the river to the Mighty Columbia.

It was more than a hundred miles from their put-in point to the mouth of the Yakima, and then another twenty or so miles down the Columbia to the mouth of the Walla Walla. The goal was to go up the Walla Walla as far as possible and land on a gravel bar for ease of unloading. Eight hours later, the landing craft passed through the delta of the Yakima and into the Columbia.

Compared to his first trip on horseback, this one was a lot faster. Tim was still amazed at the amount and variety of wildlife he saw, even more than the first trip. Traveling by fast-moving boat meant that they surprised many of the animals, showing up before being heard and recognized as a threat. Along with the ubiquitous mammoths, he saw glyptodons, herds of elk, several grizzly bears, and even a short-faced bear, its size dwarfing some nearby grizzly that were catching salmon in the river. Looking down into the crystal clear water of the Yakima, he had seen numerous salmon and steelhead. The same couldn't be said for the Columbia. It was the same dirty brown that he recalled from his timeline. Probably even dirtier, considering there were no dams on this Columbia to cause sediment to settle in still water.

As they entered the wide river, Luther commented, "Current helped us going down. Going back up'll take longer. Figure on maybe ten or twelve hours.'

Looking at his watch, Tim asked, "How much longer till we land?"

"Hour, maybe an hour and a half, max. Now that we're off the Yakima and in deeper water I can crank this puppy up and plane her."

"Planer?"

"Yeah, go fast enough we're planing, not having most of the hull in the water," Luther explained as he gunned the engine.

Soon Tim understood what he meant. The landing craft's speed increased until she was kicking out bow waves and rooster tails, her hull planing across the surface of the river. It wasn't until they reached the mouth of the Walla Walla that Luther slowed the craft down and it settled back in the water. They slowly made their way up the smaller river until they came to a gravel bar with the jeeps and trailers parked around a driftwood fire. Most of the men were sitting in camp chairs, but one was standing, rifle in the crooks of his arms, scanning the terrain around them for any overt threats. Tim estimated they were near the same site as the Washington town of Touchet on Earth, which put them about fifteen miles from where the city of Walla Walla was. One of the RHIBs was in sight, on land and tied to a large cottonwood.

"I'm gonna pull right on up on that bar, near the arhib. You get ready to drive, but don't start your engine or do anything until I say otherwise. And, leave your vest on the deck."

Tim nodded, took his PFD off, and deposited it onto the deck of the craft behind the trailer, then climbed into the jeep, keeping his hands on the wheel so Luther could be sure he wasn't starting it. With a jolt and a grinding of rocks on the hull, the landing craft grounded itself on the bar. Luther dropped the ramp and yelled, "All right. You can take her off, but go slow."

Tim started the jeep and slowly drove it off the vessel. He could feel the craft rise once the jeep was off but before the trailer was, the motion of the vessel transmitting to the jeep through the uplifting trailer. Once ashore, he turned back and waved to Luther to indicate he was clear. The ramp lifted, and Luther began backing off the bar. He would be back in two weeks.

Dave and Ken, along with a couple of the security team, met him as he pulled up to the encampment. Shutting down the jeep, he got out and asked, "How're things?"

"Going well," Dave said. "We got the one arhib moved away from the river and tied up, so if we lose the one here, we've still got an out. We're pretty much all ready to go, too, and if you don't mind, we'd like to move out, at least a couple of miles, now."

Tim had been expecting to spend at least one night on the river. "Why now?"

"Bears," Dave answered. "Damn place seems to be a bear buffet. Not just grizzlies, which are bad enough, but a fair number of short-faced bears. We already had to kill one that got a bit nasty. Seems like the salmon run is bringing them in like yellow-jackets at a picnic."

Tim thought about it. They hadn't calculated that the salmon would still be near the mouth of the Walla Walla at this time, but it made sense. The river was well downstream on the Columbia from the Snake, and subsequently the Powder, where the expected salmon run would take place later in the season.

"What are you thinking?" Tim asked his friend.

"We make for high ground. Let's get up the valley and then up the ravine to the plateau. It'll get us far enough from the river so that those monsters won't pose as much a threat, and get us closer to the gold."

Looking up at the summer sun, Tim calculated out loud, "Figure on maybe four hours, that'll still give us an hour to set up camp." In a more commanding tone, he said, "Okay, then. Let's move out. Who's riding with me?"

Two men separated from the group. "That'll be us," the shorter of the two said.

"Well, grab your packs and hop in," Tim replied. "Dave, you want to lead?"

"Sure. Let's go, guys," he said to two other security team members.

As the others loaded up into the other two jeeps, Tim introduced himself to the two men. The shorter was a Floridian named Joe Whitmire, while the taller was Bob Gebbert, from Texas. Both men put their packs in the trailer. Bob hopped in the front seat, rifle facing outward, while Joe climbed into the back. Fortunately, Tim's jeep had a backseat, unlike the other two jeeps. The seat might have been small, without a seatbelt or headrest, but it had a cushion, which Joe immediately acknowledged. "Yeah, glad I'm not riding in one of the other jeeps. Ain't neither one of 'em got a seat in the back. Only place to sit is on that flat space over the wheel well in the back or on your pack. Not my idea of fun."

Tim just smiled, knowing exactly what Joe was talking about.

"Keep an eye out, will ya? I'm gonna be focused on driving, so if a bear or Smilodon or lion shows up next to us, I doubt I'll even see him," Tim said, half-jokingly.

"Don't you worry, none, Doc. After what I've seen here over the past couple of weeks, ain't no way I'm letting my guard down," Bob said, looking outward.

"Amen to that, brother," Joe iterated.

With a clashing of gears, a clanking of metal, and a scrabbling of tires on gravel, the three jeeps made their way off the bar and up the riverbank between two enormous cottonwood trees. As Tim drove up the bank, he could tell that it had either been modified or already had jeeps up it, as the slope was nowhere near as steep as it originally was, the bank having been cut or worn away wide enough for a jeep to climb. The small convoy then began traveling up the river valley, skirting the cottonwoods and sagebrush that grew close by.

Dave wasn't kidding about the bears. Tim saw at least four during the drive up the valley. He wasn't too sure if the rifles they carried would have sufficient power to stop any one of them had they decided to attack a jeep. *I think we're gonna need something a little bigger for the next trip,* he thought as they passed one particularly huge ursine, a boar short-faced bear, half again as big as a big grizzly.

Watching the bear, Bob said, "Maybe we should bring some Barretts."

Keeping his eye on where he was driving, Tim asked, "Barrett?"

"Yeah, fifty cal rifle," Bob responded. "Semi-automatic with a five or ten round mag. Good for cars, light armor, and big freaking bears. Maybe even for mammoths."

"Sucker's got to weigh like a mother," Tim said.

"Yeah, about thirty or so pounds. Not much worse'n an M-60," Bob said, referring to the light machine gun carried by those in the military. Tim had even had to carry one for a while in Vietnam. He recalled that while the gun only weighed about twenty-three pounds, one also had to carry ammunition for it, usually a hundred linked rounds, which weighed another six pounds or so, and made the machine gun's weight about thirty pounds. Not unreasonable, but not particularly easy, either.

"Wouldn't want to hump that thing," he said.

"Me neither, but if you're in a jeep or just hanging around base, it likely wouldn't be too bad," Bob said.

"Might be worth looking into when we get back."

"Might be worth looking into now," Joe said from the rear seat. Tim just smiled.

Three hours later, they had made their way out of the valley and up one of the numerous canyons onto a plateau. Tim had done a fair amount of four-wheeling before, but never anything like this. Instead of having at least some forest roads or trails, they were bushwhacking the entire way, never doing more than fifteen miles an hour, and often slower than that. The journey was made even more challenging due to the nature of the nature: many times they thought they saw something threatening, which turned out not to exist, but they couldn't take a chance. Looking at the map, he figured that they had managed to cover only about thirty miles, if that. The drive up the canyon had been the most difficult; in some cases, men had to get out of jeeps and push them, both machines and humans slipping on the loose, dry, soil. Tim suspected it was more difficult than the famed Rubicon Trail in California's Sierra Nevada. *At least they don't have to worry about Pleistocene predators there.*

Fortunately, the slow pace meant not much dust was kicked up, so the men, while hot and sweaty, weren't also covered in a layer of dust turned to mud by their sweat.

"I recommend we laager the jeeps and trailers," Bob said when they had stopped and shut down the engines.

"What's beer got to do with this?" Tim asked.

"Not beer lager, military laager," Bob said. "You know, circle the wagons type defense. It's what we did in Armor when we'd circle the tanks and APCs at night to keep Charley out."

"Ah," Tim said. It wasn't a term he was used to, and not one he'd used in Vietnam. Usually, when the platoon or company would settle in for the night, they'd establish a defensive perimeter for a patrol base. "Sounds like a good idea. Let's do it."

After a brief discussion with the others, some of whom actually knew what it meant to laager, they had the jeeps and trailers arranged in a modified circle, with their encampment in the center. Dave, having already spent two nights out with the crew, had most of them getting firewood while he and Ken stood watch. Tim joined them on watch, scanning nearby first, then further out.

"That was fun," he commented, somewhat sarcastically.

"Yeah, my butt says the same thing," Ken chuckled.

"Be thankful you're not one of the security guys. One of my guys had to ride on his pack," Dave said.

Looking about, Tim said, "Let's make sure they switch out every hour or so while we're driving. I don't want anyone so distracted they forget to keep an eye out for threats."

As soon as the fire was going and the men began eating their meals, one of the security team, a man named John Wolfe, asked, "Hey, Doc, how much longer we gotta ride? My ass is killing me."

Both words of sympathy and derision came from the other security team. They were a pretty hard-core group. Tim held up a hand, silencing them. "Yeah, I can imagine," he said. "If I'm correct, it's about another hundred or so miles, probably half or more on relatively flat land." Looking over at Dave, he asked, "Sound about right?"

Dave nodded. "Yeah, figure on between a hundred and a hundred and twenty-five. Depends on if we decide to go up to the Sumpter area or not. I think we could probably do well enough around the Baker City area, and that'll save us a couple hours of driving."

Just as he finished saying that, there was a loud roar from outside the laager, causing many of the men to drop their plates, grab rifles, and jump up, ready to defend themselves. The only ones who didn't move were Tim and Dave, both of whom had glanced up at the sound, cocked their heads, and determined the oversized tabby was too far away to present an immediate threat. The security team saw this and felt chagrined. Here were these two academic eggheads, either too dumb to be scared or smart enough not be, and the entire security team was acting like a bunch of cherries on their first night on a listening post in 'Nam, jumping at practically every strange sound, despite having been on Hayek a couple of weeks. Even those that had been on Hayek for more than a week were surprised at how spooked they were.

Seeing their reaction, Dave commented, "You'll get used to it. First one we saw scared the shit out of us, but they don't come near fire."

"And that one's a least a mile off," Tim added. "They're quite the noisy critter."

Bob, looking outside the laager, said, "Never heard one of them before. Lion?"

"Yeah," Tim said. "American lion. About twenty-five percent bigger than their African cousins. We still haven't figured out if they're in packs like the African lion or if they're more solitary. We ran into one up close and personal last trip, so keep an eye out for them."

"Y'know," Tim said, "last time we had the horses around to give us advanced warning. Should be interesting without 'em."

All of them considered that as they finished their supper, some having to start over as their food had wound up littering the landscape when they were startled by the lion.

15

The night passed uneventfully, well, as uneventfully as a night with hungry predators patrolling outside the firelight could be. Many eyes reflected the firelight, but luckily nobody took any potshots, which would have destroyed the sleep of others. The watch rotation that Tim had set in place during the first expedition was followed now, ensuring two people were on watch at all times, with overlapping watches so nobody stood more than a two-hour stint.

Most of the gear was stowed before they had breakfast, which was mostly coffee, instant oatmeal, and dried fruit. Food was fuel on this trip, not gastronomic delight, and they all recognized it. That didn't stop people from bitching about it, though: a time-honored tradition of people in the field.

After breakfast, they finished loading up in the jeeps, with Dave taking the lead, Ken in the middle, and Tim bringing up the rear.

As they began driving across the unmarked terrain, Tim commented to Joe, who was riding in the rear of the jeep, "Hey, we made it one day without being eaten. Let's make it two. Keep a sharp eye out behind us."

"Roger that," Joe replied, looking rearward. Tim and Bob could barely hear him over the whine of the engine and the crunch of dirt and gravel. "I don't fancy myself as the *menu du jour* for Baby Puss."

"Who's Baby Puss?" Tim asked, as he ground the gears from second back to first on an incline.

"Fred Flintstone's pet saber-tooth tiger," Bob said, with a quick glance at Tim before turning his attention back to his side of the jeep.

Tim could barely hear Joe chuckle, before the smaller man said, "What he said. Yeah, you can bet I'm a bit motivated to keep a watch behind us, what with me being the most likely target of opportunity."

As planned, they stopped after the first hour and made the security team switch places. As Bob climbed into the rear, he said, "Not much legroom back here."

"Be thankful you got a seat," Tim said. "Look at what the other guys are riding in."

"Just a thought, Doc, but maybe you should consider some other vehicles next time, like maybe a Land Rover Defender or a Toyota Land Cruiser. They not only got seats, but they got hard-tops. Kind of hard for one of them saber-tooth tigers or lions to get you through that. If I recall, Toyota's got some pickup truck versions."

"You're thinking of the FJ45," Joe said, still looking outward for any threats. The lion roar the night before had left him pretty much sleepless all night. It wasn't until almost dawn that he had finally fallen asleep.

Tim had to concede the point and said he'd check into it. "First things, first, though. We need another plane and an airstrip in California."

A couple of hours into the trip, they began the descent down onto the plains north of where Baker City would be on Earth. They ate lunch shortly after they entered the flats. Like breakfast, it was fast and fuel, mainly surplus C-rations. As Tim opened up a can of Beef in Spiced Sauce with his P38 can-opener, something he had kept on his chain with his dog-tags ever since his tour in Vietnam, he was suddenly reminded of a time he and Don were doing the same thing in Vietnam. The difference was, back then they were younger, in the jungle at the edge of some rice paddies, and hadn't bathed in ages. They also weren't ducking bullets this time. As Tim looked at the can, he had another irreverent thought. *At least I'm not forced to eat Ham and Motherfuckers.* Ham and Lima Beans was the least appealing combat meal in the Meal, Combat, Individual Ration that was supposed to be for intermittent use while in the field, but in reality, was their main food source for weeks at a time. Just as he was thinking that he heard, "Ham and motherfuckers? What the fuck, over?" from one of the security team. Tim chuckled and used his plastic spoon from the ration's accessory pack to scoop the greasy ration into his mouth. It wasn't the first time he had done that, and he doubted it would be the last.

As he ate the cold, salty, gelatinous canned meat product, he rummaged through the remainder of the plain brown cardboard box, seeing what other culinary delights would emerge. *Hmm, B3 unit. Why am I not surprised?* Tim had never figured it out, but all MCIs, or C-rats as they called them, had specific combinations based on an alphanumeric system. It was even printed on the box that contained them. The M-3 unit that Tim had consisted of a specific type of meat or meat and carbohydrate combination (which is why it had the M designation - M for meat), while the B-3 can, or B for Bread, contained cookies and cocoa powder, which he thought was amazingly good. It also had a can of fruit spread. The D-3 can, which was supposed to be D for dessert, contained what was supposedly white bread. He was hoping to score the pound cake but was glad he didn't have sliced apricots. While not superstitious himself, it was taken for granted among Marine Corps armored units that eating the sliced apricots before going into action was bad luck. *Damn, no fruit cocktail.*

"Anyone wanna trade?" the unlucky recipient of the Ham and Lima Beans asked.

"Don't eat it," Tim yelled over to him. "Life's too short, and nobody's forcing you. Just grab another one. Not like we've got a shortage."

As he took another bite, he saw the man toss the unopened can over his shoulder and head for the trailer closest to him to get another box. Swallowing his bite, Tim called out, "Hey. This is our new home. Don't litter. Pick that shit up!"

Looking chagrined, the man returned to the discarded can, picked it up from the dusty ground, then returned to the trailer where he dropped it off. The others looked at Tim, surprised. It hadn't dawned on them that Tim and some of the others considered this their home and wanted it treated with respect.

Seeing their looks, he asked, "What, you think I'm staying back there? Soon as we've got enough money, I'm building up some infrastructure and moving here."

"What would it take to join you, permanent like?" Joe asked.

"At this point, not much," Tim said, "other than pay a small sum, sign the Responsibility Statement, and agree to abide by the constitution we've written. If you agree to that, you can move over permanently, become citizens, and either buy or rent some land to build on."

"What if we just decided to forgo all that and just stay here?" one of the men asked.

Tim shrugged. "You could do that, too, but pretty soon you'd run out of supplies, companionship, and it's tough living in the wilds on your own. And if you elect to skip our requirements, you can bet your ass you'll never get any support. You'd be an outlaw in the true sense of the word—outside the law. Anything happens, it'd suck to be you."

"What kind of fee are we talking about, and what's that other stuff?" Bob asked, the question on the minds of all the security team.

"We were thinking of starting out at twenty-five thousand per person. Of course, if demand is high enough, we'll raise it, so you might want to pay it now," Tim said with a smile.

"Yeah, like I got twenty-five kay lying around," Bob said, chuckling.

"You will," Ken said. "Where we're going, the gold is thick as ticks on a coyote. With your share, you'll likely have enough to pay for yourself, and likely a family of four, too."

That got a murmur among the men, and then the conversation turned to the constitution and the responsibility statement, which Tim and Dave explained to the men.

"Sure sounds better'n what we've got at home right now, what with the career politicians and such." Bob finished his statement with a disgusted look.

Lunch over, the small expedition continued on its way. A couple of hours later, they saw a small herd of bison grazing near the Powder River. These bison were distinctly different than the bison they were used to seeing, being much larger with a bigger hump and longer horns. Dave thought they were antique bisons, a species that had been extinct on Earth for about ten thousand years. "Regardless," Tim said, "they'll make a modern meal for now."

"You want to try for one?" Dave asked, rather dubiously. Considering the trailers and jeeps were full, they wouldn't be able to carry much meat if they killed one of the behemoths.

"Not yet. We know they're around, and one of them would be better than C-rats all week. We'll send a team out tomorrow."

Before reaching their destination, they ran across a herd of Saiga antelope, their large, bulbous snouts looking more like a moose with a swollen nose than the type of antelope the Americans were used to. They also saw herds of pronghorn antelope, which they were more used to.

The group continued on, eventually arriving at the location where Baker City would be on Earth. Once again, they laagered, but not before unloading the portable dredges near the Powder River. They set up their tents inside the circled vehicles and wood collected for fires. As usual, at least one person remained on watch while others worked. As they elected to set up camp away from the river, they were in a less vegetated area, with mostly sagebrush. It wasn't quite like having the beaten ground around a firebase, but it was a lot better than being in a more heavily vegetated area where visibility was obscured.

Most of the men, Ken included, wanted to get straight into looking for gold, but Tim talked them out of it. "Look, have a little fun, do some panning, but just remember, we start the back-breaking work of real gold extraction tomorrow. I want to make sure everyone's fresh. We had a long, tough day today," to which many nodded. The drive had definitely been slow and bumpy, and the constant need to pay attention for any threats had worn them out faster than just riding on a freeway would have. "Make sure your drysuits, masks, and snorkel are ready before you go play, and make sure somebody's standing watch. I'll also want a pair to take a jeep and trailer tomorrow and go back to where those bison were. One of those things'll probably feed us for a couple of days. Matter of fact, we'll probably want a team out hunting every couple of days. That is, unless you guys want to eat C-rats every day for the next couple of weeks. By the way, we actually planned for this," Tim continued. "We've got a bunch of dehydrated potatoes and veggies in one of the trailers, so you can expect a fair amount of stew. And, if anyone wants to go fishing, there're trout in the river. We brought some fly rods just in case," the last said with a smile.

"Last time we were here, we had only five of us, each pulling a two-hour shift. We're gonna continue the two-hour shift program for the rest of the time we're here, using the same system we did last night. At a minimum, we'll all get at least six hours of sleep a night. Any questions?"

Joe raised his hand.

"Yeah, Joe?"

"Just thinkin' Doc, but why don't we post a schedule? That way nobody gets confused."

"Good thinking. Do it. Any more questions? If not, I'll take the first watch and the rest of you can play."

Joe was just as surprised at Tim's response as the others. As the group split up, he managed to find a pad of paper in Tim's jeep and wrote up a quick schedule, with rows of two-hour time blocks and columns for names.

Tim was on final night watch and watched as the sun slowly crept over the mountains to the east, lighting up the trees and mountains to the west with the soft glow of early morning light. Looking at the trees reminded him of seeing the early or late sun on Mt. Rainier when it was the reddish color called *alpenglow*, a German word that meant "alps glow". The color was caused by

Rayleigh scattering, when the sun's rays took longer to pass through the atmosphere and highlighted the slower red light wave while other light waves scattered. Looking at the tall conifers with the same color, he decided that *waldenglow* would be a good way to describe them, after all, it was the forests glowing with the low rays of the sun striking them. *Waldenglow*, he thought. *Forest glow. Yeah, it fits.*

Remembering his duties, he pulled his gaze away from the *waldenglow* and looked around the camp perimeter. It was lucky he did because, despite the smoke still emitting from the campfire, there was a very large, tan-colored feline sneaking up toward him, less than fifty yards away. He knew it wasn't an American lion, and the large canines in front weren't long enough for the cat to classify as a Smilodon. *Must be a scimitar-toothed cat*, he thought. With its sloping back, due to its hindlegs being shorter than its forelegs, it reminded Tim of a hyena. Tim felt like he could actually feel the predator's eyes on him.

"Hey, Brian," he called softly to the other man standing watch with him, not taking his eyes off the scimitar-toothed cat, slowly raising his rifle to the ready.

"Yeah?"

"Slight problem, here."

Picking up on the stress in Tim's voice, Brian came running over from the other side of the laager, rifle held at the ready.

Just then, the large cat decided to attack. With lightning speed, it raced silently across the space between itself and Tim, ears back and puffs of dust being kicked up each time its paws hit the ground and propelled it forward. Wasting no time, Tim brought his rifle up, acquired the target, and shot. Doing as he was taught by Green, he dropped his rifle to the ready, jacked in another round, then brought his rifle up and fired again. By this time, Brian had joined him and was also firing. In total, the two men fired four rounds, stopping the predator just fifteen yards from Tim's perch on his jeep.

Tim could feel his heart racing, the adrenalin finally kicking in. Looking around, he said, "Look for others."

By this time, the camp was alive with men running toward the perimeter with rifles in hand. Most were in the same attire they slept in, boxer shorts and barefoot, in many cases.

"Big cat down," Tim yelled, letting everyone know what had happened.

A minute later and the word, "Clear" was echoing across the laager as each man announced there were no threats in his area.

Dave came over, looked at the dead animal, and said, "Homotherium. I wonder where the rest of the pack is?"

"Rest of the pack?" Brian asked, looking about nervously. Vietnam, where the threats were known, was bad enough. But this place, you didn't even know what the threats were, and that worried him.

"Yeah, pack. It's a Homotherium, or scimitar-toothed cat, smaller brother to the Smilodon, or saber-toothed tiger. It's likely all over the world. Was in our timeline, until about twelve thousand years ago. They usually hunted in packs, going after mammoths. Maybe even horses."

"I thought horses were brought here by Europeans," Brian said, more a question than a statement.

"Yeah, they were. But there used to be horses here before that. Matter of fact, horses originated in North America. Like a lot of other mammals, they disappeared off the face of the earth about ten to twelve thousand years ago."

By this time, several of the other members of the expedition were gathering around, looking at the dead Homotherium and listening to Dave.

"Why?" Joe Whitmire asked.

"Why, what?" Dave asked in response.

"Why'd they all disappear?"

Dave looked at the dead feline before responding, emotions playing across his face. "Overhunting."

"Overhunting?"

"Yeah. Seems like our ancestors, when they arrived in North America, set about and killed just about everything worth eating. Take out the mammoths, and that removed a major food source for

Smilodons and Homotheriums. Cascading effect of fucking with the ecosystem." Turning toward Joe, he asked, "Ever hear of the butterfly effect?" The shorter man shook his head.

"Okay, it goes something like this. A butterfly in South America flaps its wings, sending a chain of events that eventually leads to a tornado forming on the Great Plains. Little events can precipitate large changes."

"Ain't that sort of how we wound up on a different timeline?" Joe asked.

"Exactly," Tim replied, also still staring at the large cat. He hadn't wanted to kill it, but he also hadn't wanted to die. He still didn't, but he also didn't want to see this timeline's fauna, particularly the megafauna, wiped out as they had been on his timeline.

"That's enough lollygagging," he finally said. "Let's get some breakfast then get to work. We'll skin that carcass and dress it out after breakfast. No sense leaving it for anyone else. Besides, it'll save a couple of us from having to go hunting for a couple of days."

After breakfast, Tim and Dave left the laager to gather the Homotherium's carcass, which they planned to dress and skin in the comparative safety of the encircled vehicles. When they arrived at the dead animal and turned it over to gut it, Tim noticed it was a female, and appeared to be nursing, as evidenced by the swollen teats.

"Well, this sucks," he said, looking around. The last thing he wanted to do was be responsible for the death of an innocent baby animal, even if it would likely grow up and try and eat him. Keeping his rifle at the ready, he started backtracking the big cat. He didn't get too far when he heard some mewling coming from under a sagebrush. Looking under it, he saw two small Homotherium cubs, both about the size of large house cats. Their spotted coat made them almost invisible under the shrub, the dark spots and tan coat blending in with the dappled dust. They were mewling and looking up at him with large eyes, their little scimitar teeth just starting to grow out.

Looking back over his shoulder, he called to Dave, "Found 'em." Turning back to the kittens, he made calming noises. "Yeah, I bet you're scared, little ones."

Dave joined him. "So, you thinking of killing or saving them?"

Tim turned to Dave. "What do you think?"

"Knowing you, you're probably gonna adopt them."

"Well, I did kill their mom. Somebody's gonna have to take care of them until they're big enough to go out on their own."

Looking at the mewling cubs with their oversized canines, Dave said, "Yeah, good luck getting them out of there without getting bit. Those things'll probably tear your hand up worse than a regular cat would."

"One way of finding out." Shifting his rifle to his right hand, Tim reached in and grabbed the closest kitten by the scruff of the back. It started to struggle then went limp. "Thought so," he said, as he cradled the small creature.

"In for a penny," Dave said, repeating Tim's actions.

Within minutes, the two were back in the camp, organizing a small nesting area for the two cats. Tim had one of the men empty a case of C-rations and put some towels in the case. A little duct tape and the top became a side, increasing the height of the box. Once it was set up, he and Dave placed their catches into the cases. Once released, the cubs huddled together, hissing and growling at the strange creatures hovering above them.

"I bet they're hungry," one of the men said.

"Your probably right. Dig out some of the powdered milk and let's mix some up. Probably won't be enough to keep them going, but I'm betting they're already eating meat, as evidenced by those teeth."

While one of the men, Rick was mixing up the milk, Bob handed Tim a miniature bottle of tequila, the type commonly used to serve alcohol on airlines. "Here. You can either pour it out or drink it, but the bottle ought to be good enough to work as a baby bottle. Just need a nipple."

"Anyone got a condom?" Tim asked, looking around.

Several of the men reached for their wallets. Tim had suspected some of them would have been prepared for a chance encounter with a loose woman, even here on Hayek.

"Milk's ready," Rick said, handing a bowl over to Tim. "Made it thicker than usual, so it should have a bit more calories for them."

"Thanks, Rick," Tim said, taking the proffered bowl. Handing the miniature bottle back to Bob, he said, "Here. It's your bottle. You drain it however."

Cracking the lid, Bob took a sip and then offered it to everyone else. A couple of the others took a sip until the small bottle was empty and was passed back to Tim, who then rinsed it out and filled it with the milk.

Taking one of the proffered condom packets, Tim opened it and extracted the lubricated condom. Placing it over the small bottle, he held it taut, then wiped the lubricant near the tip of the condom off on his pants leg. "There, that should do."

Poking a small hole in the condom tip with his knife, Tim put the field expedient baby bottle in front of the closest cub. It backed up until it ran out of room in the small cardboard box, but the smell of the milk was enough to draw it toward the bottle. A quick lick, and then the cub chomped down on the improvised nipple, hungrily slurping. The other cub, drawn by the smell and action, joined the first cub, trying to get its fair share.

"Looks like you'll need another bottle," Bob said.

"Hold off on that," Tim said. "Anyone got a can of turkey loaf?" The turkey loaf C-ration was probably the blandest meat concoction in the Meal, Combat, Individual. Other bland M units of the MCI were tuna, boned chicken, and boned turkey.

As Tim continued to nurse the cubs, Joe squatted down next to the cardboard box with an open M-1 can of turkey loaf. Using the plastic spoon that came with the accessory packet, he slowly spooned a little into the box. The cub not nursing spotted the meat and pounced on it, in that way that all young felines do. Soon, it was eating the meat, making funny faces as it did so.

"Probably not used to the salt," Joe said.

"You're likely right," Tim agreed. "We should probably make sure we've got some fresh meat for them." Looking about, he asked, "Who's up for hunting? I don't think we should feed them their mama."

Rick and the sixth security team member, Joey Freeman, volunteered. They decided to head back to where they had seen the Saiga antelopes the day before, and if they weren't there, then to look for the bison.

"Try to be back by noon," Tim said, concern for the men's safety uppermost in his mind. Academically, he knew that their small expedition would have to split up for fresh meat, but it still made him nervous.

Soon, the cubs had drank and eaten their fill, then curling up against each other, they fell asleep. Tim figured they would likely be out for an hour or two, and suggested the men begin dredging for gold.

After the hunting team's departure, Dave stayed behind with the cubs. He took up a solitary watch, while the remaining men were either in the water or at the water's edge, paying attention to Ken as he demonstrated how to operate the dredge.

This turned out to be quite simple. Just fuel them up, start them up, get the impeller working, then stick the dredge under water. Anything sucked up would be spit out the back and have to exit through a sluice box. Each dredge was a simple, one-man operation, but since the water was cold, despite the warm air, each man was restricted to one hour of operation at a time. This would allow for a team of three to operate with one man in the water, one man on watch (or cub-sitting), and the other man warming up and keeping an eye on the dredge. Tim suspected they would work until noon, take an hour off for lunch, then probably work until six or seven.

When it was Tim's turn to operate the dredge, he got into his drysuit with some degree of difficulty. Upon Ken's advice, anyone wearing drysuits had also bought boots that were a couple of sizes bigger than their usual size. These were slipped on over their drysuit booties, mostly to protect the neoprene from abrasion by gravel. "Last thing you need is some frozen toesies," Ken had said when he made the recommendation. Tim covered his head with a drysuit hood and put drysuit gloves on.

Tim waded out into the river, and before grasping the four-inch dredge hose, placed his mask on his face and tightened the strap, put the mouthpiece of his snorkel into his mouth, and gave it a couple of test breaths. Satisfied that all was working well, he took hold of the hose and lowered himself into the water. He was pleasantly surprised to find that the cold wasn't as shocking as he had expected. He could feel it, and he knew it could have been a lot more shocking. He also knew that over time it would take its toll, and to get out before he started suffering from hypothermia. As his head ducked underwater, the chugging of the gas-powered pump became muffled, replaced by the sound of water swirling by his head, and the sound of gravel and gold clinking up the hose.

Tim worked the nozzle of the hose around and was amazed at how much gravel was being sucked up. The water remained mostly clear because Ken had set both dredges up to operate parallel in the stream, so no debris from either dredge was muddying the water of the other operator.

Losing track of time, Tim was surprised when he felt a tapping on his shoulder. Standing up in the waist-deep water, he saw Joe, dressed in a drysuit, pointing to his watch, yelling, "Time." Tim nodded, handed the hose over to the smaller man, then made his way to shore, stumbling as he did. It was only then that he realized that he had gotten quite cold in the river. Fortunately, the sun was up, as was the temperature, and he would be warm shortly.

After stripping off his mask, gloves, and hoodie, Tim made his way back into the river and took his place at the dredge, where Bob handed him a belt with a canvas pouch attached and showed him what to do. "Any nuggets come through, grab 'em and put 'em in the pouch. If the pouch gets full, empty it in the bucket over there on the left," he said, pointing to two buckets on the bank. "Other bucket's for when we rinse out the mat. Otherwise, just stay here and soak up the sun." Bob then went to take Joe's place on guard, moving to shore and picking up his rifle which had been resting on his pack. All the men had set their packs by the river and put their rifles on top of them for quick access if needed. It also meant that the rifles weren't too far away.

For the next hour, Tim was in constant motion plucking gold nuggets out of the sluice box and watching the miner's moss mat fill up with gold flakes and dust, along with a substantial number of clinkers. When the hour was up, he tapped Bob on the shoulder. Emerging from the cold water, Bob pulled his mask off his face. "Yeah?"

"Time," Tim said, pointing to his watch. While Bob took some time to take off his extraneous gear and deposit it on the shore, Joe made his way into the water, geared up for underwater operations.

When Bob returned to the dredge, Tim showed him his duties, then headed for the bank to take up his guard duties. He stripped out of the dry-suit top and put on a regular t-shirt. Looking into the box containing the Homotherium cubs, he saw they were both awake and watching him with interest. "How they've been?" he asked Dave.

"Quiet," Dave responded. Tim reached his hand in to let them smell him, and after several seconds of them backing away from him into a corner of the box, the smaller of the two, whom Tim had discovered earlier was a female, came forward and sniffed his hand. Taking the opportunity, he rubbed the side of her head with a finger, and just like a regular kitten, she curled her head down, exposing more of her neck for petting. Tim obliged her.

"I'll be back at lunch time," he said, slowly rising, trying not to startle them. He was afraid that if he did, they'd try to scramble out of the box and run away. That would be a death sentence for them, and he didn't want that on his conscience. As he looked down at them, he had a thought. *Maybe I should bring them with me. That way they won't be lonely and afraid.*

Slinging his rifle and talking calmly to the kittens, he picked up the box and walked toward the river where he would take up watch. The cubs were initially startled, but since nothing untoward was happening to them, they settled down.

The hour on watch passed slowly as Tim scanned the terrain. His eyes were constantly moving, looking around for any threats, to Bob and Joe at the dredge, then down at the Homotherium cubs in the box at his feet. As noon approached, he could hear the sound of a jeep in the distance. Looking toward the north, he saw a plume of dust approaching. *Hope they got something,* he thought, looking down at the cubs who had begun mewling again. Clearly, they were hungry.

Calling over to Dave, the only one not engaged in gold dredging, Tim asked if he wouldn't mind fetching some milk for the cubs. Dave agreed to do so, and by the time the returning jeep had pulled up to the laager, he had the milk made up in the make-shift baby bottle and handed it over to Tim. "Here. I'll keep watch while you feed the future man-eaters."

This time, the cubs recognized the bottle and fought over who should be first, the female winning out while the male continued to mewl.

It took Tim a couple of fill-ups of the bottle before the cubs were satiated enough to stop fighting over who got the nipple next. Meanwhile, one of the men from the jeep came over to Tim with a chunk of meat. "Here, they might want this."

Tim cut off several small pieces with his knife, setting them down in the box. The cubs were definitely interested in the food, attacking it with gusto.

"Wonder how old they are?" Dave said.

"Probably two or three months," Tim said, watching the two cubs eat the hunks of raw meat. "I read a *National Geographic* article on lions a while ago, and from what I recall, lion cubs start weaning at about ten weeks. I wouldn't be surprised if it was the same for these guys."

16

Lunch over, the teams returned to dredging for gold. With three teams, but only two dredges, this allowed one to relax onshore, keeping watch. In this case, it was Tim's team that got a break while Dave's dredged. Ken had recommended that the miner's moss in each sluice be changed, so one of the duties that fell onto Tim's team was to empty the gold from the miner's moss into the five-gallon buckets set aside for that purpose.

Tim was surprised at how much gold had been trapped in the moss, as he watched Bob rinse one of the mats out in the bucket. Not only did the mats trap gold, but they also trapped iron minerals known as black sand concentrates. While the black sand would hold gold, the quantities were usually so minute it wasn't considered worthwhile to keep them. But, separating the gold from the concentrates would take more equipment than they had on-site, so Tim, upon Ken's recommendation, had elected to collect all the concentrates and process them once they returned to Selah. Ken had a super magnet he said would be useful for this.

As he sat on the side of the river watching the operation, he was distracted by the sound of the two cubs fighting in their box. Looking into it, he saw them rolling around. When they noticed he was watching, they stopped their play and looked up at him.

"So, you guys want to join me?" he asked.

The cubs just stared at him, wide-eyed.

Taking a chance, Tim reached in and grabbed the female cub by the scruff of the neck. It immediately went limp. Placing the cub in his lap, Tim waited for it to resume its activity. Within seconds, it was moving about, walking on Tim's lap, going from one leg to the other. Fortunately, its claws didn't dig in too much. It moved about curiously, then stepped off Tim's lap and to the side of the box. Putting its front paws on the edge of the box, it pulled itself up so it could look over the edge. The male noticed and also pulled itself up to the top of the box edge. The two cubs mewled at each other.

"Oh, all right," Tim said, pulling the male cub out and setting it on his lap. The female came back to Tim and climbed into his lap to be with the male cub. The two cubs spent several minutes just walking across Tim's folded legs, flopping over, falling, and generally having fun exploring, little claws digging into his legs. After a while, the two cubs became tired, and Tim placed them back in the box.

Leaving the sleeping cubs, Tim waded out into the river to see how things were progressing. His first stop was at Ken's dredge. Ken was handling the sluice operation, and as Tim approached, he could see the older man plucking gold nuggets out of the sluice and placing them in his belt pouch.

"How goes it?"

Ken turned to him with a huge smile on his face. "Fifty years of prospecting and I've never seen anything like this. It's amazing!"

Tim grinned. "So, after this, you want to try the California goldfields?"

The older man's eyes lit up. "Would I? That's like asking an alki if he wants a shot of whiskey. How soon?"

"Couple weeks here, a couple days back on Earth, then we'll probably head out. Lot depends on how Don and Jack are doing."

"How much do they still have to do?"

"Not sure. Right before we left, they were finishing up setting up the fueling stations. I wouldn't be surprised if they already had it set up," Tim said. "How much do you figure going out here?"

Ken furrowed his brow. "Hard to say. But, sure is a lot more than I've ever seen before. I wouldn't be surprised if we pulled out more than 14,000 ounces today, if not more."

"Figure about 100 pounds?"

"At least that," Ken said. "Like I said, probably more than that. This is the richest field I've ever seen."

Tim raised eyebrows. "If we can go like this, we'll wind up with a ton of gold, literally."

Ken nodded, "I wouldn't be surprised. That sure is a hell of a lot of gold." As he spoke, Ken continue taking gold nuggets out of the sluice and putting them in his pouch. "And that's not even talking about whatever gold fine we find."

Tim started doing calculations in his mind. After a short pause, he exclaimed, "Holy smokes! That's over five million dollars." He looked at Ken in awe. Ken also raised his eyebrows.

"Now you're talking some serious bank," Ken said.

Looking around at the operation, Tim wondered, "Think we'll be able to keep this up?"

Ken surveyed the ground and the dredges in operation, making his own calculations. "I don't see why not. It's not like we covered everything, we're actually only scratching the surface."

"Hell, if we actually bring that much gold, we shouldn't have any problem funding that new plane and runway."

After almost two weeks, the crew had completed as much work as they were going to. On average, then pulled out about five thousand ounces of gold per day, far more than Ken had originally thought they would. In total, they had about sixty thousand ounces of gold, valued at a bit over twenty-two million dollars. Tim estimated, before taking into account the loss in value due to purity, and whatever share needed to be paid to sell gold, each person's share would be a bit over two thousand ounces, or about three-quarters of a million dollars. To say the least, everyone was rather excited when he broke the news to them.

"There is one slight problem here, though," Tim said. "Getting it all back. We've only got three trailers, each of which can handle about a thousand pounds cross country. Factor in the weight of the trailer, maybe three hundred pounds, and we're down to an actual payload capacity of about seven hundred pounds. And, we're looking at about four thousand Imperial pounds, or five thousand Troy pounds.

"No matter how we slice and dice it, we're going need six trailer loads between here and the Walla Walla." He paused. "That is, unless everyone is willing to walk and we carry nothing but gold in the jeeps and trailers. Even then, we might not be able to do it."

"So, even if we take only the gold and the important stuff with us, we're still gonna have to make a second trip?" Dave asked.

Tim nodded. "Pretty much. Possibly even a third. We can leave most of the food here as long as it's canned. Load up the essential camping equipment and enough food for five days. We'll leave the mining equipment here along with a bunch of the gold. Make sure nothing smells like food and let's stack everything together and cover it with brush."

The decision was made to carry seven hundred pounds of gold in each trailer, along with an additional one hundred pounds in each jeep. The combined weight of three men and a hundred pounds of gold was almost at the payload capacity of each jeep, but not over it. If nothing went wrong, they'd be able to complete the gold transfer with only five loads.

It didn't take long before all the extra gold, mining equipment, and spare food had been stacked and covered with sagebrush. A few trees were also cut down, the bigger branches placed over the pile to further secure everything.

"All right, let's get this show back on the road," Tim said, climbing into his Willys jeep.

In minutes, the small convoy was on its way north to the Walla Walla with three thousand pounds of raw gold and two Homotherium cubs.

The trip back to the river took them less time than the original trip to the gold field, due mainly to being able to follow their earlier tracks and knowing where to go, even though they were going slow so as not to have a problem. Going downhill was the worst; with the jeeps and trailers loaded to the maximum, it created a hazardous condition. When they made the final drop down into the Walla Walla valley, Tim had the men walk, just to reduce the loads on the brakes. When they finally arrived at the gravel bar where they had stashed the boats, they found them undisturbed.

Each boat could easily carry six men, which was the equivalent of about a thousand pounds. Tim and Dave had talked it over and determined it best to send some gold, but not all of it. They wanted the landing craft to be used for most of the gold transport. Tim made the decision to send five hundred pounds of gold with two men in each boat. Dave would command one vessel and Ken the other. The remaining gold was left on the gravel bar. "Not that it's gonna go too far, even in a flood," Ken said as they planned.

That left the gold retrieval team reduced to five. Tim would return for the remaining gold on the Powder River in two jeeps with Joe, Bob, Brian, and Doug. Naturally, one of the latter would have to ride in the back of the trailing jeep just to keep an eye out for any stalking predators. Nobody wanted a Smilodon or American lion attacking from behind. Of course, since Tim's jeep was the only one with a bench, that meant he would be driving behind Ken, sucking up any dust kicked up by the lead jeep.

As they loaded the gold onto the boats, Tim told Dave, "We'll likely be three days up and back. Once you arrive at the base camp, tell Luther to bring the landing craft back for the remainder of the gold. Before that, though, get the gold to Veronica and tell her to see about getting it smelted and sold. No sense waiting until we're back." Tim estimated three days should be a sufficient amount of time for Luther to return with Dave and Ken in the landing craft.

Before the boats left, Tim handed the cardboard box containing the two Homotherium cubs over to Dave. "Hand these over to Veronica when you get home. Make sure she understands that they need proper formula along with raw meat. If you have to kill something to feed them before you get home, go ahead and do it."

"Yeah, she sure is gonna like that," Dave said with an evil grin. "I'm looking forward to seein' the look on her face when I give her these guys."

"Just let her know that it's important to me that these guys live. She'll understand."

Taking the box with the mewling cubs, Dave said, "Your funeral, buddy."

Tim just smiled.

As the men pushed the boats off the gravel bar, Tim called out, "Stay safe out there. Remember, you're worth more than the gold is, so if anything happens, just let it go. Take care of yourselves."

With a wave of one hand, Dave gave the boat some acceleration and took off down the river, followed closely by Ken. Turning back to the remaining men, Tim said, "Load 'em up and let's go back for more gold."

17

The drive back to the gold field was, fortunately, uneventful, and even faster than their earlier trip. But, it still took more than a day. Everything was as they left it. In less than an hour, they had the remainder of the gold loaded up and were heading back to the Walla Walla. Laagering with only two jeeps and trailers had proved interesting, but it was possible. Maintaining safety and hygiene proved even more interesting. Nobody wanted latrines inside the laager's small perimeter, but nobody wanted to go outside it, either. The compromise was that urinating inside the laager was acceptable, as long as it was nowhere near where people were sleeping. If anyone needed to do more than urinate, they were advised to wait until morning, when a watch could be set up for protection.

The drive across the plain from the gold field had been fairly straightforward. They spotted lots of wildlife, mostly grazing herbivores with the occasional predator thrown in. At one point, they even saw a small pride of lions, some of them gnawing on the carcass of a Saiga antelope. Bob said, "I guess that answers the question as to whether they're pack or solitary hunters." Everyone kept an eye on the pride, who eyed them back as the jeeps slowly passed.

The final night's stop was at a campsite they had used their first night out, barely thirty miles from the Walla Walla. As usual, the five men laagered the two jeeps and trailers, gathered wood, and started a fire. It wasn't long before they were cooking C-rations over the fire, the smell of spiced pork, beans and franks, and other questionable cuisine wafting through the summer night air, mixing with the scent of juniper pines, sagebrush, and dust.

"Yeah, this is the life," Brian said, leaning back against his pack, C-rat can in one hand and white plastic spoon in the other.

"You can't be serious," Joe said, looking at Brian in disbelief.

"What? You ain't groovin' on this?" Brian responded. "Look, man. We're out in the wilderness, chowing down on food we didn't pay for, and with the exception of worrying about some hungry critters, life is pretty darn good from where I'm sitting."

Tim had to agree with the security specialist. "And, it's only gonna get better."

Doug, the security specialist who had complained about the ham and lima bean C-ration their first day out, stood up, a small brown pack of C-rat toilet paper in his hand. "Well, while you guys rhapsodize about how great everything's gonna be, I'm gonna go pinch a loaf."

"Who's gonna stand watch?" Tim asked.

"No need," the specialist said, stepping between a jeep and trailer. "I don't see no eyes, so the smoke's probably scared everything off."

"Regardless, somebody's gotta be ready." Tim set his can of turkey loaf down, stood up, grabbed his rifle, and started walking across the laager's interior. He didn't get more than a couple of steps before all hell erupted.

A great roar sounded just outside the perimeter, followed by another, different but also close. Tim immediately ran to the edge of the perimeter, but he realized he was too late when he heard screaming. Running toward the space between the jeep and the trailer where Doug had stepped out into the night, Tim raised his rifle, looking for a target, all the while listening to the man scream in mortal pain.

Joe showed up next to him, a large Mag-lite in his hand, shining out into the dark. A quick glimpse of green eyes and Tim raised his rifle. Before he could shoot, Joe placed his hand on the rifle's barrel. "You might hit Doug."

Tim shrugged the smaller man's hand off. "If I don't take the shot, it won't matter." A quick aim and he fired into the night toward the eyes. They blinked shut, then opened again with a caterwaul that made the hair on everyone's neck stand on end. Tim fired again. The screams of the giant cat ended as abruptly as they had started, but Doug's screams didn't. They just began to fade, as the man was dragged off alive into the night by the other cats.

Eventually, the screaming ended.

Tim was so angry he wanted to charge out and kill every damned lion he could see, and it was only through the combined efforts of the others that he didn't.

Bob threw more wood on the fire, making it grow, sparks flying into the night sky and the flames providing a bulwark against the dark and night predators.

"Nobody leaves the perimeter alone," Tim said, practically shouting. It wasn't just the death that had upset him, but that it was an avoidable death that happened under his command. *How am I gonna explain that one?* he thought. Calming himself down with several deep breaths, he continued. "I want two-man watches all night, like usual. We'll look for Doug first thing in the morning."

It was a long night, and none of the four men got any sleep, regardless of whether they were on watch or not. Finally, dawn came. Unlike the typical cloudless blue skies of eastern Oregon that they had gotten used to, the sky was leaden gray with a high layer of clouds, portending a weather change. The gray day matched their mood as they began the odious task of finding their dead companion. Tim made sure they had a poncho with them to use as a field expedient litter to carry the body back if they found it.

Working in two-man teams, the men tracked the spoor from the battle of the night before. The dead lion Tim had shot turned out to be a young male, not even two years old, Tim guessed. He just looked at the dead cat with a dead expression, before following the trail of dried blood from Doug.

An hour into their search, they heard the buzzing of a swarm of flies. Only one thing attracted that many flies, and whatever it was, it was usually dead. Following the sound, they came upon the remains of their companion. It was pitifully small, consisting of shredded clothing, boots still containing feet, and Doug's head, partially gnawed on, one eye missing and the other wide open in shock and pain.

"I'll do it," Joe said, taking the poncho from Tim. Ensuring the hood drawstring was pulled tied, he set it out on the ground, then gently picked up the various pieces of Doug and laid them in the center of the poncho. Once all the pieces were on the poncho, he grabbed the edges and bunched them up, tying it closed with some parachute cord he took from a paracord bracelet. Finished with the task, he took a canteen from his belt and washed his hands. Then, looking around at the others, all of whom were watching him rather than keeping watch, he asked, "Anyone gonna say any words over him?"

Tim shook his head. "We'll say words once we get back. Anyone know if he had any family?"

"Yeah," Joe said. "He's got a daughter, about ten or twelve, I think. Name's Janice."

"What about a wife?"

Joe shook his head. "Dead. Got killed by a drunk driver. From what Doug told me, they were divorced at the time, and she had custody of the kid. Happened a couple of years ago, so he became an instant single dad."

Everyone grimaced at that. Nothing worse than being an orphan. They had seen a lot of that in Vietnam.

Tim made a decision. "Well, there's no way in hell I'm gonna leave her on her own. I got her dad killed, so the least I can do is take care of her."

"You didn't get him killed," Brian said. "Damned fool did it himself, stepping out of the laager. Hell, he's been here almost a month. He knew how dangerous it was."

"Regardless, she's still my responsibility now, unless she's got family," Tim declared, mind firmly set. "Okay, let's get him back to the jeeps, and let's get the hell out of here."

18

When they arrived at the Walla Walla, the landing craft, with Luther and Dave, was already waiting for them.

As the two jeeps and trailers pulled onto the gravel bar, Dave yelled at them in a kidding manner, "What took so long?"

When the jeeps stopped, he noticed they weren't a happy crowd. His manner changed when he saw only four men, not the expected five. Taking a quick head count, he asked, "Where's Goodland?"

Tim just shook his head. Joe pointed to the poncho in the seat behind them. "Lions."

Grabbing a bag of gold from the trailer, Tim said, "Let's get the gold loaded up and get out of here."

As the men loaded the landing craft, Tim explained what had happened.

"First things first, we need to contact the police and let them know what happened. Then we'll need to find Doug's daughter. Maybe Lenny or one of the other security guys knows how we can find her."

"You sure you want to tell the cops?" Dave asked. The others were studiously ignoring the conversation while paying careful attention to the words spoken.

"Yeah. Somebody's gotta report his death."

"Why? This ain't Selah, Yakima, Washington State, or even the good ole US of A. It's our own country, and you've already reported it to the authorities."

Tim had to think about that for a moment. "Well, we've got to notify somebody. He's got a daughter that'll need taking care of. Social Security death benefits, or whatever."

"Sounds more like something Parallel should take care of," Dave said.

Tim considered Dave's words, then nodded. "Yeah, you're right. It is. I just thought we should report it to some officials, or something."

The trip back upriver consisted of only the men, gold, and Tim's jeep. The remaining jeep and trailers had been moved to higher ground, to be retrieved the next day, after the gold was safely back on Earth.

Tim and Dave discussed how best to handle the death report, and Tim finally decided that other than issue a death certificate from the Republic of Hayek, they didn't need to report anything to the police or medical examiner until such time as they announced the presence of the gate. There wasn't much the police could do against an entire planet of Pleistocene predators who could chew them up and spit them out, or not. They decided Goodland's remains would be put in the same freezer in the shed that still housed the chicken-eating Smilodon.

It was only after they had cleared the mouth of the Walla Walla and were heading up the Columbia that Tim remembered the Homotherium cubs.

"How'd Veronica like her new pets?"

Dave leaned his elbows on the landing craft's port gunwale, his gaze settled on the distant Cascade Mountains. A grin spread across his face.

"Yeah, that went over well, in a manner of speaking. She's taking care of them, but I somehow got the feeling she wasn't too thrilled."

Tim shrugged. "It ain't like she didn't watch *Born Free* a gazillion times. She used to say she wished she had her own lion. Well, now she does."

Dave just kept grinning. "In spades."

By the time they pulled up to the gravel bar near the base camp, it was approaching evening. As Luther had said on the outbound trip, the return trip would take another couple of hours, which meant ten hours in the boat, this on top of the three hours driving and the hour spent looking for and collecting Doug's remains, and another hour loading gold and stashing jeeps. While they weren't quite staggering, it was clear that the four men picked up that morning were exhausted. Dave recommended they not do any further work and to let others unload the gold.

Several of the security team were waiting for them with several four-wheel-drive vehicles and trailers. It took them less than an hour to unload the gold from the vessel and transfer it to the trailers. When they found out about Goodland, they were surprised. Surprised, but not shocked. They had seen enough of what the predators on Hayek could do to normal prey, but they were surprised one of their own would be dumb enough to leave the safety of the laager just to empty his bowels.

Trailers loaded with gold, the men boarded the vehicles and made the short drive back to the base camp. Tim was so tired, he even allowed Dave to drive his precious Willys.

Too tired to even think of unloading gold and moving it across, Tim had the security team hold on to it, while he and Dave, with Goodland's remains, crossed back to Earth from the Hayek gate, operated by the ever-flexible Luther. The rest of the expedition elected to stay on Hayek rather than return to Earth and look for accommodations for the night.

Arriving back on Earth, the two men stepped into an empty shed with only a single overhead light burning. Clearly, they weren't expected.

"Didn't you tell Veronica we'd be back tonight?" Tim asked.

"Yeah. Beats me where she is. Probably playing with your killer cubs."

Turning back to the gate, they saw Luther gleefully waving at them, stinking stogie clouding the air around his head. Then the gate disappeared, showing them only the bare metal walls of the shed where there had been a desert outpost before.

Dave placed Goodland's remains on a shelf in the walk-in freezer, crossing himself after doing so. Tim had forgotten Dave was a lapsed Catholic, vaguely remembering his friend once saying something about giving up Catholicism for Lent and liking it so much he never went back.

As they exited the shed, their eyes had to adjust to the deep twilight, one that only the high latitudes can produce. Lights were on in Tim's small house and on the deck, so they headed for the house.

Once inside, they were greeted by Veronica and Petra, both of whom were happy to see their husbands. Tim was a bit leery about Veronica's greeting, waiting to see her reaction to the introduction of a pair of Homotherium cubs into their household.

"How're the cubs?" he asked, somewhat hesitantly.

"Sleeping. I had them playing 'kill' for most of the afternoon, so they're pretty tuckered out."

Tim nodded. "Good."

That's when Veronica crossed her arms over her chest and let loose with, "What the hell were you thinking, sending a couple of saber-tooth tiger cubs home for me to take care of? Are you out of your freaking mind?"

Tim just looked at her for a couple of seconds, seeing the steam rise off her. Dave and Petra tried to act invisible.

"I killed their mom," was all he finally said. That was enough to deflate Veronica's anger. Uncrossing her arms, she came up to him and wrapped her arms around him. Burying her head into his chest, she said, "I thought it was something like that."

Letting go and stepping back, she continued, "Well, you broke it, you own it. What are you thinking of doing?"

"We can either raise them as pets or raise them to release them. Sort of like in *Born Free*. What are your thoughts?"

"I don't know the first thing about teaching saber-tooth tigers how to hunt."

"Homotheriums," Tim said, absently.

"Huh?" Veronica gave him a confused look.

"They're Homotheriums. You're probably thinking of Smilodons, the saber-tooth tigers with really big teeth, like the one Dave shot on day one. Different species. Smilodons have longer canines."

"They're also smaller," Dave chimed in.

"Homotheriums?" Veronica asked.

"No, Smilodon. Smilodons are about the size of a tiger and Homotherium are bigger, about the size of a lion."

"Just to get this straight," Veronica said, putting her hands on her hips, "you sent home two baby saber-tooth tigers that'll grow up to be as big as lions?"

Tim looked askance, while Dave looked away, like butter wouldn't melt in his mouth.

Looking back at Veronica, he slowly replied, "Well, if you put it that way, yeah. I guess so."

At that moment, one of the baby saber-tooth tigers under discussion made its way into the kitchen, blinking its huge eyes as it adjusted to the light.

Tim squatted, and called to the small creature. "Hey, little guy. How you doing?"

Hearing Tim's voice, the cat scrabbled along the linoleum floor to him, practically jumping into his lap and almost knocking the scientist over. It began purring as Tim stroked its back.

Looking at the scratched floor, Veronica said, "You are aware that their claws don't retract?"

Picking up one of the cub's paws, Tim looked at it, seeing the small, sharp claws extended. "You mean, like a cheetah's?"

"Cheetah's claws don't retract?" Petra asked.

"Yep, only big cat whose claws don't," Tim said. He didn't know much about animals, but he had read a science fiction novel about nuclear war several months ago, one where the protagonist, a bounty hunter, had a pet cheetah. For some reason, that factoid stuck with him.

Just then, the cat's sibling made an appearance.

"Well, if it ain't Timmy the Terror. Missing out on all the action, little fella?" Veronica asked the cat, who made a beeline for Tim, now sitting on the kitchen floor.

"Timmy?" he asked, looking up at Veronica.

"They needed names, so the boy is Timmy and the girl is Tiami, but I just call her Tia."

"Tiami?"

"Yeah, I figure these cats are gonna take a helluva lot of time and energy, so I decided to name her after an acronym my dad used with us kids as we went off to college: This Is A Major Investment."

That caused the tension to break as everyone laughed.

"I love it," Tim said, as Tia climbed into his lap, pushing her brother out of the way.

Looking back up at his wife, he changed the subject."One of our guys got killed over there."

That statement put a chill in the air, despite the playfulness of the cubs.

Tim explained what happened, and the fact that a daughter needed notification.

"What about the mom?" Veronica asked.

Dave piped up. "From what I understand, she's dead."

Looking between the two men, Veronica said, "Don and Jack returned yesterday morning. Might be a good idea to tell them. You might want Jack along to help out with the notification, being he's still a kid."

"Did they return to Kirkland?"

Veronica shook her head. "No. Eileen rented a place here. Said she got tired of having to wait even more for them when they got back."

Tim nodded. "I'll call in the morning."

19

Early the next morning, Tim was awakened by the sound of mewling and the feeling of drowning. Opening his eyes, he was surprised he couldn't see. It took a second to realize one of the cubs was lying on his face. He could feel the other lying on his stomach. Reaching up, he removed Tia from his face, holding her above him with both hands. She looked down at him in total trust, then let loose another mewl.

"Hungry, are you?"

Setting the cub down on the floor next to him, he then picked up Timmy the Terror and did the same. Before getting out of bed, he looked over to Veronica, who was sleeping on her side, facing away from him, and snoring lightly. Sometimes her snoring could hit epic proportions, but she always denied it, claiming, "Women don't snore. I'm a woman, so I don't snore." Tim had thought of recording her one night, but decided against it, recognizing a losing battle from afar.

Getting out of bed, he almost tripped over the two cubs as they climbed around his legs, rubbing against him. *Just like regular cats,* he thought, picking each one up in a hand and making his way out of the bedroom.

A quick visit outside gave the cubs the opportunity to empty their bladders. Tim was impressed that they didn't make messes in the house.

Stepping back inside with the two cubs in tow, he found the formula mix that Veronica had picked up. After reading the instructions, he mixed up enough for the two cats. He spotted two small baby bottles with latex nipples in the dish drainer, so he filled them with formula, then had to figure out how to feed two small, hungry Homotherium cubs at the same time as both of them started putting their front paws on his legs, reaching for the formula. Luckily, Veronica came into the kitchen then, rubbing her head, causing her long, black hair to flow back and forth. Seeing Tim looking helpless, holding two baby bottles while two Homotherium cubs tried to climb up his pajama-clad legs, she burst out laughing.

"Give me the bottles and get some coffee going," she said, holding out her hands. Tim gratefully turned them over to her.

Sitting down on the kitchen floor cross-legged, she held the bottles in such a way that both cubs climbed into her lap to begin suckling.

"After you get the coffee going, there's some raw meat in the fridge. Pull out a couple of pieces."

The cubs had finished the formula and were working on the hunks of raw meat, their little canines ripping it, while Tim poured coffee for the two humans.

As they sat down at the kitchen table, situated to keep an eye on the cubs, Veronica asked, "So, what's the plan for the day?"

Tim looked down at his coffee, then back up at his wife. She could see the sadness on his face. "Next-of-kin notification."

Veronica just raised her eyebrows. "The guy that got eaten by lions the other day."

"As I said last night, he's got a small daughter. Ten or twelve years old. So, first thing I need to do is find her, then notify her."

"Does she have any living relatives?"

Tim shrugged. "Don't know. If she doesn't, where does she go? I'm feeling kinda responsible for her."

Looking down at the gnawing cubs, then back up at her husband, Veronica said, "Well, we're taking in all sorts of strays these days. I think we can find some room for her here, if necessary."

Tim couldn't say a thing due to the lump in his throat, so he just nodded. After a couple of minutes, he finally got out, "I'll contact Lenny Gross after breakfast. Maybe he knows where she is."

"You thinking of asking him to tell her?"

Shaking his head, Tim said, "No, that's my job. But I do want him along."

"Don't forget to call Jack."

After breakfast and a shower, Tim got on the phone and got in touch with Gross. Fortunately, the head of the security firm kept pretty good tabs on his employees and had them constantly update their next-of-kin notification list. Doug's daughter, Janice, who turned out to be eleven years old, was staying with a friend of Doug's in the small town of Enumclaw, southeast of Seattle. Tim got the address and asked Lenny to meet him somewhere in the town. As it would take at least two to three hours to get there, going through Mt. Rainier National Park on Highway 410, Lenny suggested meeting at The Mint, a local diner in downtown Enumclaw.

"Food's good, and pretty cheap. It'll also give us time to talk before going to see Janice."

His next call was to Don Lewis. Luckily, Veronica had written down their new phone number and thumbtacked it to the corkboard next to the telephone on the wall, so he didn't have to waste time tracking it down. In the brief conversation with Don, then Jack, all agreed that it would likely be good if Jack were along. The Bowmans would pick him up on the way to Enumclaw.

Hanging up, Tim wondered what to do with the cubs.

"Bring them with us," Veronica said. "Kids love cats, and it'll help her connect if she comes with us."

"Yeah, but her dad was killed by a cat."

"Doesn't matter. Different type of cat."

Based on that, they took the Willys wagon, putting the cubs in the back storage area behind the back seats, on a pile of blankets. Tim doubted the two adventurous cats would remain there.

It was almost nine o'clock by the time they picked up Jack at the Lewises new residence. Don explained that Eileen was in the process of selling their old house. They planned to move over to Hayek as soon as there was enough infrastructure in place.

Jack climbed into the back seat of the Willys wagon after being introduced to Timmy and Tia, who, as Tim suspected, refused to remain in the wayback. They decided riding in the back seat with the teenager was a lot more fun. Jack seemed to enjoy it, especially when the two cubs fought over who got to sit in his lap.

The drive up Highway 12, then Highway 410, was beautiful as ever, but Tim couldn't help comparing it to the unspoiled beauty of Hayek. As usual, Mount Rainier, which he was now beginning to think of as Mount Tahoma, came into full display in all its snow-shrouded glory soon after crossing over Chinook pass. The winding road down from the pass caused it to disappear, but then it came back into view several times.

An hour later they passed through the small town of Greenwater, unknown to many except for the wool caps produced by the small outpost of Wapiti Woolies, made famous on many a trip up Mount Everest. Had they not already had lunch plans in Enumclaw, they would have stopped for burgers at Buzzy's Greenwater Cafe or burgers and beer at the Naches Tavern, both old establishments in an otherwise culinary limited environment. Tim particularly loved eating at Buzzy's, usually getting the Chinook burger whenever he made the trip over to the Wet Side, as western Washington was known. It was also fun to look at the walls covered with currency from all over the world, some of it from countries that no longer existed.

Another half hour and they pulled into the outskirts of Enumclaw. The vinegar scent of cucumbers being turned into pickles permeated the air as they passed Farman's Pickle Factory. A couple of minutes later and they were parked in the public parking lot downtown, under a large big-leaf maple tree.

The cubs had fallen asleep during the drive, so they elected to crack the windows and leave them sleeping on the back seat. The last thing they needed was for the Homotherium cubs to be wandering the streets of a modern post-Pleistocene town.

Entering The Mint Restaurant and Alehouse, the three were greeted by a cloud of cigarette smoke and dark lighting. A wood bar ran through the center of the room from front to back and tables were strewn along the opposite wall. As their eyes adjusted, Tim could see Lenny in the back of the room waving toward them. The three headed over.

Taking seats, they shook hands with Lenny, commiserating on the loss.

"I called the lady who's watching over Janice," he said. "She's expecting us after lunch."

"Has she told Janice, yet?" Tim asked.

Lenny nodded. "Yeah, I didn't see the sense in having her hear it from total strangers. Said she'd let the girl know. Wants to know what do to now. She was only expecting to watch her for a couple of weeks."

Just then, they were interrupted by a waitress. After placing drink orders, consisting of coffee, iced tea, and root beer, the waitress left them alone, leaving them with paper menus.

A quick glance and they all decided to go with the house special burgers and fries.

During lunch, the three adults discussed all options. Lenny was unaware of any other family members, so the conclusion was that Janice would stay with the Bowmans until such time as a willing family member was available to take her.

"I'm adamant about the willing part," Veronica said, before taking a sip of her iced tea. "I don't want the poor thing feeling like she's not wanted. If she needs a home, she's got one with us."

Unsaid, and known only to Tim and Veronica, was the fact that the reason the couple was childless was that Veronica was incapable of having children. Not that they hadn't tried. Several pregnancies had wound up self-terminating, leaving the couple frustrated. They had never adopted, hoping that one day they would have a child of their own, but it was not to be.

Lunch over, the group made their way to a small dairy farm on the south side of town. By now, Timmy and Tia had woken up and exhibited some hunger. This was sated by giving each cub a small can of dog food, which they ate from bowls which Jack had set in the back of the wagon.

As they pulled into the driveway, a large, yellow Labrador retriever came out to greet them. Clearly, it was a vicious dog, as its large happy tail wagged vigorously enough to knock any of them over. After the obligatory hand and crotch sniffing, the dog allowed them to pass up to the house, where an elderly woman was sitting on the porch with a small, black-haired girl. The dog hung around the wagon a bit, sniffing with curiosity, before joining the humans on the porch. The elderly lady rose as they approached.

It was clear the girl had been crying; dried tears streaked her cheeks under bright blue eyes and dark bangs.

Veronica immediately went up to where the girl was sitting in a wicker chair.

"Hi," she said, squatting down in front of her, so their eyes were level. "I'm Veronica. I'm betting you're Janice."

The small girl nodded.

"I thought so."

Tim could only stare, a lump developing in his throat. Next-of-kin notifications were not something he had ever done, and having to do so with a pre-teen orphan wasn't one he was fully prepared for.

"I'm so sorry, hon," Veronica said, holding her arms out, inviting Janice into them. With a wail, the girl launched herself into the open arms. Veronica, still kneeling, wrapped her arms around her, and started stroking Janice's head, giving her soothing sounds.

After several minutes, Janice finally decided to separate herself from Veronica. Wiping her nose with a sleeve, she asked, "My daddy's never coming home again, is he? Just like Mommy."

Veronica couldn't speak, either, at that point. She just looked Janice in the eyes and shook her head. Finally, she was able to say, "No, honey. He's not."

Tim was expecting another outburst, so he was surprised when Janice, looking first at the elderly lady she had been staying with, then at the two men and boy on the porch, and finally back at Veronica, asked in a small voice, "What's gonna happen to me?"

"Well, that's partly up to you, hon. If you're up for it, my husband, Tim," Veronica indicated who he was, "and I would be happy to have you live with us until a relative can be found who would want you to stay with them."

Janice looked at the elderly lady. "Can I stay here with you, Mrs. Eaton?"

The elderly lady wrung her hands together for a minute, turning to look out over the small cow pasture, where black-and-white cows chewed contentedly on their cuds. Turning back to Janice, she said, "I'm sorry, dear, but I just don't think I'd be a good parent for you, being as old as I am. You really need somebody younger to help raise you, and I think these fine folk would be better."

Janice nodded, understanding but not understanding. She knew Mrs. Eaton was old but didn't understand why the elderly lady couldn't take care of her. Walking over to her, Janice wrapped her arms around Mrs. Eaton's waist, burying her head in the older lady's bosom. "It's okay," she murmured into the woman's dress. Mrs. Eaton gave Janice a hug, a look of pure anguish on her face.

Releasing the older woman, Janice turned back toward Veronica. "What now?"

"Now, we go home. Are you packed?"

Janice nodded.

"Well, let's go get your stuff." Veronica took Janice's hand in hers, and the two went into the small farmhouse.

As they entered, Tim could hear Veronica asking, "So, do you have any special stuffed animals?"

The two returned within minutes, Veronica holding a suitcase and Janice's hand, while Janice held onto a stuffed elephant. Veronica introduced Janice to Jack, who had been silently waiting on the lawn with Tim and Lenny.

Tim took Janice's suitcase and went to put it into the back compartment of the wagon, noticing that the cubs were still awake. He set the suitcase in the back, leaving them enough room between it and the back seat. As the others opened the doors to get in, the two cubs took an interest in this, placing their front paws on the back of the back seat.

Getting into the back seat of the Willys wagon, Janice was surprised to see the two cubs poking their heads above it.

She reached out and rubbed the head of Tia, saying, "These are some pretty big cats. What're their names?"

"They're special cats, Janice," Veronica said as she got into the front passenger seat. "We call them Timmy and Tia. The one you're petting is Tia."

"Hi Tia," Janice said to the cub, who decided that was an invitation to climb over the seat and into the child's lap to lick her on the face. That's when the girl noticed the extra-long canines.

"Wow, he's got some pretty big fangs."

"That he does," Tim intoned from the driver's seat as he got in and started the wagon.

The drive back to Selah started out quiet, with Jack and Janice riding in the back seat, both playing with the rambunctious Homotherium cubs.

Eventually, Janice asked what happened to her father. Before Tim or Veronica could respond, Jack started explaining about Hayek and the portals between different dimensions, and how her father was actually on a different dimension when he died.

Tim listened as he drove, and was impressed with how Jack addressed things. Looking in the rearview mirror, he could see the small girl's eyes get large and round as she took occasional looks at the animal in her lap, recognizing it wasn't a normal tabby. Rather than telling Janice that her dad got eaten by lions while trying to go to the bathroom, he explained about how her dad helped get a lot of gold, and that his death was caused by Pleistocene animals who attacked his camp, catching him unaware. "He probably didn't even know it," the teen said. Tim knew differently.

As they approached the town of Greenwater, Veronica leaned back over the front seat, facing the two kids. "Do you guys like honey sticks?"

While Jack responded with an emphatic, "Yes" Janice asked, "What's a honey stick?"

Veronica was floored. She had never known anyone that didn't know what a honey stick was.

"We'll just have to show you." Turning to Tim, she said, "Pull into Wapiti Woolies."

Tim pulled into the gravel parking lot, shut the car off, and turned to Veronica. "We probably oughta let the cats out to go to the bathroom. Why don't you take Janice inside? Jack and I'll handle the critters."

As Veronica took Janice inside the small log cabin that served as a store, Tim put leashes on the two cats, and with Jack's assistance, got them out of the wagon, over the gravel parking lot, and into a grassy spot in front of the store. Both cubs figured out what needed doing, and did so. Fortunately, they didn't leave any piles for Tim to clean up. *Hope they don't in the Willys*, he thought, watching the cubs sniff about.

Before they could head back to the wagon, the store's door opened and Veronica, followed by Janice and a young woman with dirty blond hair exited the store. Tim could see that Janice had discovered honey sticks, as she was sucking on one, holding it in one hand while squeezing it with the other. Tim knew exactly what that was like, with the sweet, tingling rush of honey one got from squeezing it out of the tube directly into the mouth. The honey sticks from Wapiti Woolies were usually from beekeepers who kept their bees around wildflowers, so the flavors reflected that.

Coming over to her husband, Veronica introduced the blonde as the store's owner. "Debbie saw the cats from inside and asked to meet Tia and Timmy." Tim could tell she was a bit nervous, probably didn't want others to know what the real deal was, but decided to go along with it rather than create waves or suspicion.

"Sure. I think they're pretty calm now."

As the young lady squatted down to cat level, both cubs scrambled over to her in their awkward cub runs. She rubbed their heads, commenting on their size.

"They're a special breed, from China," Tim said. "They're supposed to be big, bigger than a Maine Coon cat. I hear they may get over twenty pounds."

"Looks like they're almost pushing that now," Debbie said, with a grin.

"Honey, don't we need to be back in Yakima soon?" Veronica asked in an effort to pull Tim and the cubs away from the unaware store owner.

Tim looked at his watch, then exclaimed, "Holy smokes. Why didn't you tell me how late it was?" Picking up Timmy, he said to Debbie, "Sorry, but we're late." Turning to Jack, as he walked toward the Willys in an apparent rush, "We gotta get going."

Taking the hint, Jack picked up Tia and made his way to the wagon, barely arriving after Tim, who placed Timmy in the back seat while Veronica shooed Janice in with the young cub.

The group arrived in Selah an hour and a half later, delayed by the usual summer crush of tourists traveling to and through Mt. Rainier National Park. Tim was glad the cats were napping when they passed a National Park Service Ranger near Tipsoo Lake. *I'd have a hard time explaining two wild cats that shouldn't exist on this timeline*, he thought as they drove under the large log sign cum pedestrian overpass over Highway 410 welcoming them to the Wenatchee National Forest. Tim knew if he looked back, the other side of the sign would say Welcome to Mt. Rainier National Park.

By the time they had arrived home, Janice knew just as much about Hayek as Jack, and she was intrigued. He had also impressed upon her the need to keep it a secret. What had really impressed her was understanding that Timmy and Tia weren't just any normal cats, but orphaned Pleistocene Homotheriums. "Just like me," she said sadly, stroking the head of Timmy, whose turn it was to cuddle in her lap, his head draped in her lap, his body on the seat between the two young people. Tia's head was resting in Jack's lap, both cubs sound asleep.

The stopping of the Willys caused the cubs to wake up and take an interest in their surroundings again.

"Better get them out before they have an accident," Veronica said as she got out of the wagon.

As Janice got out, the two cubs jumped down after her, tumbling on the ground. "Oh, you poor things," she said, squatting down to their level. This brought on a round of face-licking on their part as they lapped up the attention.

Tim retrieved Janice's suitcase. As he was about to carry it inside, Veronica called, "Janice, you want to follow me and see your new bedroom?"

As the girl followed her, Tim turned to Jack. "Could you watch the cubs until I get back?"

Jack nodded. "Sure."

Before Tim went into the house, Jack added, "Can we take her over today?"

Tim thought about it. Then, shaking his head, he said, "I don't think so. Let's give her a day or so. Then, maybe."

After giving Jack a ride home, Tim returned to the ranchette. It was almost five o'clock, and he found Veronica and Janice playing with the cubs in the backyard. The horses had elected to get as far from the tiny predators as possible and were nervously grazing on the far side of the paddock.

Stepping inside to grab a couple of beers, Tim heard the phone ringing. He answered it, and a strange male voice asked for Veronica. With a small amount of suspicion, he asked who was calling. It turned out to be a land-use planner that Veronica had hired to help design a town.

"We've pretty much finished the design. Would you like to come to our office, or should we come to yours?"

"Let me talk to my wife, first. Can you give me your number and call you back in five or so minutes?"

Back outside, handed one of the beers to Veronica and told her of the phone call.

"It'd be easier to have him meet us here since his office is in Bellevue. But I'm not sure that's the best thing, what with everything we've got going on here."

"How about we meet at Poe's office?" Tim suggested. "We can ask Eileen and the girls to come on over and keep an eye out on Janice and the cubs while Don joins us."

Veronica nodded. "Yeah, that'd be best. You want to call him back, or do you want me to?"

Tim smiled at his wife. "Your game. You call it."

Veronica nodded again. "Let me call him back." She got up and headed into the house while Tim spent time with Janice and the cubs. Tim didn't have a whole lot of experience with kids, but he suspected that Janice was probably on the smart end of the bell curve.

20

Late the next morning, all five Clarks showed up at the Bowmans'. Eileen had agreed to stay with Janice and the twins while Don and Jack attended the meeting. Tim hadn't considered asking Jack to join, but since the boy held a stake in the company, it made sense.

The twins both oohed and aahed over the small Homotheriums. They also seemed to get along well with Janice, being only a year apart in age. They had never met anyone whose parents had been killed, so the twins were suitably impressed and awed by Janice.

Veronica hugged Janice, telling her that they'd be back in a couple of hours. "Don't feed the fur-babies too much while we're gone," she chided the girl as she let go of her and stood.

Tim didn't know what to do, and as he was prepared to wave and head out the door, the young girl came up and gave him a hug. Tim hugged her back, looking at his wife with consternation. He wasn't sure about this whole hugging kids thing. She just smiled back at him. Releasing him, Janice turned and ran over to where the twins were playing with Timmy and Tia in the living room.

The short drive to Poe's office was uneventful, and soon the Bowmans and Clarks were seated with Dave, Bob Poe, Jeff Shimazu, and the land-use planner, Patrick Teppos, in Bob's small conference room. The planner was a relatively young man, barely in his thirties. For somebody from the Wet Side, he was more tanned than usual, and small lines around his eyes indicated that he spent a fair amount of time outdoors.

During the introductory phase, the team learned that Teppos was a navy veteran who had served on a nuclear submarine and put himself through the University of Washington with the GI Bill. He was also a believer in sustainable development and permaculture, which was what had prompted Veronica to seek him out and hire him.

Teppos removed several plans from a cardboard tube and spread them out on the conference table. Then he looked up at Veronica. "You presented me with an interesting problem. If you hadn't paid up front, I likely wouldn't have done this, despite how intriguing it sounded." His eyes then traveled among the men. "Plan a town from scratch, starting with a population of ten thousand, then plan on it increasing to fifty thousand over a couple of years. Make it pedestrian and mass transit-friendly. Include all infrastructure, including power and a fixed mass transit system, while minimizing the impact on the environment. Consider all renewable energy sources, but don't include fossil fuels. Have a town square and numerous parks." He shook his head. "That was a lot to plan for, but I think you'll like what I've come up with."

Looking at the plans, Tim could make out the topography of the town of Selah, but the layout was different. The plans had streets, parks, and a town square where Selah did not. Other plans had what appeared to be power, communications, water, and sewer infrastructure.

"You may not like the price tag, though," Teppos continued. "Based on what you gave me, you can figure on at least twenty-six million dollars for basic power and water facilities, along with another two million for each mile of basic infrastructure, such as roads, power, water, and sewer."

Teppos noticed the shocked looks on the assembled faces but plowed on.

"Of course, these prices are based on what it'll cost to do it in the US. Overseas prices can be less or more expensive, depending on labor costs and material availability.

"Things I had to consider; livability, streets, water, sewer, stormwater, electricity, communications, mass transit, and waste management.

"Addressing the livability issue first, we decided on small pedestrian-friendly city blocks, with plenty of parks and greenspace. As you can see," Teppos pointed to various features on one of the plans, "the town square is close to the big river, with a waterfront park along both the big and small rivers and this small creek," Teppos pointed to Wenas Creek on the map, "connecting them." Unknown to Teppos, he was referring to the Yakima and Naches Rivers. "The terrain pretty much precludes building near the smaller river. The street pattern will be more like the gridiron system of the twenties than our modern system of cul-de-sacs and freeways. Residential streets will be wide enough for two-way traffic, but not much parking. Sidewalks on either side, and alleys in the middle of the blocks, behind the houses. Residents are expected to park on their own property, that is, if they have a car. The downtown area, around the square, will be mixed-use, with commercial and retail on the ground floors and residential above. Any manufacturing would be south of town, downriver.

"When I considered mass transit, I immediately thought of Vancouver, the one in Canada, that is, which is considering a new type of mass transit, an automated system that's driven by electromagnetic propulsion. It's mostly elevated, which makes it more expensive per mile, but it has less impact on the ground, both in footprint and in any impact on vehicular traffic. We can't even estimate the cost of such a system at this point, but we'll know more soon. Another option is a suspended rail system, like what's opening in Germany soon."

Teppos put a picture of a suspended rail system on the table. It showed towers with steel beams between them, and cars that rode under the beams.

"Like the Vancouver system, this one has minimal impact on the ground. Far more flexible than running rails at grade, and you don't have to worry about train-pedestrian or train-car accidents.

"Getting back to the cost issue. Figure that a city block is about a hundred thousand square feet, or roughly two and a half acres. We made the block length three hundred feet by a hundred sixty feet, so each block's gonna need nine hundred twenty feet of infrastructure. That means each block will run you about three hundred thirty two thousand, or three hundred sixty bucks a linear foot.

"If you require on-site composting and greywater treatment for residences, you can keep the cost of the waste treatment plant down a bit, maybe. If not, you'll be able to produce biosolids, suitable for fertilizer, which you can resell. Figure on about thirteen million for the first stage, with probably another thirteen million to build out for increased population.

"For fifty thousand people, you're gonna need thirty megawatts of power. As with the roads, sewer, and water mains, this is something that can be scalable, meaning you don't have to build it all at once. You can add on to it over time, keeping the initial cost down. Figure on six megawatts to begin with, the diversion hydro will run about thirteen million dollars.

"Planning parameters were no fossil fuels, so no natural gas or oil, no coal, or anything similar. Even though running water's available, there should be no dams. Everything had to be manufactured off-site but easily deployed or installed on-site. I reached out to a buddy of mine who's more familiar with energy systems, and here's what we propose: a hybrid system using grid-tied net-metered solar, nuclear, and low-impact hydro."

As Teppos was pulling some photographs from his briefcase, Tim asked, "Grid-tied net-metered?"

Teppos placed the photos on the table. the top one was some sort of hydroelectric system.

"Let's say you've got an energy-producing piece of equipment; in this case, solar panels. You use the energy you need, but if you're producing more than you need, you sell it back to the utility at their wholesale price, and they either pay you for it or credit it to you when you have a deficit. Companies then sell it to other consumers at the retail rate. It's kind of a win-win situation, but you wouldn't know that by listening to most energy producers.

"The reason we recommend grid-tied is because it won't require batteries in each house. Everything goes into and out of the local power grid."

Tim, along with the others, were impressed enough to have eyebrows rise on that information.

"So, along with the grid-tied solar, we figured some other good options were diversion hydro, pumped storage hydro, and possibly mini-nuclear." Teppos spread the photos out on the table. One was a picture of a river with a small building next to it. He pointed to a spot next to the small building. "This is a diversion hydro plant. You don't dam up the river, as you can see; instead, you put in a canal or tunnel and divert water into that. That water hits the turbines, and you get electricity. That's probably your best bet for low-impact power generation. Great thing about it is that it works twenty-four seven, unless the river freezes." Then he shrugged. "Well, unless there's also a drought. That may throw a kink in the system."

He pointed to the next picture, where they could all see a pond on top of a hill. "This is pumped storage. During the day, solar energy is used to pump water up the hill to this pond. At night, the water runs downhill into a turbine, generating electricity. Another good option, but a bit more complicated than the diversion hydro."

Teppos then pointed to the third and fourth pictures. One was a simple building, and the other a complicated piece of machinery. "Mini nuclear. Navy's been doing it for decades, but some enterprising companies are trying to get these to market. As you're probably aware, the early nuke reactors were basically mini-nukes, generating less than three hundred megawatts. To give you an idea, current reactors generate about eight to thirteen hundred megawatts. What we're interested in, though, are the really small ones, like the La Cross boiling water reactor, which generates fifty megawatts. "

"How is nuclear environmentally friendly?" Veronica asked. "I mean, we've all heard about Three Mile Island."

The others nodded. Teppos shook his head.

"Three Mile Island was a success. The design prevented any real radiation from leaking out. Nobody died from it, and more importantly, there's no evidence anyone was hurt by it. Of course, we don't have to go with nuclear, or even start with it, but it really is more environmentally sound than coal or gas. First, no emissions, so no air pollution; second, no real waste. Most anything produced can be reused through reprocessing. The French do this all the time. Third, it doesn't take up a lot of space. Finally, it allows you to use electric-powered vehicles, which also reduces air pollution. Just think if they used those in Los Angeles, how clean the air would be."

"Your recommendation?" Tim asked.

"Start with the diversion hydro. Plat out the town, put in the diversion hydro, then begin developing infrastructure. You'll want to put in water, sewer, and electric before you put in the roads. I recommend having single-family residences install composting toilets with gray water systems to reduce the impact on the rivers from waste treatment."

"What's graywater?" Poe asked.

"To put it bluntly, anything that doesn't have fecal matter in it. Showers, dishwasher water, stuff from the bathroom sink. All of it is polluted, but minimizing the amount of fecal matter in a wastewater system reduces the environmental impact. That's what you want, isn't it?"

Again, everyone nodded.

"Once the population starts increasing over ten thousand, then you'll want to install a mini-nuke plant. Moving on. Once you've got everything set up, and once people start moving in, then you can consider adding nuclear. The hardest part's gonna be getting permits. The EPA and NRC take forever to issue them…" Teppos petered off as he saw the grins on the assembled group's faces.

"Permits won't be a problem," Tim said.

Teppos looked confused.

"Don't sweat it for now," Poe said. "Just run with it."

Teppos shrugged.

"Anyhow, that's our recommendations."

"How long would it take to build the basics?" Tim asked. "Like the hydro, water and waste treatment, and infrastructure, for say, the town square and a couple of blocks?"

"Just the permitting will take months, if not a couple of years."

"Forget the permitting," Dave chimed in. "Just rough estimates on construction times and costs."

Teppos thought for several seconds, running his hand through his hair. Finally, he said, "Hydro shouldn't take more than a month or so, maybe even a couple of weeks if you had all the parts. Roads and such are pretty quick, if you lay the pipes and electricity in place first. Maybe a month for those, if all you're doing is the square and a couple of blocks."

Teppos then shook his head. "The one that'll likely take the longest would be the water and waste treatment plants."

"What if we built smaller waste treatment facilities, such as those used by schools and businesses. Maybe have one per block?" Dave asked.

"That would certainly reduce the initial investment," Teppos agreed.

"And it would make users more invested," Tim said.

For the next hour, the group went over Teppos' plans, eventually coming to a consensus on what should be done, by whom, and with a rough idea on how to pay for it. When discussing the financial portion of the project, they asked Teppos to step out of the conference room.

"Okay, if we're lucky, we brought back about fifteen million in gold, give or take," Tim said to the group. "And, that doesn't take into account loss to purity and reselling it. If we're lucky, what, ten mil?"

The others nodded.

"And we need a million for the plane, so now we're down to about nine million. That leaves us seventeen million shy." Tim turned to Don. "How soon before we're ready to head to California?"

Don shrugged. "We can go any time. We've got plenty of fuel in place and can haul more while you're in California.

"Okay." Looking around at the others, Tim said, "Tomorrow we prep. We go in two days. I want to have enough money to get the power up and running along with some of the basic infrastructure. At least the town square and a couple of blocks, including a mini-waste treatment plant. Then we can make the move."

Turning to Veronica, he asked, "Do you think you can continue to head this up?"

Veronica paused. "I think so. I mean, I don't have any experience or anything, but I'm sure I could find people to help out."

"What about Luther?" Jack asked. "He's built everything else, why not the basic stuff we're talking about?"

Once again, Tim was impressed with the teen's intelligence. He had briefly considered asking Luther but figured they needed somebody with an actual civil engineering degree, not a degree in on-the-job training for combat-related civil engineering. He mentioned that to the group.

"Uh, he has one," Jack said, a bit uncomfortable correcting an adult, especially one with the title of Doctor.

The rest of the group just stared at Jack.

"He has one, what?" Dave asked.

"A civil engineering degree," Jack responded. "From the Colorado School of Mines."

"How'd you learn that?" his father asked.

"He told me. He was trying to get me interested in civil engineering. Figures there's gonna be a lot of construction and big projects on Hayek, and thought it'd be good for me to be involved."

"Interesting," Tim murmured, rubbing his chin. "I wonder why he wasn't a naval officer?"

"From what I heard, it had something to do with the war," Jack said. "But you'll have to ask him. He didn't really tell me much about that."

"I bet he'd jump at the chance," Poe said, "with a sufficient economic incentive."

"Make him Chief Engineer for Parallel?" Tim asked.

"I'd also give him free passage, as long as he sticks with Parallel for at least two years," Don said.

"He'd be working under you," Tim said to Don.

His buddy nodded. "Roger, that."

"And, after you drop us off, find us a Caribou," Tim continued. "I want an operational airfield in California in two or three weeks. That means get the bird and whatever construction equipment Luther needs. We'll need to airdrop everything, so find a loadmaster who's got low altitude airdrop experience. Lenny might know somebody. Also, I don't want to try and haul a dredge and gas over Donner Pass, so we're going to airdrop those, too."

"How about we go in, do a rough LZ, and airdrop equipment and people?" Don asked. "Jack and I drop a bunch of you off at Donner Lake, you cross over the Sierra, find a good spot to dredge, and then we come back with everything you need and drop it?"

Tim and Dave looked at each other, eyebrows rising. They looked around at the others and saw the same contemplation in their eyes.

"I think that'd work," Tim said. "We go in with Ken, some basic mining equipment, and security. Scout around a bit, and when we find the best place, we clear a drop zone for everything." He looked around the group. "Yeah. That's what we'll do."

He turned back to Don. "You get a list from Luther on everything he needs. I'll contact Gross about a dropmaster and chutes."

When they called Teppos back into the conference room, Poe laid the ubiquitous non-disclosure agreement in front of him, as Tim said, "You agree to this, we'll keep you busy. If not," and he pointed to the door, "that's the way out."

Teppos reviewed the NDA, but finding nothing questionable or obviously illegal, signed it.

Once signed, Tim told the younger man that he'd be working with Veronica for the next several months. "That includes providing lists for every project she wants built. Don't worry about permits or anything else, just make sure things are designed to work and that we can get what we need pretty much off the shelf."

Teppos clearly struggled a bit internally, shifting in his seat and crossing and uncrossing legs and arms, before finally asking, "How are you going to get anything done if I don't worry about permits?"

"That's our job," Tim said. "You get any push-back, you give 'em Bob's number and tell them to talk to him. How soon can you get started on the exact specifications of the power plant and town square needs?"

CALIFORNIA

21

Two days later, the original crew of four met in the shed on the Bowmans' property, the sun barely above the horizon. Joining them were Ken Wilson, Lee Orange, and the security team of Joe and Bob. Tim was starting to think of them as the Joe-Bob Show, as the two seemed inseparable on Hayek, and even back on Earth. Each man had a pack stuffed with basics, along with his rifle.

Ken had cobbled together a couple of all-terrain trailers that could be broken down and stored in the plane. "It'll help us haul the mining gear and food down the mountains, and the gold to the airfield, if we have to," he explained when he'd showed it to them the day before. One trailer held a sluice with a couple of pairs of drysuits, shovels, and a metal detector, while the other held tents, cases of freeze-dried meals, a couple of cases of C-rations, and a battery-operated PRC-25 radio with spare batteries. They expected to be out three weeks this time but brought enough food for four. The radio was a surplus military one, familiar to all those who had served in Vietnam, and had a range of three to five miles. Enough for what they had planned. But if that wasn't, they even had the long wire antenna, which greatly extended the range.

In addition to their regular supplies, Lenny Gross had managed to procure them some smoke grenades, dynamite, and detonation cord, all designed to assist with the initial airdrop. Tim had used det cord in Vietnam, but it was Dave, Ken, and Lee's first exposure to it.

"Real simple," Tim said, showing them how to assemble the rope-like explosive. "You wrap a length of this stuff around something, attach a blasting cap, then blow it." He held up the finished product, a non-electric blasting cap attached to a length of det cord by a det cord connector, a small piece of plastic that fit over both the blasting cap and the det cord. "Wrap this around a tree with some dynamite, boom, instant logging."

When they were finally ready, Veronica opened the gate, and after a brief kiss from her, Tim led the team back to Hayek.

Within an hour, they were aboard the Grumman Goose, Jack in the pilot's seat, Don in the co-pilot's, and the rest sitting on the bare floor in the passenger compartment, scrunched in among the supplies. The passenger seats had been removed for transporting fuel bladders, and nobody saw the need to spend time reinstalling them just for one trip.

Take-off from the gate airfield was uneventful, and soon the plane was crossing the high desert east of the Cascade Mountains. While the view was now old hat for the Clarks, this was the first time that any of the others had seen Hayek from any perspective other than ground level. They still couldn't get over the lack of human infrastructure. No highways, no power lines, the Columbia River looking turbulent as they crossed over it at an altitude of several thousand feet.

Less than an hour and a half later, the plane passed over a large lake. Jack got on the intercom and announced that it was Goose Lake, one of their refueling points, located on the California-Oregon border on Earth. "We've got plenty of fuel to make it to Donner Lake and back, so we're not stopping today."

Another hour later and the small amphibian plane was circling over a long, east-west running lake, which Tim suspected was said Donner Lake. Sure enough, Jack came on the intercom and announced, "Prepare for landing. It'll be a bit bumpy, so hold on to whatever you can."

Tim watched the water slowly approach until touchdown. The small plane hit the water with enough force to cause a huge splash, then bounced up and down, hitting the water a second time, but gentler, but still tossing the loose men about the cabin a bit. Slapping the lake's waves, throwing up water with each hit, the plane slowed until it was barely underway, bobbing up and down in the small waves.

Jack gunned the engines to move them toward the eastern shore of the lake. Don got on the intercom, and in a serious voice, announced, "Thank you for flying Pleistocene Air. We hoped you enjoyed the trip down, and hope you survived the landing. I'm glad I did. Before leaving the airplane, please be sure you've collected all your valuables, particularly your rifles—you're gonna need 'em." This brought a chuckle to all those in the cargo-turned-passenger compartment.

Soon the plane was pushed up on the eastern shore, protected from the winds. Tim had initially thought they would deplane on the western shore, but Ken, who had some familiarity with the California Gold Country, had set him straight the day before.

"If we land on the western shore, that means we've got to cross Donner Pass, the hardest of the three passes in the area. Instead, we'll walk up the Coldstream Valley and over Coldstream Pass, just south of Donner Peak. It's a longer walk from the eastern shore, but a helluva lot easier. Especially with these carts. We won't be trying to raise our equipment up cliffs with ropes. It's also easier going down the western slope there."

Before exiting the plane, Don and Tim confirmed that the two pilots would return in a week, and overfly the Central Valley around noon. Once contact was made, they would begin the process of airdropping men and material for the new airstrip.

In order to keep their clothing dry, the men stripped down to their skivvies, and while Dave stood guard, the others formed a bucket brigade to unload all the food and equipment from the plane. Fortunately, the water was shallow and warmed up, but it was still cold, as all alpine lakes are.

Unlike their prior trips, the men were carrying packs this time, with sleeping gear, spare clothing, and food. The two trailers were mainly for the sluice, mining equipment, and additional food.

Fortunately, once they cleared the lake and got dressed, the underbrush was clear enough to make pulling the carts easier. Each cart had hand-grips that could be held while pulling them, but they also had belt straps, so they could be attached at the waist, leaving the hands free to carry rifles at the ready.

Tim and Bob had the first shift hauling the wagons, not an easy task, particularly since each wagon weighed over two hundred pounds fully loaded. But rather than complain, Bob pointed out, "Hey, at least we ain't carrying this shit on our back, or trying to drive or ride five hundred miles over rough terrain, especially in those jeeps that don't seem to have any seat padding."

As they walked, Tim thought about Bob's comment, playing in his mind West Coast geography, and then said, "Well, technically, we'd only have to drive around three hundred fifty, maybe four hundred miles, as the crow flies."

"How do you figure?" Bob asked, grunting as he pulled the small trailer over the dry landscape.

"Simple. Use the landing craft to go down the Yakima to the Columbia, then up the Willamette. Then again, we'd have to get across the entire Siskiyou Range, which would prove rather daunting," the last said with a grunt as his trailer hit a rock and bounced.

"Yeah, think I'd rather walk four or five days than deal with driving in your jeep for two weeks."

Tim got a chuckle out of that.

Time passed slowly as the six men made their way up the valley to the pass, a distance of only seven miles, but it took them up almost two thousand feet in elevation, from six thousand to over seven thousand eight-hundred feet. It only took four hours, but it was mostly uphill in rough country, and the need to constantly keep watch for predators also wore on them. By the time they finally made it to the pass, it was well past noon. Flopping to the ground, they elected to stop and eat lunch there. None of them were used to climbing, or any other activity, at these elevations, and none of them were spring chickens, either, so the break was greatly welcomed by all. The cool breeze dried the sweat off them as they ate C-rations brought specifically for quick meals on the go, such as this. The dehydrated meals would be when they set up camp.

As this was Lee's first time away from the gates, he was suitably impressed by what he was seeing. "It isn't just the lack of human intervention on the landscape or the truly exotic wildlife, but it's the whole *gestalt* of the situation—the beauty of the untrammeled environment," he said. The others agreed with him.

Donner Peak rose above them on one side and Mt. Judah on the other. Toward the east were mountains, blocking the views of Donner Lake and Lake Tahoe. Tim was disappointed. He was hoping to be able to see them both from this vantage point.

"Well, it's all downhill from here," Ken said as he chewed a cold spoonful of beans and franks, his face still red with the exertion from the climb.

Looking toward the west, Tim could see the conifer-covered slopes leading toward California's Central Valley.

The eventual goal was to get to the confluence of the Feather and Yuba Rivers by way of the Yuba. When they had plotted the route out two days before, they had estimated it would be around one hundred miles and take them five or six days, depending on how rough the terrain was. Looking at his watch, Tim came to the conclusion it would probably take closer to six than five days.

A large shadow passed over at that moment. Looking up, the men could see a California condor flying overhead, its gracefulness in the air and almost ten-foot wingspan a sight to behold. "That's something you'll likely never see on Earth," Tim said.

"Yeah, I hear they're almost extinct," Dave added. "Be a shame if that were to happen here."

"I wonder how we can prevent that from happening?" Tim mused. It was something to ponder on. How to protect the environment with the constitution they had developed?

22

Tim was correct in his assessment: it took the team six days to make it to the Feather River. While the trip had been mostly incident-free, it was still a struggle, particularly in some of the tight places on the Yuba River, when the canyon narrowed precipitously.

"Imagine if we'd try to get to Rich's Bar," Ken said, as the group stood on the banks of the Feather River. Ken was referring to one of the richest gold deposits on the Feather, about seventy miles and countless canyons north of Donner Lake, and well over one hundred miles from their current location, up the North Fork of the Feather. "I still think we oughta explore up to Bidwell's Bar, if we can. That's only another thirty-five or so miles from here."

The other men stared at him as if he were insane.

"Ken, you try hauling these damned trailers over this terrain," Joe said. "It ain't easy." The others agreed, with Bob chiming in, "Damned if I'll haul this thing another mile further than necessary, let alone thirty-five."

Being the oldest in the party, Ken had been exempt from hauling the trailers, letting the younger men do it. As such, he wasn't quite as exhausted as they were. He relented, rather ungracefully, as his desire to hit one of the richest gold strikes in history practically overrode his common sense and the situation facing the small group.

Fortunately, it had been a mild winter, and the flow in both the Yuba and Feather Rivers was low and slow. Good conditions for gold dredging. But the Feather looked a bit deeper than what Ken found comfortable working in, so he recommended they start a little upriver on the Yuba. "We might want to consider putting the airfield on the north side," he said as they looked around.

"Why?" Tim asked.

"Fewer rivers to cross if we want to head up to Bidwell's Bar or up the North Fork of the Feather."

The men agree that was a valid point, so dragging the two trailers, they made their way back up the Yuba and crossed over at a shallow spot, making camp north of the Yuba and east of the Feather.

The team set up camp in the central oak woodland, dominated by valley oaks and bunchgrass. Closer to the river were towering cottonwoods, alder, blue elderberry, and wild grapes and blackberries. What was most evidently missing were the imported plants, such as eucalyptus, pampas grass, and the European annual grasses that gave California its tawny hills on Earth. The group had been surprised to see green hills herein the summer; most of them associated California with hills covered with dry grasses. Tim also spotted what appeared to be poison oak. Just brushing up against it would cause the plant's oils to transfer to skin, causing an allergic reaction.

"Cold water and friction, just like with stinging nettles," Ken said when Tim pointed out the poison oak to the others.

When asked what he meant, Ken explained. "You ever brush up against stinging nettles? You get oil on your skin, just like poison oak. That's what causes the allergic reaction. Back home, we use the undersides of sword fern to rub the oil off. Same thing here. Just douse it with cold water right away, then rub it off with a bandana or some other plant's leaves. Just make sure you rub hard enough you get some friction going on. That's what'll get the oils off."

"Why not use warm water?" Dave asked.

"It'll open the pores, lets the oil get in under the skin," Ken replied. "Trust me, you wouldn't like that. It'd take days or weeks to finally get rid of."

Once the tents were set up and firewood was gathered, Tim and Joe erected the long-wire antenna for the PRC-25, or prick twenty-five as they called it, while the others set up a tripwire around the camp's perimeter. They didn't expect Jack and Don to fly over until noon the next day, but Tim figured it was best to get things set up early, rather than miss making a connection with the aircrew.

The perimeter tripwire was a new take on an old application. Rather than just concertina or other wire with pebble-laden cans attached, this tripwire was attached to a military surplus M49A1 flare, left over from the war. The flare was set on a small post, and connected to the perimeter wire. If the wire got bumped into by an animal, the flare's pin would be yanked out, which would ignite the flare and light up the surrounding area with a bright light for about a minute. Tim, Bob, and Joe were familiar with them from Vietnam, and Tim suspected any flare lighting up would scare the living bejeesus out of anything unfamiliar with it, which included all animals on Hayek. The wire was strung in a pentagon shape around the camp, with five flares set out. If a flare went up, they'd have a good idea where to look first. Rather than taking a chance of having the flare go off in their hands by accidentally tripping the wire, Joe and Bob took care to connect the wire to the flare after stringing it out. They also attached high-visibility marking tape to the wire so everyone could clearly see where it was, so that the flares wouldn't be set off accidentally.

The fauna was similar to that surrounding the gate, ranging from mastodons to Smilodons to giant sloths, dire wolves, American lions and cheetahs, and the ever-present, and feared, short-faced bear. Grizzlies were also abundant, along with pronghorn antelope, elk, and mule deer. One animal that the team hadn't seen in their previous explorations was the California tapir, a pig-like animal with a long snout. All in all, just the typical Hayek fauna and megafauna they had become accustomed to.

"Hope we don't have to deal with another lion attack," Lee said, staring out into the surrounding landscape, rifle at the ready while standing watch as the rest of the team strapped TNT blocks to oak trees with det cord in preparation for creating a landing zone.

While the three Vietnam War veterans had experience clearing helicopter landing zones with det cord, none of the men had any actual experience in airdrops from airplanes, but they understood they needed a clearing at least a couple of hundred feet long to ensure everything dropped close together. Tim had paced off the distance and wrapped high-visibility tape around trees that defined the perimeter. Anything within that perimeter was coming down, and while Lee and Ken, both of whom had little or no experience with explosives, stood guard, the rest of the men worked industriously to make it happen. It wasn't just enough to bring the trees down; they had to ensure they were destroyed completely, turned into matchsticks, so the equipment and personnel could drop safely.

For the next couple of hours, the valley and surrounding foothills echoed with the sounds of explosions as trees were blasted into oblivion. When finished, they had a two hundred by fifty foot stretch of land cleared of all trees, many of which had been rendered into very large toothpicks. Fortunately, despite the dry climate and high temperatures, none of the explosions turned into wildfires.

Only after the drop zone was cleared and enough wood gathered for a fire, did the team finally take a break. They had been hard at it for the past six days, hiking over rough terrain for most of it, going from almost eight-thousand feet to fifty feet of elevation, and wrapping it all up by blasting out an airdrop zone in the middle of a wilderness in the blazing, humid heat of a Central Valley summer day. They decided cooling off in the Yuba River, then maybe looking for some gold, was in order.

The water was certainly cooling. It wasn't anything like the near-freezing temperatures of the Powder River, but still respectably cool, close to seventy-five degrees. After the initial shock of the cool water, the men spent time swimming and warming up on the sandy beach. Knowing they might be swimming in water warmer than they were used to, the men had elected to bring swimsuits with them, and wore said suits. As Dave had said when he initially recommended bringing the attire, "You really don't want to get burnt down there if you're skinny dipping."

Eventually, they dug out the sluices and shovels and began mining for gold, still wearing just swimsuits, but also putting on neoprene booties to protect their feet.

All of them had become used to finding lots of gold when mining in the Powder River, but their prior experience was nothing like what they experienced on the Yuba. From the first shovelful of sand and gravel, gold nuggets began emerging.

None of them wanted to take a break for supper, but they eventually realized it was for the best. "Gold'll still be here in the morning," Tim said, making his way to shore, shovel in hand, water splashing around his bare thighs, hitting the gold-laden bag dangling from his waist.

The sluices were dragged out of the water and deposited on the shore, close enough to the water's edge so they wouldn't have to spend more time dragging them to the water in the morning.

Supper consisted of boiling river water and using it to rehydrate their dehydrated meals. None of them were surprised at just how much of an appetite they had, not after having spent the past six days walking over rough terrain and burning up thousands of calories each day. All six men wolfed down two packets of dehydrated meals each, meals supposedly designed for two people.

It wasn't long after supper that those not on watch crawled into their tents and fell into deep sleeps, well, as deep as their bodies were willing to let them, considering the situation. That meant they slept like the dead on edge. Joe and Bob took the first watch, with Tim relieving Joe after the first hour, and Dave relieving Bob after the second.

"Sure will be nice to have a little more company to keep watch," Dave murmured as he added some more brush to the fire.

"If they got it set up right, we should see at least another half-dozen tomorrow," Tim replied, all while keeping an eye out on the camp perimeter. He didn't want to have another Goodland on his hands.

23

The night passed uneventfully, and as with their first trip, the men were somewhat sleep-deprived, although having six people alternating watch was a lot better than four. Throughout the night, the men could hear the trumpeting of mastodons and the roaring of lions. It was a sound that, while somewhat terrifying, was becoming comforting. The one thing that surprised them was the preponderance of mosquitoes, something they weren't used to. Those on watch were kept busy swatting and swearing at the little blood-suckers. As Tim sat through his watch, seemingly being devoured by them, he wondered if they were carriers for any of Earth's diseases. "Sure would suck to get malaria or dengue fever, especially after getting through a tour of 'Nam without it," he said to Bob in a low voice, staring out into the star-studded landscape. Bob agreed.

Gotta come up with some way to kill them, at least, where we'll be. I wonder if I can find any DDT? Finding legal DDT was much harder since it had been banned in the US in 1972. The more Tim thought about it, the more he came to the conclusion that allowing some DDT, such as around living areas, would be good, but wholesale use of an insecticide would have a severe negative impact on the bird and bat populations, wiping out their main food source.

A glance up showed the Milky Way in all its glory, stretching from horizon to horizon, starting to fade as dawn approached.

As the dawn slowly broke over the Sierra Nevada, a cacophony of noise arose from the multitude of avian life that occupied the water-fed Central Valley. It was unlike anything that any of them had heard before: not on Earth or on their limited travels east of the Cascades on Hayek, a much more arid environment, despite the rivers. Screeching, cawing, and whistling abounded. Tim could only recognize a few of the bird sounds, such as the warbling, guttural call of a raven, the call of a loon, or the quacking of a duck. Going beyond that for identification purposes was beyond his ken. He couldn't even imagine the sounds and sights that would greet anyone watching the annual migrations along this important flyway between Mexico and northern latitudes.

The increasing light and noise from the birds woke the rest of the team up, and slowly, one by one, like larva emerging from the egg, the men crawled out of their tents into the cool morning air. Well, relatively cool compared to the heat and humidity of the day before. The humidity was still up there, adding to the damp coolness of the dawn.

A coffee pot was strung up over the campfire, kept going constantly by whoever was on watch. It was a welcome treat to those just awakening.

Dave joined Tim on the perimeter, coffee cup in one hand, rifle in the other. "Anything?"

Tim shook his head. "Just the usual. Guess the fire trick is still working."

Dave looked around the landscape. "Yeah, guess so. Y'know, I thought this area would have a lot less brush, be more cleared out than it was. I guess, without the Indians here to have controlled burns, this is pretty much what Earth must've looked like before the first Indians crossed over the Bering Strait."

Tim looked at him with a puzzled expression. "Controlled burns?"

Dave nodded absently. "Yeah. Indians used to burn the land to maintain for their use. That's why the first settlers in Washington saw all those prairies. Indians would burn them regularly to ensure there was food for deer and elk. I read somewhere that Indians in California would keep the underbrush burned down so they could grow oak trees. One of their main foods was acorns. If it weren't for the Forest Service tamping down on any fires, it would probably look more like this."

Tim hadn't even heard of such a thing. All his years growing up, the Forest Service was around stomping out fires; Smokey the Bear, and all that stuff.

It wasn't long before the rest of the team was up, dining on dehydrated scrambled eggs and instant oatmeal. Tim helped himself to a box of C-rats, this one containing ham and eggs, chopped. Digging into the box, he found the B-1 unit contained cookies and chocolate disks, much like a Nestle's Crunch Bar, while the D-1 was a can of fruit cocktail. *Not too shabby*, he thought, setting aside the D and B unit cans as he used his John Wayne to open the can of ham and eggs, chopped. Once the can was mostly open, he stopped, put away the small can opener, and bent the lid back, creating a handle. Carefully, he set the partially open can on the bed of coals at the edge of the previous night's fire.

Only after he was certain the can wouldn't tip over into the fire did he tackle the next can, the one containing the fruit.

As they ate, the men talked about the day's activities. The airfield construction team was supposed to drop in some time around noon, which gave them about six hours to undertake whatever they wanted. In this case, they all agreed that getting more gold was important, rather than just sitting around keeping an eye out for hungry critters.

Breakfast was a quick affair, and within a half-hour, the team was back at the edge of the Yuba River. Since it wasn't quite as warm as the afternoon before, they elected to have two people don the drysuits and work the shovels and sluices. The lucky two were Joe and Bob. Ken chose to use the metal detector to find gold on land, asking Lee to do the digging while he did the spotting. That left Dave and Tim to stand watch until it was their turn to spell the Joe-Bob show and don the drysuits.

As noon approached, the team hauled the sluice back out of the river and made their way back to their rough camp in anticipation of the airdrop. An early lunch consisted of more reconstituted freeze-dried meals. Lunch over, they made their way to the edge of the drop zone.

Tim extracted his binoculars from his pack and began searching the sky to the north for any evidence of the seaplane. After fifteen minutes, he turned to Dave. "No sense keeping all this fun to myself," he said as he handed the binoculars to his friend, letting his arms sink down to his sides, giving them a break, and turned his attention to the PRC-25.

Less than ten minutes passed before Dave announced, "I think they're here." The balding astronomer pointed to the north with one hand, the other still holding the binoculars to his eyes. "Right over there, about thirty degrees above the horizon." He handed the binoculars back to Tim, who trained them where Dave had said to look. Sure enough, the ungainly plane came into view, still small with distance, despite the multiplying effect of the binoculars.

Over the radio's earphone, which Tim had set down on the radio, they could hear a voice tinnily calling out.

Handing the binoculars back to Dave, Tim picked up the radio's handset and listened for a few seconds. Squeezing the handset's push-to-talk button, Tim answered. "Goose, this is ground control. Do you copy, over?"

Tim heard Don's voice come back clear and strong. "Roger that, ground control. Copy five-by-five. How copy, over?"

Tim smiled. "I copy five-by-five. We've got you north of us about ten miles, over." Even Tim was surprised that the PRC-25 was reaching the aircraft at such a distance.

A slight pause on the other end, then Don came back. "Roger. We should be over in a couple of minutes. Pop smoke, over."

"Wilco. Standby. Out."

"Pop smoke," Tim ordered, "and blow a couple of blasting caps. Let's scare any critters away from here." Within seconds, there was a pop and a hiss. Soon, purple smoke started swirling around the drop zone, drifting to the west. This was followed by a number of sharp explosions as Joe and Bob set off several blasting caps.

Not too long after that, the men could hear the throaty roar of the twin turboprop engines which had replaced the original radial engines, giving the Grumman Goose increased speed, distance, and carrying capacity.

Tim's PRC came alive. "Goose to ground control, I spot goofy grape. I say again, goofy grape. Over."

"That's affirmative, Goose. You can drop any time, the delta zulu is clear. I say again, the delta zulu is clear. Out." Tim used the military phonetic alphabet to refer to the drop zone.

The plane circled over the field, and Tim could see young Jack looking down at the field from the pilot's seat. The window was open and Jack's red hair, which had grown over the summer, was whipping about in the slipstream. The cargo/passenger door was open, and a man was standing in the doorway, hands on either side of the door's exterior.

Jack, clearly seeing what direction the wind was blowing the smoke, lined the plane up and made his first run high above the runway from the south, slightly to the east. As he passed the threshold of the drop zone, first one man, then a second fell from the plane. A third exited just before the plane crossed the northern edge of the field. As the plane circled about, three parachutes blossomed. Dave and Lee headed to the north while Bob and Joe headed to the south, the four intent on providing the falling men with security against any potential fauna threats. Ken stayed with Tim, providing security at the radio site.

The second run was identical to the first, with three men jumping. Unlike the first drop, though, this one didn't result in three blossoming parachutes; rather, only two of the chutes deployed. The third chute refused to deploy and streamed after the rapidly falling man. As the men watched in horror, expecting him to hit the ground, the malfunctioning chute separated from the falling man and he was able to deploy his reserve chute. It barely deployed fully just before impact, slowing his descent, but not stopping him from slamming into the ground faster than he would have had his main chute deployed properly.

While everyone else ran to the downed man, Tim got on the radio. "Goose, standby. I say again, standby. We had a streamer. Out."

Turning to Ken, he said, without hope, "I hope he's okay."

Ken nodded. Both men could tell it didn't look good, not at the speed that he'd hit, nor the screams that echoed across the field.

One of the new men came running up to Tim. Panting, he said, "We're gonna need a medic, maybe even a doctor. He's got two broken legs, likely compound fractures."

Tim winced. "Okay. Let's get him off the field, if we can, so they can finish the drop. Maybe we can get a medic down here in a couple of hours. In the meantime, give him a shot of morphine and get him off the field."

The man nodded, then began running back to the crowd that had formed around the injured jumper.

"Goose, this is ground control, over."

"Go ahead, ground control. Over."

"One of the guys is hurt, bad. Once we get him off the field, complete the drop, then head back to base and get us a medic or a doctor. Possible compound fractures in both legs, over."

A slight pause.

"Ah, roger that, ground control. Complete the drop, romeo tango bravo, and return with a medic or doctor." A slight pause, then, "Any suggestions on where to get one? Over."

Tim and Ken looked at each other, bewildered.

"Stand by while I check with the drop team, out." Setting the handset down, Tim told Ken, "Watch the radio. I'm gonna see if any of the new guys have any suggestions."

Holding his rifle in his right hand, Tim jogged out to the field. By the time he arrived, he was panting. The injured man was no longer screaming, but it was evident he was in a great deal of pain. Both legs were bent at awkward angles above the ankles, with white bones visible below the pulled-up trouser legs. *Thank God, it's not the femurs*, Tim thought, catching his breath.

"We gotta get a medic or doctor here, asap. Any suggestions?"

Luther, on the ground attending to the injured man, looked up and said, "Lenny's got a doctor on stand-by in Seattle. Usually helps when one of our guys gets hurt and they don't want to go to a hospital. Y'know, discreet like."

"Think he'll come out?"

Luther thought a moment, then nodded. "Yeah, I wouldn't doubt it."

"Okay. Let's see if we can get him, then." Looking down at the moaning man, Tim said, "Get some splints on those legs and let's get him off the field. We've got more gear that needs to come down." With that, he turned and jogged back to the radio.

After catching his breath, he radioed Don with the news on the medical doctor. "Get in touch with Lenny as soon as you can and see how fast you can get this guy here. Likely won't be until tomorrow, but make it happen. As soon as I give the word, commence the rest of the drop, over."

"Roger that. We'll drop on your word and get Lenny to get the doc here. Out."

It didn't take more than a couple of minutes to make a field-expedient stretcher from a poncho and get the injured man off the field. Once he was out of the way, Tim notified Don to commence the operation. Two more passes later, all the gear was on the ground, most of it consisting of hand tools and demolition explosives to clear the way for the airstrip.

Luther informed Tim after the Goose had departed that the construction crew had completed construction of an airstrip near Goose Lake, and had laid in sufficient fuel to allow for operations for the DHC-4 Caribou that was recently purchased.

"They're gonna come back a couple of times and airdrop the rest of the construction equipment, maybe even some Marston Mats." Luther nodded in the direction of the injured man. "Hope this doesn't slow 'em down too much."

Looking about at the site and the makeshift aid tent set up to deal with the injured man, Tim replied, "I doubt it'll slow 'em down. I'm gonna recommend they drop the equipment tomorrow, so let's get crackin' on this airfield."

The rest of the day was spent preparing the field. By the time the crew had wrapped up for the day and were settling into a late supper, they had made tremendous headway. Most of the cut brush had been pushed off to the sides, leaving mainly tree stumps and an almost level ground to deal with. Luther even commented on how it shouldn't take too long to finish clearing.

"Mini-dozer we're bringing in'll take care of the stumps, and that and the roller'll flatten out the rest," the former Seabee said, taking a bite of his chili. One of the items dropped was a camp kitchen, complete with stove and sink, along with several cases of number 10 cans of various meals, such as chili, chicken and dumplings, beef stew, and other complete meals that only needed reheating. Each can contained enough to feed four to six men, or in this case, four hungry adventurers. It was still better than eating the glop that freeze-dried meals consisted of.

"How goes the development at Milton?" Tim asked the former Seabee.

"It goes. Veronica and that Teppos guy have already assembled everything we need for the hydro-power and a couple of mini-waste treatment plants. I found a gravel deposit, so we won't have to be trucking stuff through your shed," this said with a grin. "I also gave a couple of guys directions on how to excavate and prep the roads. I wouldn't doubt we'll be ready to install everything a week after I get back."

"Cool," Tim said, shoveling a spoonful of beef stew into his mouth, then getting a faraway look on his face as he slowly chewed.

24

Dawn of the second day was similar to their first dawn, only this time the new men were introduced to the cacophony that made up morning in the Central Valley.

"Noisy neighbors," Luther complained as he drank his black coffee from a surplus military metal canteen cup, one that looked like it had been around since World War II.

Tim only grinned. "You'd rather hear lions roaring at the wire?" he asked, his grin growing wider.

Luther just shook his head.

Looking toward the north, he asked, "Any idea on when they might get here with the doc?"

Tim shrugged. "Earliest I can imagine would be about eight, maybe eight-thirty, if they took off at dawn. That's even if they managed to get a doctor."

"Lenny looks after his own," Luther said stubbornly, taking another sip of his coffee.

"Well, until then, anything we can do on the field?"

Luther shook his head. "Not without the heavier equipment."

"Well, we might's well do some prospecting while we wait."

With only the one sluice, two drysuits, and one metal detector, there wasn't enough equipment to keep them all occupied, so Tim suggested the newer members get the opportunity to find some gold, reminding them that a portion of it was theirs to keep. Ken looked forlorn, being kept out of the prospecting action, but Tim made it up to him by putting him in charge, having the men determine the best spots in the river to excavate.

While the other men were prospecting or standing watch, Tim, Dave, and Luther remained in the camp, keeping an ear on the radio and taking care of the injured man. Not that there was much they could do for him, other than give him the occasional shot of morphine.

Finally, at almost eleven o'clock, they heard the sound of a plane in the distance. Turning to the north, the trio could see a plane approaching. Tim got his binoculars out, and once he spotted the plane and got the focus dialed in, he could see it wasn't the Grumman Goose. "Looks like they got the 'Boo."

Tim handed the glasses over to Dave, who looked at the oncoming plane.

Heading for the radio, Tim called over to Luther, "Get some smoke ready."

He had just turned the radio on when he heard Don calling. "Caribou to ground control, over."

Picking up the handset, Tim pushed the PTT button, "Caribou, this is ground control, over."

"We've got the delta zulu in sight. Medical personnel ready to jump. Pop smoke, over."

"Wilco. Stand by, over."

"Pop smoke!" Tim yelled to Luther.

A pop followed by a hiss followed his command. Soon, there was green smoke swirling around the small camp.

"Ground control to Caribou, smoke popped, over."

"Roger. We see lime, I say again, lime, over."

"Affirmative, Caribou. Lime it is. Out."

The twin-engine plane lined up on the drop zone and was soon passing over it. Instead of people jumping out the side door, as they did from the Grumman, this time a couple of people exited the rear of the plane, where a cargo door was lowered as a ramp. Fortunately, both jumpers' parachutes deployed successfully, and their occupants settled to the ground without injury, both of them landing well within the drop zone. As Tim and Dave ran out to greet them and provide security, they saw the jumpers, one a man, the other a woman, were struggling out of the unfamiliar harnesses and hadn't even apparently given a thought as to their surroundings, particularly the precarious position they were in.

"Welcome to Hayek," Tim said to the pair, while also keeping watch for any threats.

After struggling out of his parachute harness, the man, about Tim's age, introduced himself.

"I'm Dr. Martine. Where's the patient?"

Usually, if somebody introduced themselves as doctor, Tim's hackles would rise a bit. It was the natural reaction those with doctorates of philosophy had when confronted by their medical doctor counterparts, most of whom made a hell of a lot more than the academically inclined Ph.D. This time, Tim didn't mind, as it was truly a professional greeting and letting Tim know that the man was the medical expert. Tim hoped he had experience in rough conditions.

Tim waved over to the camp. "Over there."

As the woman joined the two men, Martine introduced her as Judy Lowe, a paramedic with King County's Medic 1. The Medic 1 program was the county's medical first responder unit, operating in Seattle and its environs.

Tim nodded, then said, "Let's move it. We need to get out of this drop zone asap."

As the four jogged away from the discarded chutes, Tim asked Martine where his medical supplies were.

"I've got some here," he said, patting a small pouch that Tim hadn't seen before, slung over the physician's shoulder. "I've got more coming down in a minute. And in case you're wondering, this ain't my first rodeo. I was a battalion surgeon for the 173rd Airborne in 'Nam."

He said that just as they made it back to camp, which was now full of the rest of the team. Tim pointed out the injured man, and as the physician and the medic went to check on him, Tim got back on the radio.

"Caribou this is ground control, over."

"Go ahead, ground control, over."

"Successful drop. Start the second run, over."

"Roger, wilco. Hope the drop zone's clear, 'cause we're coming in low. Over."

"That's affirmative. Drop zone is clear. Go for it. Out."

This time, instead of staying more than a thousand feet up, the olive-drab painted plane came screaming in at what Tim calculated to be an altitude of about four or five feet above ground level, barely above the blasted trunks of the trees still on the nascent airstrip. The plane's wheels were extended, but Tim knew the plane wouldn't be landing. Hoping they wouldn't catch on a tree stump or other hazard, he could just imagine the concentration on the young pilot's face. It was a lot to ask of a boy not even sixteen years old, but young Jack seemed to be handling it well.

As the plane crossed over the threshold of the drop zone, a parachute deployed from the rear, opening up before whatever piece of equipment was attached to it even exited the plane. Tim had seen this type of low-altitude parachute extraction technique used in Vietnam, usually under hot conditions. Luckily, nobody was shooting at the cargo plane here.

The cargo came out of the plane on a large pallet, landed in a cloud of dust, and skidded along the drop zone, crushing whatever got in its way. Before the plane was halfway down the drop zone, a second parachute deployed, and another pallet came out . This time, the equipment skidded to the end of the drop zone and beyond, missing a large oak tree by a matter of feet.

"Caribou to ground control, over," Tim heard over the radio, watching as the plane increased altitude.

"Go ahead, over," Tim replied.

"We're gonna need the delta zulu cleared before we can make our next drop, over."

"Roger, that. Clear the delta zulu. On it. Out."

"Okay, let's clear the DZ," Tim called out to the surrounding crowd.

In less than five minutes, they had one of the two pieces of equipment unstrapped from the pallets and off the drop zone. It was a small bulldozer, the smallest Tim had ever seen. The engineer who was unstrapping it said it was military surplus from World War II. "It's a Clark Airborne tractor," he said. "They used to drop them in gliders to make airfields during the war. Luther figured it was our best option."

The other piece of equipment was a small fuel bladder on top of a pallet. Tim estimated it was a two-hundred-gallon bladder. Rather than unstrap it, the engineer connected a cable to it from the tractor and pulled the pallet to the edge of the drop zone, close to the camp.

Tim got back on the radio and let Don know the field was clear. This time the bird came in at a slightly higher altitude and only a single parachute exited, this one consisting of whatever medical supplies Martine had packed. As Tim watched the cargo descend, Don informed him that this was the last piece and that they'd be returning to base for more.

"We'll return in about five, six hours. This trip was near max payload. See you soon. Over."

"Roger. See you then. Out."

With that, the plane, which had already gained height and made a turn to the north, continued on its way.

Luther clapped his hands and rubbed them together in anticipation. "Okay, now we can start. Shouldn't take too long to scrape a runway out of this dirt." He looked around at the tule reeds and cottonwoods flanking the rivers. Rubbing his chin, he said, almost to himself, "All this water, hope we don't hit a bunch of soft dirt." Shrugging, he said in a louder voice, "Get that thing fueled up, and let's start scrapin'."

When the Caribou returned late in the day, the engineers had managed to scrape a basic runway out of the raw land, extending the drop zone so it was twelve hundred feet long and one hundred fifty feet wide. All that was needed to complete it was compacting it flat. Of course, a more permanent field would require adding Marston Mats and gravel, but that would wait.

Martine had also declared that the injured man would live, did not appear to have any internal injuries, but needed to get to a hospital soon. "We've got enough IV fluids and antibiotics to stave off any immediate infections, but if we don't get him back soon, he'll likely lose both feet," the physician said shortly after seeing his patient. Fortunately, the physician had brought a sufficient amount of morphine to last several days.

As with the last equipment drop, Don made sure that smoke was popped, indicating wind direction, and the field was clear before Jack made a screaming run down the field, this time barely three feet above the raw earth, releasing first one then a second pallet of equipment using the low-altitude parachute extraction method. As the plane gained altitude into the late afternoon light, Don radioed Tim, saying they'd be back early the next afternoon. Further conversation before the Caribou slipped out of range gave Tim the understanding that the plane would take off an hour before noon, so as to allow the crew on the ground sufficient time to compact the airstrip. With any luck at all, they'd be able to evacuate the injured man the next day.

The pallets turned out to contain another bladder of fuel and a small walk-behind compacting roller. Luther had a smile of pure bliss on his face when he saw the piece of machinery. Turning toward Tim, he said, "Greatest things for compacting sidewalks. Let's see how this one works on a runway."

The crew worked on the field until it was nearly dusk, only stopping due to the potential threat posed by predators they couldn't see. "For all we know, they might think the dozer and roller are just a couple of fat, slow, noisy prey," Dave said as he helped Tim wrangle up all the engineers.

They left the equipment on the edge of the field, not bothering to move it far. They were just going to use it in the morning.

Joe, who had wound up being the master of the watch schedule since the Powder River, assigned the watch rotation, leaving the two medical personnel off it. His explanation to Tim was that he figured if anyone needed to be sharp, it was the people who might be able to save them if they got attacked. Tim shrugged, just grateful that he had first watch, so he wouldn't have to have his sleep interrupted.

Other than the two medical types, everyone else had been on Hayek in one position or another for the past couple of months, either prospecting on the Powder River or building airstrips, roads, and bridges near the future site of Milton. Luther was sharing the first watch with Tim, so Tim brought up the idea of Luther becoming Parallel's chief engineer.

"Y'know, I tried to avoid anything resembling normalcy and responsibility ever since I graduated college," the former Seabee said, "but damned if you guys didn't get me all excited about this. Don asked me if I'd be interested, and I gotta say, it didn't take too much talkin' to convince me." Holding out his hand to Tim, he said, "Count me in, Doc."

That was a load off Tim's mind. Now, if they could only raise enough money.

Morning arrived with the usual cacophony of birds, but this time, it was also greeted with the cacophony of machinery, as the engineers got the roller up and running. It was barely dawn, but light enough for the men to work, and work they did. Walking behind the compactor-roller was energy draining, having to hold onto the machine and guide it while it hammered and rolled across the ground. The vibrations worked their way up the men's arms to their shoulders and necks, practically beating them. Taking turns every half-hour, they were able to get the center strip of the runway completely compacted for its entire length and a width of almost seventy-five feet. Luther was hoping to get all one hundred fifty feet of the strip's width compacted but elected to compromise with the center portion compacted all the way from end to end.

Luther had the men break for lunch at noon, announcing, "Ain't no sense working on it anymore for now. We ain't gonna do enough to really make a difference. We'll get back to it after the evac."

Tim was feeling guilty about not letting himself get pummeled walking behind the machine, but only slightly. The engineers got to fly the entire way to gold country; they didn't have to walk almost a week through unchartered wilderness, humping a ruck and rifle while dragging heavily laden trailers over boulders and through rivers.

The crew, with the exception of the medical team and one of the security, took a break from the humidity and heat by swimming in the Yuba River. Part of the swimming involved diving to the riverbed and picking up gold nuggets.

By two, everyone had returned to the campsite to await the arrival of the Caribou. Thirty minutes later, the plane was spotted coming from the north. Martine and Lowe were standing next to the injured man, whose name Tim didn't even know. He had been moved from his tent onto a stretcher that had been in the medical drop with the medical personnel. He was still medicated, but not so much that he wasn't aware of his surroundings.

Ten minutes later, smoke was popped and everyone watched with a combination of dread and anticipation as Jack lined the aircraft up for the dirt airstrip's first landing. *Christ, I hope he doesn't crash*, Tim thought, watching the plane come in with what he considered a sharp nose-down attitude, not remembering that the sharp angle of attack was necessary to get the bird on the ground. The wheels deployed, and shortly before flying into the runway, Jack pulled the nose up and gently landed the plane on the dirt strip. Tim was impressed. He had seen far worse landings in Vietnam, where the grunts would jokingly refer to the pilots as Captain Kangaroo due to the multiple bounces the plane made when landing.

Tim heard the familiar pitch of the propellers change as Jack put them in reverse to stop the plane, and in less than half the field's length, the cargo plane came to a halt, its reversed props pushing it slightly backward before Jack put them back in forward operation and stopped the motion. Jack then turned the aircraft around and powered to the end of the runway from whence he had just landed.

Once there, he turned the plane around again, preparing to take advantage of the slight wind from the south.

Tim saw waving coming from the co-pilot's window, then a window in the upper fuselage of the plane behind the co-pilot's seat opened and a figure wearing a Nomex flight suit and olive drab aviator's helmet stood up and waved them over, the visor down covering the figure's face.

"Okay, let's get him loaded up and get the rest of the equipment off the plane," Tim yelled at the men. Luther, Joe, and the two remaining engineers grabbed the stretcher's handles and began trotting over to the plane with Martine and Lowe alongside them. Tim and the others joined them, mainly keeping an eye out for any threats. It reminded Tim of his time doing similar things in Vietnam. Fortunately, nobody was shooting at him this time. As the cargo master saw them approaching, he disappeared back into the plane, closing the window behind him.

The group circled wide around the plane, ensuring nobody pulled a Cuisinart with the plane's still-spinning propellers.

Before Tim arrived at the back of the plane, the injured man was already set on the ground near the ramp and the men had begun the process of moving equipment out of the plane. Tim noticed that just like the Caribous he saw, and flew in, in Vietnam, this one had canvas seats against the interior wall, folded up to allow room for cargo. The floor had temporary rollers set on the sides to allow palletized cargo to rapidly slide in and out. In this case, the cargo consisted of the dredges, along with a Willys jeep and trailer. In the trailer were several drysuits.

Don, also wearing an aviator's helmet, came down the cabin and met with Tim. Yelling over the din of the still-running propellers, he told Tim that he figured they'd need the jeep and trailer to move the equipment and gold. "I'll bring more fuel tomorrow, along with some Marston Mats. We'll try to get two runs in a day, bringing essentials and enough mats to at least give us a solid runway and ramp." Tim nodded, then asked to talk with Jack. Don waved him forward and went to unlatch one of the benches from the cabin's wall in preparation for the flight back. Martine would be returning with the injured engineer, but Lowe would be staying on as the medical staff. When she found out about the possibilities, she had immediately drafted a resignation letter in a small medical notebook she had brought, giving up her position with Medic 1 just so she could get in on what she saw as a groundbreaking opportunity.

Tim made his way to the cockpit where he found Jack sitting in the pilot's seat. The young man was writing on a clipboard, and it wasn't until Tim tapped him on the shoulder did he look up. A smile broke his face and he pulled off his earphones. "Dr. Bowman, great to see you," he yelled. The noise in the cockpit was louder than in the cabin, mainly because the cockpit windows were open to allow fresh, relatively cooler air in.

"No, great to see you, Jack. Helluva job you're doing here." Tim could see the redheaded boy blush from the praise. "How'd you learn to fly this thing so fast?"

Jack shrugged. "Don't know. Seems natural-like. A couple of hours in the co-pilot's seat, then a couple as pilot, and I felt ready. The IP said it was the darndest thing he'd ever seen." The IP Jack referred to was the instructor pilot. What Jack didn't say was that the couple of hours was more like dozens of hours, with many eight- and ten-hour days spent in the cockpit and with his nose buried in flight manuals.

"Any suggestions on the field?"

Jack thought about it for a couple of seconds, then said, "We need a windsock and a basic weather station. You know, air temperature, barometric pressure, wind speed; that kind of thing. Those things are important to know when landing and taking off. Especially landing. And a beacon, that would help."

"You get what you need and bring it back. We'll set it up. In the meantime, keep up the good work." With that, Tim left a smiling Jack and exited the cockpit.

The cargo had been unloaded and the injured man was strapped in on one of the benches. Martine gave him a thumb's up, indicating he was ready to go. Tim and Don shook hands while the cargo master disentangled himself from Dave. At first, Tim was shocked, then recognized that the cargo master was actually Petra, kissing her husband goodbye as she prepared to return to Selah. She waved to Tim as he passed her on the way out of the plane. Once off the ramp, he saw her speaking into the microphone attached to her helmet, which she had plugged into the aircraft's onboard intercom system. Another wave, and then the aircraft's props began revving up.

25

After the plane took off, the men loaded one of the dredges into the trailer. Dave got into the driver's seat with Ken in the passenger seat, and one of the engineers hopped into the back, rifle at the ready. Unfortunately, this wasn't Tim's jeep, so there wasn't a cushioned seat for the man to sit on. Tim didn't envy him the bouncy trip to the river.

Luther requested Tim stand watch over him while he used the small dozer to cut a path from the camp to the river. "No sense parking the jeep and trailer far from the river, not with the animals we got wandering around," the crusty ex-sailor said as he started up the dozer's engine, adding more smoke into the air to go with the foul-smelling cigar he had clamped in his mouth. The particular area Luther was referring to was the area closest to the river, where the vegetation was thick and difficult to penetrate or even see through. Joe and Bob joined Tim in keeping watch, the three men slowly advancing whenever Luther plowed a trail through the brush.

"We're gonna have to find a gravel deposit," Luther yelled at one point, as his dozer broke through a dry, mud-crusted vernal pool and sank several inches into the damp ground under the crust, settling onto the hardpan. The vernal pool was one of an immeasurable number that dotted the floor of the Central Valley. Temporary wetlands that were water-filled in the winter and spring, they usually dried up in early summer, leaving a carpet of cracked mud or plants uniquely adapted to the region's

Mediterranean climate. What kept the water in the pools was the underlying hardpan, a dense layer of soil impenetrable to water.

"Remind me to have Don check the Yellow Pages for rock quarries. No sense looking for them when we can just let our fingers do the walking," Tim yelled back, quoting a relatively recent television commercial for the telephone book.

Once the road was cut through, Luther trundled the small dozer back to the main campsite, tagged along by Tim and Dave. It wasn't more than a few minutes before he shut the dozer down outside the camp's perimeter. Climbing off, he grabbed his buttocks and vigorously kneaded them. "That thing's a butt-numbing machine," he said.

Still looking around for any threats, Tim asked, "Any reason why you need to remain here, or can your guys handle it?"

"Lots of reasons to go, only one to stay, and that's the gravel."

"How so?"

"My guys are pretty good at building stuff and blowing shit up, but unless they have the materials, they aren't all particularly adept at adapting, if you know what I mean. Let me check out the gravel, and depending on how it is, I can tell the guys what to do to make it usable."

Tim nodded. "Sounds good. I want you back at the gate and working on the hydroelectric project."

"Me, too. Soon as that and the water and sewage treatment plants are in, we can all move over, sorta permanent-like."

That evening, as the men and Lowe gathered around the campfire, Tim announced that he and Dave would be returning to Selah the next day. "Luther, here," he continued, waving to the engineer, "is gonna stay another day or so and check out some gravel deposits. Once he surveys them, he's gonna pull out and leave one of you other Seabees in charge of finishing up the airfield and helping Ken develop the mines."

Tim then nodded to Lee Orange. "Lee's gonna be in charge of security here, so if any of you have any issues with the local fauna, talk to him." Despite the gallows humor reminder of what happened to Goodland, a chuckle rose among the gathered.

"Finally, Ken's in charge of mining ops. Over time, we're gonna be bringing in more and heavier mining equipment, along with more people to operate the equipment. Don't be surprised if they aren't all white men, either." As the only non-white amongst the group, Tim wanted to ensure he didn't remain such. He had given it a fair amount of thought, and considering the growing number of Hispanics in the Yakima area, he was willing to bet he'd be able to find a large number of non-whites who would be interested in higher paying mining and construction work over the back-breaking fruit and vegetable picking jobs they mostly had. Unlike many of the others, he also knew some of the minority history of the Yakima Valley, particularly the small town of Wapato, which once had the highest concentration of Japanese in Washington outside of Seattle. It was bad enough there was a lot of anti-Japanese sentiment by white farmers, but when it culminated in Roosevelt's Executive Action 9066, the entire town's Japanese population was wiped out by "interning" them. It didn't matter if the Japanese had been born in Japan or America, they were all interned in what were essentially American concentration camps. Tim had heard about them from some of his classmates, who had parents and older siblings interned.

"I'm hoping to make Hayek as diversified as possible, but with some common, unifying themes: freedom, responsibility, and respect. So, if any of you've got problems with little brown brother, you better drop it right now or take the first gate home."

It wasn't long before the silence was broken by Bob, who said in a joking manner, "As long as little brown brother ain't trying to kill me like he was in 'Nam, I'm fine with that." That broke the tension that had developed with Tim's speech.

When the Caribou returned late the next morning, Tim was surprised to see writing on it - Air Hayek in a sans serif font that reminded Tim of something, but he wasn't quite sure what. As he walked toward the parked plane, he could see more writing, in smaller font, under the name. It was a slogan: *Somethings, Somewhere, Sometimes, Semi-Professionally.* Then it struck Tim, and like a hammer hitting between his eyes, he flashed back to his year in Vietnam, watching a shiny, silver unpainted C-123 Provider land on one of the dirt airstrips his unit operated out of. The airplane was operated by Air America, a Central Intelligence Agency front company that was used to transport all sorts of things around Southeast Asia. Tim had heard they transported "hard rice" in Laos, code for arms and ammunition, a way to circumvent the International Agreement on the Neutrality of Laos, a "peace treaty" agreed to in 1962 and ignored ever since then until the fall of Laos to the Pathet Lao government shortly after the fall of Saigon in 1975. Air America's slogan was *Anything, Anywhere, Anytime — Professionally.* Someone had a sense of humor, co-opting the CIA's pet airline slogan. Tim had later learned that the helicopter supposedly evacuating the US Embassy in Saigon was actually an Air America helicopter evacuating people off an apartment building almost a kilometer from the embassy.

The ramp dropped, and a minute later, the cargo master, whom Tim assumed was Petra Jaskey again, was waving men over to assist. The load consisted of three rows of Marston Mats, each row containing fifteen of the pierced steel planks. As the load was pulled out one plank at a time, Tim calculated that it would probably take over a hundred flights to get enough planking down for a decent runway. *And that's only if we make it fifty feet wide. At two trips a day, that's gonna take at least fifty-five days. We're gonna need a couple more planes for this. I wonder if we can get a C-123?*

While Tim spoke with Ken, Luther, and Lee, the remaining men unloaded the pierced steel planking and a box containing a windsock and the basic equipment necessary for a portable weather station: a barometer, thermometer, and hygrometer, along with an anemometer to measure the wind speed. After leaving last-minute instructions with Ken and Luther, Tim joined Dave in hauling one of the small all-terrain trailers they had brought with them on the trek from Donner Lake. This time, instead of supplies, it was loaded with canvas bags full of gold nuggets. Future loads would be transported by jeep-towed trailers. They rolled the cart into the plane and were greeted by Petra, who helped the two men lash the cart down to the cargo deck. Once the trailer was secured, Petra dropped one of the red canvas benches that lined the cargo bay's walls and gestured for them to have a seat, red canvas webbing attached to the walls serving as their seatbacks. Before they had managed to strap in, the aircraft started rolling down the runway. The takeoff wasn't as steep as Tim had experienced in Vietnam, which surprised him for some reason. *Then again, ain't nobody trying to shoot us down with an RPG or anti-aircraft missile.*

The flight back to the site that was becoming known as Milton Air Strip took three hours, including a short stop at Goose Lake to add more fuel.

"Don't want to arrive home on fumes," Jack had announced when they sat down at Goose Lake. Unlike the other two airstrips, there was nobody at this one; nothing but fuel bladders and a small shack set up, just in case the crew had to remain overnight. Jack used a manual pump to transfer fuel from a bladder to the aircraft while the others kept watch.

As they approached their final destination, Tim noticed a small tower was set up adjacent to the runway, opposite the gate. Petra informed him that it was set up to better handle landings, with a weather station like the one recently delivered to the California strip.

"One of Lenny's guys serves as the air controller. Says we might as well get used to having one, as we'll probably have more planes, soon."

Tim could also see the outline of streets marking the new settlement of Milton. It was apparent that several streets extending from the Yakima River were ready for development, albeit with gravel instead of concrete or macadam. He could see machinery and men moving around, and a dump truck dumping gravel. It was amazing to see how much work could be done by a dedicated group of individuals who didn't constantly have government workers overseeing everything they did or unions to slow them down. *Set up a way to have independent inspections for safety purposes,* he thought, as the plane dipped lower and he lost sight of the small grid-iron street network.

The landing at Milton Air Strip was unremarkable. As they exited the craft with the cart of gold, they were met by Veronica, Janice, and the two Homotherium cubs, both on leashes held by Veronica. Both cubs were looking larger than the last time Tim had seen them, not even two weeks ago. As the men exited the aircraft through the lowered ramp, they were pleasantly surprised to find that the summer heat that typically blanketed eastern Washington had been replaced with a cold front that had swept through the night before, leaving the air cool and clear.

Before Tim could reach Veronica, Janice came running up to him and grabbed him in a big hug. He was surprised, but not surprised enough to not return the small girl's hug.

"Hey, look at you! How're you doing?" he asked the girl, who finally let go.

"Better, now that you're back. Missus Veronica was worried, and so was I."

Ruffling the girl's hair with one hand, Tim said, "Well, I'm back now, and not going out for a while. Is this your first time on Hayek?"

The girl nodded, clearly excited. Taking Tim's hand, she walked with him back to where Veronica was holding the two impatient Homotheriums.

"What are you feeding these two?" he jokingly asked his wife, squatting down to rub the spot behind an ear on each cub. They purred a low rumble and rubbed their heads against his hands.

"Whatever they want," she replied. "And, a lot of it." Nodding toward the trailer, she asked, "How much this time?"

Tim stood. "Probably close to fifty pounds, just for a couple of days' work."

Dave interrupted them. "Figure around a quarter mil, before refining. So, around a hundred eighty to two hundred kay."

"And that's just with us doing some placer mining and sluice work for less than a day," Tim continued with some excitement. "It

really is rich down there, a lot more than I actually expected."
Turning to Janice, he asked, "Wanna see some real gold?"

The girl's eyes lit up. "Yeah, can I?"

"Sure."

Dave opened one of the bags in the trailer and let Janice look into it. The girl's face lit up again. "Can I touch it?"

"Sure," Dave said, "but just be sure you don't take any," the last said in a mock warning.

As Janice pulled out a particularly large nugget, even Veronica and Petra looked surprised.

"Wow," was all Veronica said.

"Exactly, wow," Tim repeated. Switching gears, he asked, "How goes the planning and development?"

"Pretty good. Teppos has gotten us most of what we need for the hydro-plant, and we've got the first waste treatment plant being delivered in a couple of days, along with everything we need for water. Luther has a couple of his guys already clearing for roads and houses." Veronica then paused, and looked worried. "We've also had company at the ranch."

"What kind?" Tim asked suspiciously, noting that Dave and Petra were also paying close attention.

"Some guys from the county permitting office. Said they had a complaint that we must be doing some unauthorized construction without a permit."

"Did you let them into the shed?" Tim asked. He wasn't too worried. Anyone entering the shed would only see an un-powered gate that resembled nothing more than a large, steel door frame or engine lift, big enough for a truck.

Veronica shook her head. "Told them nothing was happening, and if they wanted to come onto the property, they'd better show a warrant. They tried to tell me they didn't need a warrant, as they were code enforcement, but I told them that since they worked for the government, they sure as hell needed a warrant, and if they didn't leave immediately, I'd be calling Poe."

Tim nodded, and out of the corner of his eye, saw Dave doing the same thing.

"Yeah, we might want to think about moving our operations a bit," the astronomer said.

"Might be a good idea," Tim agreed.

"What about over by the fruit packing plant?" Petra chimed in. "I hear they've got some spare warehouses."

Tim looked thoughtful for a minute, the cool wind playing across his face, causing his black hair, which had gotten long over the summer, to move across his face. He thought about where the packing plants were located, mostly on the edge of the town of Selah, close to the freeway. Swiping the hair back, he said, "Aren't those in the actual town limits of Selah?"

"Yeah, but considering how much stuff we're taking over, and all the truck traffic we're gonna have while we build out Milton, it might be a good idea," Dave said.

Tim shook his head. "Just when you think you're caught up on all the planning…"

As the group made their way to the small Hayek gate, Veronica brought up another subject. "Have you guys considered how we're gonna build this city out, and everything?" She waved around with one hand, the other still holding the leashes to Timmy and Tia. "I mean, one that's not dependent on stuff from Earth?"

The group stopped, and in unison, turned around to look over the landscape past the airstrip. While currently sagebrush-covered desert, with the occasional Pleistocene critter popping into view, a small shack, and a bunch of fuel bladders, they could all imagine it covered by a small city, based on Teppos' drawings.

"I've been pondering that for some time now," Tim said. "What we need is somebody, or somebodies, who can help us realize this dream of ours; one in which we're not tied to Earth. Lots to do here, such as finding raw materials, setting up a manufacturing base, getting agriculture established. We're gonna need a whole lot more people and some basic infrastructure."

Tearing his gaze away from the horizon, he looked at the others. "We need people who understand about resources and development. Any suggestions?"

"I know a guy," Dave said. Everyone turned to him, even Timmy and Tia.

Tim made a come-along motion with his hand.

"Guy's a geographer at Central. Adjunct instructor. Just finished his Ph.D. at U-dub. I used to see him in the adjunct offices when I taught there."

"What can a geographer bring to the table?" Tim asked, rather skeptical. He thought geographers were only good for teaching students what countries were where and what the capital of who-gives-a-darn-istan was. "Don't you mean geologists for the resources?"

Dave shook his head. "No, geographer. You want to know where stuff is, like natural resources, you ask a geographer. They live for this stuff. They also know a lot about economics and development. Matter of fact, I think Harrison's work focused on sustainable development."

"Sustainable development? What the heck is that?"

Dave shrugged. "Not exactly sure, but has something to do with having development that can be sustained without depleting resources, somehow."

Tim nodded. "Give him a call. Let's meet with him. Sooner the better."

"Will do."

With that, the group turned and made for the small gate back to Earth. As they approached it, Tim and Dave saw that a second small watchtower had been built near it while they were in California. The watchtower was barely big enough for two people, but it had a roof to provide whoever was on watch with some escape from the heat of the sun. Tim approved of this new construction, as it allowed whoever was in it to see further than if they were standing at ground level. This meant increased awareness and warning of any oncoming threats.

The security team member on watch looked down at the approaching group and nonchalantly waved at them. Everyone waved back.

HAYEK

26

Tim was having a late breakfast the next morning, with Timmy and Tia playing around his legs at the kitchen table, when the phone rang. Disentangling himself from the two rambunctious predators, he got up and answered the phone.

"Hello?"

Dave's voice came through the earpiece. "You free for lunch?"

"Yeah. What's up?"

"We're meeting Harrison up in Ellensburg, at the Frontier Tavern. Pick you up at 11:15?"

Tim looked at his watch. Barely past eight. *Guess getting up at daybreak makes this a late breakfast.* "Sure."

"Great, see you then." Dave hung up, not even saying goodbye.

Hanging up the phone, he looked down at the two Homotherium cubs, who had stopped playing to pay attention to him while he was talking. "Looks like I'll have to leave you guys again. Now, where's that wife o' mine?"

A bit before 11:15, Dave's Ford Bronco pulled into the gravel driveway, dust following behind it like a rooster's tail. He didn't even bother to shut the engine down as Tim came out of the house.

Climbing into the passenger seat, Tim asked, "So, what's this guy like?"

Dave looked over his shoulder as he backed the Bronco up and did a T-turn in the driveway. It wasn't until he started driving forward toward the main road that he replied. "Light in the loafers."

Tim was surprised. It wasn't the answer he was expecting. He was expecting something along the lines of geeky, outdoorsy, academic. Light in the loafers was the furthest thing from his mind.

"Waddaya mean, 'light in the loafers'? As in, 'he's a faggot'?'"

"He's gay, is what I mean. They don't like being called faggots, or even fags. You got a problem with that?"

Tim shook his head. "No. Just surprised. Can't say that I know any fags."

"Gays," Dave said, absently, as he turned onto the pavement. The sound of the tires changed from crunching gravel to a high-pitched whine.

"Fine. Gay, happy, whatever. Other than being 'light in the loafers,' what else is he like?"

"From what I can tell, guy's pretty sharp. I think he'll be a good addition to the team."

The drive to Ellensburg took barely over a half-hour. Tim and Dave were both used to the climb over Untanum Ridge. Tim kept his eye on the Bronco's engine temperature. Cars were known to overheat on the climb. Once over the ridge, they dropped down before climbing back over Manastash ridge. As they made their way north along Interstate 82, they talked about what Hayek needed to succeed. Clearly, along with infrastructure, industry, and agriculture, they needed people and more money.

"What'd you tell Harrison about us?" Tim asked.

"Said we were writing a science fiction novel about the multiverse and wanted to get some idea on what it would take to establish a colony."

Tim nodded. Sounded as good as an alibi as any.

After a bit over thirty minutes, the Bronco left I-82 and merged onto I-90 and less than a mile later, left the freeway, entering the outskirts of Ellensburg, home of Central Washington University—

one of six state universities, usually just called Central by locals and most Washingtonians.

The city was once a contender for the state capital but lost out on that honor after a fire destroyed the town on July 4th, 1889. A quick rebuild of the city in its vain attempt to become the new state's capital led to the construction of many one- to three-story brick buildings. Unfortunately, the bricks used weren't the best in quality, and as they drove down Main Street, Tim looked out over the man-made landscape. Many buildings had pieces of brick crumbling from them, or large cracks extending along their faces. A couple were boarded up. Tim, having attended Central, was aware of the city's history. Driving into Ellensburg was always a bit of a homecoming for him, despite the town starting to show evidence of growth.

Within minutes, Dave turned onto West Fourth Street and pulled into a parking space in front of a low brick building with the brick painted over and a false front on it, declaring the establishment to be the Frontier. Not Frontier Tavern, just Frontier. The original saloon on the site, established in 1873, burned to the ground during the 1889 fire, and it wasn't until a few years later that the current building was constructed. The folks at the Frontier liked to claim it was Washington's oldest bar, despite the slight gap after the fire.

Getting out of the Bronco, neither man bothered to lock their door, leaving the windows rolled down. It was Ellensburg, after all, not a crime hub like Seattle or Tacoma. Of course, compared to many cities, those two probably wouldn't qualify as crime hubs, but for those in eastern Washington, they did.

Entering the tavern, it took a moment for their eyes to adjust to the gloom after the bright, cloudless summer day. The smell of stale cigarette smoke and beer assailed their nostrils. It had been a while since Tim had been in the tavern. Quite a while. *Christ, has it really been about twenty years?* he thought. It was a place he sometimes hung out with college friends to drink cheap beer and shoot some pool, but that was before Vietnam. The place looked and smelled the same.

Dave nudged Tim. "That's him, over there."

Looking past the bar along the east wall, Tim could see a young man waving to them. Dave waved back they headed over.

Dave made the introductions, and Tim and Harrison shook hands. Timothy Jarrod Harrison, or TJ as he like to be called (mainly because he was in horror at the thought of somebody calling him 'Timmy' and having the nickname stick) was in his late twenties, with fine blond hair and blue eyes; practically a walking advertisement for Nordic heritage or a fishing boat crew based in Seattle's Ballard neighborhood. Just looking at him, Tim couldn't tell he was gay. Not too many people in eastern Washington were willing to face the social stigma consequences of coming out of the closet, and Ellensburg was far from San Francisco, so Tim couldn't say if he knew anybody who was gay. Clearly, he couldn't tell if somebody was just by looking at them.

"I ordered a couple of burgers from the Tav next door for you guys. I forgot the Frontier doesn't serve food," Harrison said as the two men from Selah sat down.

A waitress appeared at the table asking what they wanted to drink. The Frontier wasn't the type of place that offered a wine or drink list; you could either have beer or something stronger.

"I'll have an Oly, please," Tim said. Dave ordered a Rainier. Both were local Washington beers. Tim remembered drinking many cans of Olympia beer in Vietnam. It was one of the very few good things about his year spent there.

The men exchanged pleasantries while waiting for the beer and food. Tim learned that Harrison had graduated with a Ph.D. the year before from the University of Washington geography program and was looking for a tenure-track position. He also enjoyed some of the minor things in life, like eating, a place to live, and clothing, or as he quipped, Maslow's needs of water, food, and shelter. Hence, his teaching as a visiting professor in Central's geography program while he continued to apply to tenure-track positions throughout the US.

The beer arrived first, and while the men were taking their first sips, a young lady came into the bar carrying three brown bags. The food had arrived. Harrison waved her over, and within minutes, the three men were digging into greasy burgers, fries, and cold beer.

As they ate, they talked, with Dave giving Harrison the story of them writing a science fiction novel and seeking assistance. He spoke of Hayek as if it were a fictional place, and the need to develop a civilization in a world with none.

Harrison nodded, then said around a mouthful of burger, "Bullshit."

This took the two men by surprise. Tim was the first to recover. "What do you mean, bullshit?"

Harrison swallowed his food, took a sip of beer, and repeated himself. "Bullshit. I decided to do a little checking up on you guys when Dave called this morning."

Ticking off on his fingers, he continued, "One, you're a physicist. Two, he's an astronomer. Three, you both quit your jobs, tenured positions, I'll remind you, at Yakima Valley College. Fourth, nobody gives up a tenured position unless they found something a whole helluva lot better than teaching at a college. And, fifth, nobody gives up a job to co-write a science fiction novel without having a real plan on what to write, or even a publisher who's paying advance royalties."

Leaning forward, so only those at the table could hear, he said, "So, the only conclusion I can come up with is somehow you invented a way to access parallel worlds, and I wanna see it."

Tim and Dave settled back in their chairs, shocked. Tim's mind went blank for a couple of seconds, then he thought, *If some guy who doesn't even know me can figure out what we're doing, who the hell else can?*

"This might not be the best place to discuss this," Tim finally said, low voiced. Dave nodded, looking about to see if anyone else had heard Harrison.

"Tell you what," Harrison said, leaning back in his chair, "how about we take this conversation on the road. Like, maybe on the road back to your place?"

Tim and Dave looked at each other, coming to a silent agreement with shrugs and eyebrow raises.

"We can do that," Tim said. "You got a car, or will we need to ride in Dave's and bring you back?"

"I got a car. But if it helps, I'll be glad to ride with you guys."

Tim thought for a moment. "Any reason you can't stay the night?"

Harrison shook his head. "None right now."

"That's settled," Dave said. "Let's finish eating, we can follow you back to your place, and once you pack an overnight bag, we'll head back to Selah."

The rest of the meal was eaten quickly in silence.

Harrison lived in a small bungalow near the university, and it wasn't long after he parked his little gray Datsun station wagon in front of it that he emerged with a small leather overnight bag.

Tim had to lean forward as Harrison tipped the seat forward and climbed into the back of the Bronco. Settling himself in, he said with a boyish grin, "Let's go."

Rather than take the freeways back to Selah, Tim had Dave drive down Canyon Road, through the Yakima River Canyon. Without air conditioning, talking at forty-five miles per hour with the windows down would be a bit easier on the two-lane highway than if they were doing fifty-five on a busy freeway.

Along the way, Tim and Dave explained the situation they were in. Harrison was fascinated and asked numerous questions, not only about the organization's needs but about Hayek. He asked about specific animals and was surprised to hear just how many different species existed. He professed a vast amount of ignorance of Pleistocene animals, but he knew that many had still existed locally until approximately 10,000 years or so ago, when they were supposedly all killed for food by Native Americans. "Some people think they died off when the climate changed, but who knows?" he summarized.

After Tim explained about the plans for Milton, Harrison, who had both arms resting on the front seats, nodded. "Makes sense. Looks like you guys are already planning some form of sustainable development long term."

"Dave mentioned something about that sustainable development thing you've been working on, but wasn't totally clear on it," Tim said. "What's it all about?"

"In a nutshell, developing an economy based on reducing or limiting the impact to the environment. Let me give you a couple of examples, starting at the micro-level and then moving up to the macro-level. Most American homes, especially those in the suburbs, have nice little yards of grass, with maybe a fruit tree or two in the backyard. Most often, though, the owners are planting ornamentals, like Japanese maple trees or arborvitaes, or around here poplars as wind breaks."

Just then, they drove past a typical eastern Washington home, a rambler with a row of poplars on the east side, planted to block the constant wind blowing down from the Cascade Mountains. The green, grass lawn, carefully watered and manicured, contrasted with the surrounding dry grassy shrubs and sagebrush.

"What if, instead of the whole white picket fence with a yard thing, people planted mostly edible plants? It not only reduces the need to transport food a long distance, cutting down on fuel costs and the associated impacts, but provides the landowner more food security.

"There's a guy in Australia that's developed this concept called 'permaculture' that does that. It's a combo of two words, permanent and agriculture, hence *permaculture*. He basically set out zones in land, sort of like von Thünen's isolated state model."

"Von who?" Tim asked.

"Von Thünen," Harrison replied. "German economist back in the 1800s. He came up with an economic model based on the ideal European city or state. In the center was the city, and it was surrounded by various rings of economic activity, mostly related to agriculture. You gotta remember, this is the early 1800s, when everything traveled by foot or hoof. The first ring was the high-value stuff that needed to get into town fast before it spoiled, such as dairy and what we'd call truck farms now. Fresh veggies, eggs, stuff like that.

"The second ring was forest. Mostly because people needed to burn wood for cooking and heat, and wood being so heavy, you didn't want to have to carry it far. If you've ever been to Europe, you might have noticed them. Usually, they're coppicing trees, like maples, elm, alder, and cherry. You can cut those things practically to the ground, and they'll grow back."

"Sort of like when the city trims all the cherry trees way back?" Dave asked.

"Exactly! They do that so more branches can grow and give a lot more flowers. Anyhow, the third ring is crops, such as wheat, barley, and oats. The kind of thing that doesn't take up a lot of time while it's growing, but weighs a fair amount when harvested. Ever lift a bushel of wheat?"

Both men shook their heads. "I've had to carry bushels of apples," Tim answered. Growing up on an apple orchard gave him plenty of experience with bushels of apples, first with actual baskets that held a bushel's worth, then with bags. The advantage of bags over baskets is that, while they both held the same amount, you could pick with two hands rather than one if. That meant more apples picked in less time, and if you're getting paid by how much you pick…

"Probably weighs the same, about forty pounds or so. Wouldn't want to carry that too far. The final economic ring was raising of livestock, such as cows, sheep, pigs. The kind of food that can walk itself to market. They require a fair amount of space for grazing, and since they could walk into town, no need to keep them close.

"Anyhow, that's von Thünen's model in a nutshell. A bunch of people, led by Fukuoka of Japan, and Mollison in Australia, are coming up with similar ideas. Fukuoka's work deals mostly with agriculture, while Mollison is taking a more holistic approach, touching on not just the agricultural component, but the entire holistic human experience. He calls it permaculture, and instead of rings, he defines zones. It's pretty much the same concept, but at the micro-level. Stuff you need daily, you plant close to the home. Stuff that doesn't need immediate care gets planted further and further out until you've got an outer ring, or most distant stuff, being planted with stuff you only need to access once in a while. It uses the concept of synergy, with things working together to create food, not working against each other. It's not just about planting stuff, it's about reducing the impact on the environment while still providing for food and biodiversity.

"But, that's just the agricultural side. There's basically three things permaculture focuses on; earth care, people care, and fair share."

"Fair share?" Tim asked. "Is that like 'from each according to his abilities, and to each according to his needs'?" Everyone in the car recognized the Marxist quote.

"Not really. Some think so, but it's more along the lines of setting limits to population and consumption. Look around you," Harrison said, waving one arm expansively out toward in front of the Bronco.

As the men looked at the barren landscape, with only a road, river, and sagebrush-covered canyon walls and hills, Harrison chuckled. "Well, maybe not around here, but around the world. We've got a population explosion going on, famines happening around the world, people using natural resources so fast that we're constantly having to find new resources, which are usually harder to extract and cause even more damage to the environment."

"Yeah, well, if we can just pop over into a parallel world to get the easy stuff, we won't have to worry about that too much," Dave said laconically.

Harrison paused for a bit. "True, but is that what you really want to do?"

Tim shrugged, looked out the window, then turned back to Harrison. "We're not sure. That's why you're here. All we know is we want to move over, but we also don't want to remain dependent on this Earth."

Changing the topic, Tim asked Harrison, "You any good with a gun?"

Caught off guard, Harrison replied, "Not really. Never had any use for them, so I haven't ever used one."

"You're gonna need to learn, because where we're going, there ain't no police to protect you."

For the remainder of the drive, Harrison taught Tim and Dave more about permaculture and how it fit into the whole concept of sustainable development. While they could clearly see the advantage of both, they also recognized that to develop fast enough to meet their requirements, they were going to have to take advantage of the easily obtained resources from Hayek, and even possibly other parallel Earths. That, along with the finished goods from Earth they would need to make things happen.

"Y'know," Tim said, as the Bronco pulled into the outskirts of Selah, "all this is well and good, but to get up to speed, we're gonna need more than sustainable development at the beginning. We're gonna need enough resources, manufacturing capacity, and agricultural capacity to stand alone. Is this something you can help us with?"

A huge grin split Harrison's face. "Is this something I can help you with? Hell, yeah! I'm a geographer. Of course, this is something I can help you with. I've already got some ideas floating around, but let's see what I've got to work with first of all."

27

It was almost two o'clock when they pulled into Tim's yard, the bronco kicking up a cloud of dust from the dry gravel driveway. Tim had been thinking about the firearms issue while they drove, and broached the subject with Harrison.

"You've *never* fired a gun?"

"Nope. Never."

As they got out of the car, Tim said, "First time for everything. You're not going over unless you're proficient enough with a gun to protect yourself and others."

"What about a shotgun?" Dave asked, looking over the roof of the Bronco at Tim and Harrison, who had just emerged from the car with his overnight bag.

Tim nodded. "That might work. Doesn't take too much learning." Turning to Harrison, he continued, "Looks like you're gonna learn how use a shotgun."

"It's not really all that dangerous near the gate, is it?"

Both men nodded, which caused Harrison to raise an eyebrow.

"We had a guy get eaten by a lion. You wouldn't want to be that guy," Tim said, "and I sure as hell don't want to be that guy because you couldn't protect me."

Harrison nodded, practically in resignation. He had gone almost thirty years avoiding violence, and he wasn't too happy to break his streak.

"Hey, look at the bright side," Dave said. "You might not have to shoot anything."

Looking about, Tim realized that Lee Orange was still in California, so training Harrison was going to fall to him. Fortunately, he had a shotgun he kept in his bedroom, one that had the butt-stock replaced with a pistol grip so it was easier to maneuver in the close confines of the house. It was also something Veronica felt comfortable using.

"You guys wait here. I'm gonna get the shotgun and some shells. We can cross over and practice there."

Veronica came out of the house, shading her eyes with her hand. Tim waved to her and she waved back. As he approached her, he said, "Need the shotgun." She just nodded, getting a kiss from him on his way inside.

She then introduced herself to Harrison. Seeing her perplexed expression on learning he was the geographer that was supposed to help them with their fictional world, Dave explained with a shrug. "Seems like Harrison figured out what we're up to and wanted to see it."

Nodding, she said, "I hope you're good with guns. It ain't exactly friendly over there."

Only then did Harrison's mood change a bit. Up to now, it had seemed like a lark, but after Tim, then his wife, talked about the danger, he started considering the possibility that it was maybe a bit more dangerous than he had reckoned. He shook his head. "Never fired a gun before. Looks like I'm about to learn, though. Tim's getting a shotgun for me."

"Makes sense," Veronica replied. "Easier to learn and it's a great close-up weapon."

The door to the house slammed, causing all to turn. Expecting to see Tim with a shotgun, Harrison was surprised to see a young girl trailed by two giant cats coming toward them.

"I don't think I've ever seen cats that big," he commented.

Dave and Veronica chuckled.

"You've never seen these types of cats before," Dave said. "They're from Hayek. Some of the local fauna left orphaned by our great leader, who then adopted them."

Looking closer, Harrison asked, "What type of cats are they?"

"Homotherium, cousin to the Smilodon, better known as a saber-toothed tiger."

Tim came out of the house, shotgun in one hand and a box of shells in the other. The two cubs pounced their way to him, practically causing him to trip as they stopped in front of him, seeking attention.

Janice called the two cubs back to her, and Tim continued on his way to the Bronco, where he placed the box of shells on the hood and held the shotgun up for Harrison to see. "Operating it's pretty easy," he said, pointing the shotgun out over an empty field as he racked the slide back. "To shoot, just make sure the safety is off," he clicked off the safety, "point, and pull the trigger. No need to aim, just point. It'll kick, but if you're holding it right, like this," Tim held the shotgun at waist level, one hand on the pistol grip and the other on the foregrip, "you should be able to hit what's coming at you."

Handing the shotgun over to Harrison, he said, "Why don't you try?"

Harrison held the shotgun warily.

"Ain't loaded," Tim said. "But, you'll want to check anyhow. Point it in a safe direction."

The younger man pointed it at the same field Tim had.

"Rack the slide by holding onto the slide," Tim pointed to it, "and pushing down on this button in front of the trigger guard, then pulling the slide to the rear."

Harrison did so, awkwardly.

"Look in the side there, into the barrel. Anything there?"

Harrison shook his head.

"Rack it a few times 'til you feel comfortable."

Harrison looked at him in confusion.

"Rack the slide, back and forward."

After several tries, Harrison began to operate the slide with more ease.

Within fifteen minutes, Tim had Harrison dry-firing and operating the shotgun as if he had been handling one for years. Another ten minutes was spent loading fake shells Tim had retrieved from the house, and having Harrison operate the shotgun as if he were really firing it.

"I think we're ready," Tim finally said.

Before heading over, Tim gathered what he was now starting to call his "Hayek Survival Kit" from his house. It consisted of a small pack with poncho and poncho liner, spare food, a mess kit, a first aid kit, some toiletries, and spare ammunition for his rifle. Dave had a similar one stashed in his Bronco.

Wearing his pack, Tim led the way into the shed, where Harrison had his first look at the gate. As the two former college instructors took web belts with canteens and ammunition pouches off hooks on the shed wall and donned them, Veronica headed toward the gate's controls. Tim pulled a small pack off a hook, which he handed to Harrison, indicating he should put it on.

"Survival kit," Tim said. "Got enough stuff to maybe keep you alive a couple of days." After Harrison had put the pack on his back, Tim handed him a web belt similar to the ones he and Dave wore.

"Load all the spare shotgun shells you can into the ammo pouches," Tim said as Harrison strapped the belt about his waist. Tim waited as Harrison put shells from the box into the ammo pouches.

Veronica started the power to the gate while Tim and Dave grabbed their rifles off a rack bolted to the wall near the belts. Checking his rifle to ensure it was loaded, Tim commented to Harrison, "Now would be a good time to load that thing for real. Anything we see on the other side might not be all too friendly."

Awkwardly, but not as awkward as a short fifteen minutes ago, Harrison loaded first one shotshell, then another, and another, until the shotgun held five shells.

"Rack and load another," Tim said. "You want as many loaded as possible."

Harrison's eyebrows rose, but he did as commanded, looking down to ensure the shotgun was on safe once he finished.

Tim gestured Harrison to follow him, and the three men stopped in front of the gate, all with firearms at the ready. Tim looked over to Veronica and nodded. "Now would be a good time to open the gate."

A slight humming and the gate opened onto the dry landscape of Hayek. One of the security team was standing in the small watchtower. The man glanced down at the open gate, then back over the surrounding landscape, saying "All's clear" loud enough for the others to hear.

The three men stepped through the gate, which shut down once they were several steps into Hayek. The air smelled different, drier with more of a sagebrush scent. All three immediately noticed it, and Tim could see Harrison's eyebrows rising and his nostrils flaring.

Glancing about as the security man, whom Tim recognized as Joey Freeman, rose from his seat, Tim asked, "Quiet?"

Joey nodded, with a curious glance in Harrison's direction. Anything new was automatically suspect. "Yeah, ain't much happening right now."

"Where're the Clarks?"

"They took a load of perforated planks to California this morning. Should be back in another hour or so."

Tim nodded. "Okay. Guess we wait. Which airfield are they coming back to?"

"Supposed to be coming back here. Quicker for transferring things." Joey didn't want to mention gold out loud to this stranger. Who knew what he was supposed to know or not know?

Tim introduced Harrison and told Freeman that they'd be spending the night and doing some exploring.

Gesturing to the shotgun the geographer held, Freeman asked, "You know how to use that thing?"

Harrison shrugged slightly, looking down at the foreign object in his hands. "I hope so. Just spent the last half-hour with it."

"Well, don't hesitate if you need to use it. Critters here are big and nasty." Harrison nodded his understanding.

Breaking what had become a slightly awkward silence, Tim waved his free hand to the field. "Let's head over to the airfield and wait for them."

They made their way to the airfield. Along with the control tower, Tim learned that a small open-sided shed had been erected adjacent to a perforated steel plank apron set up to keep the planes off the runway. The Grumman was currently parked on the apron, looking sad in its solitary state. The men decided to wait in the shade of the shed, where they took their packs off and set them on the ground. They took a seat on a jury-rigged bench that had been made by throwing a plank over a couple of log rounds.

None of them let down their guard, knowing that at any moment a Smilodon or mastodon might make their way across the open ground and head their way. In less than the expected hour, they spotted the Caribou coming in from the south. Tim glanced over at the windsock to verify that the wind was coming from the southwest, as usual, then watched as the plane circled about the field to land from the north.

After stopping at the end of the runway, the plane turned around and started heading for the perforated steel planking apron that had been constructed near the windsock. As it moved down the runway, the rear ramp started lowering. Once parked on the apron, the plane's ramp lowered until it was touching the metal. The men stayed in the shed until both engines shut down and the propellers stopped spinning. A minute later, two flight-suited figures and one wearing jeans and a surplus Vietnam War rip-stop shirt emerged from the rear of the ramp. The two in flight suits turned out to be Jack and Don. The other person was Bob Gebbert, of the Joe and Bob show.

Before Tim could approach them, Freeman drove up in one of the jeeps. Stopping near the plane, he hopped out and unhooked the trailer. He got back into the jeep, and with guidance from Jack, backed the jeep into the aircraft. A minute later he emerged, towing a different trailer, this one sunk low on its springs. The left-behind trailer would be loaded into the plane later, and used to transport gold from the river to the airfield to Milton.

"Good haul, huh?" Tim asked as the three figures stepped over to him while Freeman drove the gold-laden trailer away.

"Yeah," Don replied, looking askance at Harrison. "It's amazing how much they can pull out with those dredges."

Tim introduced Harrison to the two Lewises, explaining that he had figured out what was up and wanted a look around before helping out.

"How do you like it so far?" Don asked.

Harrison looked around, taking in the airfield, the landscape empty of most man-made features, and the clear skies, devoid of airplane contrail lines. "Pretty freakin' amazing," he finally said.

Don looked at Tim. "You wouldn't be standing out here waiting if you didn't want something. What's up?"

"We were hoping you or Jack might be interested in flying us around a bit, maybe over the Sound and back in the Goose." Tim was referring to the Puget Sound, the large glacial scoured waterway where the major western Washington cities of Bellingham, Seattle, Tacoma, and Olympia were located.

Don looked over at Jack. "I'm bushed. You?"

Jack looked anything but bushed. The excitement of more flying seemed to energize the young man. Don just shook his head. "Youth," he muttered, turning back to Tim. "Yeah, he'll be glad to take you up. Have him home by supper time, though. I don't need his mom jumping all over me 'cause he ain't there."

With a wave, Don and Bob continued on their way to the gate.

Jack waved the three men toward the Grumman. "What's a geographer do, Dr. Harrison? I mean, other than memorize where things are."

Harrison chuckled. "Let me guess, you had a geography class in high school and that's what it was about?"

Jack nodded.

"I hate it when teachers do that," Harrison said. "Let's see if I can sum this up in a few words." Ticking off by holding up a finger from his free hand, he continued, "First, geography is the spatial science. That means we analyze things from a spatial perspective. Such as, what's located where, what patterns exist across the Earth, and what type of interactions happen between places. Lots of interactions always happening. Just look at the apple industry. Grown in eastern Washington, trucked to Seattle, and either put on trains for the East Coast or ships for the Asian market.

"Second," another finger went up, "we study regions. What makes one region different than another? Again, let's use Washington State, made up mainly of eastern and western Washington. One's mostly desert and grows apples and the other is practically a rainforest." At that, Harrison shrugged. "Well, not really, but you get the drift."

Tim was impressed listening to Harrison instruct Jack in a manner that was neither condescending nor in lecture mode, more like a conversation between two equals.

"You'll notice that both have that location thing going for them. It's not just a matter of what is where, but how those locations matter. We call that site and situation. You might think you have a great site, but if you don't have a good situation, then it's not a good site."

At Jack's confused look, Harrison explained further. "Look around you." The teen did, taking in the airfield and surrounding desert.

"Not much here, but it's a good site for an airfield, right?"

Jack nodded. Tim and Dave were just taking it in, learning about geography themselves.

"Is the situation good, though? Can you connect to other places?"

"Well, we can connect to the airfields in Oregon and California," Jack replied.

"So, there you have it. You've got good site and good situation, for the limited stuff you're doing. But what if you needed to bring in iron ore for steel manufacturing?"

"That'd be hard to do with small airplanes," Jack said.

"Exactly! What you need is a transportation system set up to handle bulk ore and coal. This might be a good site for it, but not really. Something along a navigable waterway is better here. So, thinking along those lines, where might you set up steel manufacturing?

Jack thought for a moment. "Along the coast? Maybe where Tacoma or Seattle are?" His responses were more a question than a true answer.

"Exactly! Along the coast. And knowing Washington's geography, I'd be more inclined to consider Tacoma over Seattle."

As Tim listened, he began to have an understanding of why Dave wanted a geographer on the team. It now made sense—Harrison had a viewpoint neither Tim nor Dave had, and likely one that none of the rest of the founders had.

"There's a reason a lot of our heavy-duty manufacturing, such as cars, trucks, and trains, take place near iron ore and coal deposits, and why we developed a pretty extensive railroad and inland shipping transportation infrastructure system—it's cheaper to build close to the sources than to have to ship things from far away. Site and situation. Keep that in mind."

By that time, the group had arrived at the Grumman. Jack opened the side door. "You might want to wait a minute or two after I open the doors and windows. This puppy's been baking in the sun all day."

After a quick, mostly unsuccessful attempt at cooling off the plane's interior, and a very thorough preflight inspection, Jack taxied the plane onto the runway, talking to the control tower as he did so.

A minute later, the plane rose into the air.

Harrison, who was given the opportunity to ride in the co-pilot's seat, stared in awe at the landscape beneath him. As far as he could see, there was only nature—no sign of human impact anywhere, with the exception of the two airfields and the new townsite.

Tim and Dave rode in the back, sans seats. It didn't bother Tim too much, as he was standing, hunched over, behind Jack and Harrison, elbows resting on the seats.

"Whaddaya think?" he yelled, trying to be heard over the roar of the twin turbines.

Harrison yelled back, "It's amazing!"

"Wait until we get over the Cascades. That's when it really hits you. Not much over on this side, but on the west side…" Tim let the rest of his response fade away.

At its cruising speed of 166 knots, they passed Mt. Rainier to the north in only twenty minutes. While most of this area was forested on Earth, here there was no patchwork quilt of clear-cuts, where logging had taken place. The entire mountain range was covered in a verdant carpet of evergreens, mostly ponderosa and lodgepole pines on the eastern side of the range, followed by Douglas fir and western hemlock on the western side.

Another ten minutes later and they were flying over Puget Sound. Looking down, Tim could see where the glacial-flour-laden Puyallup River was dumping its white waters into Commencement Bay. It looked a lot different without the Port of Tacoma's new container gantry cranes and concrete terminals covering everything. Gone were the piers, the warehouses, the city, the freeway. All that existed were huge evergreens covering the hills and drumlins surrounding the bay and sound, and wetlands occupying the mouth of the Puyallup. Madrona trees, with their peeling bark, could be seen lining the cliffs north of the bay, as were the large western red cedar. As they dipped down and flew lower over the Puyallup, they could see numerous bears in the river and on the bank.

"Salmon run," Tim yelled, pointing to the bears. Harrison nodded, not saying a word.

"You mind if I run us a bit south, Dr. Bowman?" Jack asked.

"Go for it," Tim said.

In just a couple of minutes, they were flying over the Nisqually delta, a flat floodplain and marsh-covered delta nestled between where Tacoma and Olympia would be on Earth. Jack pointed down. "Dad's hoping to claim some of the land down there," he said.

Tim nodded. "Don't see a reason why not. I'll talk to him when we get back." Turning to Harrison, he asked, "Wanna see Seattle?"

Harrison nodded, still not speaking.

Jack put the plane into a two-G turn and got it heading north. They passed over the Tacoma Narrows, a deep, sinuous waterway that connected the major part of Puget Sound to the South Puget Sound. It looked naked without the green suspension bridge that connected Tacoma to the Kitsap Peninsula on Earth. The next landmark they flew over was Vashon Island, devoid of all human habitation. As they approached the site where Seattle was on Earth, they could clearly see Lake Union and Lake Washington. The two lakes, though, weren't connected by the man-made ship canal, the Montlake Cut, that Harrison was so familiar with, having spent a considerable amount of time at the University of Washington, located on the cut's north side. Further to the east was smaller Lake Sammamish, one of the many lakes throughout the Puget Sound lowlands created by the Puget Lobe's retreat during the last glaciation, the Vashon stade.

Elliot Bay looked strange without all the piers, terminals, cranes, and ships. The Duwamish River ended in a swampy delta and muddy tide flats, rather than the straight channel they were all used to seeing. Looking toward the south end of Lake Washington, they could see the now-defunct on Earth Black River feeding the lake's overflow into the Duwamish.

After several minutes of flying over this familiar but not-familiar geography, Harrison turned back to Tim. "I've seen enough. Let's head back."

Jack turned the plane eastward.

For the rest of the flight, nobody spoke. They only looked out the windows and watched the unspoiled wilderness pass beneath them.

It wasn't until they approached Milton Air Strip that Jack got on the radio and requested landing instructions. Minutes later, they were on the ground.

Those in the back of the Grumman exited first, rifles back at the ready. As Harrison emerged, he saw the others at the ready, so made sure his shotgun was also ready before exiting the plane.

With the noise level reduced to only the passage of wind across the airstrip, Tim asked, "Well, what did you think?"

Harrison shook his head. "Amazing. Abso-freaking-lutely amazing."

"You want to spend the night here or back on Earth?"

"If it's all right with you guys, I wouldn't mind spending the night here, just to see what it's like."

"Well, not me," Dave said. "I've got a wife I haven't seen enough of, so I'll leave you guys here. Jack, you coming?"

Jack, who was just exiting the plane, said, "Sure thing, Dr. Jaskey. Let me do a quick post-flight inspection and I'll join you."

As Jack conducted his inspection, Harrison said, "If you plan on keeping this place viable, you're gonna need a whole lot of things. Foremost among them is people, followed by some basic infrastructure, manufacturing, and agriculture. You can't just go with a minimum viable population and expect it to work."

"Minimum viable population?" Tim asked.

"Yeah. Or MVP as we call it. It's the minimum number of people you need to survive. At one point in time, the entire human population was down to about 10,000 people. From that number, we've grown to about four and half to five billion, expected to hit six billion by the end of the century. Anyhow, for a viable basic industrial civilization you'd probably need a minimum of four to six million people."

"That much?" Tim was shocked. He was expecting to hear, at most, a million. He was hoping for far less than that.

That statement also stopped Dave and Jack in their steps, just as they had started walking away.

"How do you come to that number?" Dave asked, turning back to Harrison.

"Simple: let's look at the population numbers for a few relatively isolated societies; Australia, New Zealand, and Cuba. Australia tried to keep everything homegrown with rather large tariffs in place for most imported products." Harrison's facial expression changed, indicating internal deep thought.

"Let's see, Australia's population right now is about fifteen million. It can manufacture pretty much everything it needs. They've been pretty active in manufacturing since the mid-to-late nineteenth century, and I'm including automotive and shipping, even when their population was less than five million. They don't have much of an aviation industry, although they did manufacture some planes during World War II.

"They're currently a food exporter, and were during the First World War, so that population number includes agriculture.

"New Zealand's current population is about three million. It doesn't have much of a shipbuilding industry or an automotive industry. Most of its shipbuilding is small, coastal stuff. Even during World War II, they had a pretty limited shipbuilding industry. They pretty much rely on others for all international shipping. They've never really had an automotive industry.

"So, looking at the two countries, it looks like three million is pretty much the lower limit, with four or five million being better."

"What about Cuba?" Tim asked.

"Yeah, what about Cuba?" Harrison replied. "It's a mess. Pretty much cut off from the rest of the world due to the US embargo, Soviet stuff ain't all that good, so it's had to be pretty much self-sustaining. Population about ten million, limited resources, command economy with no real direction, some iron ore deposits, but lacking in coal deposits. Hell, they're still using cars left over from the revolution.

"Cuba's a good example of a cut-off population, but for your purposes, not the best example. You're looking at being able to access virtually unlimited resources, if you can get to them and get them where you need them. And for any civilization, the two biggies are coal and iron ore. Of course, aluminum, rubber, and nickel are all also important, as are a bunch of other resources.

"So, yeah, minimum three million. I'd shoot for five or six million, though, if possible. Reason being, you've got a lot of infrastructure that needs developing. Fortunately, there's both coal and iron ore in Washington."

"Wow," Tim said. "I wasn't expecting that."

"Hey, you want to live life civilized, or not?" Harrison asked.

After Jack and Dave passed through the gate to Earth, Tim took Harrison on a tour of Milton, or what was to become Milton. It was Tim's first tour, too, so Joey Freeman volunteered to show them around.

"Luther should be back in another day or so, but things are progressing fairly fast," Freeman said as they rode in Tim's jeep from the airstrip to the townsite. Once it migrated to Hayek, the jeep remained, giving those who needed it some means of transport. There were currently two jeeps near the airstrip, Tim's and the old surplus military model he bought early on, the one Freeman had used to haul the gold-laden trailer from the airstrip. The third jeep was still in California.

The road from the gate to the townsite was an undeveloped dirt path beaten into dust with the consistency of flour by the numerous trucks transiting it. The jeep raised a rooster tail of dust as it traveled along the road, dust that drifted forward onto the passengers and settled on them in a fine patina. It reminded Tim of riding in the back of deuce-and-a-halfs in Vietnam, the only difference being this dust was a light brown, not the red of Southeast Asian roads.

Their arrival at the future home of Milton was shocking. The contrast between the outlying sagebrush-covered wilderness and the orderly grid-iron layout of a city was sharp. There were gravel roads in place, pieces of machinery moving dirt, and equipment and piping laid out in preparation for installation.

Tim noticed there were more men he didn't recognize, and mentioned that to Joey.

"Yeah, Lenny brought in some more guys. Figured we didn't have enough security on hand, what with most of it being in California." He waved at one of the guards as they passed.

"Can we see where the hydropower's going in?" Tim asked. Joey nodded and turned the jeep toward the river.

Soon they were parked next to a small, dry ditch that ran away from the Yakima, then back toward it. The final cuts connecting the ditch to the river weren't made yet.

"From what I understand," Joey said as they stood by the edge of the four-foot-wide ditch, "they're gonna be laying pipe in here to feed the generator, and they're gonna install some of them metal things to keep crap like logs and fish out of the pipe. I also hear they're gonna dig it down below the river's level, and make a sort of pond or pool in front of the pipe so it's always underwater."

"Weir," Harrison said.

"We're what?"

"Not *we are* we're, but *double-u ee aye are* weir. It's a pond you dig to keep the penstock always submerged."

"Learn something new every day," Tim said, understanding what the geographer was saying.

Turning away from the river, Tim asked Joey, "What's the status on sleeping space?"

"Basic bunkhouse and dining facilities set up near the gate." Then Joey grinned an evil grin. "You're gonna love the latrines."

"Let me guess. Fifty-five-gallon drums cut in half?" Tim was referring to the military practice of cutting barrels in half, welding handles on the side, then using them to collect human waste, instead of a hole in the ground or a porta-potty.

Freeman laughed and nodded.

"Who's got shit detail?" This was the task of pulling the drums out from under the seats, filling them with diesel fuel, and burning the human waste—an extremely odious task that stank like shit— literally. It was a smell that was sure to give Tim some flashbacks to Vietnam.

"We've got a roster. That way everyone takes a turn."

At Tim's upraised eyebrow, Freeman continued with a grin, "Except you. Ain't no way, no how, any of us would consider asking the guy who's paying for everything to do that."

The evening was spent in and near the security of the bunkhouse. Tim and Harrison got to meet more of the security and construction team, many of who had worked for Gross in the past in one capacity or another. All were excited about the work they were doing and made sure Tim understood that they wanted to migrate over permanently.

"First thing first," Tim said during the group chat. "We've gotta make sure we've got enough things going to support us, both in terms of food and technology. Any of you guys want to move over here and devolve down to the stone age level?"

Everyone shook their heads.

"In that case, I want you guys to consider this. According to Dr. Harrison," Tim nodded in Harrison's direction, who was seated in a folding chair sipping on a McNaughton's blended whiskey out of Canada, "we're gonna need about three to five million people to make sure we can actually run this as an independent society. Got any friends?"

That brought a laugh to the crowd.

Joey Freeman piped up with a take-off on an old joke, "No friends, but I know people."

"Well, we're gonna need 'em."

The next morning, Tim and Harrison made their way back to the gate and returned to Earth. The sun was barely up and Harrison was dragging. It seemed that the screeching of some of Hayek's Pleistocene predators had been enough to keep him awake all night.

"Guess I'm a bit more used to civilization than I thought," he said once they were back in the shed.

"Yeah, it takes a while to get used to it."

Inside the shed, Tim hung his spare pack and ammo belt back on the hooks. Waving toward the gear Harrison carried, he said, "Keep it. You'll likely need it again. That is, if you're interested in going back."

"Oh, I'm interested all right. Sounds like you're already working on the kind of place I'd like to call home."

"You mean, one where everyone's accepted."

Harrison threw him a suspicious look. "Such as?"

"As far as I'm concerned, I don't give a damn what color somebody is, what their gender is, or what their sexual preferences are. As long as they're a decent person, don't hurt others, and do their damn job, I want them on board."

"Even if they're gay?"

Tim shrugged. "As long as they're not hitting on me, I could care less." Then, with a shrug and a grin, he said, "Y'know, my philosophy on homos was always that if they're a guy, they were less competition for me, and if they're a girl, they like the same things I like. What's not to like about that?"

"When you put it that way, not much. I wish others would adopt that philosophy. But, don't say homo. The proper term is gay."

"Yeah, that's what Dave said, too." Tim shrugged. "Guess it'll take me a while to break old habits."

With that, the two men got into the old Willys pickup truck and Tim drove Harrison back to his small apartment in Ellensburg.

During the drive, they continued their discussion on the needs for Hayek's growth and basic economic independence.

As Harrison got out of the truck, he said, "I'll have some rough plans drawn up for you in a couple of days."

Tim nodded. Looking at his watch, he could see from the analog dial showing the day that it was Sunday. He had stopped paying attention to the days of the week. With everything that needed doing, it didn't matter if it was a weekend; for Tim, every day was Monday. "Think you can be back down on Tuesday to present to everyone?"

"Yeah, as long as it's in the late afternoon."

"Good. You remember how to get to my house?"

When Harrison indicated he did, Tim continued, "Okay then. See you about four or five."

"Will do." With that, Harrison closed the truck's passenger door, causing the slightly rusted hinges to squeal.

28

Two days later, all members of Parallel, Incorporated, were gathered on the back deck of Tim's ranchette. While most drank beer, some were enjoying the fruits of labor produced by Covey Run, a local start-up winery, one of the first in the newly dedicated Yakima Valley AVA, or American Viticulture Area. Some people thought the wines were pretty good, actually better than good, and claimed the area to be the next Napa Valley of fine wine production. Tim wasn't too sure about that, being more a beer guy than a wine connoisseur.

Poe had just arrived and was shedding his suit coat, accepting a glass of merlot from Veronica when Harrison drove up in his Datsun. Tim could see another person in the passenger seat and presumed it was Harrison's partner. He still wasn't sure what type of terminology to use. Partner, boyfriend, butt-buddy? They all flew around in his mind. While academia had become more liberal and less stodgy over the years, there still weren't all that many openly gay people at Yakima Valley College. *Guess I'll know more when he brings it up*, Tim thought as the two men exited the dust-covered small car.

It turned out Harrison's passenger was a light-skinned black man in his mid-to-late twenties, about the same age as Harrison. As he stood by, Harrison reached into the back seat and pulled out a large pad of paper and an easel. Handing the easel to his partner, he pulled out a cardboard box, then the two men made their way to the group on the deck.

Tim stepped off the deck to greet them. "This is my partner, Bill Evans," Harrison said. Nothing exciting or dramatic, just a basic introduction.

"Nice to meet you, Bill," Tim said, shaking the man's hand.

Turning back to the assembled crowd, Tim introduced Harrison and Bill. As Bill set up the easel, making sure it was set in such a manner that nobody could see from outside the group, Harrison handed out three-ring binders to everyone. Tim got them some drinks. Both chose the Covey Run chardonnay over the Olympic beer he was drinking.

Taking a sip of the wine, Harrison nodded his gratitude. "This everyone?" he asked, looking around at the assembled group.

Veronica was sitting next to Petra, who was sitting next to Dave. Don, Eileen, and Jack Lews were all gathered together, while Poe and Shimazu were seated a bit apart. Janice and the Lewis girls were inside the house with Timmy and Tia, who were hidden from the two strangers. *Probably tearing up the house, knowing those two,* Tim thought, as he nodded toward Harrison.

"Let's get started then," Harrison said. "What's everyone know so far?"

Tim grinned a slight grin. "Only that you're gonna be breaking some pretty important news to them."

"Okay, then. Well, let's do it." He flipped over the cover of the pad, which had '3,000,000' written on it. "Tim asked me to come up with a basic plan to develop Hayek into a self-sufficient economy. To do that, the first thing you're going to need is a population big enough and with a diverse enough background and education to make it happen. The lower limit on that population, as I explained to Tim and the others the other day, is three million."

Harrison briefly described the population conversation from a couple of days prior before launching into his next item on the agenda.

"As you can imagine, you're not going to want to put three million people here in the Yakima Valley. First off, that won't do anything but lead to problems. You need people at places where you can either extract the resources, process the resources, or get them to market. To do that, you're going to need a lot of infrastructure, and I mean a lot!

"First though, let's talk resources." Harrison flipped over the page, displaying another page that contained a list of resources. "You'll find this information in the binders I handed out, so I'm just gonna go over the basics.

"Basic resources you're going to need are iron ore and coal for steel; limestone, aggregate, gypsum, and wood for construction; oil for fuel, lubricants, plastics, and fertilizers; rubber for tires, gaskets, whatever; copper for electricity; silicon for glass; materials for porcelain insulators, such as clay, feldspar, and quartz or alumina; bauxite for aluminum; uranium if you plan on going nuclear; and the list goes on, chromium, molybdenum, sulfur, titanium, nickel, lead, diamonds, tungsten, et cetera.

"As you're probably aware, it's the abundant and cheap hydroelectric system that was developed on the Columbia River that led to the development of the aluminum industry in the Pacific Northwest. That's because aluminum is one of those energy-intensive industries. You're gonna have to come up with something similar if you want to have cheap aluminum. Either hydro or nuclear. For that, you're gonna need concrete and uranium, which means a nuclear energy industry.

"As you can see, I haven't even touched on agriculture yet. We'll get to that later.

"So, where are these necessary resources?"

Harrison turned the page over, this time showing a map of Washington State. On it were a variety of variously colored blobs and symbols.

"Here in Washington, we're pretty lucky. As you can see from this map, we've got a fair amount of minerals, both metallic and non-metallic, but none are readily accessible right now. Luckily, a bunch of it is around Puget Sound, like iron ore, coal, clay, aggregate, bauxite, silica, limestone, so any industrial base you have will have to be located there, just like it is on this timeline.

"The iron ore we've got isn't a whole lot, so you're going to have to consider getting it from other locations, such as Utah, Michigan, Minnesota, or even overseas, like Western Australia or India.

"Same with copper. We've got some, but not a whole lot. North American deposits are scattered throughout the West, the biggest being in Utah. The closest big overseas deposits are in Chile.

"We've got some uranium, but not a whole lot. Most of it's in the northeast part of the state, in Stevens County. Matter of fact, the two mines there just recently shut down. That's something you'll eventually want to go elsewhere for."

Pointing back at the long list, Harrison said, "In short, most of what you need is local, but not in big quantities. I've given more detail to their locations throughout the Pacific Northwest in the documents I handed out."

Harrison pointed to the map. "Things we don't have in Washington, or even the Pacific Northwest, are oil, rubber, diamonds. Heck, the list goes on, as you can see in your folders. You can get oil down in California, but for rubber, you're going to need to set up some plantations in tropical areas, like the Caribbean or Hawaii.

"Which brings us to agriculture. Pretty much, anything you *need* can be grown in Washington. Not luxuries, like coffee, tea, bananas, sugar, cacao for chocolate, most nuts, or a bunch of spices, but all the basics like wheat, barley, lentils, apples," the last brought a chuckle among the group, as Washington State was the leading apple producer in the world, "and even sugar beets for sugar. We can even grow hemp for rope. Of course, if you like rice, fuggedaboutit. Closest place to grow rice is California's Central Valley.

"You want spices? Most of them will likely need to be grown in tropical places; black pepper, cumin, cinnamon, cumin, nutmeg, vanilla. Again, the list goes on.

"So, based on this info, here're my suggestions." Harrison flipped the page, showing another map of Washington State, this one with dots where the major Puget Sound cities were located.

"First, you need to locate where you want your major population centers to be. They've got to be accessible to transportation infrastructure, such as sea lanes, and enough land for industry. That pretty much rules out Milton. Once again, you're looking at Puget Sound. Commencement Bay, Budd Inlet, Bellingham Bay, and Elliot Bay are your best locations, just like they are here on Earth. Oh, that's Tacoma, Olympia, Bellingham, and Seattle, in case you're unfamiliar."

Flipping another page, this time he showed a map of the West Coast and the Pacific Ocean out to Hawaii, including the entire states of Washington, Oregon, and California.

"Agriculture centers should be established in Hawaii, California's Central Valley, Oregon's Willamette Valley, and throughout Washington, including the Puget Sound lowlands and Central Washington, maybe the Palouse.

"You'll need to establish some form of energy production so you can process raw material into finished goods. Other than hydroelectric, your only other real options are natural gas, oil, or nuclear. I'd opt for nuclear if you can. Small nuke plants, something bigger than a nuclear sub, but smaller than the WPPSS mistake." Everyone recognized the WPPSS comment, pronounced whoops by Harrison. The Washington Public Power Supply System had recently halted construction on several nuclear power plants, forcing the company to default to the tune of over two billion dollars. "Maybe something like the MH-1A the army used to power the Panama Canal back in the sixties and seventies."

At the confused look of his audience, Harrison elaborated. "The army put a small nuclear reactor on a Liberty ship, something along the lines of ten megawatts.

"No matter what energy source you use, you're eventually going to need POLs—petroleum, oils, and lubricants. Gas, diesel, jet fuel, et cetera. You can get oil in southern California, but to get it back here you need shipping." Another flip of the easel page, this time showing a cargo vessel.

"To that end, I recommend setting up a basic shipbuilding program based on the Liberty or Victory ships of World War II.

Easy to construct, relatively durable, and with a range of about seventeen thousand miles for the Liberty ship and over twenty-three thousand miles for the Victory. I'd personally opt for the Victory ship, mainly due to the better design and longer range. You can build both general cargo and tanker versions, both of which were built during the war, so the plans should be available.

"For overland transport, such as to eastern Washington, you're gonna need rail lines. You could start off with gravel roads and trucks, but any serious infrastructure requires rail. Double-track for cargo, if you can. And, if you can, design a set of lines from the start to be like the Japanese Shinkansen lines, or bullet trains as you know them. Of course, if you really want to be cutting edge, you could always consider magnetic levitation trains."

"What's the difference between them?" Tim asked.

"Mainly the means of propulsion and how they ride. Regular trains operate with steel wheels on steel rails. They use either electric motors powered from overhead or diesel-electric motors, whereby the diesel engine powers the electric motors. The motors turn the wheels.

"A mag-lev train gets the propulsion from magnets set in the rails and the train. One set of magnets causes the train to levitate, just like if you tried to push two magnets together with the north ends, and another pushes the train. They naturally repel each other. Same concept, only on a grander scale.

"Another difference is cost. Mag-levs are more expensive to construct but are cheaper to run. Main reason you don't see many mag-levs is because it's hard to justify building an expensive system if you've already got a good system in place. Of course, if you're building from scratch, mag-lev might be the best option, especially if you can run it through an evacuated tube or tunnel. From what I understand, the hypothetical speeds can reach up to four or five thousand miles an hour. Imagine being able to cross the continent in less than an hour."

That caused everyone's eyebrows to rise.

"Let me get this straight," Tim said. "What you're suggesting is two sets of rail lines, one for cargo and a high-speed system for passengers?"

Harrison nodded. "Yeah, pretty much."

"Why not just use planes and regular trains for passengers?" Dave asked as a follow-up.

"You could," Harrison responded, "but it's not as sustainable or environmentally sound. I thought you guys wanted a society that was more environmentally friendly than our current slash-and-burn one?"

That brought nods from everyone.

"Correct me if I'm wrong," Poe piped up, "but, isn't this gonna take years to develop?"

"I estimate at least three to five years before you can even think of approaching self-sufficiency. And that's going to take a lot of monetary and human investment."

A quiet overtook the gathered group. Tim stared at the easel still showing the image of the Liberty ship. Breaking the silence, he asked, almost rhetorically, "You know the best time to plant a tree?"

The others all turned to look questioningly at him.

Looking around at each person, he said, "Twenty years ago." A slight pause, then, "The next best time to plant a tree is now."

The meeting continued on through the afternoon and into the evening, with the issue finally settled on where and how to start.

Poe would find a warehouse in Tacoma where Tim would set up a gate. While gold mining operations continued in California, they would complete the basics of Milton, then start a similar process in Tacoma, or Tahoma as they decided to name the new town. Instead of just housing, though, Tahoma would be set up as an industrial town, one designed for shipping, steel manufacturing, shipbuilding, and turning out the necessary components to build the transportation infrastructure Hayek would require.

Since Tim wasn't letting anyone know how to build the gates, he was also responsible for opening a few more, one in Hawaii, one in the Palouse, and one in southern California. These were all going to be temporary gates with the sole purpose of moving the necessary equipment to get things going—tropical agriculture in Hawaii, temperate grain production agriculture in the Palouse, and POL production in California.

When the topic of immigrants came up, the biggest questions involved where to house them, how to feed them, and how much they should pay to cross over. Tim had already decided to charge twenty-five thousand dollars per person, preferably in gold. Part of that fee was also going to be returned to each adult in the form of basic military equipment as part of the militia. Tim had calculated that to be about five to six hundred dollars, going with a modification of the M14 instead of the M16 or AK47. What he wanted was a slightly smaller version of the M14 using a smaller cartridge than the 7.62x51mm NATO round. That was something that was going to have to be developed on Hayek, though, once the industry could support it. In the meantime, they'd likely be stuck with M14s, M16s, or AK47s.

Harrison brought up the concept of using indentured servants. While initially rejected out of hand by the group, it was Harrison's partner, Bill, who argued most vociferously for it. "Think about it: say you don't have the money to come over, but you really want to. Maybe because you're looking for adventure, or maybe because you really want to escape Earth. If you're poor, you can't afford it. This gives even poor people an opportunity. Make it a two or three-year payback period, and have people working on the important infrastructure, like the rail lines. Basically, put them to work where it will benefit everyone."

"But, isn't that like slavery?" Veronica asked.

Bill shook his head. "Nope, 'cause it's both voluntary and for a limited time. If the company is the one that's doing it, and you set the parameters right, it should prove beneficial to all."

"Actually, it's illegal," Poe said. "Thirteenth Amendment prohibits it."

Tim thought for a moment. "Doesn't that relate to slavery and *involuntary* servitude, not *voluntary* servitude?

Poe shook his head. "Nope, doesn't matter if one enters into it legally, once entered, it's considered illegal. Courts have already ruled that this includes peonage, which is when a person is compelled to work to pay off a debt."

That's when Dave piped up. "Maybe here, but not on Hayek. US laws don't apply there. Remember, we've got our own constitution."

After a moment's hesitation, Poe said, "He's right. Hayek has its own constitution, so it's legal there. But, good luck promoting it here where it's illegal."

"First Amendment?" Tim asked.

"What about it?" Poe replied.

"Can we advertise, then have people sign the contract once they're on Hayek?"

"What if they won't sign?"

Tim's look became a little harder. "Simple, we push them back to Earth."

The nods of the others showed they supported this action. Poe took this in. "Well, that's one way of making it work. But, if you're going to take this one, you have to devise a way in which it isn't anything like slavery."

"What if you gave them a salary, maybe one that's a quarter to a third of what the normal salary would be, along with room, board, weekends off, medical care, and allow them to use whatever they want to from what they earn to pay off their debt early?" Harrison asked.

"That would work," Tim agreed. "Let's do it."

"One thing you're going to want to consider," Harrison said, "is the culture you want to introduce."

"The what?" Dave asked.

"The culture. Every part of the world has culture. The New England culture is different than the culture of the South, and vastly different than the mañana culture of Latin America. Whatever tone you set from the beginning, and practically impose on all those who follow, is what type of culture will develop."

The conversation that ensued came to the conclusion that the culture sought would be one of a love for freedom and independence, a strong work ethic, one that valued education, and one more caring of the environment than what was happening on Earth.

HAYEK

TWO YEARS LATER

29

Two years after the planning session with Harrison, Tim sat in a new Willys jeep and looked out over the completely changed landscape of Commencement Bay, renamed Tahoma Bay on Hayek, as the sun rose over the Cascades, illuminating it. There was still a lot to do, but the shoreline had changed considerably. A small shipyard was in the process of turning out another Victory ship. Other smaller shipyards were turning out a T2 tanker, an FS Design 381 light cargo ship, and smaller fishing vessels, tugs, and barges. The three bigger ships were replicas of the venerable World War II ships made in the US. The Victory ship and the T2 tanker were getting to keep their names on Hayek, but the FS Design 381 was renamed the LCS-1 for Light Cargo Ship, Type 1.

While most people recalled the Liberty ships of World War II, many didn't recall their larger cousin, the Victory ship. At 445 long and a range of over 23,000 miles, it was ideally made for crossing Hayek's unpopulated oceans, as long as it could also carry fuel for the return trip or have a tanker along for supply. When operating alone, resupply was done using barrels of fuel stored inside one of the cargo holds. The FS Design 381 light cargo ship, limited to 4,000 miles, was good for coastal operations, but was especially ideal for those shallow ports where its ten-foot draft was considerably less than the twenty-eight-foot draft of the larger Victory ship. The T2 tanker was useful for transporting oil from the southern California oil fields to Tahoma, and future coastal settlements. This was another of Harrison's ideas. Not only was the design proven, but the ships would be able to work in tandem, with the larger ships transferring cargo to the smaller ship to access more ports. The geographer was full of such arcane knowledge.

Small concrete marine terminals with metal cargo warehouses dotted the landscape along the bay's shore. The Puyallup River, still named that on Hayek, was dumping its whitish glacial flour sediment into the bay. In the winter, when the glaciers atop Mt. Tahoma stopped melting, the river would be clearer and less sediment-laden.

Along the hills of Tahoma were more manufacturing, including an entire factory to manufacture Willys jeeps that Tim had purchased from Mitsubishi in Japan. It turned out the Japanese company was still manufacturing CJ3B Willys, known as the J series in Japan. The jeep Tim had purchased the tooling for was for the J54, the venerable high-hood flat-fender jeep, but instead of a gas engine, it had a diesel engine. The only major modification he had made was to convert the right-hand drive back to left-hand drive. They were just now producing the first jeeps, which Tim had decided to rename back to Willys.

Thinking about it as he looked over the landscape, Tim realized they were stealing a lot of trademarked names and ideas from Earth, but he didn't care. *Not like their laws matter here.*

It had been a rather contentious two years for Parallel, Inc., especially the last year when the scope of the project became fully known on Earth. The US government wasn't all that thrilled when they discovered Tim had several gates operating throughout the West and was moving a vast amount of material from Earth to Hayek. They tried to shut him down, stating that he was involved in international trade without going through customs, but Poe had worked his magic and gotten the government to realize that just about all trade was export trade to Hayek, so there was no need for most customs, and the only stuff flowing back to Earth was gold, which the IRS was already getting a cut of as part of Parallel's tax payments, and the taxes from all the shareholders. The gold was now being smelted on Hayek.

As a precaution, Tim had moved all gates over to Hayek, operating in Tahoma, Milton, Multnomah in the Willamette Valley, Tongva in the Los Angeles basin, and Kalihi Kai, near Honolulu. The process of constructing all those gates, most of which were big enough to drive semi-trucks through, took months, but it was finally done. The gates were still tied to warehouses on Earth but were now beyond the physical reach of the US government. The only inhabited place without a gate was the Central Valley mining district, as the goldfields were now called.

Gravel roads now extended from Tahoma through the valleys of the Duwamish and Puyallup, across Snoqualmie Pass to Milton, and down to the Walla Walla area. There were also gravel roads from the oil fields in the Los Angeles Basin to the small port on the Pacific Ocean near Tongva, where the first oil refinery was located. The first tanker load of Hayek-produced POLs had made its maiden voyage just two months ago, mostly diesel fuel, as that was what most of the construction and transport machinery used.

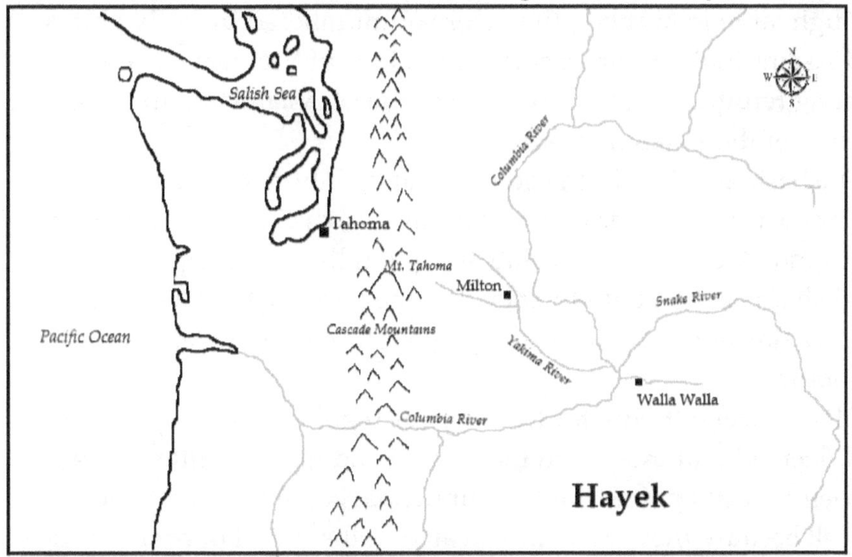

The first set of train tracks was already approaching Snoqualmie Pass at about two miles a day, coming from both Tahoma and Milton. Crews were already working in the pass to ensure that when the lines reached it, the ground would be prepared. With any luck, the train would be running before the snow fell.

Rather than go with Harrison's suggestion of one mag-lev line and two regular rail lines, a decision was made to operate a double mag-lev line to serve both passengers and cargo. The double line would have to wait, though, likely for several more years. The emphasis was on getting at least one line running as soon as possible connecting the far-flung settlements. It would likely be at least a year or more before they made it to southern California even with all the indentured servants they had recruited, and there were a lot of those. Turning his head slightly, Tim could see the tracks that were making their way south from Tahoma toward Multnomah, then eventually Tongva.

The indentured servant program had worked out incredibly well. Many of the indentured servants, or *indents* as they were called, were from poor families who had heard of the opportunities of Hayek and wanted to escape Earth. Lots of migrants were from poor black or Hispanic areas in the US that were being overrun with drugs, or illegal immigrants from south of the US border. Though large in number, they were outnumbered by both whites and Asians looking for opportunities. Lots of Vietnamese, Lao, and Hmong refugees from the war in Southeast Asia made up a good portion of the Asian migrants.

The basic cost had been settled on at twenty-five thousand dollars per person. For families, though, each child was only five thousand. All those who didn't speak English were required to take English classes to attain fluency. For the parents, they worked six hours a day and were in class for two. The children were in class for six hours.

Classes weren't only for language or regular school topics; Tim had decreed that they learn the culture and financial literacy as part of their education. He didn't want people being in poverty on Hayek because they were uneducated in the world of basic finance. His goal was for those who wanted a home to be able to get one, once they paid off their indentured servitude. At ten thousand dollars per year, most would pay it off in a matter of two to three years.

Indents weren't the only ones to arrive. Not by any stretch of the imagination. With worldwide advertising, Hayek was able to attract hundreds of thousands of middle-class and well-to-do immigrants. Many even brought their businesses with them, or as much of their physical components as was possible.

Everyone who migrated to Hayek was required to sign the statement of personal responsibility, indicating that not only was he or she responsible for him or herself, but that they would respect others and the private property of others. The first two were to instill the cultural traits that Harrison had brought up, but the third was mostly mercenary on Parallel's part, as all of the planet was effectively owned by the company, to be sold, leased, or doled out as seen fit by the company's board, which was mainly one each Tim Bowman, Ph.D.

While a lot had been done, there was more to do. Unfortunately, there were still several years to go before the rubber and coffee plantations would be up and running. For construction projects, one could throw men and material at them to make them happen fast. Nothing could be done to speed up the growth of plants, though. It would be at least another five to seven years before they would even get their first rubber harvest. Fortunately, the coffee would be ready sooner, only another two or so years to go.

If only the United States would allow them to, that is.

"Penny for your thoughts," Veronica asked. She was sitting in the passenger seat of the Willys.

Tim turned to her, hands still grasping the steering wheel. "Thinking of what we've accomplished, and what needs doing."

"That's a mighty big thinking," Veronica said with a grin.

"What's a big thinking, Aunt Veronica?" piped up a small voice from the rear of the jeep inquisitively.

Turning back to the barely teenaged girl seated between two rather large Homotherium in the back seat, Veronica answered, "It means somebody is thinking up some big ideas, thoughts, and concepts."

"Oh," Janice said.

"Uncle Tim's been doing a lot of big concept thinking about what we need to do to make Hayek independent of Earth."

"What's it gonna take?" Janice asked.

Tim turned and answered her with a grin. "Oh, just about a million things, and about two million more people."

"That's a lot of people," Janice said, scratching Tia's ear. The big cat purred, reminding Tim of nothing more than an oversized tabby. Tia wasn't just an overgrown tabby, though. She and Timmy were still considered cubs, but now they were about three-quarters their potential adult size, weighing in at over two hundred pounds, or about ninety kilos each. Tim was a bit worried that the big cats would overwhelm the carrying capacity of the little four-wheel-drive vehicle, so he had hooked up a small trailer to the back of it. The trailer, made by another plant owned by Parallel, not only served to carry the big cats, who considered themselves Janice's siblings, but also new things from Tahoma to their new home in Milton. This trailer was modified to provide an enclosed area for the cubs, in an effort to ensure they didn't jump out of the moving vehicle.

"Yes, it is," Tim said. "Fortunately, there're a lot of people who want to move over, so I'm not too worried about that, but we want the right people, those who are good and do the right thing, even when nobody's looking."

Starting the jeep's engine, he said, "Well, enough gawking. Time to test this baby out and get home. Janice, could you put the cubs in the trailer?"

The drive back to Milton took considerably longer than a similar drive from Tacoma to Selah would have taken, considering the only road was rough gravel, and speeds were pretty much limited to between thirty and forty miles per hour. Any faster, and the trailer would start sliding all over the place. Tim didn't want the cubs hurt or scared. They also had to watch out for wildlife. It wasn't just deer or elk they had to worry about running into. On several prior trips, Tim had had to stop and wait for herds of mastodons and saiga elk to cross the road. He also saw numerous predators, which is why they still traveled armed.

It was early afternoon when they pulled into Milton. The town had also changed. No longer was it just gravel roads laid out in a wilderness. Now it was populated with commercial and residential buildings, some as tall as four stories. Tim expected to see more of the taller buildings, which mixed residential with retail and commercial, rising in the near future. The elevated rail was also progressing. Just like in Vancouver, the Milton rail system was called the skytrain. Fifteen meter tall towers were popping up a hundred meters apart with metal rails running between them, suspended by a metal latticework. The trains, once installed, would be suspended below the rails, about seven and a half meters above the ground, well out of the way of any surface transportation.

Tim was amazed at how much they had accomplished in two short years. *Imagine how much we'll get done in another four or five*, he thought.

Recognizing that safety from the megafauna and predators lay in numbers, the Bowmans eschewed living in a ranchette like their home on Earth. Instead, they lived in a small bungalow near downtown Milton. The horses were now being kept in a stable on the edge of town—one that had extensive electrically-charged wires strung around it to deter any hungry critters from eating the horses.

While the streets were now paved, the alleys behind the houses weren't. More dust was added to the Willys' and the trailer's occupants as Tim guided the small jeep down the narrow alleyway. He had a small garage behind the house where he stored the vehicles.

After parking, he told Janice to wash the cubs. "Don't need them dragging in all sorts of dirt into the house. Aunt Veronica would *not* be happy."

"At least they're housebroken," Veronica said, as Janice released the two cubs, who were more than happy to be out of their dusty confines.

Tim undid the straps holding the wire cage to the trailer and lifted the cage out, revealing a number of metal boxes with handles buried in the bottom of the trailer. The boxes, also made by Parallel, were designed to fit in the trailer to keep things dry and secure while being transported. The boxes contained spare parts for the jeep, along with some personal items that were easier to get in Tahoma than Milton.

"You going in to the office?" Veronica asked as they made their way to the back door of the bungalow, passing a garden containing a variety of greens and vegetables.

"Naw, it can wait. I'd rather relax with a cold beer or two than deal with whatever the crisis of the day is."

The cold beers turned out to be Hayek-brewed porters from The Giant Sloth Brewery, a small brewery set on a hop farm in the Duwamish Valley. Hops grew well in the marine West Coast climate of the Salish lowlands. The area around Walla Walla, in the drier Yakama Canton climate, was well known for growing wheat, not just sweet onions, but it wasn't as suited for hops. Of course, barley was one of the first crops put in when a number of young farmers moved to Hayek. The plan was to move barley production eastward, in what was eastern Washington on Earth. It seemed that a lot of the back-to-nature crowd, leftover hippies from the sixties and wannabe hippies from the late seventies and early eighties, really grokked on the idea of moving to a more natural environment, one where they could raise crops using their own environmentally sound practices, and not having to rely on the big fertilizer, herbicide, and pesticide producers. It was interesting to note that not many of them got into meat farming, focusing on grain and truck farming.

Getting people to move to Hayek turned out to be a lot easier than Tim had thought it would be, he reflected, as he and Veronica sipped the cold brews on their front porch, watching pedestrians pass by. It was keeping them safe and fed that had taxed the burgeoning community's logistics. Everyone needed a rifle for protection, communities and agriculture had to be protected, and people needed to eat. Many a ramshackle shed had gone up the first several months. It wasn't until the gravel road connected Tahoma to Milton that real housing started to develop, with lumber from the Salish lowland being used for home construction, and locally made bricks and imported steel being used for the larger commercial buildings.

The town of Walla Walla presented a special problem, being located at the confluence of the Walla Walla and Columbia Rivers, a point about forty kilometers west of Earth's Walla Walla, and on the wrong side of the Columbia. A bridge wasn't in the works any time soon, so a lot of trade between Walla Walla and the other settlements was via the navigable waterways of the Columbia and Yakima Rivers, although a road did extend from Milton to a point on the Columbia across from Walla Walla. It used basically the same route that the team had used on their first expedition to the Powder River, with the exception that instead of crossing Horse Heaven Hills, the route ran the length of the Yakima Valley. A couple of large ferries, big enough to hold a couple of laden trucks, operated across the Columbia between the two shores, keeping the communities connected. Plans were to construct some bridges, particularly for the trains, but those wouldn't be happening for at least a couple of years.

After some time sitting and sipping beers, Tim and Veronica were joined by Janice and the cubs, all three of whom wanted to know when supper would be served. It was still fairly early, but considering they had been up before dawn, Veronica figured an early meal and early to bed was probably best for all. As she and Janice went inside to fix supper, Tim sat on the porch, still sipping on his beer, scratching Tia's ear, and people watching. Many who passed would wave to him. They knew who he was, but he would be hard put to put any names to faces.

30

"Okay, we've got a lot to cover in not a lot of time," Tim told the assembled group, which consisted of all stakeholders in Parallel, Inc. The meeting was taking place in the conference room of the company's new three-story building in downtown Milton. The plate-glass window overlooked the town square. All were seated around a polished wood table, created from a single giant slab of big leaf maple, the yellow wood glowing with fine grain lines. Tim sat at one end of the table, with Dave, Don, and Jack on one side, and Poe and Shimazu on the other. The swivel chairs they sat in were made from local flora and fauna—mostly mastodon skins and big leaf maples.

"Seems like we've got more issues with the US government. Bob?"

Poe started the discussion. "Earth's still being a pain in the ass on the gate issue, most importantly, the US government. Several issues we're working with on them.

"First, even though we've got a terminal rented at the Port of Tacoma and everything that comes across the land-water interface goes directly through the gate, US Customs and the INS are complaining about it, saying we're bringing stuff onto US soil without declaring anything."

"Well, technically, aren't we?" Don asked.

Poe nodded. "Technically. But we had already worked out an agreement with the government to allow us to trans-ship without going through customs—basically unload from ship onto the dock and then straight through the gate to Hayek. Somehow, they got wind that we managed to bring our mini-nuke plants in from Japan and, for some reason, aren't happy with us. Now they're trying to stop us from importing more nuke plants and fuel, mainly because they're afraid somebody's going to hijack a shipment and let a dirty bomb loose in an American city."

"Aren't we all?" Tim asked, almost rhetorically. Turning to Poe, he asked, "Have you told them that we're worried about the same thing?"

Poe shook his head with an evil lawyer grin, the kind that's just compressed lips presenting a facade of humor. "I've refused to acknowledge that there were any nuclear shipments at all. They can wonder all they want, and they might have heard we have them, but unless they can actually prove it, there's nothing they can do."

"They didn't detect anything?" Don asked. "I thought they had some sort of nuclear detection equipment around Seattle."

Poe shrugged. "Apparently not.

"Second point," he continued. "The whole world is leaning on us to tell them how the gate works. Just about every government and big business wants the plans, claiming that it's in 'the public's interest'. Of course, this is being led by the US, which is applying even more pressure to get the secret from us. Again, we're being threatened with being shut down by the US government if we don't play nice."

"They aren't getting the gate's secret," Tim said rather hotly, slapping his palm down on the polished table.

"Then you better never go back to Earth," Poe replied. "Otherwise, they'll snatch you up so fast it'll make your head spin."

"Yeah, don't I know that already," Tim said. "Veronica hates the fact that we can never go back to Earth, but them's the facts."

Getting back to the original topic, Tim asked, "How would they shut us down?"

"Legally, they would likely get a cease and desist operations court order, which we would have to comply with. That's best case scenario. Worst case scenario, they find some reason to get a warrant to seize the gate."

Tim chuckled. "Good luck with that."

At Poe's confused look, Tim said, "We've got every gate rigged to destruct if anyone tries to take control of them."

Now Poe's look went from confused to horror. "You don't have explosives on them, do you?"

"Nope. But we do have them rigged with thermite."

"What's thermite?"

"A simple pyrotechnic composition of metal powders and oxides," Don explained. "Used a lot for high temp welding, like rail lines. Also used by the military in thermite grenades to destroy equipment, like artillery cannons, when they have to."

"Isn't that illegal?"

Don shrugged. "Maybe, but so what? It's not a weapon, nor designed as one, so I highly doubt it. Either way, if the feds try to take over the gates, all they'll be getting will be slagged metal."

"Let's keep a sharp eye on this," Tim said. "Last thing we need is to be shut down before we reach critical mass. And besides, I really don't want us having to cut the cords to Earth until we're at a point where we're self-sufficient."

Turning to Don, he said, "Find a couple of more places on Earth, maybe in Seattle or Portland or LA where we can rent warehouse space. Make sure you use a dummy corporation, so our name isn't tied to it. I'll build some more gates and we can open them up on this end. At least we'll have some way of getting stuff over here if the government makes a move on us."

Don nodded, jotting down a note on a yellow legal pad. It seemed all of them had taken up Poe's habit of taking notes on yellow legal pads. It's not something any of them would have considered a couple of years ago.

Tim looked at Poe. "Anything else?"

"Yeah," Poe continued. "Yet again, another issue with the US. This time from the INS."

Tim rolled his eyes, as did just about everyone else in the room. "What's the Immigration and Naturalization Service got to do with us? Not like we're moving people from Hayek to the US."

"They're not issuing visas to everyone who wants to migrate."

"Huh?"

"They're not issuing visas to everyone who wants to migrate," Poe repeated. "Lots of people want to migrate from all over the world. Right now, our only gates are in the US, so most people have to get a visa to visit the US. And even if a person gets a visa, Customs can refuse them entry. We're also seeing a lot of that. It's a messed up situation."

"What are our options?"

"It'd be great if we could open gates in those other countries, but that ain't happening for a while," Poe answered with a shrug. The thought of attempting to cross thousands of miles of wilderness to allow migration from an Earth country to an unsupportable Hayek wilderness wasn't an option. It might be in a few years, but not at the present time.

"Other than that, continue to negotiate with them."

"Smuggling?" Don brought up.

"You mean like the nuke plants?" Dave asked, shaking his head. "Too difficult. You'd have to have people in containers and smuggle them through. Too risky." Looking about the table, Dave continued, "I don't know about the rest of you, but I don't want accidental deaths on my hands. Let's find another way, one that works for all."

"What if we increase the gate fee to thirty or forty thousand and give the US government a portion of it as a fee?" Shimazu asked. "I'm sure those who really want to come will pay it."

"Yeah, they likely would, or we would for indents," Don said, "but then we're getting into the whole corruption and payoff world that we're trying to escape."

Tim nodded, turning his gaze outside the window. The Cascades were already dusted with a light frosting of snow, clearly visible from the conference room.

"Yeah, I'm not into letting those greedy bastards get even more," he said. Almost rhetorically, he asked, "When is government greed enough."

"Never," Shimazu said.

Tim thought about it for a couple of more seconds, then turned to Poe. "Okay, let's try Jeff's idea, but make damned sure that anyone migrating understands that it's the US government wanting their hard-earned dollars just to transit the country, and that it's beyond our control."

"Sorta like when the county raises property taxes," Shimazu said. "Landlord's gotta raise rent to cover it. If the renter doesn't know why, they usually blame the landlord. Let the renters know why."

Poe jotted a note down. "You want I should start small, maybe a hundred a head?"

"Yeah, do that," Tim answered. "Make them make the first big offer, then negotiate down. It's not as if they actually have to do anything to make the money." Tim turned to look out the window again, and in a more quiet voice, but one that everyone heard, muttered, "Greedy bastards. Always wanting something for nothing."

Turning back to the group and visibly collecting himself, he asked Poe, "Anything else?"

Poe grinned. "Yeah, and this one is kinda funny. They're claiming that people are taking advantage of the situation by taking out loans then migrating to Hayek, never paying."

"That sounds like their problem, not ours," Tim said.

"Yeah, but enough people do that, then they might try to shut us down, saying we represent a national risk to the economy."

"What, one or two million people? That's what, not even one percent of the US population. How many are doing that? I bet it's such a small percentage, it's probably about on par with the number of people who default or declare bankruptcy."

"Can't people just declare bankruptcy before moving over and keep their money and stuff?" Jack asked.

"Doesn't work that way," Poe said, turning to Jack. "I'll be glad to explain it after the meeting, but not right now."

Jack nodded, understanding that time was short.

"Thoughts?" Tim asked.

"Ignore the feds?" Don asked. He was always a bit more of a risk-taker than the others.

"Not a good idea," Dave said.

Tim agreed with Dave, as did the others. "That ain't gonna work, at least for a couple of years."

"I say we just put it out there that we won't accept migrants looking to skip debt," Poe suggested.

"That might deter people from moving." Dave, like the others, didn't want to prevent people from coming to Hayek, even if it meant them skipping out on debt. The planet was capital-poor in people.

"I didn't say we wouldn't let them in," Poe continued with another of his patented grins, "I'm just saying we put the word out. Let the feds figure out what to do as we play along."

Tim thought for a second, then said, "Fine. Let's play their silly games. Put it out, in writing and through press releases, that Hayek does not condone migration to escape debt. Put a big sign at every gate announcing this. We'll see where that gets us. I'm betting people will ignore it."

"You're likely right, but at least it'll get the feds off our case on this one."

"Got any more surprises for us?" Tim asked, more in dark humor than anything else.

"Not me," Poe said, looking around.

Shimazu tapped his pen on the table, causing all to turn to him. The pen was a refillable fountain pen, green with a gold band circling it. With limited resources on Hayek, most of the things being manufactured were long-lasting and durable, not disposable. Tim hoped to keep it that way. He hated seeing America become a disposable society and didn't want to see that type of wasteful consumerism on his new home.

"Financially, we're fine," he started. "As a matter of fact, more than fine. We've had roughly a million people migrate to Hayek, with only about ten percent coming as indents. Lots of families, but also lots of single people, mostly men. We're likely gonna need an infusion of women soon," that last said with a chuckle.

"So far, we've brought in about eight and a half billion dollars, not counting the money brought in by selling gold on Earth."

"Did you say billion with a B?" Don asked. Tim already knew the numbers, but this was the first it was being told to the group.

Shimazu nodded. "Yep, and more on the way. We've been able to pay cash for the nuke plants, and should be able to complete the rail construction without having to float any bonds or take out any loans from Earth or here."

"Better yet, we won't have to sell any shares," Tim interjected.

"There's that," Shimazu agreed. "But, we do have one minor problem. The US government is after us for 'unpaid' taxes, saying our filings are fabricated."

"Are they?" Jack asked with a touch of suspicion. A couple of years on Hayek had changed him. He was now a young man, barely seventeen, but very much a self-assured one. He was also the chief pilot for Air Hayek, which now consisted of a veritable fleet of DHC-4 Caribous, along with some C123 Providers and C130 Hercules. Unlike some teenagers, who would be cowed to be among older, wiser, and more educated men than themselves, Jack knew that his experiences and the responsibilities he had undertaken over the past year had made him into a more mature individual. Jack not only felt he was their equal, but the men reciprocated, viewing him the same way.

Shimazu shook his head. "Not until we all give up our US citizenship am I willing to doctor any tax forms. Just not worth it. Besides, thanks to the new tax changes Reagan gave us back in '81, we're only paying fifty percent of *our* money to the government. The company rate is still at forty-six percent of its profits. The question to ask now, though, is whether or not we want to cut our corporate ties to Earth, especially with more than eight billion dollars in revenue?"

"Can we do that?" Tim asked.

Shimazu nodded. "No reason we can't. Collect all money on Hayek, none on Earth. Toward that end, I'd recommend taking all payments in gold and silver. As shareholders, you have to pay taxes on whatever dividends you get, but those are all long-term capital gains, which are taxed at twenty percent, a huge difference between what you'd pay if you were taking it in salary. If you like, we can reduce salaries and dividends for several years, so you don't have to pay much in taxes. Better yet, take only salaries. Nothing says we have to pay dividends."

"That's an idea," Tim said. "Go back to that gold thing, are you suggesting we move to a gold-based economic system?

Shimazu nodded. "Yeah. I don't see why not."

"How do we value it, then?" Tim asked. "Right now, we're looking at dollars per troy ounce, but that's always changing. I mean, when we started up, gold was running, what, three seventy-five a troy ounce. What's it at now? Three fifty? Earlier in the year, it was over four hundred."

"We could start by valuing it at whatever we say it is, for us. One troy ounce is equivalent to, let's say, three hundred seventy dollars, and then take into account inflation every year. It won't matter here on Hayek, but it will mean more on Earth."

"Come again?" Dave said, with a come-along gesture.

"Simple," Shimazu said. "For us, the value of an ounce of gold is worth the value of an ounce of gold. It doesn't change. But, on Earth, the value increases as the price of gold increases in relation to the dollar. That means whatever we purchase from Earth will likely cost us less."

"That makes sense," Dave said. "Are you thinking of silver for the lesser coinage?"

"Why not?" Shimazu responded. "It's been used that way for centuries. Let's not invent the wheel all over again."

"What kind of ratio would it be?" This from Don.

"I was doing a bit of research the other day," Shimazu said, "and, it's been all over the board. When the US was founded, it was fifteen to one. But when silver was found in quantity throughout the West, the ratios bounced all over the place, as high as ninety-eight to one under FDR." Shimazu was referring to Franklin D. Roosevelt, who manipulated gold prices during his presidency. "On average, it's been hovering around forty-seven to one for most of the century. So, we could either set it for forty-seven to one, or we could round up or down to an even number to make it easier for people to calculate."

"So, either forty or fifty to one?" Tim asked.

"Yeah, that's what I'd recommend," Shimazu responded.

Tim thought about. "Okay, let's go with forty to one. Easy to do the calculations, and since the Bank of Hayek and Parallel Credit Union are the biggest games in town, and they set the monetary policies for the rest of the planet, for all intents and purposes, all the other banks and credit unions will fall in line."

Don chuckled. "Doesn't hurt that the Bank of Hayek and the Parallel Credit Union are owned by Parallel, Incorporated."

"No, no it doesn't," Tim agreed, with a smile. "Okay, then. Let's do it."

"Gotta love decisive leadership," Shimazu said with a grin.

Changing topic, Tim turned to Don and asked, "How's the militia program coming along?"

"Pretty good. Everyone coming through the gate is being issued basic equipment, so they've got at least the minimal necessary. The R-1's fully developed and we've started issuing them to the militia." The R-1 was a locally developed rifle similar to the M14, but even more similar to the Ruger Mini-14. It was not only chambered differently, but also made with three butt-stock sizes, designed to closer fit the various heights of people. The cartridge was a shortened .270, slightly smaller than the 7.62 NATO used in the M14 and slightly larger than the 5.56 NATO used in the Mini-14. It was more suitable for the longer distances of the dry West, despite being shot out of an eighteen-inch barrel. The official caliber was 6.8mm x 48mm.

"What are you doing with the rifles you're replacing them with?"

"Mostly, putting them in storage, just in case. Anyone wants to keep theirs, we sell it to them for a price. This way, they've got an issue rifle that'll take the ammo we use, and they get to keep their original piece."

"Good." Tim looked around the table. "Anything else that might have some bearing on our operations or growth?"

Don raised a hand.

"Yeah?"

"Y'know, I've been thinking about our operations on Hayek, and how we should maybe be doing things slightly different."

"How so?"

"Well, when you think of it, we just kinda opened the gate and sashayed in, not even really looking all that hard to make sure there weren't any other sentient species here. Maybe we should really look, and I mean look, like with eyes in the sky and boots on the ground look."

Tim rubbed his chin between thumb and forefinger as he thought about it.

"Yeah, but we still haven't found anything," Dave said before Tim could say anything.

"But have we really looked?" Don said. "Last time I checked, we haven't even put boots on the ground on the East Coast yet. I should know, as I'm still running Air Hayek."

Putting his hands back down on the table, Tim said, "Don's got a point. We only think nobody's here, based mainly on limited observations and a lack of radio and television activity. What do you have in mind?"

"We need to have a systematic search over most of Hayek. Either people are here, or they're not."

"Wouldn't matter if they were," Dave said. "Not like we're leaving or anything."

"Valid points from both of you," Tim said. "We're not leaving, but what if there're Neanderthals or Homo Erectus living in Europe? Do we want to cause an inadvertent genocide like what happened when the Europeans landed in the New World? I don't." Leaning back in his chair, Tim asked Don, "So, what are you proposing?"

"We need to set up an organization whose main goal is exploring planets. Think about it: we're already talking about opening up other planets to let people migrate. Do we want to unleash them on unsuspecting human populations?"

"What would it take?" Shimazu asked, thinking about the fiscal costs.

Don nodded to Jack who reached under the table and pulled up a banker's box filled with three-ring binders. As he handed them around, Don said, "This here's a plan Jack and I came up with. We need airplanes for aerial surveys, we need to put in small runways, and we likely need some way of conducting ground surveys, either on foot or using jeeps. That all requires a logistics team to handle constructing bases and airfields, fuel, food, and parts.

"It's all laid out in those binders."

By now, everyone had a binder and had flipped them open.

"That's far fewer planes than I thought," Tim said as he read. "Two Boos, two Providers, and a CL215 to start? Why the CL215, and what's this 'high-altitude survey plane'?"

"The 215 is a seaplane, so it can land on water," Jack answered. "The teams might need to do that, like around the Caribbean. As for the high-altitude survey plane, we're thinking we need something that goes high and far, like the U2 or the RB57 Canberra. Only thing is, we need it to be comfortable enough for a crew of four, two pilots and two aerial photographers. That way they can take turns working and resting on long missions."

"How long a mission are we talking about?"

"If we can build it right, maybe a couple of days."

That caused a stir around the table.

"But, that's a ways off," Jack continued. "For now, we just need planes that can get up high enough to be mistaken for a bird. Both the Boo and the Provider can do that, but the crews would need to be on oxygen, most likely."

Looking through the binder, Shimazu asked what the expected costs would be.

"Not gonna lie," Don said. "Figure on millions per planet just in operating costs. Capital costs are gonna be millions more, but most of that'll be long-term capital investment, planes, a base here on Hayek, more jeeps, construction equipment, fueling equipment, it's all there. Imagine it like the California trip, but more."

"California on steroids, ja?" Dave joked, using his best Arnold Schwarzenegger accent.

Don grinned. "Yeah, pretty much."

Tim set his binder down on the table, got up, and walked to the room's door. Opening it, he called out, "Alice, could you bring coffees in for everyone, and let's see about getting some lunch ordered. Looks like we'll be here a while."

An hour later, the binder had been read by all, discussed, and plans made. Don was going to be put in charge of a new organization under Parallel, the Corps of Discovery, a name provided by Jack. The teen freely admitted that he stole the name from the Lewis and Clark expedition, whom he and his father admired greatly, even saying that they'd be doing a reverse Lewis and Clark expedition, looking eastward first.

"If we're gonna practice what we preach, let's get this thing going. How soon before you can begin?" Tim asked Don.

"Give me a week to scrounge up enough people and equipment, and we can start. Equipment-wise, we only need a couple of planes, some runway construction equipment, fuel bladders, and photographic equipment. Maybe a couple of jeeps. Immediate personnel needs are pilots, photographers, a dark-room technician, mechanics, some Seabees, and somebody that can handle logistics. I could probably get by with less than forty for a bare-bones operation.

"Long term, maybe a year to be fully operational. With the land in the Naches Valley, we should be able to develop a base and use the Yakima airstrip as the main airfield, although I'd rather develop a dedicated strip, one that won't impact other operations. One that's closer to the valley."

"Pick out the land you need and develop it," Tim said. "I'll notify the Land Office to set aside whatever land you need. You can have the Yakima airstrip. Have Lee Orange and Lenny Gross help you with some of the planning. I'm sure weapons will be involved in there somewhere. And Lenny's 'Nam experience should be helpful for something."

"Roger that," Don said.

31

For the next several months, things ran rather smoothly. More migrants made their way to Hayek, mostly Americans with a sprinkling of refugees from the Vietnam War, many of whom were Hmong from Laos. The Americans migrating were a mix of Asian, mostly Japanese and Filipino, whites, and blacks, which surprised Tim. He had expected more Native Americans might want to live on the untamed planet. He later found out that several tribes had approached Poe about possibly opening another planet, one which the tribes could migrate to. Not that they were anti-white; they just wanted to be free of the burden and culture imposed on them, and they didn't want to be on a planet where that could happen again. Tim personally felt that it didn't matter where they went, somebody would try to take over, but it was their money, so he was trying his best to determine how to make it happen.

More people were trained in basic gate operations, all of whom agreed to stay on Hayek and were sworn never to tell anyone how the gate operated, not that they knew the physics behind it. Tim sort of did, but sometimes even he was baffled by it. He knew how to open and calibrate them, but was still trying to formulate a good hypothesis for the science behind it all.

Poe spent considerable time working to convince the US government that allowing foreigners access to US soil to migrate to Hayek was a good thing. Shimazu's suggestion about upping the migration fee and paying off the government helped on that front, at the cost of only five hundred dollars per person. Indents were required to pay the fee. Parallel wasn't covering that portion of their expenses. The Hayekers, as the founders were now calling themselves, expected to see greater migration due to this agreement.

The US government was also slightly mollified when Parallel announced its effort to prevent people from bailing on debt. No other action was taken by Parallel, but just getting the word out seemed to have slowed the number of people taking out home loans then ditching those houses and using the loan proceeds for residency on Hayek.

One area that appeared to bother the feds a great deal, though, was when Parallel, Inc. asserted its foreign corporation status, informing the IRS that it was no longer a US corporation on US soil and would not be paying taxes on revenues generated outside the US. As all payments by migrants were being made on Hayek, either directly to Parallel once they crossed over, or from Parallel to Hayek-based banks for indents, that was completely true. None of the shareholders resigned their positions, but they did reduce their salaries to those commensurate with the same salaries of similar positions of US companies, which meant reduced earnings for all. They also voted to defer share dividends, thereby avoiding capital gains taxes. While the IRS wasn't happy about any of this, there was nothing they could do, as it was completely legal.

The flow of gold from Hayek to Earth also stopped, thereby reducing the revenue the IRS and US Customs could obtain. Most gold was now smelted on Hayek and minted into bullion, either ingots or coin, most of which was held in the Bank of Hayek or the Parallel Credit Union. Several new banks had sprung up after Parallel had granted mining rights to a couple of companies who were mining gold at Washington's Blewitt pass and the old diggings on the Powder River. Those banks were also minting their own coins. The only common denominator amongst the various mints was the purity and weight. All gold coins had to be .9999 purity and list their weight in troy ounces, or portions of it, the smallest being one-tenth of an ounce, about the size of a US dime. The Bank of Hayek coins usually had an animal on them, progressing in size from the smallest having a Smilodon to the largest having a mammoth. The latter was known as a Manny.

On the Hayek Militia front, the militia's rifle was a huge success, especially among those military veterans who had fought with the M-16 in Vietnam. While slightly heavier, they liked the sturdiness of it along with the extra punch of the bigger round and the fact that it wasn't so finicky that it would jam up if it got slightly dirty.

Also in the works were knock-offs of the M-2 machine gun and Barrett M-82, both of which fired the .50 BMG round, a bullet a half an inch wide and longer than a hand was wide. Both were good against soft and hard targets. Another product already in the pipeline was a grenade launcher, based on the South African Milkor Stopper, which could fire a forty-millimeter grenade almost four hundred meters.

A new addition to the militia's armory was the introduction of the RPG-7, a Soviet-designed recoilless rifle that fired a high explosive anti-tank rocket-boosted projectile. Tim had always thought RPG stood for Rocket Propelled Grenade, so when he was informed that it was the Russian acronym for *Ruchnoy Protivotankovyy Granatomet*, which translated into "hand-held anti-tank grenade launcher," he was a bit chagrined. While the militia didn't have any armored threats on Hayek, the fear was always that the US or another government would attempt to invade. The RPG was already proven to be able to destroy most of Earth's armored vehicles, but it wasn't considered good enough to destroy an M-1 main battle tank, the new workhorse of the US Army. Nobody wanted to fight the US, but it was always in the back of everyone's minds, especially when the government started making threatening demands.

Toward that end, Tim had spent several weeks constructing a couple of more gates on Hayek's side of Tacoma, along with additional gates around Selah and Yakima. These gates were built adjacent to warehouses rented in dummy corporation names, so the feds were hopefully unaware of their existence. Most of the goods moving across these stealth warehouse/gates were those that Hayek couldn't manufacture on its own yet, but still needed. One of these new things was computers. Tim and Dave both saw the immediate benefits of this new technology but didn't quite know how to get a computer industry up and running on Hayek. Until they could, they were relegated to importing IBM PCs and Macintosh computers.

At Japan's request, hidden from the US and the rest of the world, Tim even opened a gate near Hiroshima. The Victory ships built on Hayek were now involved in the nuclear fuel and factory trade directly with Japan, obviating the need to smuggle the fuel and equipment through the US. Ships were now sailing between Nippon, Hawaii, and Tahoma on Hayek.

Japan was hoping to see more raw material come in from Hayek, including fuel oil, as the Hayek oil industry developed, and wood from the vast forests on the islands of the Nippon archipelago, forests that had been decimated on Earth's Japanese islands. Plans were in place to develop storage tanks and pipelines on Hayek to feed oil through the gates from Nippon to Japan.

Tim had just returned from Nippon after ensuring gate operations were functioning fine and was sitting in his bungalow's small living room, watching two nearly full-sized Homotheriums play 'beat each other to death.' The only furniture in the living room were some chairs and end tables, one of which held a folded over newspaper, the *Hayek Globe*. The center of the room was left open to allow the rambunctious almost-adult cubs to be able to engage in play activity without tearing the house apart. Tim wondered how long that would last, as he sipped on his coffee, watching the sun slowly rise in the east. Veronica and Janice were in the kitchen making breakfast while Timmy tried to gnaw Tia's ear off. She wasn't having any of it.

As he watched the two cats tussle about, he realized he was glad to be home, even if it was a smaller two-story bungalow in a town lot, rather than his old rambler on several acres. It had been an amazing adventure to finally leave the west coast of Ti'icham, as they were now calling North America, but he was glad to be home.

Something about the North Pacific with big storms and a small Victory ship that seemed to bob up and down on what Tim considered were monstrous waves, but Luther said were pond ripples, just didn't fit for him. That, and the fact that he discovered he got seasick once they passed through the Salish Strait out into the Pacific, and stayed that way until they entered Hiroshima Bay. Harrison referred to the bay as a ria, a drowned river valley that developed during past glaciations but was now flooded due to the end of the glaciation and the rise of sea levels. Like Luther, he didn't get seasick. Just Tim.

If it hadn't been for the fact that Tim spoke Japanese, a skill acquired by listening to his mother speak in her native language from birth, he likely wouldn't have made the trip. But he did.

One of the things that made this possible was the Corps of Discovery had already surveyed the Japanese archipelago and found no sign of human habitation. Don had instructed Jack to complete a survey of North America first, then South America, and then head across the Pacific to survey the islands and archipelagos that stretched around the ocean's western edge. Asia and Oceania were currently being surveyed, with Africa and Europe next. Tim was amazed at the amount of time and energy it took to complete a survey and now understood why Jack wanted a plane that could remain aloft and travel further than anything they currently had in inventory.

Due to the short range of all the available planes, forward airstrips had to be developed, which required air-dropping teams and construction equipment, constructing the strips, then bringing in fuel bladders and spare parts. Fortunately, they didn't require Marston mats, so the initial cost was relatively low, usually only in the thousands of dollars. Most of the forward airstrips were being constructed on coastlines to make resupply by ship easier and less costly.

Getting to Europe was going to be interesting, as interesting as getting to Nippon was. None of the planes on Hayek were able to make a direct flight from Tahoma to Nippon, so they had had to go the northern route, constructing airstrips along the west coast and across the Aleutian islands, something that couldn't be safely done in the winter. As with the island-hopping across the Pacific, the Corps was going to be island-hopping across the Atlantic, using Greenland, Iceland, and Ireland as stopping points. They had already developed multiple airstrips across Ti'icham during the initial aerial survey, so at least that didn't need to be redone.

Currently, ships were able to supply the Pacific routes, and once a foothold in Europe was made, the plan was to take a trio of ships there: a Victory ship, a tanker, and an LCS-1. The Victory ship and tanker would rotate between Tahoma and whatever main port was designated on the east coast and Europe, a journey that necessitated going around the southern tip of South America, the treacherous waters of the Cape Horn.

This was all on Tim's mind when Tia roll-crashed into him, causing him to spill some of the Earth-imported coffee into his lap. That was the end of the Homotherium mosh-pit. Tim's bellow caused the two cats to stop their assaults upon each other, lower their ears, and try to slump down into the floor in their attempt at a disappearing act.

Tim got up, still glaring at the Homotheriums, and made his way into the kitchen to get another cup of coffee.

Taking the Willys after breakfast, Tim drove down the river toward the new Corps of Discovery base. While he drove alone, he didn't go unarmed. Despite the increase in population and the subsequent push of wildlife away from Milton, there were still plenty of critters out there that could do harm.

It was much nicer being out in the outdoors, enjoying the fall, and seeing the changing color of the cottonwood alder, larch, and quaking aspen. The smell of sagebrush and other fresh scents hit him full force as he drove along the gravel road. There was even a tang of dust from vehicles that had recently traveled the road.

As he crossed over Wenas Creek, he recalled the first trip for gold. He couldn't believe that was less than three years ago. The wooden bridge over the creek was big enough to handle trucks, so his little jeep didn't have too much of an impact.

Crossing over the Naches River was similar—a wood bridge designed to take the weight of trucks. There were already skytrain towers extending down the valley toward the newly established Corps of Discovery base.

It had been a while since Tim had made the trip down here, so he was surprised when he arrived to see how much it had been developed. The first thing he noticed was a big building, with a number of small houses behind it. The streets, like Milton, were laid out in a gridiron pattern behind the big building. As he pulled up in front of the building, parking next to a row of Willys jeeps, he could hear firing off in the distance, up the Naches Valley. A sign on the building announced it was the Corps of Discovery headquarters.

Tim was exiting the jeep, rifle in hand, when Don came out, rifle in hand. "Well, you finally made it," the elder Lewis said.

Taking his outstretched hand, Tim answered with a grin, "In case you haven't noticed, I've been a bit busy."

"Yeah, that's what I hear," Don agreed. "More issues with the feds?"

Tim shook his head. "No, just the usual." Looking around, he took in all the new construction. "So, show me around."

Waving his arm around, Don said with a chuckle, "Well this is the core of the Corps. Headquarters, motor pool, and basic housing. We expect to expand housing and build a cafeteria soon. I figure we'll have thousands of Explorers operating from here, so we're planning for that."

The two men began walking along the gravel road near the housing. "Other things we've got planned include a classroom training facility, auditorium, warehouses, apartments, commissary, base exchange, pool, and a school for dependents. Y'know, just like an army base back on Earth." More shooting could be heard. "As you can tell, we've already got a rifle range set up. It's a basic known distance range, but we'll be expanding that, too. Making it more realistic."

"How so?"

"Pop-up targets, mostly Smilodons and other predators, but the occasional mammoth. We're also looking at setting up a couple of survival schools, which means we need more land."

"What, isn't this enough?" Tim asked. The base took up a bunch of the Naches Valley.

"Not for alpine or jungle survival," Don said.

"Ah, okay. Well, pick some spots, let the Land Office know, and I'll have the surveyors plot them out for you."

"Already got some picked out."

After a quizzical look from Tim, Don continued, "For alpine training, we figure on the Olympics. For the arid lands, we'll need a base near here, but a bit further east. Last, but not least, we'll want a tropical base down on the Yucatan Peninsula."

Tim nodded.

The two men walked in silence for a bit, Tim seeing all the work Don had accomplished. It didn't take too long, as the base was still in its infancy.

"Want to see the airfield? It's been updated, too."

"Sure. Why not?"

"Walk or drive?"

Tim was enjoying being outside away from the office. Besides, he needed the exercise. All that desk time was starting to give him swivel spread, something Veronica wasn't too pleased about. She hadn't said anything, but Tim could tell. "Let's walk. It's only a mile or so."

As they approached the field, Tim could see that the airstrip consisted of two concrete runways, a flight line, with an actual control tower and several hangars on its edge. The runways were crossed at sharp angles, apparently due to the natural winds. One runway ran east-west and the other southwest-northeast. Nearby was a larger building that Tim assumed was a combination passenger terminal and base operations. Several fuel trucks were parked on the flight line, but well away from the building. There were also a C123 Provider, and a DHC-4 Caribou parked on the flight line. A sign welcomed them to Bowman Field.

"I thought we had more planes than that," Tim said, more a question than a statement. He had recalled signing off checks for several million dollars specifically for that purpose.

"We do, but they're out surveying right now. These are for the local runs. We've got a Provider, a Boo, and a 215 out right now. The Goose is over at Milton field."

"A 215?"

"Canadair CL-215. Twin-engine seaplane made up in Canada, eh," Don replied with a fake Canadian accent.

Tim nodded, now recalling the conversation several months ago. "So, how's it work?" he asked, referring to the actual survey operation.

"Pretty straightforward. The Boo does an initial surveillance run. If it doesn't find anything, it'll drop a crew of eight with det cord and demo to clear a field. Once they're done, the Provider drops the same equipment we used in California. The crew sets up a field expedient strip, and the Boo is back with supplies and fuel, then they do it all over again. We can cover a fair amount of ground that way."

"So why the seaplane?"

"We figure it'll be safer to land people near shore than airdrop them. Also, as we got further from land, it gave our crews a sense of safety knowing that if they had to, they could land on the ocean and survive."

"Are you planning on any ground surveys, I mean, like boots on the ground stuff?"

"Yeah, but not right away. We figure once we've surveyed the entire planet, we'll start ground ops. We need more people for that. People trained in staying alive out there."

"Lenny and Lee helping out with that?"

Don nodded. "Yep. Matter of fact, they're out on the rifle range right now, teaching the first group of Explorers."

"Explorers?"

"Yep," Don said with a grin. "Jack came up with the name. Said that anyone who joined the Corps would likely be exploring new worlds, going boldly, and all that shit."

"They aren't wearing red shirts, are they?"

Don laughed out loud at that one. "Naw, no red shirts. But we do have a uniform."

At that point, the two men arrived at the terminal. Stepping inside, Tim could see it was very spartan. A chalkboard had a list of airplanes with crew members and last known positions. A desk next to the board was occupied by a young lady wearing a brown long-sleeve shirt and pants.

Don introduced her to Tim, who promptly forgot her name.

"This here's the uniform I was telling you about," Don said, indicating her outfit. It took a moment of looking at it before Tim realized it reminded him of another uniform. He didn't say anything at the time, just nodded. *Somebody's been reading too many issues of Soldier of Fortune magazine, and decided to copy the South African Army uniform*, was his thought.

"I've got a hat, too," the young lady said, reaching behind her and pulling it from the edge of the chair. She set a wide-brimmed hat on the desk.

"Another Canadian import," Don said, picking up the hat. "Note the mesh around the crown. Keeps the noggin cool even in hot weather. Not like a boonie cap."

Don handed it to Tim, who turned it around and looked at it from various angles. The inside read "Tilly Endurables" and it had two straps, apparently one for the back of the head and one to go under the chin. A half-inch mesh ran around the top of the crown.

"Comfortable hat," Don said.

The young lady agreed with him.

"I'll have to see about getting one," Tim said, handing it back to the lady, who placed it back on the back of the chair, using one of the straps to hold it in place.

Tim noticed that a rifle was leaning against the wall behind the lady, and pointed to it with his chin. "Looks like your rifle, Don."

Don held his up. "There's a reason for that. We've standardized the Corps' rifle. We call it the ER-1."

Leaning his rifle against the desk, Tim took ahold of Don's. It was very similar to those first made when they started exploring Hayek.

A bolt-action rifle with an 18-inch barrel and a low power scope chambered in 7.62 NATO. Unlike their original rifles, this one incorporated many new features. First was an integrated bipod in a composite stock, the second a ghost-ring rear sight, and finally, there was the 10-round magazine. Keeping the rifle pointed in a safe direction, he turned it around, looking at all angles. It was then he noticed another magazine was inserted into the bottom of the stock. He looked questioningly at Don.

"Five-round mag. Just in case."

Tim's eyebrows rose on that.

More examination showed a trapdoor in the butt plate of the stock, the point where the rifle rested against the shooter's shoulder. Opening it, he found a small rifle cleaning kit.

Ejecting the magazine, he saw it contained what looked like full-metal jacket bullets, larger than the NATO rounds he had used in Vietnam. Another questioning look to Don for explanation.

"Dangerous game, especially big ones, requires bullets that can penetrate and break bones. Not the expanding bullets one uses for hunting deer or even elk. All bullets are 220-grain non-expanding. We consider it the minimum. It'll take large game, but it's really designed to *hopefully*" Don made air quotes with his fingers, "stop any big critter coming at you, like a Smilodon or Homotherium."

Tim replaced the magazine in the rifle, handing it back to Don.

"I'm impressed," he said.

"Thought you'd be," Don said with a grin, slinging his rifle.

Nodding their farewells to the young lady, the two left the terminal and began the walk back to the headquarters.

"So, whaddaya think, so far?"

"Like I said, I'm impressed," Tim replied. "Not only with the rifle but everything you've done so far. How soon do you think you'll finish surveying Hayek?"

"Aerial survey, a couple more months. You want a full ground survey? That'll likely take a year or so."

"Okay. Let's keep it going. I've got some customers looking for another Earth, so once we finish up here, let's see about another survey for them."

"Get me my long-range plane, and it'll happen faster."

As the two men walked along the gravel road, Tim thought about a solution.

"Y'know, U-dub has an aeronautical science engineering program. I'm sure some smart grad student can design one for you. See what you can find out."

Rather than return to his bungalow, Tim made the drive back to the office. Another appointment with Poe regarding more demands by the federal government. Tim was a patriotic American, but damnit, the government was pushing just a bit too much for his liking. It wasn't like Hayek was a hotbed of communists looking to overthrow the USA. As a matter of fact, it was just the opposite, a bunch of people looking to make a living and be left alone by what they perceived to be an intrusive and overbearing government.

As he walked into the headquarters, he was once again struck by the incongruity of a modern building and town stuck in the middle of a wilderness. He knew none of this would have been possible if close to a million people hadn't wanted to leave Earth for better opportunities. And none of it would have been possible if he hadn't been able to construct the gates. *Need more gates in more areas*, he thought as he walked up the stairs from the lobby. No elevator for him, especially since the building was only three stories tall. His office, where he was meeting Poe, was on the same level as the conference room.

When he got to his office, the young attorney was already sitting in one of the leather-stuffed guest chairs. In this case, it was leather from a mastodon that had attempted to overrun one of the early gates a year ago as construction was just starting to ramp up. Tim figured the large mammal was rather irked by all the activity and elected to show its displeasure by rampaging through the new town and toward the gate. It was amazing what damage a bunch of .50 BMG rounds could do.

Closing the door behind him, he asked, "So, what's the word?"

"Not looking good," Poe said as Tim took a seat in the leather swivel chair behind his desk. A desk made from local wood. None of that cheap particle board shit for him.

"Feds?"

Poe nodded. "Yep. They're starting to push more, saying we need to give them info on how the gate works. Congress is also starting to get involved. I heard rumblings about having you testify before them."

Tim shook his head. "Ain't happening. I go back, they'll try to force me to stay."

"They might consider you in contempt of Congress if you don't go."

"Screw 'em. This is my home now, not Earth, and not the United States. I'll continue to pay taxes until we're completely independent, but not a minute longer."

Poe jotted something down on the yellow legal pad he held in his lap.

"So, we just let them know their jurisdiction doesn't apply here," he said, "and if they decide to come after you?"

Tim's grin was a bit feral. "Good luck with that. Sure wouldn't want to be the guys enforcing those rules. I'll shut the gates down and move to another Earth if it comes to that."

"It just might. Want some advice? Not legal, just planning."

"Go ahead."

"Find another planet now. One that's got a similar timeline, but maybe just a bit off."

"Already in the works."

Poe nodded. "What if they decide to take action before then? I'm talking military-type action."

Tim answered with a shrug. "If they do, they do." Then, with a more thoughtful look, he asked, "What's the rules of warfare if a country attacks another country unprovoked?"

"Self-defense?" Poe answered, more as a question.

"Find somebody who knows. Would we be able to go after whoever ordered the attack? I mean, let's say Reagan orders an attack on us. Can we go after him?"

Poe set his pen and pad down. "Going after the Gipper would likely be a huge mistake. Huge."

Tim turned his chair, looking out the window toward the Cascade Mountains to the west. He stared at them for what seemed an interminable amount of time before turning back to Poe.

"Check whatever laws of warfare apply. We're a sovereign nation. If they decide to attack us, I don't want us fighting only the grunts. Remember, I spent a year in 'Nam because people in power thought it'd be good to send us there. I'm not about to put up with that bullshit anymore."

32

Searching for an Earth similar to the one he was from proved a bit challenging for Tim. One of the requirements was that it be similar enough to his Earth to have a United States, but also dissimilar enough that he wouldn't be meeting his doppelgänger. He also had to do the searching mostly on the sly, where most other people wouldn't see what he was doing. Added to that was the requirement that the "host" Earth not become aware of him and his activities. The last thing he needed was more people trying to get the secret of the gate from him.

Opening a gate in a populated area was a sure way of attracting unwanted attention, so Tim had to establish a gate in an area not likely to be populated, but one that would allow for accessing radio and television transmissions. Toward that end, he elected to move his base of operation to one of the ridges west of town. He figured that if the ridge wasn't occupied on his timeline, it likely wasn't occupied on a similar timeline.

He had a small shack built there, and over the course of a couple of weeks erected two gates, a regular sized one that would allow a person to walk through, and a smaller one that was barely a square foot in diameter. The smaller gate would be opened first, to search for radio and television transmissions. Both gates faced west, toward the Cascade Mountains, another of Tim's attempts to keep things as covert as possible. Fewer people were likely to live in the mountains than the valleys, so the odds of anyone spotting an open gate would be reduced. The biggest concern was the generator needed to power the gates. The best Tim could do was keep the generator out of the shack with a barrier between the two. With any luck, the noise coming through the gate would be so minimal it wouldn't attract any attention.

With Dave and Veronica's assistance, he began a systematic search. Over the course of several weeks, he was able to refine the search from purely Pleistocene timelines to ones that more closely paralleled his Earth. Some of the timelines he opened were ones he had no desire to ever see again. Eventually, he came upon one that looked like it would fit the criteria.

Using a brand new Sony Trinitron television with an antenna extended through the small gate, the three would watch television from the timeline, paying particular attention to news shows and historical documentaries. It was when Tim saw an episode of "War in the Pacific" that he realized this timeline might be the one. The episode, titled "Operation Downfall" was about the invasion of Japan in 1945 and the battles that raged through 1946 into 1947. Instead of dropping two nuclear bombs which caused the Emperor of Japan to order Japan's unconditional surrender to the US and its allies, the US invaded the Japanese islands. Nuclear bombs were never used in the war, apparently not having been developed in time.

Tim was appalled to learn of the massive loss of life on both the Japanese and American sides. The entire Japanese military was wiped out almost to a man, almost four and a half million dead. The Japanese population was decimated by half. Part of this was due to the US bombing campaigns which thoroughly destroyed every city and major town. To a greater degree, though, the great loss of civilian life was due to the Japanese government's "Operation Ketsugo," in which the entire population of Japan was committed to its defense. This was done with a propaganda campaign that told the Japanese subject that it was glorious to die for the holy Emperor of Japan, and that every man, woman, and child should so when the Allies invaded. It was called "The Glorious Death of One Hundred Million."

American losses approached a million dead and another three million wounded. All American POWs held by the Japanese up to that point had been slaughtered the first day of the invasion.

Considering that his parents had met in 1946, and he was born in 1947, Tim suspected that he wouldn't find a doppelgänger on this timeline. It was likely his mother had been killed in the invasion, and it was probable that his father didn't survive, either.

Only one way to find out, Tim thought, as the show wrapped up, the credits scrolling across the television's screen.

"You want him to what?" Don practically shouted the question, leaning forward and placing both elbows on the conference table.

Tim leaned back in his chair. They were seated in the conference room, along with Veronica, Dave, Petra, Jack, and Jack's mother, Eileen.

"I want him to explore a new timeline, in person."

Jack piped up. "Dad, it's not like we haven't planned for this."

Don turned to his son. "Yes, it is. We haven't planned for this. We've planned to explore worlds *without* people. He's asking you to go to a world *with* people. Huge difference! Huge!"

"Who do you suggest, then?" Tim asked reasonably. "A kid on a bike riding to a library is a lot less suspicious than one of us walking, riding, or driving a car or jeep.

"Look, we've been listening to the radio and watching television for the past month. This timeline's pretty similar to our Earth. If you're not breaking the law or looking suspicious, the cops leave you alone. The big difference is the lack of Asians, of which I'm one. I go there, I'll stick out like a sore thumb. Jack goes, nobody'll notice him, except maybe the girls," the last said with a grin.

"He's right, Dad."

Don turned toward his wife. "What do *you* think?"

Eileen leaned back in her chair and steepled her fingers. She looked around at the others, taking her time answering, the shock of the proposal still hitting her.

"I don't like it," she finally said, lowering her fingers and placing her hands in her lap. Tim couldn't see them, but he was mentally betting that she was wringing her hands. "But, it's probably the right thing to do. Does he have to go by himself?"

Tim shrugged. "I don't think so. I mean, if he's got somebody he thinks will be good to take, I'm all for that, but it can't be an adult."

"What about Janice?" Jack asked.

This caused Veronica to sit up. "What about Janice?"

"If we were to go into town together, it'd look like we were brother and sister," Jack said. "Even less suspicious."

"She's only thirteen," Veronica said, with what sounded like finality.

"She may only be thirteen," Tim said, "but she's an uncommon thirteen-year-old. And, she's had plenty of time exploring here on Hayek."

"But, that's always with Timmy and Tia."

"So?" Tim countered. "It's not like she doesn't hear what's going on at home. I agree with Jack."

Veronica glowered at him but didn't argue any further.

Tim turned back to Don. "If Janice agrees to go, will you agree to let Jack go?"

"Hold on there a second," Jack interrupted. Everybody turned to look at him, surprised. "Last time I checked, I signed the Responsibility Statement. Any decision made here is my decision, and mine alone. Not Dad's and not Mom's." Looking at his parents, seated across the table from him, he said, "Sorry Mom and Dad, but that's the truth. I'll listen to your concerns, but you don't get to make this decision."

The look of realization dawned on both parents simultaneously. Jack had signed the document the year before when only sixteen. Since then, even though he still lived at home, he acted independently in all other things, including being the chief pilot for Air Hayek and helping his father establish the Corps of Discovery.

Don didn't like it, but he looked over at his wife, shrugged, and said, "The boy's right. His responsibility, his choice."

A couple more weeks passed before the pair of Explorers, as Jack was referring to Janice and himself, were ready to venture out into the new Earth. Hours had been spent watching television, which translated into having bicycles and clothing made that more closely resembled what was seen. Apparently, three-geared banana seat bikes with high handlebars were all the rage, as opposed to the BMX and ten-speed bikes that dominated Tim's Earth, or the more rough-terrain utility bikes used on Hayek.

Each Explorer was also issued a small pack with enough food for a full day and a stainless steel military surplus canteen for water. The canteens were left over from World War II. When Janice saw the date stamped on the bottom of hers, she exclaimed, "Wow, 1944. I can't believe anything can be that old." Tim and Veronica just rolled their eyes.

"Keep them upright," Tim warned her. "Otherwise, they'll leak all over your back."

Both teens also had notepads and pens. It was mostly up to Jack to do the research, but it gave Janice the feeling of being a full member of the team, and she was told she could draw or take notes of the town. Jack also had a few small gold nuggets. In the event he needed any cash, he could sell them at a pawn shop or jeweler. His excuse would be that he found them prospecting with his dad earlier in the summer, had wanted to keep them, but needed the money.

Jack had already made a few expeditions to try and determine the best way into the small town at the bottom of the ridge. It looked almost like their timeline's Selah, but with some visible differences, most notable of which was, it appeared smaller. Tim was pretty sure Yakima was on the other side of the Naches Valley based on the city glow visible at night. Well, that and the fact that they had picked up the news broadcasts on both radio and television from Yakima.

The plan was for the two teens to ride their bikes down a dirt road from the ridge into the valley to the north, then down a macadam road into town. Once in town, they'd visit the library and search the phone books for any listings of Tim or his parents. "See if you can find any mention of Dave at the college or any of the other board members anywhere," Tim said before sending the two on their way.

It was an hour before dawn when Tim opened the big gate. The shed had been darkened with only a subdued flashlight used to operate the gate. Light was barely showing in the sky to the east, while the land to the west was shrouded in darkness. Stars were still visible overhead. A quick glance around to ensure nobody was nearby and would witness the event, and then two teenagers were rolling their bikes out onto the high desert. Jack looked around, then gave Tim a thumbs-up sign that the coast was clear. Tim nodded, returned to the gate controls, then shut the gate down. He would re-open it after sunset. Hopefully, the two Explorers would be there. If they weren't, Tim wasn't looking forward to telling Jack's parents or Veronica.

At the appointed time, Tim darkened the interior of the shed, and with Veronica using only a small flashlight to illuminate the controls, opened the gate. Stepping toward the gate, he looked through it, trying to see movement in the darkness.

"Dr. Bowman?" a voice called out quietly. Tim recognized it as Jack's.

"Over here," he said in a normal voice, one that wasn't too likely to be heard from more than a hundred feet.

Scrunching of feet and tires on dry soil came closer, with the occasional whisper of jeans against sagebrush, and then the two were in front of him.

Tim stepped back into the shed so they could roll their bikes in. Once they were all the way in, he shut down the gate and turned on the small, bare overhead light. The two put their hands up to shield their eyes, despite it being only 15 watts. Tim felt relief surge through him as he saw they were unharmed. Veronica practically rushed forward and hugged the small teenaged girl who had become her *de facto* daughter. Holding her at arm's length, Veronica asked, "You okay?"

At the girl's nod, Tim could see the tension leave his wife's body. "Good. Hungry?"

"Not really. We ate the food you packed us."

"We got back up the ridge early," Jack explained. "Figured we might as well eat before it got dark."

"Good idea," Tim said, opening the door to the shed. "Leave the bikes here. I'll get 'em in the morning. Everyone's waiting to hear what you found."

A short trip in the jeep later, the four pulled up to the Bowmans' bungalow, where the Lewises and Jaskeys were waiting. Tim could see Tia and Timmy, front paws and snouts pressed against the living room plate glass windowpane, fogging it up with each exhalation from their nostrils, their hind ends wagging with excitement at seeing their goddess return.

Entering the home, they were practically bowled over by the two Homotheriums, who couldn't seem to get enough of Janice, sniffing her up and down to ensure she was safe, all while taking in strange smells that had latched onto her on the other timeline.

Once the rest of them managed to get through the traffic jam at the front door, they were greeted by the adults.

"How'd it go?" asked Don, while Eileen came forward and hugged her son, doing the exact same thing Veronica had done with Janice less than fifteen minutes beforehand.

Jack nodded. "Went well." He turned back to look at Janice and the big cats. "If they ever settle down, we can tell you what we found."

Janice took that as a cue to stop frolicking with her pets, and joined the rest in the living room, taking a seat on the couch next to Veronica, the two big cats plopping down at her feet. Eileen took the love seat and Petra sat next to her. The men elected to stand, even Tim, who could have easily claimed his favorite recliner. Don handed beers out to Veronica and Tim. Turning to his son, he asked, "You want anything?"

"A coke?"

"Got it. You?" The latter was addressed to Janice.

"May I have a root beer, please?"

Don nodded and disappeared into the kitchen, returning a minute later with two bottles which he handed to the teens. The coke bottle was identical to the trademark Coca-Cola bottle on Earth, an outcome of the Coca-Cola Bottling Company opening a plant in Tahoma. The root beer was similar, with the words "Pop's Root Beer" emblazoned across the bottle at an angle.

The adults waited until the teens had taken a few sips of their drinks, before Tim asked, "Well?"

Jack and Janice looked at each other before Jack nodded to the younger girl. "You first."

Janice pulled her notebook out of her pack, which she had set on the floor in front of her. Opening it to the first page, she began her tale with a self-assured voice. "Well, first we rode into town, like you said to, Uncle Tim. It looks different than Selah on Earth. Smaller." She took another sip of her root beer. "One of the things we saw was a war memorial with a lot of names on it. It was sorta like the Washington Monument, but smaller and black, and the names were on a base surrounding the pointy thing."

"You mean an obelisk? Four sides, tall, with a pointy top?" Veronica asked for clarification.

"Yeah," Janice said, nodding. "It was in a park called Memorial Park."

Tim didn't recall any parks named Memorial Park, nor any monuments to fallen soldiers. And an obelisk was certainly something he would have remembered. After all, he had spent most of his life in or near Selah.

Looking at Tim, she said, "One of the names on the base was Richard T. Bowman, US Army. Killed in Japan in 1946."

Tim felt a weird sensation of *deja vu* all over again. It was like when he first heard of his father's death. His father's middle name was Timothy, which was where Tim got his name. Tim got control of his emotions. Janice was looking at him sadly. The rest were looking at the teenager with surprise or shock.

"Well, that was unexpected," Tim said, trying to lighten the mood. "Anything else?"

Janice turned toward Jack, who took up the narrative.

"Like you asked, I went into the library and looked up your name and your dad's name. Nothing in Selah, Yakima, Ellensburg, Bellevue, Seattle, or Tacoma. When I looked up Dr. Jaskey's name, I couldn't find it either. I even borrowed the library's phone and called the college. Nobody with that name works there. As a matter of fact, nobody's name was in the phone book."

"Interesting," Tim said, a bit more in control of his feelings. "So, it looks like we don't exist on that timeline."

"We passed a pawn shop in town, near the library," Jack continued. "It had a sign saying they buy gold, so we could probably sell some gold there if we need some cash."

That was a piece of well-received news.

Janice reached over and kicked Jack, giving him an exasperated look. "Oh, I almost forgot," he said, reaching down for his own pack. "I got a book."

"You what?" asked several voices.

"I got a book," he repeated, pulling a book out of the pack. "It was on a table at the front door of the library. They were giving away old books and I thought it'd be useful."

He handed the book over to Tim who read the title out loud. "*US History of the 20th Century*. Well, this ought to prove interesting." Looking back up at Jack, he said, "Smart move Jack."

"Told you," Janice said to Jack.

"Yeah, I know," he replied. Turning to the others, he said, "Janice spotted it first. She told me about it."

Veronica ruffled the girl's hair. "Good on you, my little Explorer."

The girl practically beamed. Turning to Veronica, she said, "That's what I want to be when I grow up. An Explorer."

33

The decision was made to send Poe into the new world to connect with the federal government. This time, instead of doing so as a US citizen, he would be doing so as a representative of one of Hayek's private industries, specifically Parallel, Inc., not the government. Representing the newly elected government was a character named John Foster.

Foster was practically a zealot when it came to Hayek's form of government. He was appointed ambassador plenipotentiary by the newly elected president, with the authority to contact other governments irrespective of what Parallel was doing. Of course, he could only do so through the good graces of Parallel, which was run mostly by Tim. Knowing that, he had reached out to Tim when initially appointed to the position, letting him know that he supported Hayek's constitution and would do whatever was necessary to ensure its survival.

What made Foster a character was that he was a little different than many of the other Vietnam vets who had migrated to Hayek, to put it mildly. He had been drafted just before the war, serving in Vietnam from 1965 to 1966 as a door gunner on a Bell UH-1 helicopter with the US Army's First Cavalry Division. While he loved the thrill of riding in a helicopter and oftentimes hanging out the side, he didn't enjoy having to shoot people with a machine gun. As he liked to say, "I'm a lover, not a fighter." He also didn't like crashing, something the young warrant officers flying the helicopters he was in seemed to do all too often. Not that it was their fault. It's kind of hard to keep a bird in the air when unfriendly forces are blasting it with AK-47 and 12.7mm DshK 38/46 heavy machine guns. While fortunate to walk away from all three gunfire-inspired crashes, the same couldn't be said of his pilots, co-pilots, and fellow door gunners. On one of those occasions, Foster was the sole survivor. He wondered whether he would have even been had it not been for some twenty-something-year-old crazy-ass warrant officer who landed his chopper in the middle of a fire-fight to rescue him, just as the Viet Cong were about to overrun his hiding position near his shot down chopper. That crazy-ass warrant officer was killed a week later, shot down attempting to rescue a shot down Air Force pilot. Foster left Vietnam with a Purple Heart with oak leaf cluster, a Bronze Star with a V for Valor, and a serious jones against war.

Instead of being a veteran who tried to settle down after his service, he joined a hippie commune in northern California and then became active with Vietnam Veterans Against the War. His long, now-silver hair was usually tied up in a ponytail, and his attire was most often blue jeans and tie-dyed Grateful Dead T-shirts and leather bomber jackets. He found marijuana in Vietnam and liked it so much he decided to keep using it when he returned to "the World," as the US was known by those serving in 'Nam, using northern California's Emerald Triangle as his base of operation. He was now the CEO of the biggest and most successful marijuana/hemp operations on Hayek, taking advantage of the various climates in the Yakama and Cascadia Cantons to grow his products.

Foster's enjoyment of his product wasn't restricted to the smokable type; he also was invested in what he called "Joyous Edibles." This included marijuana and hashish-infused foods, such as brownies, cookies, and taffies. Toward that end, Foster's enjoyment had led him to gaining the stature of a well-fed nearly middle-aged stoner—definitely not thin, but not obese. Just heavy enough to show a substantial paunch, one that would be called a beer belly if he drank beer, which he didn't.

Foster, along with newly-elected Hayek president Larry Finerty, sat down with Poe and Tim in Parallel's third-story conference room to go over the logistics of introducing themselves to the authorities on the newly opened planet. Finerty was, like anyone who held office or voted, a veteran of the military or law enforcement on Earth. In his case, he had been a twenty-year cop with the Seattle police, having served as a state representative in Washington's legislature, before bailing Earth and moving to Hayek. Politics seemed to be in his blood, which is how he wound up as Hayek's first president. He had no illusions, though, realizing that the real power on Hayek emanated from the building he was sitting in, with those who controlled the gates.

"As you know," Poe said from his usual chair, one that gave him a view of the Cascade Mountains, "the US government isn't playing nice with us. As a matter of fact, we're fast approaching the point they might take action to kidnap Tim and take him back to Earth."

Finerty and Foster looked over at Tim, seated in his usual position at the head of the table. Tim shrugged.

"Based on that," Poe continued, "and, again, as you already know, we've identified a timeline similar to our Earth, but different enough that several of us don't exist on it, at least to our knowledge. Hence, the reason for all of us being here." Nodding to Foster, Poe continued, "Along with John and me, we'd like to have Jack Lewis go."

"Isn't that the boy who flies the planes for Air Hayek?" Finerty asked.

Tim leaned forward and put his elbows on the table, interlocking his fingers. "Yep, and he's not a boy. Took the Responsibility Oath a while back. Plus, he's already made one run into this new timeline. That history book we loaned you, well, it's one he picked up there."

Both Finerty and Foster were impressed with that. Teenagers already running covert ops was definitely something out of the ordinary.

"Look, it's real simple," Tim continued. "You guys know TJ Harrison, the geographer?" At their nods, he continued, "Then you know he pointed out that we can't advance or sustain ourselves as a civilization with the limited number of people we've got, and the limited resource extraction and manufacturing. While we'll likely retain a connection with Japan, we need access to another civilization. That's where you guys come in. You send the rep, we fund it."

"You're saying you'll pay for everything?" Finerty asked. Considering the limitations on government, particularly the funding, this was a serious matter.

Tim nodded. "Within reason. I'm not gonna pay for John to be smoking pot all the way across the country, but otherwise, yeah."

Poe took over the conversation. "Based on what we've been able to learn, the US on this new timeline is pretty similar to our old US, but with far fewer Asians. Seems like the door shut pretty hard on Asians after World War II, unless one was Filipino.

"We figure that we should be able to exchange some gold for cash, get a car, and drive to DC. We can also sell gold along the way, so we don't stick out as a big-time gold seller at the beginning, causing a bunch of questions. The tricky part is figuring out how to get in contact with the person who we need to talk to, the Secretary of State."

"Would that be George Shultz?" Finerty asked.

"Interestingly enough, it is," Poe replied. "And in case you're wondering how we're going to show them we're from a different timeline, we're gonna bring some contemporary history books with us, particularly ones focusing on the War in the Pacific."

"Is that wise?" Finerty asked. "I mean, if they didn't have the bomb back then, how do we know you won't be giving it to them now?"

"Oh, they've got the bomb," Tim said. "A bit late to drop on Japan, but they've had it since 1948. It helped stop Nazi advances after the war. Which, again, shows the difference in our timelines. On this Earth the Nazis beat the Soviets. Brits are still hanging on, but apparently not by much."

The men soberly took in this new information.

"So, other than borrowing John, what do you need from the government?" Finerty finally asked.

"Just diplomatic support," Poe said. "We want Hayek recognized as a sovereign state, and then we want to open up for trade and migration, using the same system we've already got in place."

"From what I can tell, it looks like I'm the one that gives the go-ahead on diplomatic missions," Finerty said. He turned to Foster. "Think you can pull this off as ambassador plenipotentiary?"

"Only one way to find out," Foster said, "and that's to give it a try."

Turning back to Poe, Finerty asked, "How soon before you want to start this?"

"Give us a couple of days, and we should be good to go."

"Okay. You've got my blessing, especially since I don't have to pay for it," Finerty said with a slight chuckle.

Just then, there was a knock on the conference door, which opened almost immediately after, and a young woman entered the conference room. Looking very nervous, she walked over to Tim and handed him a note, stepping back in case he needed her.

Tim quickly read the note, his brow furrowing. Looking up at the others, who were looking at him expectantly, he said, "Looks like the US got tired of waiting."

Looking at Hayek's president, Tim said, "The US just tried taking over our gates, using armed men."

"A military invasion?"

"Doesn't look that way," Tim said, shaking his head. "More like some federal law enforcement types." He passed the note over to Finerty. "Show Bob after you've read it."

Finerty read the note, eyebrows rising even more, then passed it to Poe.

"Looks like both an invasion of Hayek and an illegal attempt at an arrest warrant service," Finerty announced. "What we might call an attempted kidnapping."

"They come over here with guns, shooting up my people, and trying to take me into custody?" Tim responded. "Yeah, I'd call that an invasion and attempted kidnapping, and if any of my people are hurt, we can add on more charges."

Standing up, Tim announced, "I'm going to the situation room to better find out what's going on." The next question was addressed to Finerty. "You want to join me and see what the hell just happened?"

"I think that'd be a good idea," Finerty said as he rose from his chair. "Can we both come?"

Tim thought it over a second. "Yeah, might's well bring John. He might be needed for this. Bob, you come along, too. We might need some legal advice."

The situation room was on the opposite side of the building from the conference room, overlooking the Yakima River and the eastern desert landscape. It occupied a full quarter of the floor and had numerous maps hanging from three of the four walls. One map showed the west coast, another showed the Japanese islands, known as Nippon on Hayek, while a third, larger scale, was more focused on the area of the Pacific Northwest mostly occupied by Hayekers. There were numerous red pins stuck in this map, along with a few green pins. Several desks were occupied by people on phones, all talking at once. In one corner was a radio with a young man talking into a headset.

"What's the status?" Tim asked as he walked in the room, trailed by the others.

A young lady with her blond hair cut short and spiked with some sort of gel, holding a clipboard, turned to Tim. "Incursion by an unknown US agency; we suspect either FBI, ATF, or Secret Service. Nothing firm yet, but it looks like they're all from the same agency, decked out in blue military togs with badges. Fighting's still going on at some of the gates."

"How're the gates?" Tim looked at the board.

"The red pins are gates that were destroyed by the operators. The green ones show gates still operational."

"How many of our people were hurt?"

"Don't know, yet. Situation's still fluid."

"Okay. Carry on. We're just gonna observe for now. I'm here if you've got any questions."

"Yessir," the blonde said, turning back to those manning the desks and phones.

The four men took places against the wall, standing and watching as the blonde directed her teams on the phones and radio, who directed teams on the ground.

A few minutes later the situation became clearer, as both armed staff from Parallel, which was anyone employed by the company, along with public safety officers and Hayek Militia responded to the incursion. The invaders were overwhelmed, and the situation well in hand within another fifteen minutes. With the exception of a few of the gates that had been hidden from the US government, all gates on the continent had been destroyed. The thermite charges surrounding the gates and controls had been set off by dead-man switches almost immediately upon the incursion. In all, fewer than a hundred of the US government's agents had made it to Hayek, and fewer than twenty were still alive. It turned out that they were US Marshals.

Unfortunately, Hayek losses were also high, caught by surprise as they were. Almost every gate operator at the overrun gates had been shot, several of them dying. That pissed Tim off mightily. These were men and women specifically chosen by him to guard the secret of the gate, and given the opportunity and power to run them.

Grinding his teeth, Tim looked at Poe and Finerty. "US Marshals. So, definitely a government-run op. What are our legal options?"

"We can put those we've caught on trial. Those who ordered this, and we likely won't know who for a while, we can try *in absentia*," Poe said.

"So, we give 'em a fair trial and hang them, right?" Tim asked, seething with righteous vengeance.

Poe shook his head. "No can do, Tim. Constitution won't allow for the government to kill anyone."

Tim turned away, looking out the situation room's control window. A brief pause, then an exhalation of air. "I knew that. I helped write the damned thing. Damn!"

"Tim, this is Hayek's business," Finerty said. "We'll handle the legal stuff, including finding out who ordered the attack, and why. Then we're gonna ask for extradition. Nobody comes into our home and does this much damage without paying for it. And those who decided to attack, well, we'll just let the citizens of Hayek and the relatives of the victims determine their fate, be it a lifetime of servitude to pay off the lost income by those killed, or ostracism to whatever hellhole planet you can find.

"In the meantime, I need you to get that diplomatic mission to this new Earth underway ASAP. I don't think we've got a lot of time to mess around, and we're gonna need more material soon."

Tim looked at Poe and Foster. "How soon do you think you'll be ready to go? You can take a Willys and some gold right now if you want. They've got Willys over there. Might not be comfortable, but it'll be quick."

The two men looked at each other for a second, then back to Tim. Foster was the first to speak. "Give me a day or two, and I'll be ready."

"Me, too," Poe said. "We still need to find Jack and get him on board."

"I'll handle that. Start getting ready, and meet me back in the conference room at eight in the morning, two days from now. We've got a new world to explore." Tim turned and looked out the window again. "Make that new *worlds* to explore."

AFTERWARD

Dear Reader,

Thanks for buying *Openings*, the first in *The Hayek Chronicles* series. I hope you enjoyed it. As an independent author, I don't have a marketing department or the exposure of being on bookshelves. If you enjoyed *Openings*, please help spread the word and support the writing of the rest of the series by writing an Amazon and/or Goodreads review or telling a few friends about the book.

Thanks again,

James S. Peet
Enumclaw WA

About the Author

James S. Peet is a modern-day Renaissance Man. He's lived on four continents, six countries, and visited countless more. He's been a National Park Service Ranger, a police officer, a tow-truck driver, a college instructor, a private investigator, a fraud examiner/forensic accountant, an inventor, and an entrepreneur. His other writing endeavors include *The Corps of Discovery* series, several articles on modern sea piracy, economics, and the private investigation of fraud. He lives on the top of a small mountain in the foothills of Washington's Cascade Mountains with his wife, dogs, barn cats, and whatever adult daughter returns to the nest. He's attended 10 colleges and universities, two law enforcement academies, and has three degrees (all in geography) and multiple certificates (he really likes learning). *Openings* is his first novel in the *Chronicles of Hayek* series. Check out his *Corps of Discovery* novels set later in the timeline, *Surveyor*, *Trekker*, and *Explorer*. Be sure to watch for future releases.

In Memoriam

Sometimes friendships peter away, wilting in the passage of time. Other times, friendships explode like a rotten tomato, leaving a stain on all affected. The best friendships, though, are those that end in death. To be friends with someone until the very end is a special type of friendship. It means you both cared enough about the other that only death can separate you.

On September 7th, 2020, one of my friendships ended in exactly that way. David Jeschke, whose name was bastardized to David Jaskey for this series and the *Corps of Discovery* series died from complications cause by pancreatic cancer.

Dave and I had been best buds for over 20 years, meeting as grad students at the University of Washington in 1997. He was, for all intents and purposes, an uncle to my kids. He is greatly missed. This book is dedicated to fellow geographer and world traveler Dave. I'm glad he was fine with letting me use his name.

Join My Mailing List (I don't spam!)

This is my first novel in the *The Hayek Chronicles* series. If you'd like advance notice of future releases, please join my e-mail list at https//jamespeet.com. You can also find my other series, *Corps of Discovery*, available on Amazon through my website at https://jamespeet.com/.

9 780999 609361